A DEADLY DEAL

Tony swallowed and said, "Where do we go from here, Edward?"

"Tony, this is a major problem. Not just with this Walker person. I'm not at all happy with you. The rules are very clear. Nobody gets in once the con is on. Nobody sees inside our operation or inside our heads once we're up and moving. Nobody." Brand slowly turned his head and faced his visitor, his gray eyes cold and penetrating. "Where do we go? Good question."

"Jesus, Edward, it was a one-time thing. It'll never happen again. I swear." He was shaking now and concentrated on keeping his beer steady. He swallowed heavily, his throat dry.

"You're a good guy, Tony, but business is business," Brand said. He remained motionless, and the room was absolutely quiet. A log shifted slightly in the fireplace and a few sparks shot up the flue. "I tell you what," he finally said, "I'll make you a deal."

"What sort of deal?"

"We need to take care of the problem we've got in New York. She's a very real threat to our safety. You take care of her, and everything's fine."

"Kill her?" Tony asked.

"Seems almost barbaric when you just come right out and say it," Brand said, finishing his beer....

SHELL
GAME

JEFF BUICK

LEISURE BOOKS NEW YORK CITY

To my sons,
Tyler, Shawn, Justin and Matthew.
Thanks for keeping me on my toes all these
years. While I don't think it made me taller,
I do think it made me wiser.

A LEISURE BOOK®

April 2007

Published by

Dorchester Publishing Co., Inc.
200 Madison Avenue
New York, NY 10016

ISBN-10: 0-8439-5846-4
ISBN-13: 978-0-8439-5846-1

Visit us on the web at www.dorchesterpub.com.

ACKNOWLEDGMENTS

Huge thanks to C. J. Woods for the invite to his private villa in Cabo.

Thanks to John Norrish for the name, *Shell Game*.

This is my fourth book—time to say thanks to some key people who kick-started my writing career and kept it moving forward.

Chrystal Boscoe—a dear friend who started the ball rolling when she met Paul Pearce and told him she knew a writer. Despite his protests, she finally pinned him to the ground and extracted a business card.

Paul Pearce—my Canadian distributor and my friend, who, when faced with that crucial decision —root canal or read Jeff's manuscript—chose wisely. And for hand-delivering it to Don D'Auria in New York. Paul, you're the best.

Don D'Auria—my editor at Dorchester Publishing. Every author should be so lucky to work with an editor who is as professional, honest, fair and insightful as Don. I love writing, and Don gave me the chance to share my work with the world. Thanks is a mighty small word for all you've done.

SHELL GAME

PROLOGUE

They moved through the night with stealth and speed.

Eight figures, dressed in dark clothes, jockeyed the desks, boxes and filing cabinets through the loading area into waiting trucks. No one spoke; there was no need. They were orchestrating a plan just as a pro football team runs a play—every player knowing exactly what to do the moment the ball is snapped. And this was one play the team knew very well.

The boxes and filing cabinets they were removing from the offices were light. They should be. They were mostly empty. Paper of any sort was heavy, and it left incriminating evidence, even after it was shredded. Most of the letters and memos that had been in the offices, and that was a very small amount, had been removed over the past few days. When they were finished, not one sheet of paper would remain. In fact, there would not be one desk or telephone or garbage can left. The work area, five hours earlier a fully functional office, would be stripped clean. It was Friday night and the building was deserted. No one would notice the barren space until Monday morning.

The solitary wall-mounted security camera aimed at the loading dock was disconnected, the wire dangling beneath the lens. When they had picked the office space for their San Francisco operation eight months ago, part of their decision to sign this lease was the lax security in this section of the building. Everything thought out. Nothing to chance.

It's the details that will trip you up.

When they were finished loading the unmarked vehicles, they closed and bolted the rear doors, and the four trucks pulled out onto the dark side street, single file and moving at exactly the speed limit. Four of the eight drove the trucks; the other four remained in the building. They returned to the empty offices and wiped down every surface that might have contained a fingerprint. It took them less than ten minutes.

Three of the remaining four headed directly to a black Lincoln Navigator parked in the shadows a block north of the building. The fourth returned to the loading dock, reconnected the security camera and dialed a number on his cell phone. He let it ring twice, then hit End. The vibrating phone on the other end of the line was the signal that they were finished on the loading dock. Their accomplice, whose job it was to distract the security guard, could wrap things up and leave. The man who dialed the number joined the other three in the SUV. When they were a mile from the building, one of the two in the backseat finally broke the silence.

"That went well," he said.

"Was there ever any doubt?" the man in the front passenger seat asked. His name was Edward Brand, and this was his operation.

All three laughed. The kind of laugh that comes easily once a dangerous job is finished and the adrenaline surge begins to subside.

"Not for a moment," the first man said.

They reached an unmarked intersection where two

narrow back streets met, and the driver pulled over to the curb. He switched off the ignition. Parked at the curb were three identical, nondescript cars. Brand turned in his seat so the men could see his face, dimly lit by a streetlight half a block up the road.

"Everyone knows exactly what to do," he said, and all three nodded silently. "There is no deviation from the plan. None whatsoever. Understood?" Again, all three nodded. "Then that's it. We meet again when and where it's arranged. Until then, be cool."

He extended his hand, and they all shook. The driver stayed in the Navigator and Edward Brand and the others walked up the deserted street to their vehicles. One at a time, they started the motors and pulled away from the curb, each heading in a different direction. Brand's car was the last to leave. As he pulled onto the deserted street, he allowed himself a smile. Christ, were they going to be shocked.

They always were. They never saw it coming.

Never.

CHAPTER ONE

Taylor Simons kept her mouth shut. The next person to speak would lose.

She let her gaze drift about the boardroom. Six other people sat on the stainless-steel and leather chairs. Three of them were her staff, the key personnel and designers who had spent eight weeks putting together the ad campaign. The other three were the executive team with Hammer-Fire Inc., an international corporation out of New York that developed and marketed fitness equipment. Their newest line of cardio machines was sleek and very expensive. Their target market were the rich and pampered who thought they were devoted enough to work out at home, and every high-end fitness facility in America and Europe that catered to the same people when they found buying the equipment was the easy part. Actually using it was completely different.

Her staff was quiet, unmoving and focused on nothing in particular. They were masters at this segment of the game. Deliver the presentation, answer any questions, then shut up. Let the clients make their decision based on the work. It seldom failed.

"So the bottom line is six-point-two million," said the most senior of the Hammer-Fire executives.

She had them.

"That's correct, Don," Taylor said.

"And there'll be no cost overruns."

"None. We have the quotes for television and print guaranteed for the time frames you need. Our figures are accurate to the dollar."

"Okay, Taylor," he said, standing and extending his hand. "You've got the contract."

"Thanks," she said, shaking his hand. She turned to one of her staff members. "Do you have the paperwork, Reg?"

The man nodded and flipped open a file. "Right here." He slid it across the table to the executive. "I'll need a couple of signatures."

Twenty minutes later, Taylor Simons retreated to her corner office and dropped into her padded chair. She hated the uncomfortable and harsh chairs in the boardroom, but her clients expected a cutting-edge advertising agency to project a certain appearance. And since they were paying the bills, they got the image. She touched her wireless mouse and the computer screen came to life. Seven new e-mails since she had left for the boardroom two hours ago. She was responding to the sixth one when a man walked into her office. He was one of the three from the boardroom, the head of her Web design department.

"Nice work today," he said, leaning on the door jamb. His name was Kelly Kramer, a young-looking thirty-six-year-old and one of Taylor's most trusted and valuable employees. He had thick dark hair, parted in the middle and creeping down over his ears, a goatee that suited his rugged face and a quick smile. For almost five years, he had been a fixture in Taylor's inner circle and had grown close enough to be called a friend.

"Thanks," she said, leaning back in the soft leather. She loved her chair. "Twelve percent of six-point-two million. Not bad for two months' work."

"Our ideas were original," Kelly said. "We deserved the contract over New York and Chicago. They were serving up rehashed concepts."

"Whatever it was, it worked."

"I'm out of here," he said, glancing at his watch. "Been in since four this morning prepping for the meeting. I'll see you tomorrow."

"Tomorrow."

Taylor Simons returned to answering her e-mail. At thirty-seven, she was successful beyond even her own high expectations. She owned G-cubed, one of the most sought-after advertising agencies in San Francisco, with 122 staff and annual revenues topping 150 million dollars a year. Her offices occupied seven thousand square feet of prime space in William Polk's brilliantly designed Hobart Building on Market Street. She was an attractive woman, with high cheekbones, vibrant red hair, green eyes and a facial shape close enough to Nicole Kidman's to warrant second looks from passers-by. People in restaurants often spent more time stealing glimpses of her and whispering among themselves trying to figure out if she was the famous actress than they did eating. All the downside of fame without the upside. But genetics were genetics. There was no changing how she looked.

Her private line rang, and she glanced at the call display. Earl Hinks, her personal banker at Bay City Trust. She picked up the receiver. "Hello, Earl. Calling to tell me I won't be paying any bank fees this month?"

"Taylor, something's happened," Hinks said. His tone was ominous.

"What?" she asked, leaning forward on her desk.

"Call Alan and have him meet you in my office in half an hour. Can you do that?"

"Yes, of course. What's wrong?"

"Not over the phone. I'll see you in half an hour." The line went dead.

Taylor punched a button for an outside line and dialed her husband's work number. He answered on the third ring.

"Hi, honey. What's up? Thought you had a meeting with the Hammer-Fire boys."

"The meeting's finished. I just got a call from Earl Hinks at the bank. He said something happened, but he wouldn't tell me what it was. He wants us to meet him at his office in a half hour."

"What? Why? What's going on?"

"I don't know. He wouldn't say. He wants to meet."

"Christ, Taylor, I'm busy. We've got deadlines on this unit we're designing."

"I know. But he told me to call you and for both of us to be there in half an hour."

"Okay. I'll get there as quick as I can. Half an hour's tight, though."

"See you there," she said, hanging up. She shut down her computer, stopped at the reception desk on the way out to let them know she would be out of the office for an hour or two, then took the elevator to P6, where her Audi A4 waited. The drive to the bank, on Sacramento Street, near Lafayette Park, was quick for a Monday afternoon. The September sun was high in its daily arc, and the temperature hovered in the mid-eighties. There was little breeze from the bay and no chill in the air. It was a perfect day.

Taylor pulled into the small parking lot behind the bank and squeezed the Audi between two SUVs. She slid out, her long legs cramped between her car and the truck. She entered the bank through the side door and headed for Earl Hinks's office, down the hall on the left. The receptionist looked up as she approached.

"Hello, Lois," Taylor said as she walked past the woman's desk. Earl Hinks was the manager of the branch, but his door was always open to her, and she never waited.

"Ms. Simons, Mr. Hinks has asked that you and Mr.

Bestwick go in together today. He'd like you to wait in the reception area until your husband arrives."

Taylor stopped and cocked her head. "What is this all about?" she asked.

The woman shrugged. "I don't know."

Taylor teetered between steps, then moved back to the small grouping of chairs where clients waited for Hinks or one of the high-end personal bankers who worked in the branch, serving financial advice to the wealthy. She had been waiting about ten minutes when her husband came in the side door looking confused.

"What's going on?" he asked, taking the seat beside her.

Taylor still liked what she saw when she looked at her husband. Alan Bestwick was thirty-eight, one year older than she was, and in peak physical condition. He had a ruggedly handsome face, with strong lines accenting his cheeks and jaw, and steely blue eyes beneath a mop of curly off-blond hair. He was dressed in jeans and a loose-fitting shirt rolled up to expose his sinewy forearms. Taylor didn't have time to answer before Earl Hinks appeared in the hallway entrance.

"Come on in," Hinks said, turning and shuffling down the hall to his office. Earl Hinks was in his late fifties and a poster boy for a heart attack. He was sixty pounds overweight, ate junk food three times a day, didn't exercise and drank to excess. And he smoked.

Taylor and Alan followed him and sat in the comfortable chairs facing his desk. Hinks closed the door and sat down, his chair groaning under the weight. He wiped his brow from the exertion and tucked the handkerchief in his inside suit pocket. He adjusted his glasses and opened the lone file sitting on his desk.

"There's no easy way to say this," he began, clearing his throat, "but the bank is calling your loan."

Alan sat forward. "What? Calling the loan? Why, Earl? Why would they do that?"

Now Hinks looked really uncomfortable. He fidgeted

in his chair for a moment, then said, "NewPro has disappeared."

Neither Alan nor Taylor uttered a word for the better part of ten seconds. Then Taylor said, "What do you mean, Earl? How can a company disappear?"

"Our bank regularly sends out teams of inspectors to monitor new companies our clients have used our funds to invest in. Strictly due diligence, nothing else. We do it all the time. When our man arrived at the NewPro offices this morning, they were empty. Everything inside was gone: the desks, the computers and servers, the copiers, even the coffee machine." Hinks was quiet for a moment, then said, "This looks like it could be fraud." He cleared his throat, a strange gargling sound. "Do either of you know about this? Did Edward Brand mention he was moving to a new location?"

Both shook their heads. Alan said, "What does this mean, Earl. For us?"

Earl Hinks took a couple of deep breaths. "The loan has to be repaid."

"When?" Taylor asked, her voice barely a whisper.

"Now."

"Define now," Alan said.

Hinks glanced at the file on his desk. "When you invested in NewPro, you gave them one-point-six million in cash and levered another thirteen million using the equity in G-cubed. The cash was yours, but the thirteen million was our money, and according to the contract, the money is due immediately if the bank decides the risk is too great. That's why it's called a demand loan. And obviously, if the business you invested in has packed up shop and disappeared, the risk is no longer acceptable."

"You didn't answer the question, Earl," Alan said.

"We need the money from the sale of G-cubed to cover the loan," Hinks said. "That would mean you need to put the business on the market immediately. At a price where it will sell. We can wait a bit for you to find a buyer and for the deal to close, but we're talking within one to three months. Any longer and the guys in the head office are going to force the sale, and that'll mean you'll be taking a fire-sale price on the business."

Taylor stared at the banker, the room about her swaying. "Earl, it's all we've got. The cash plus the business. Aside from our house, there's nothing else."

Hinks didn't respond. He was taking shallow breaths and repeatedly wiping his brow despite the cool air being pumped into the enclosed room. Finally, he said, "I'm sorry. Maybe the police . . ." He let the sentence trail off.

Alan slumped back in the chair. "Jesus. We're ruined."

Taylor didn't say a word.

CHAPTER TWO

Taylor caught a glimpse of her husband as she walked past the door to their home gym. He was on the treadmill and running hard. Probably still in shock, as she was. The Monday afternoon meeting with Earl Hinks, only three days ago, seemed surreal. A tasteless joke with no redeeming value. But she knew in her heart it was no joke. The paperwork on Hinks's desk had detailed the bank's position in black and white, no gray area.

The loan was due. Now.

Thirteen million dollars. Money they did not have.

She felt her knees buckling and ducked into the office, sitting on a stool before she collapsed. Everything she and Alan had worked for was gone. The business would have to go on the block. Finding a buyer to purchase the company she had worked twelve years to build would not be difficult. Letting it go would be next to impossible. She had put her heart and soul and an interminable amount of hours into the business, and her employees were like family. What was happening was impossible.

She glanced about the room, quiet elegance with dark, teak furniture and wall units. The brick fireplace was clean and ready to be lit. One wall was covered with plaques, framed accolades and awards her company had won over the years for its savvy in the highly competitive advertising world. Her eyes came to rest on Alan's degree from Stanford, set in a simple black frame against the taupe wall. No matting, nothing fancy—it was so Alan. When they had met three years ago, it had been packed in a box and stuck in his bedroom closet. They were learning about each other, talking to all hours of the night, when the subject of education had come up. He had never mentioned his Master's degree in Electrical Engineering. Nor did he wear the ring. It took him almost a week to find the box where the degree was tucked between a *Sports Illustrated* and a handful of *National Geographic* magazines. He didn't hang it on the wall until after they were married, almost seven months later. He did wear the ring, though. But only at her insistence.

That was a real difference between her and her husband. Alan didn't care about the house or what car he drove, and he certainly didn't care if anyone knew he was a Stanford graduate. What he did care about was doing things right. It wasn't the degree that mattered; it was putting the knowledge into action. He worked for one of San Francisco's most forward-thinking corporate security companies, and when he designed a new system for his clients, it was perfect in theory and in implementation. They had talked about it and planned it since they were married, and he was only a year or so from starting his own company. Silicon Valley was a veritable gold mine for companies that could provide secure environments for the software and hardware designers. Price was not an issue when it came to protecting a billion-dollar idea. But what had been a dream within their grasp was now a fleeting thought. The start-up costs were high and the carrying costs for the first year staggering. There was no chance Alan Bestwick would be controlling his own destiny for some time.

And Taylor's tangible dream was in tatters. G-cubed would have to be sold. Twelve years of novel ideas that grew to become national icons for some of corporate America's most innovative clients were history. And the six- and seven-figure billings that accompanied the print and television ads were gone. The good news was that the company carried no debt. And the net worth of G-cubed was at least thirteen million, which covered the loan Taylor and Alan had taken out to purchase a chunk of NewPro. That left them broke, except for the equity in their house.

It was a nightmare.

But to Taylor, the nightmare went far beyond the financial. She had invested heavily in her company not only financially, but emotionally. She couldn't count the number of times she had sat alone in her corner office with red eyes and a half-empty box of tissues. She remembered the day Amy Reid, one of her copy editors, had phoned in on a regular Monday morning. She could barely speak. Her baby had died of SIDS over the weekend. She wouldn't be in to work for a while. Taylor had met the baby three weeks before at a company picnic. Charles Reid. A perfect little boy, wide eyed at the newness of the world that surrounded him. Now deceased.

Taylor had called a meeting of all the staff. They were to contact the clients who knew Amy and let them know what had happened. She wanted a trust fund in Charles's name established immediately, the proceeds to go toward university education for Amy's other two children. She had gathered the women separately, setting a firm timetable for them to be at the Reid house, helping with dinner and the grind of daily chores. And just being there for the grieving family. They had set a minimum of three months. In the end, the women kept up the vigil for almost seven months. They cooked and cleaned, but more importantly, they gave Amy and her husband a new lease on life. Taylor spent more time at Amy's house than any other woman.

There was a low sound, and Taylor turned toward the door. Alan stood in the doorway, sweat dripping from his forehead, his shirt soaked. He wiped his brow with a towel and walked over to where she sat on the stool. He knelt on the floor in front of her.

"We'll survive this," he said, touching her lightly on her knee. "We've got the house, I'm working, and you're about the most employable person on the planet."

The tears started. Again. She wiped at them, but they streamed down her face. Alan dabbed them with his towel. "How could this have happened?" she said, her voice choked with emotion.

"The police have a forensics crew looking into it," Alan said. "Maybe they'll come up with something."

"Your money," she said. "My business. They took everything we had."

Now it was Alan's turn to choke back the tears. "It's just money," he said after a few moments. "Feeling guilty isn't going to change anything."

"Only money," she said. She took his hand and squeezed. "You worked your entire life to save that money. And it's my fault it's gone."

"No," Alan said, taking her by the shoulders and locking eyes. "You can't think that way, Taylor. We both agreed that NewPro was a good investment. Either one of us taking the blame and feeling guilty about what happened isn't healthy. We've got to focus on where we are right now and hope the police can catch these guys."

The doorbell rang, and Alan asked, "The real estate agent?"

She nodded. "He wanted to see the house before he did the market analysis."

Alan gave her shoulders a gentle squeeze. "I'll show him around."

"Thanks," she said.

She heard the front door open and muffled voices in the hall. Footsteps echoed off the hardwood as her husband and the Realtor moved through the main floor of the two-story Victorian. She stood and walked to the window, looking out over Octavia Street. They had purchased the house two and a half years ago when they got married. The San Francisco real estate market had been increasing steadily since then, and their location in Pacific Heights was ideal. Taylor figured the house would fetch about one-point-four. After expenses and the mortgage, that would net them about nine hundred thousand. How much of that would have to go toward paying off the bank was the only real variable. And that depended on what they could net from the sale of G-cubed. The word was already on the street that they needed to sell, and she knew there would be low-ball offers from competitors looking to capitalize on their misfortune. She turned from the window as Alan and the Realtor entered the office.

"Honey, this is Dave Bryant," Alan said.

She walked across the room and shook the man's hand. "Thanks for coming so quickly," she said.

"Not a problem. Referrals are important. I jump when someone puts their name on the line for me." Bryant's name had been passed along to Taylor through one of her office staff who had used him to sell their house in San Mateo and find them a condo in the city. He glanced about the room, then followed Alan back into the hall. Their voices diminished as they moved to the back of the house.

Taylor checked her watch. Almost three o'clock. On any normal day she would be at the office working on an ad campaign or at a client's office making a presentation. Not so now. In two hours someone from the corporate fraud division of the San Francisco police would be paying them a visit.

Corporate fraud.

Why didn't they see it? How could they have fallen so hard for the scam? Why did they invest so heavily? Questions, so many questions. And right now, no answers.

She closed her eyes and wondered if there would ever be any answers.

CHAPTER THREE

Detective Sam Morel shook his head. He'd seen clean-out jobs before, but nothing quite like this one. The office space was absolutely bare, not a stitch of furniture or paper. The forensics crew dusting for fingerprints was almost finished and they had yet to find one usable print. Morel snapped his notebook shut as two men in dark suits entered through the main doors. Morel knew cops, and these ones reeked of feds. He waited for them to approach him. At ten feet the badges came out, and at five feet one of the suits introduced himself.

"Detective Morel, I'm Special Agent Hawkins, and this is Special Agent Abrams. We're with the San Francisco office of the FBI."

Morel glanced at the creds. He didn't quite loathe FBI agents, but it was close. They always dressed the same, talked the same and most importantly, thought the same. Brent Hawkins was six feet tall and thin, his face chiseled rather than formed. He wore his dirty-blond hair short to his scalp, which only served to highlight his intense blue eyes. His hawklike nose was a touch too big for his lean face, and his jaw was set in a permanent scowl. John Abrams was softer, in the eyes and around the midsection. He topped out at five-ten, and his face was caught somewhere between full and chubby. His hair was at the maximum length the Bureau would allow, and his suit was off the rack, not tailor-made like his partner's. Both men were mid-thirties.

"What makes an agent special?" Sam Morel asked. "As compared to just a regular agent?"

Hawkins ignored the barb. "We understand you're in charge of this operation," he said.

"Yes, I am," Morel said, knowing full well that he wouldn't be for long. FBI agents didn't show up at white-collar crime scenes for no reason. Somewhere, somehow this scam had crossed state lines, and it was now federal.

"We have reason to believe that the people involved in this fraud were also operating in New York, Chicago and New Orleans. The information is still coming in, but this appears to be a well-organized setup, with offices across the country. And if they are tied together, then the case will come under federal jurisdiction."

"I understand," Morel said. There was no up-side to arguing with the suit. The best approach was to cooperate and hand over the file. Hell, his department was already busy, he hardly needed the business. The FBI could have this one if they wanted. In fact, just that morning he had stared at himself in the mirror, seeing the creases running back from the corners of his eyes to the tufts of hair he called sideburns. His face was thicker than when he was in his thirties. Not pudgier, thicker. He didn't seem to have as much neck either, almost like his head was settling into his shoulders. That wasn't good; he'd never been taller than five-nine at any point in his life. He still had all his body parts, a healthy head of graying hair and sturdy teeth. And his prostate was in fine form. Life was good; no sense letting a few wrinkles mess with his mind-set.

Morel said, "We had the place sealed for two days until we got search warrants, so we only got in this morning. My CSU guys are almost finished. If you want to bring in your own experts I'll arrange for access."

Hawkins nodded. "Thanks. Have you requisitioned the phone logs?"

"First thing. The company operated out of this space for eight months. We've got a request in for a complete list of incoming and outgoing calls over that period. We've also identified the bank they used to pay their operating expenses and have asked for copies of the corporate seal, the directors' names and all transactions since inception. I'll forward that ahead to your office."

Hawkins raised an eyebrow, then handed Morel a business card. "We appreciate the cooperation, Detective Morel."

Morel smiled. "We're on the same side, Agent Hawkins. I try to keep that in mind."

"Thanks."

Morel glanced at his watch. "I've got a meeting with two of the victims in half an hour. Want to come along?"

"That would be good," Abrams said. They had planned on conducting their own interview within twenty-four hours. This just made things easier.

Morel scribbled Alan and Taylor's address on a piece of paper and held it out. Abrams took it. "See you there at five," he said. He started toward the door, then stopped. "Hey, I've gotta know something."

"What is it, Detective?" Abrams asked.

"Do you guys take a course on always talking in proper English? You know, never using slang or saying 'Sure' instead of 'That would be good.'"

Abrams looked like he was going to blow, but Hawkins smiled. "They teach us to be polite, Detective. And to never swear."

"See you in half an hour," Morel said, grinning. Life at the Bureau was certainly different from SFPD.

Morel was fifty-two and three years from a full pension with the department. His waistline, a steady thirty-six for fifteen years, had recently ballooned to a forty. Grecian formula couldn't stop the constant flow of gray hair, and he needed an hour a week now just to pull out the unsightly nose and ear hairs. This was early fifties. What the hell was coming when he hit seventy or eighty? His energy levels were dropping as fast as his waistline was expanding. There was a time in his career when he would have fought the feds tooth and nail for jurisdiction, but not now. That surprised him, given the scope of what was fast becoming a major scam. White-collar crime in America was huge, and this one was shaping up to be one of the largest he had ever seen. First indications were that this was going to run into the tens of millions in San Francisco alone, even before the dollar amounts from the other cities were added in. He slid behind the wheel of his unmarked car and checked the map. Octavia Street—Pacific Heights. The high-rent district.

Twenty-five minutes later, he parked outside the restored Victorian belonging to Alan Bestwick and Taylor Simons. He called in his location, locked the car and hoofed it up the stairs to the front door. An extremely attractive woman with red hair and pale skin answered the doorbell. He slipped his badge out and held it up for her.

"Detective Sam Morel from the major crimes division," he said.

"Taylor Simons," she said, scrutinizing his ID. "Please come in."

"Thanks," he said, entering the house. He went through the introductions again as Alan Bestwick appeared. "Someone from the District Attorney's office will be here shortly. The FBI as well." He thought it best to warn them before the doorbell rang and more warm bodies began showing up.

"Well, I suppose that's a good thing," Alan said, leading Morel into the living room. He and Taylor sat beside each other on one of the couches, and Morel chose a wingback. "Is this normal procedure?"

"Yes and no," Morel said, settling into the chair. It was uncomfortable. "The DA's office is on the front lines in consumer and corporate fraud. We secure the site and then share the information with them. They handle some of the investigation and all the prosecution. Having someone from the District Attorney's office is normal, but the FBI isn't."

"Then why are they coming?" Taylor asked as the doorbell rang.

"That's probably them," Morel said. "I'll let them explain, if that's okay."

"Fine," Alan said. He disappeared into the hallway and returned a minute later with the two FBI agents. A woman dressed in a gray pantsuit and carrying a briefcase accompanied them. Sam Morel nodded to the woman and she returned the gesture.

The woman introduced herself to Taylor. "Julie Swimaker. I'm with the District Attorney's office."

Taylor shook her hand. "Detective Morel said to expect you."

Hawkins and Abrams flashed their creds and took a seat on an empty couch. Hawkins started the conversation. "Mr. Bestwick, Ms. Simons, fraud cases such as this one would usually be handled by the San Francisco DA's office, but the FBI is involved in this investigation because we have evidence that suggests this fraud is country wide. We have confirmation of similar scams being run in New York, Chicago, New Orleans, and we just received a call that the perpetrators were also active in Dallas. Since the crime is in more than one state, jurisdiction is federal."

"I understand," Alan said.

"What we need from you are the details of your involvement with NewPro," Hawkins said, taking a small tape recorder from his pocket and placing it on the coffee table. "I'm going to tape this conversation, if that's okay with you."

Alan and Taylor both nodded, and Hawkins hit the record button.

"Who introduced you to NewPro, and how did you first meet?"

Alan glanced at Taylor and gave her a nod. She replied, "I met Edward Brand, the president of NewPro, when he came to my advertising agency about seven months ago, looking for a firm to handle an upcoming ad campaign. His business idea was brilliant. He had researched a number of products that had been off the shelves for a long time. Products that had household names." She named off about fifteen of them from memory. "All of these products had one thing in common: Their manufacturer had dropped them, and let those household names get stale. The companies that held the trademark didn't care. They had other consumables on the market that were generating enough income to satisfy their shareholders and had little desire to reintroduce an old product to a new market. In fact, a lot of the companies had let their exclusivity to the product expire. They couldn't care less if NewPro walked in and retabled the product."

"Edward Brand wanted your company to devise a marketing strategy to reintroduce these products," Hawkins said.

"Yes. It would have been a substantial account. The up-front costs to our firm, just for initial design concepts, research and planning were high. I asked him for a hundred thousand–dollar retainer. He wrote the check on the spot. When it cleared the bank and the money was in our account, we did a creative presentation for him. He loved it. He wanted a few minor changes, but went with the concept as we designed it. The total cost of a nationwide advertising campaign would have been over twenty-eight million dollars. I asked for another hundred thousand—dollars so we could begin to secure print and television space. Again, the check was in my hand inside two minutes. I was impressed with how he did business."

"How did you come to invest in his company?" Swimaker asked.

"That's a good question," Taylor said, scratching the top of her head. "I don't think there was ever a defining moment. It wasn't like he ever said, 'Hey, why don't you guys invest in my company' or anything like that. There were a lot of times when Alan and I would sit around and talk about what an excellent idea Brand had. He was organized, focused and well financed. NewPro had the legal rights to at least twelve of the products I mentioned, and was in negotiations for a handful more. They had manufacturing plants in New Jersey, Pittsburgh and Seattle ready to begin production given about three months' lead-in time."

"Did you visit any of the manufacturing facilities?" Hawkins asked.

She turned slightly to face the two FBI men. "We did, but not until a bit later, after we decided we might want to invest in NewPro."

"Sorry, getting ahead of the game," Hawkins said.

Taylor forced a smile, and Alan reached over and clasped her left hand. Her emotions were kicking in, and the brave face she had put on was beginning to crack. "I think the idea of getting involved may have surfaced when he talked about his intent to take the company public a couple of months before the products were scheduled to hit the shelves. He expected the Initial Public Offering, or IPO, would raise about four hundred and eighty million dollars, with an error margin of about three percent. The prospectus was already filed, and getting registered on the New York Stock Exchange was almost a rubber stamp."

"We looked at the prospectus very closely," Alan interjected. "It was extremely well done. There was no reason to suspect it was false."

Hawkins nodded. "We pulled a copy of it. It *was* professional. And very believable."

Taylor continued. "Brand's projections for the company's stock were amazing. Sixty million common shares would hit the market, priced at eight dollars a share. The IPO would sell out in less than a month and then, if someone wanted in, they would have to pay resale prices on the shares. According to the models he was using, the share prices would double in about six to nine months."

"Did you see the models he was using?" Hawkins asked.

Taylor nodded. "Yes. We had full access to them once we expressed an interest in buying in. At first we thought we might invest a couple of million, but as time progressed and we realized what a gold mine NewPro was sitting on, we decided to up the ante."

"Who decided?" Julie Swimaker asked. "One of you, or were you influenced by Brand?"

Taylor swallowed. "I did. Alan was the cautious one, but I thought the opportunities NewPro presented were too good to pass on. If Brand's company had been legit and if they had met the targets he was projecting, we could have cashed out in two years with more than twenty million dollars and full ownership in G-cubed. It was almost like winning the lottery."

"Almost," Sam Morel said.

"When I see something I consider to be risky, I check it out," Taylor said. "If it falls within my boundaries of acceptable risk, I go for it."

"We felt it was manageable," Alan agreed.

Taylor continued, "That was when we asked to see the manufacturing facilities. Brand told us we could pick any one of the three, or all of them if we wanted. We decided on New Jersey, mostly because we thought a few days in New York would be a nice break."

"And the facilities were believable?" Julie Swimaker asked.

"Absolutely," Alan answered. "The building was about forty thousand square feet, with a lot of equipment. There were packaging and labeling areas, lots of conveyors to move the product, and a large loading dock to get the product onto trucks and into the stores. The facilities were impressive, but what really sold us was the guy who showed us through. He explained the equipment, even going into how much money they had saved by buying used rather than new. I think that was one of the deciding factors for us. They were sitting on a gold mine, yet they were being very cautious about how they spent their seed money. In retrospect, we suspect the equipment was used because they leased the space with everything already in place."

"I pushed Alan to invest heavily after we got back from New York. He had about a million-three in accessible funds, and I had about three hundred thousand. It was my idea to lever the extra money from the equity in G-cubed."

"Your company must be in good stead for the bank to loan one hundred percent of its value. That's unusual," Julie Swimaker said.

"We had a very good relationship with our banker," Alan said, then added, "unfortunately."

"So your idea was to invest in the company before it went public, then reap the benefits of the IPO?" Julie Swimaker asked.

"Yes," Taylor answered. "We knew there would be a lock-up period of two years from the IPO, but that didn't worry us."

"Lock-up period?" Sam Morel asked. "What's that?"

"It's one of the Blue Sky laws put in place to protect small shareholders when a firm first goes public. The large shareholders are required by law to hold their shares for two years from the IPO. That prevents them from driving up the price of a stock that's based on a false prospectus and dumping their shares at an inflated figure right after it goes public. The two-year period gives the company time to establish its true value in the marketplace."

Alan added, "It was the two-year lock-up that influenced our decision to invest. Brand couldn't sell his shares for two years, and that gave us confidence in the company."

"But NewPro never went public," Taylor said. "They just disappeared in the middle of the night."

"This is sure starting to look like a shell game," Morel said, shaking his head.

"What?" Taylor said. "What's a shell game?"

"It's a con. A guy sets up a board in a back alley or a street corner—wherever—and puts three half shells on it. You know, walnut shells, something like that. Then he puts something under one of the shells. He moves them around and you have to guess which shell it's under. But he always makes one move that you don't see. Your chances of picking the correct shell are a whole lot less than one in three. They're almost zero."

"What's going to happen now?" Alan asked dejectedly. "What can we expect from your investigation?"

Hawkins answered, "We'll be working hand-in-hand with Ms. Swimaker and the rest of the San Francisco DA's office to try to track down Edward Brand and his associates. We'll run a complete forensic audit on the company, concentrating as much as we can on hard evidence, like the information they gave to the SEC on their stock exchange application. We'll coordinate the investigation with the district offices in New York and the other centers we think are involved in this scam. Right now, Mr. Bestwick, I can't give you any assurances or guarantees. But we'll try."

"Thanks," Taylor said. She was verging on tears. "Anything you can do is appreciated."

Taylor and Alan shook hands with the FBI agents and Julie Swimaker as they left the house. Sam Morel lingered for a minute after the others had departed.

"The FBI is going to take over the investigation," he said. "But that doesn't mean I can't stay up to date with what they have and keep you in the loop. Sometimes these guys tend to hold things a little close to their chest. If it's okay with you, I'll call and let you know what they've got."

Taylor touched him on the arm. "Thanks, Detective Morel. That would be helpful."

"Not a problem," he said. He grasped her hand for a second, then left.

Alan closed the door and caught his wife as she fell into his arms, the tears bursting forth. Her body was wracked with convulsions as she cried. Her knees collapsed, and her feet slipped out from under her on the hardwood. Alan clutched her tight and slowly lowered himself to the ground, leaning against the front door for support. They lay on the floor in each other's arms for ten minutes, silent and unmoving.

CHAPTER FOUR

Detective Sam Morel glanced back at the old Victorian house. The paint was new, the wedding-cake trim impeccable and the small garden well tended. By all appearances, a beautiful home where the cares of the world refused to rest. Appearances could be so deceiving.

Sam Morel was no fool. He knew exactly what a two-year lock-up was, and he was well versed in the Blue Sky laws, which had been instituted after the turn of the century and brought into the limelight during the Depression. By asking the question in front of the FBI agents, he had relegated himself to a nonentity in their eyes. That was just fine. It was so much easier to operate under the radar. He was now positioned to work hand-in-hand with the FBI, getting access to all the current information in their files while their expectations of what he could produce would be minimal.

He was also well versed with a man named Robin Malory and his company, Morgan Fay. Robin Malory was a Fortune 100 castoff. He spent twenty-eight years of his life scratching his way to the top, only to receive the kiss-off when he was finally in line to be the next CEO.

He left the firm and started Morgan Fay, a company that specialized in revitalizing old brand names and bringing them back to market. Morgan Fay had received SEC approval and had gone public. The stock price had shot upward, and for the first seventeen months had performed admirably. But the truth behind the company's success was far different.

The truth was a four hundred million–dollar scam. Morgan Fay was being manipulated by a management company called Avalon Partners, and creative bookkeeping was the order of the day. Not to the scale of Enron or WorldCom, but four hundred million was hardly small potatoes. Sam Morel could see a lot of differences between the Morgan Fay case and NewPro, but he suspected the brainchild of Edward Brand's company was none other than Morgan Fay. And that gave him an inside track to how Edward Brand and his accomplices thought. Knowing how a criminal thinks was important.

Morgan Fay was a company that existed on testosterone and guile. When Robin Malory said something was possible, or plausible, people assumed it was. It wasn't until the forensic auditors had marched through the front doors of Avalon Partners that the scope of what had happened became apparent. If Sam Morel was correct in his thinking, Edward Brand was another Robin Malory. Christ, the man had taken on an alias that mocked the very scam he was perpetrating. Edward Brand, revitalizing brand name products. The guy had balls.

Morel pulled into the parking lot off Vallejo Street and hoofed it into the Central District station. He took the elevator to the fourth floor and picked up his mail on the way by the reception desk. His office had a window, but the view was nothing spectacular, another building and a bit of the street. It provided enough light to keep his plants alive. That was something he cared about. His personal life was a mess, his ex-wife in rehab for her drinking, his daughter three months into a trial separation with her abusive husband and his son sitting on a beach somewhere in India wasting his life smoking pot every day. At least he had his plants.

He checked the soil, and his finger came away slightly damp. They'd be good over the weekend, but Monday would be watering day. Morel dropped into his chair and smoothed his hands over his scalp, feeling his thick gray hair on his fingertips. He was a dinosaur, one who believed in holding doors open for women and paying for dinner and a movie. But he was a staunch supporter of equal pay scales for the sexes. He was a technological dichotomy as well, and he knew it. He understood computers and was well versed in the newest forensic methods of hunting a criminal by following even the faintest electronic trail. But he was the first cop to call for a CSU team to physically search the crime scene for tangible clues. His contact list on his e-mail server was full, but he carried an address book with the same numbers written in by hand. It was as if he couldn't quite make the break from paper to bytes. Whatever it was that drove him, he got results.

Corporate fraud in San Francisco was handled mostly by the District Attorney's office, but there was always a need for an investigative presence outside cyberspace. When Assistant DAs, like Julie Swimaker, showed up at a crime scene, they always looked for Sam Morel. He was their contact to SFPD, the one who secured the area and ordered the crime scene unit. He was the cop; they were the law. Julie Swimaker and the other Assistant DAs knew Sam Morel, and they knew he was no idiot. Morel could only imagine what Julie was thinking when he asked the question about the Blue Sky laws. That didn't matter. What did matter was that the FBI agents working the case thought he was incompetent. That meant that they would share information freely, under the assumption that he wouldn't have a clue what to do with it. That worked just fine for him.

Morel checked his Day-timer for a number, then picked up the phone and dialed. A man's voice answered. "Billy, it's Sam, how are things?"

"Fine. What can I do for you?" The voice was guarded, the kind of voice from a man who knows he's talking to a cop, doesn't want to, but has no option.

"There was an operation that shut down three days ago. My guess would be fifty to sixty computers, servers, printers, copy machines, desks and all the stuff that goes with a complete office. I want you to watch for it, call me if you see it come through the back door somewhere."

"That's easy," Billy said, relieved that Morel's request was generic and not specific to the hot merchandise he traded daily. "I'll keep my eyes open."

"Thanks. You get something that might be it, call me right away."

"Done."

Morel hung up and searched out another number. The FBI was smart about some things, but they didn't always see the whole picture. That picture included getting rid of the equipment that had been used to keep the office up and running for the past seven or eight months. Putting it into storage was dangerous. It kept all the equipment together, and with that many computers and servers, a forensic audit was bound to turn up something. Dumping it in a landfill was akin to lighting a neon sign asking to be investigated and arrested. That left letting it filter out to the second-hand market. Not all at once, but a bit at a time. He didn't have to explain that to Billy; the fence knew how these things worked. They would release them in a few batches; a handful of computers here, a couple of servers and printers there. Nothing that would raise too many eyebrows. The market for resale computers and office supplies was an interesting one. But it was who they would release them to that was the key. The papers were full of used computer equipment, but no self-respecting thief would ever leave a phone number where the police could simply call him, set up a meeting, then bust him with the gear. They relied on fences to middle the merchandise, and Sam Morel knew those fences. Billy was one in the know, and Sam relied on Billy a lot. In return, Sam made sure no one ever touched his source. Tit for tat. Lots of rubbing each other's back going on. That was how things worked on the street. And that was the part of the equation the FBI often missed. They stuck out like a fat man in a marathon. They didn't like to work the sordid little details in case they got their suits dirty. It wasn't that Morel didn't like the feds—he was indifferent.

Morel found the number he was looking for and dialed. A man answered, but the voice sounded young. That's because the person talking was only twenty-two. Two years over twenty and already a master at recovering information from hard drives that had been wiped clean by their owners. So good at it, in fact, that he had spent six months in juvie for hacking into the Department of Defense's mainframe and changing all the employees' pay scales. Nobody complained when their pay was deposited, but the accounting department went ballistic. The judge found the stunt mildly amusing, but still serious enough for a short stint in one of the minimum-security juvenile detention centers. He ordered the young man to perform two hundred hours of community service. Sam Morel wormed his way to the front of the line and got the two hundred hours for his department.

"Jamie," Sam said. "How ya doing?"

"Hey, Sam," the kid said, his voice upbeat. He liked working with Sam. It sure beat spending time with other kids who thought mainlining heroin was fun. "What's up? You got something for me?"

"Might have. I've got one of my guys watching for some computers that were used in a corporate fraud. If we get our hands on them, I'll need you right away."

"Not a problem. I'm in college Monday through Thursday, but I've got evenings and Fridays, and the weekends of course."

"Good. Just make sure you don't check out for any length of time. No more than twelve hours between checking your voice mail and your e-mail, okay?"

"Sure, Sam. This one sounds cool."

"It looks big, Jamie. Real big."

"Man, I hope you find one of those babies."

"Me too. Talk to you later." Sam hung up and leaned back in his chair.

Edward Brand. Who was he? The FBI would be running him through their computers, just as he was running records checks on every police computer he could access. Brand was, without a doubt, not the man's real name, but sometimes aliases emitted clues. Sometimes. But one thing was for certain: Edward Brand had pulled off one hell of a scam. If the initial figures were correct, the man had scooped up more than one hundred and eighty million dollars from unsuspecting investors. And he had done it wisely. At no time had he completed the Securities and Exchange Commission requirements and taken the company public. If he had, the microscope NewPro would have been operating under would have made pulling the scam off almost impossible. No, Edward Brand was no dummy. By all appearances he had succeeded in doing exactly what he had set out to do: relieving a lot of rich people of their money.

Sam Morel knew one thing. Once criminals had the cash, they didn't like to give it back. If Brand was organized enough to pull this off, then he had enough insight to look ahead and plan what to do once he had the money. Morel closed his eyes and replayed the looks on the victims' faces. Alan Bestwick, ashen white with heavy bags under his eyes. Taylor Simons, a strong woman driven close to her breaking point, desperately trying to keep her emotions in check. For a moment he wondered what would happen to them if no one could find Brand and they lost all their money. It wasn't pretty. What made it so reprehensible was that the odds were overwhelmingly in Brand's favor at this point. Sam had one more thought before he got up and went in search of some stale coffee. If he were a betting man—and he was—his money would be on the bad guy.

CHAPTER FIVE

Edward Brand stood on the balcony overlooking English Bay. The sun had been out since he had arrived in Vancouver three days before, but the weather forecasters were calling for a massive cloud bank to sweep in off the Pacific Ocean in the next twelve hours. Brand knew Vancouver well enough to know the meteorologists were seldom wrong when it came to soggy weather. He sipped his coffee and stared at the bay.

Brand was a charismatic man, the kind of guy people noticed in a crowded room. He was six feet with thick blond hair to the top of his ears and penetrating gray eyes. He had a quick smile and an easygoing nature. There was little body fat on his frame, the results of a good diet and a strict workout regimen. His handshake was as firm as the hand he was shaking, and he was either an intellectual person and a highly interesting conversationalist, or quiet as a hawk circling on the updrafts. He was whatever he had to be. Edward Brand was the ultimate con man.

Every part of him could mutate to fit the moment. If his marks were looking for a man they thought could

run a multi-billion–dollar company, he was the articulate
and informed CEO, dressed in Armani business casual.
When the scam needed him in the pits at a Formula One
race, he was there in coveralls and a Ferrari hat. On the
beach in Monaco, in a five-star Paris restaurant or braced
against the howling Arctic winds at a northern Canadian oil rig—Edward Brand could pull it off. He had
grown rich from his talent, but rich wasn't enough. He
was driven, much like the CEOs he pretended to be, to
rise above average and reach the pinnacle. Rich was
good, but Brand aspired to super-rich. So he continued to
take people's money. Lots of it. The NewPro scam had
been his best to date. Now that job was history. He had
wrapped it up and flown to Vancouver, a much richer
man than a year prior.

In his mind, Vancouver was the most beautiful city in
the world. The layout was very similar to San Francisco,
but the similarities ended there. The city was built into
the heavily wooded foothills surrounding the Fraser
River, and right from the start the urban planners had refused to cede to developers by allowing them to over-
build. The amount of green space in the city was
staggering, Stanley Park alone covering 1,000 acres of
prime real estate. The mixture of mountains, old-growth
forests with intimate walking paths and water was almost magic. He loved Vancouver, but not just for its
beauty. He loved it because it was in Canada, and if you
ever want to leave the United States and not be hassled at
a border, head for Canada.

The Canadian authorities were almost British in their
politeness. They questioned why he wanted to visit the
country, but never asked more than the most perfunctory
questions. Then, invariably, they let him enter. When he
wanted to leave, they smiled and helped load his bag on
the nearest conveyor. God he loved the Canadians.

Although he was American, it was the United States
Customs and Immigration officials who worried him

most. They were extremely efficient, and since he always traveled with a forged passport, exiting and entering the country of his birth was a harrowing experience. He had been sweating as he departed San Francisco, and he didn't sweat unless it was a hundred degrees and a hundred percent humidity. This con had been different. Bigger. Much bigger. And wildly successful. He turned slightly at the sound of another person exiting the house onto the balcony.

"Tony," he said when he saw who it was. The man leaned on the railing next to him. They didn't shake hands. "Any problems getting across the border?"

"None," Tony replied. The newcomer was a tall man, almost six-three, with close-cropped blond hair and penetrating blue eyes. His build matched his height, sturdy and toned. He rarely smiled and when he did it was with his lips, never showing his teeth. He was clean-shaven and the paleness of his skin spoke to his Scandinavian heritage. "Came across in Montreal, then flew Air Canada across the country."

Brand nodded. "Everything wrap up okay in New York?"

"Without a hitch. We had the offices emptied out by nine and the factory in New Jersey wiped down and locked up before midnight. Joey's still in New York, and Frank's already moved on to Mexico."

"Good. Joey leaves tomorrow?"

"Yup. He'll be in Rio by this time tomorrow. That's the last of our New York crew."

"Excellent job, Tony. Do you know what your final numbers were?"

"Somewhere close to nine million, I think."

"Over nine. Closer to ten. We got Stilling's money just before cut-off time. That was almost a million."

Tony Stevens grinned. A hint of white showed. "Got the fucker. He was so damned tough. I didn't think we'd see anything out of him or that shrew of a wife of his.

Christ, what a pair. He reminded me of a pig farmer every time I saw him. I think it's because he looked like a pig. Ugly bastard. And his wife, what a total bitch. I don't think she ever said one nice word to him."

It was Brand's turn to smile. "It sounds like you're happy we got their money."

"Fucking ecstatic. Couldn't have happened to a nicer pair of total shitheads."

"You did well. Ten million."

"What was the final count in San Fran?"

"Eighteen-five. Most of it from the couple who owned G-cubed."

Tony whistled. "Eighteen-five. Wow. What was the total?"

"With your extra million coming in just under the wire, about two hundred and twelve."

Now the man smiled, his teeth visible. They were crooked and the front ones pushed back, like someone had punched him in the face the day his adult teeth came in. "Christ, Robert, we really fucked them, didn't we?"

"What did you say?" Brand said, his head snapping around, the tone of his voice absolute ice. "What did you call me?"

"Christ, sorry. Edward. Edward Brand. Never our real names. I know the drill. Damn it, that was stupid. Like Mr. Pink and Mr. White and all that shit on *Reservoir Dogs*. Sorry, Edward."

Brand cooled. "Okay, Tony. But for Christ's sake be careful. We use the names until the job is over. It's the little things that fuck you up. Remember that."

"Yeah, the little things."

A silence settled over the balcony, just the slight whisper of wind coming in off the ocean. "Who was your favorite?" Brand asked after a minute.

"What?"

"*Reservoir Dogs*. Who was your favorite guy?"

"Shit, no doubt about it, Mr. Pink. Loved Steve Buscemi

in that movie. Thing about Buscemi I can't figure out, is why he doesn't get his teeth fixed. The guy must have enough money by now."

Edward Brand leaned over the railing and focused on the water. "I liked Mr. Blonde."

"Yeah, he was cool."

"They sure fucked up the robbery, though. What a mess. Too much testosterone."

"And a police informant. That's where the wheels came off. The snitch."

Brand shifted slightly and glanced at Stevens. "Yeah, the snitch." He was silent for a minute, then said, "You know, Tony, we've got a lot of people in the know on this one. Crews in New York, San Fran and six other cities. That's a lot of people."

"What are you saying?" Tony asked, concerned.

"Nothing. Just wondering how long we can keep expanding before one of our key people is on the wrong side."

"Shit, that would be bad. Really bad."

"Yeah. Worse than bad. We'd have to take care of them."

Tony Stevens wasn't smiling now. "Kill them?"

Brand finished his coffee and looked north to the mountains. The view from the upscale neighborhood of Kitsilano was stunning. The skyline of Greater Vancouver was framed against Mount Seymour and directly across English Bay was Stanley Park, lush green resting on the tranquil waters of the Pacific Ocean. He took a deep breath and tasted the salt air. When he answered the other man's question, it was in a soft voice, but one that was unmistakably serious.

"Yes, Tony. We'd have to kill them."

CHAPTER SIX

Alan Bestwick was worried about his wife. She was lethargic, a ghost of the person he had known only eight days ago. He had to constantly remind her to eat, and she had stopped exercising on the treadmill. Her color was washed out, pale except for the dark shadows under her eyes. Even her normally vibrant red hair looked muted. He finished filing his nails and set the file on the night table beside their bed. He walked over to where she sat looking out the second-story bay window and placed his hands gently on her shoulders. She glanced up and smiled. It was forced.

"It'll be okay," he said. "Your staff will understand. They knew the company had to be sold."

"Of course they will," she said, turning again to the street. "But what about the campaign to raise money for the children's hospital? We're donating all our time on that, Alan. Will the new owners live up to our commitment? That's important. There are a lot of sick kids out there who need a good facility. We were making a difference. And all the other charity work we did at G-cubed. What's going to happen to that?"

"Maybe they'll be community minded."

"I shouldn't have to sell my company. I mean that for a lot more reasons than just the money we took out of G-cubed."

He rubbed her shoulders and neck, feeling the knots in her muscles. "No, you shouldn't." What else could he say? G-cubed had gone on the block four days ago and a smaller, almost unknown firm out of Los Angeles had snapped it up in less than forty-eight hours. A few details remained to be ironed out, but the deal was done. Thirteen-five for the company, and after selling expenses, they would net about twelve-eight. That left them two hundred thousand dollars short on the loan to the bank. The house would have to go.

"I talked to the Realtor this morning," Alan said. "He'll be over tonight to list the house. That okay with you?"

She nodded, almost imperceptibly. "What price does he want to put it on at?"

"One-point-four-five. He feels we will get one-point-four million. That nets us about what we expected. After covering a two hundred thousand shortfall with the bank, we should have about seven hundred thousand left over."

"Well, that's not enough to buy a place in the city. We'll have to look at San Mateo or one of the other suburbs."

He continued to rub her neck, the knots diminishing under his touch. "That's not so bad."

Silence crept through the room, and they both watched a woman walking her dog on the far sidewalk. She chastised him for peeing on a bag of garbage left by the curb and Alan could feel his wife's body shake slightly as she chuckled at the absurdity of it. At that moment, the woman's greatest challenge in life was to get her dog not to pee on someone's garbage. The dog only cared about emptying his bladder on something that smelled good.

"Life should be so simple," Taylor said quietly, as though reading his mind.

"It will be someday. Just not right now."

She glanced at her watch and stood up. It was nine-thirty. "I need to go. I asked the staff to be in the board-room for ten o'clock."

He kissed her and held her tight for a minute, then let go. She left quietly, locking the door behind her. Her car was parked at the curb, and she turned the alarm off and slipped in behind the steering wheel. The Audi didn't feel as sporty today, but she knew it was just her. The car was simply metal and glass, plastic and wires. It didn't care who drove it. For that matter, she thought, money didn't care who owned it. Right now, Edward Brand owned a whole bunch of her money. She floored the car and felt some of her tension melt away as the high-performance vehicle shot ahead. The tachometer red-lined before she reached for the gear shift. When she finally up-shifted, the car responded and the speedometer crossed over seventy. She eased off the gas and brought her speed down to the legal limit. Somehow, that simple exercise made her feel better.

Taylor reached her office and parked in her assigned spot. Her entire staff was waiting in the boardroom when she arrived. It was five after ten. She took her place at the head of the table and had a quick look about. All eyes were focused on her, waiting. Waiting to know whether they still had jobs.

"The company has been sold," she said. "But no one in this room will be let go. That was the first condition of the sale. Everyone is still employed." There was a silent, collective sigh in the room. She could feel it more than hear it. "I've got all the details of the sale, including when it will be effective. I'll get into those in a few minutes, but first, I want you to know that I will not be staying on. In any capacity. This is it for me."

There were groans of dissention, but she raised her hand and her staff quieted. She was closer to tears than anyone in the room could have imagined. "It was my choice," she said. "I can't continue to work inside the organization that we, as a team, built from scratch. Not with someone watching over my shoulder."

The meeting continued for another hour as Taylor detailed what the new owners would like wrapped up before they took over. They were heavily tied to the West Coast but had no presence in San Francisco. With the client base G-cubed had built and the office space and staff already in place, the deal worked perfectly for them. Thirteen-point-five million worked well for Taylor.

She finished her speech and spent another half hour hugging everyone and wishing them the best. She left her personal items in her office. Removing everything was going to be painful, and she would rather do it when there was no staff present. She pulled up in front of the house and parked behind a dark car that she'd seen before. She just couldn't place it. The moment she entered her house, she remembered. Sam Morel's voice carried down the hall to where she was removing her shoes. When she entered the kitchen, she saw Morel and her husband sitting at the table. Alan rose when he saw her.

"How did it go?" he asked.

"They took it okay," Taylor said. "They're glad no one is getting laid off." She smiled at Morel and checked her watch. Five to twelve. "Good morning, Detective."

"Ms. Simons," he said, rising.

She waved him back into his chair and sat down at the table. "Please call me Taylor."

"Sam," he said.

Alan rejoined them at the table. "Sam was just going over the latest news from the FBI and the DA's office."

"We appreciate you taking the time to keep us up to date," Taylor said.

Morel nodded, then cleared his throat. "I was telling Alan that the FBI has identified eight centers Brand and his colleagues targeted. The operation in San Francisco was one of the eight."

"The others were all in major cities?" Taylor asked.

"Yes. New York, Dallas, Denver and the like. Nothing under a million people and all cities with vibrant economies. The sting was the same in each city. They used the NewPro name, told people that they would be revitalizing old products and gave each investor a copy of the false prospectus. From what we can gather so far, they ripped off about two hundred million dollars."

"So it's not just us," Alan said. "There are lots of people out there in the same predicament we're in."

Sam nodded. "I have a list of the victims. Some can easily afford the loss, others were hit very hard. Brand didn't care. He took whatever money he could get his hands on. Hawkins gave me a detailed report on New-Pro's accounting. Once they had the corporate accounts set up they established lines of credit with suppliers and pushed most of those dates to September fifteenth. Then they packed up a week before that and skipped out on the payments. Some of their suppliers wouldn't extend the dates that far and all those companies were paid up to date."

"How much money did they invest in this?" Alan asked. "I mean, setting something like this up isn't cheap."

"No, it's not. The FBI tally on what Brand's crew paid out is somewhere around eight million dollars. That includes paying their office staff, who had absolutely no idea what was going on and covering up-front costs like the two hundred thousand they paid to G-cubed for your initial setup fees on the advertising campaign. They were well financed. And that's got Hawkins and his guys thinking that maybe these guys have done this before. They're looking in their history databases for similar scams." Morel brightened for a moment. "There's one thing that might be helpful," he said. "The FBI office in New York might have something."

"What?" Taylor asked, sitting forward in her chair.

"Don't know. Hawkins said they had a source that was feeding them information, but he wouldn't elaborate."

"I'll keep my fingers crossed," Taylor said. "We need some sort of a break." Alan grasped her hand.

"We've finished interviewing the staff who were working at NewPro," he said. "We did it jointly with the FBI, and we've identified two other men beside Edward Brand who were involved. The rest of the staff look to be innocent dupes."

"Who are the other two?" Alan asked.

"Ben Wright and Roger Tate. Do you know them?"

Alan and Taylor both nodded. "Wright was VP—Western Region Sales, and Tate was the financial guy. Brand introduced him as a Certified Public Accountant."

"Well, we've accounted for everyone but them. They're ghosts, like Brand. No one living at their addresses, no mail, no trace of either man. We suspect they kept an address just for show, but that all three were living together somewhere else. Where, we have no idea."

"So the entire office, with the exception of these three guys, all thought NewPro was a legitimate business," Taylor said.

"It appears that way." Morel sipped his coffee and continued. "Fraud, or white-collar crime or whatever you want to call it, is out of control. The FBI has an entire division, the White-Collar Crime Investigation Team, set up to monitor fraud and money laundering through the Caribbean. It's not just drug money flowing through the Bahamas and the Caymans and all the other islands. More and more it's money from fraud that's being deposited into the banks. Since it's not drug money, the bankers are more accommodating on stretching or breaking the rules."

"Why don't they stop it?" Alan asked. "We've got the

Securities and Exchange Commission regulating publicly traded stocks. Why can't something be done to control private corporations?"

Morel shook his head. "Computers changed everything. It used to be that in order to pass a bad check, a fraud artist would have to physically move into an address, search the public records for someone about his or her age who had died, assume the identity by ordering a birth certificate and get a driver's license once the proof of birth arrived in the mail. Then they would go to the bank, open an account and order checks with their address on them. They'd wait for the checks to be printed and mailed out, then they'd go on a spending spree. Now, with computers and the Internet, they simply place an order with a firm that prints checks and have them sent to a P.O. box. Turnaround time is less than a week, and they don't need an address. I don't know if any of you saw the movie *Catch Me If You Can*, with Leonardo DiCaprio, but one of the scams they showed in the movie still works just fine. Say someone wants to write a bunch of bad checks in New York State. They take the checks and modify one number on the routing numbers the banks use to designate the Federal Reserve Bank in that region. By changing two to twelve on the routing number, the checks are sent to Hawaii for processing rather than New York. That buys them another two weeks. When the checks finally start to come back to the bank, they've scammed thousands and thousands of dollars from merchants and the bank and have moved on to the next set of checks they ordered. The losses to the banks are in the hundreds of millions of dollars. That's just checks. There are hundreds of other frauds going on out there every day. We're talking billions of dollars in fraud every year. Yet for some reason, everyone seems to think this is acceptable. It's all Greek to me."

"How do you catch them?" Alan asked.

Morel shrugged. "Usually we don't. The criminal has

to make a mistake to get caught. If they're smart about what they're doing, keep moving and don't get too greedy, they get away with it. In fact, most of the small ones just get written off. It's the big ones, like this, that get the attention."

"That's not good news," Taylor said.

Morel finished his coffee and set the mug on the table. "We might have a line on some of the computers they used. And sometimes there is still usable information on the drives. Sometimes. Usually they wipe the drives clean by writing a series of zeroes over the data."

Taylor nodded. "Kelly told me about that," she said. Both men looked at her. "Kelly Kramer, he's my computer specialist at G-cubed. Well, *was* my computer specialist. He took some kind of Master's program in some sort of high-technology crime investigation from some college in Arlington."

"He's working for an advertising firm?" Morel asked. "What's with that?"

"He was involved with some woman, and she wanted to move to San Francisco. When he followed her out here, he needed a job. I was the first one to make him an offer. He's great with computers and CAD, and he loved the job. So he stayed."

Morel scratched his head thoughtfully. Jamie was an asset when it came to dredging information off a wiped hard drive, but Jamie wasn't always reliable. There were times when he was AWOL. It would be wise to keep Taylor Simons's computer specialist as a backup. "Maybe we could use him," Sam said. "We're run off our feet just trying to keep up with all the fraud that's happening. We've got a hiring freeze on. It's all about money these days. Anyway, one of my sources has a line on a batch of computers that just came on the resale market. I'm meeting with him later today."

Alan managed a slight smile. "Well, good luck. Any news these days is good news. It's been over a week since they took off with our money. I don't imagine the trail gets any warmer with time."

"No. It's not like a murder investigation where time is often crucial, but the longer Brand and his crew have to settle in somewhere, the worse it is for us."

"If the trail goes cold . . ." Taylor let the sentence die off. She didn't have to finish. The money had disappeared into a black hole, and that hole was closing.

CHAPTER SEVEN

Alicia Walker glanced over her shoulder. Two men were about eighty feet behind her and matching her pace. She ducked into an alley and sprinted fifty feet to an overflowing Dumpster, crouching low in the shadows. She could feel the pressure of the government-issue Glock pistol against her back. It felt good.

The two men walked past the alley entrance without a glance. She waited a few minutes, then moved through the garbage-strewn lane back to the street. It was dark, the only light coming from a streetlamp halfway down the block. She looked both directions, her eyes taking in every detail. The street front was lined with retail shops: a butcher, a bookseller, a tailor and a small deli stood on the far side of road. Her eyes saw into every doorway, every shadow, every niche. Nothing. She ventured out from the alley until she could see into the recessed doorways on her side of the street. There was no sign of the men. She resumed walking north on the street, her senses on high alert.

Some people would call her actions paranoia. She

called it common sense. And not just because she lived in New York.

Alicia Walker was undercover FBI, working in the corporate fraud division. She was trained to notice the small details and to recognize and eliminate danger before it eliminated her. Six years with the Bureau and so far she had managed to sidestep the violence that so often plagued undercover work. She had pulled her weapon three times, but had never fired. That was something she was extremely proud of. Most of her working days were spent in posh offices with white-collar criminals, amassing enough evidence for the boys from the J. Edgar Hoover Building to swoop in and arrest the major players before they could pull their scam and close up shop. She had been successful many times, but this one hadn't gone well. Not that it was really her fault; she had come in at the last moment, too late to stop the con from going down.

Six weeks ago, Alicia had met Tony Stevens at a SoHo art gallery featuring a new Manhattan artist. He was attractive and charming, and from minute one she had suspected he was involved in some sort of con. The signs were all there. He was more than willing to talk about himself, but reluctant to reveal too much about NewPro, even though she showed a real interest in his company. She didn't push too hard, but spent some time going over the company's SEC application. Bells started to go off immediately. She dug deeper and after two weeks was convinced that Tony Stevens and his cronies were not interested in going public, but were setting up their victims for a big crash. She kept in touch with him, as a new friend, not a business associate. He revealed precious little to her, but with the scraps she managed to pry loose, she was positive NewPro was a scam.

Twelve days ago her suspicions had proved correct. Overnight, NewPro had vanished. The front doors were locked and the offices inside stripped bare. Any paper trail at the New Jersey manufacturing plant was gone, and the key players, including Tony Stevens, had disappeared. With them, they took almost ten million dollars of their investors' money. She was disappointed but not surprised; she knew the scam was wrapping up when she got involved. Another week, maybe two, she might have had enough on Tony Stevens to get a positive ID. From things he had said, she suspected he was from Stockholm, but she had no idea what his real name was. The FBI and Interpol computers had no record of anyone matching his description, and that worried her more than anything else. Usually by the time a con artist was scamming his victims for ten million dollars, he was in a criminal database somewhere. But not Tony Stevens. This meant whoever was running the operation was bringing in partners with no prior arrest records. That made them tough, if not impossible, to find.

Alicia reached her apartment on West Twentieth Street in Chelsea. It was a typical New York brownstone walk-up, with eight steps leading from the street to the landing. She checked the street, then let herself in, locked the door behind her and headed straight for the bathroom. She filled the bathtub and lowered herself into the steaming water after securing her gun in a small cavity next to the tub and hidden by the shower curtain. The warmth felt good, even though it was a mild mid-September evening. She let her mind drift back to Tony Stevens and NewPro.

Even though the con hadn't taken her by surprise, the size of the scam had. Including the other cities they had targeted, the take was more than two hundred million. That number was huge. The Bureau was treating the case with the attention it deserved. District offices in every city where Stevens and his accomplices had been active had agents working the scene and trying to identify the players. To date, they had very little. The best penetration into the group was her attachment to the New York chapter. Although Tony Stevens had been tight-lipped, he had inadvertently given them something to work with. Tony had talked about a luxury boat he owned and kept moored in the Bahamas. She wasn't sure where exactly, but he had spoken a couple of times of Freeport and Port Lucaya on Grand Bahama Island. The boys stationed in the Caribbean were running the registered owners of every boat over thirty-five feet, trying to find a connection back to the mainland. It was a long shot, but the best they had right now. The phone logs and utility accounts had netted them exactly nothing. Tony Stevens was no fool. He had been extremely careful to leave no clues.

Alicia pulled the plug and stepped out of the bath. She toweled off and rubbed on some body cream. A full-length mirror was affixed to the back of the bathroom door, and she stood staring at her reflection for a few moments. She was twenty-nine and in prime physical condition. There was no tummy or weight on her hips and no fat on her legs or arms. Her body was lean, her B-cup breasts just the right size for her chest. She had dark hair that fell just past her shoulders and a face that was attractive, but not beautiful. She could turn some heads when she put on makeup, but if she really wanted to get noticed, she just needed to dress in Spandex. She never did.

Alicia slipped into her bathrobe and headed for the kitchen. Tuesday night and no date. No friends calling on the phone to have coffee. Nobody wanting to spend time with her. Such was the life of an FBI agent. All the glamour of getting to carry a gun to work, none of the James Bond love life. But tomorrow was a new day, and her boss had hinted he may have another assignment. Time to go undercover again. No truths, all lies. Never let anyone close. Never let your guard down. Never.

CHAPTER EIGHT

Alan Bestwick pulled up in front of the old Victorian and left the motor running. He stared at the FOR SALE sign and took a couple of deep breaths. This just kept getting better. The U2 song finished on the radio, and he switched off the ignition. He locked the five-year-old Mazda and made his way slowly to the front door.

Inside the house was dark, the curtains and blinds drawn, cutting off the afternoon sunlight. He slipped off his shoes and walked silently in his sock feet through the house to the kitchen. Taylor was sitting on the window bench in the bay that overlooked the tiny backyard. A closed hardcover book rested in her lap. She was staring into the yard as he entered. She glanced up, then looked at the clock.

"You're early," she said.

He sat beside her and put his hands on her knees, which she tucked up to her chest so he could sit. "Gus is shutting down the company," he said. "I'm laid off, effective immediately." Angus Strang owned the corporate security company he worked for.

Taylor stared at him. "What?" she said, her voice a whisper. "When did this happen?"

Alan swallowed. "Gus has been talking about retiring for about a year now. He decided that this was as good a time as any."

"But the timing . . ."

"He apologized. He feels really bad about it, but if he doesn't shut operations down now while we're between jobs and he takes on another big contract, it could be a couple of years before the opportunity comes up again. He wanted to come and talk to you personally, but I told him it was okay."

She nodded but didn't say anything.

"He paid me out for the rest of September and cut a severance check as well."

"How much?" she asked, not believing she actually said that.

"Fifty thousand."

"That was nice of him."

"It'll help."

She looked out the window again. "There's a showing this evening. The Realtor says the people who are interested are serious buyers. They've looked at a few houses in the area, but he thinks this could be the one. If the house has to sell, let's hope nice people buy it." She forced an upbeat tone into her voice. "It's a wonderful house, Alan."

He held her as she cried, feeling her body tremble. She was a strong woman, but even strong people had their limits. She had worked so hard for so many years to build G-cubed, and then to lose it overnight had been devastating. The house was equally as stressful. He knew Taylor was a nester, not a wanderer. She needed roots, and without that anchor she was a lost soul.

For ten minutes they sat silently on the window bench, just holding each other. Finally, she said, "I'm going to lie down for a while."

"Okay." He kissed her forehead.

Taylor forced herself to walk down the center of the swaying hallway. Her equilibrium had been getting worse in the last week or so, probably a combination of low blood pressure and an iron deficiency. She'd always had problems with low blood pressure and had had a few instances of light headedness, but nothing like this. The bouts were almost constant now, and she was having trouble functioning. She didn't want to alarm Alan and had seen the doctor without telling him. Her doctor had prescribed iron supplements and told her to rest. She was trying to do as she was told, but her rebellious nature kicked in and she often missed her pills.

She sat on the side of their bed and stared ahead. Her eyes were drawn to the night table and she opened the drawer and opened the book on Picasso to page 108. A four-by-six photograph of Alan on a street corner stared back at her. It was her favorite picture of him. Every part of him was laughing, especially his eyes. The background looked European, but she had never asked him where the photo was taken. She just loved the man in the moment. It was her private piece of him, and she cherished it. She tucked the photo back in the book and closed the drawer. At least she still had him, she thought. How bad can life really be when you have the person you love?

Not bad, she decided as she slipped under the covers. She was asleep in seconds.

CHAPTER NINE

A light rain had settled in, and the lower mainland was awash in clouds and mist. It was beautiful but depressing, a week from the start of October and already the wet winter weather was settling in. Vancouver was like Seattle, wonderful when the clouds cleared, sunlight-deprived when they settled on the mountains surrounding the city. Edward Brand buttoned his coat against the wet cold that penetrated right into his bones. He was tired of the rain and wanted to leave. But plans were plans, not to be messed with. He was in the Canadian city for at least another week. He sipped his tea and leaned on the railing, watching the small craft navigate a misty English Bay.

The front doorbell sounded, and Brand walked to the door and opened it. Tony Stevens was folding his umbrella as he waited under the portico. Brand waved Stevens into the house and sat in the living room near the wood-burning fireplace. Flames were licking at the birch logs, and an occasional snap broke the silence in the room. Stevens sat on the couch across from Brand. The room was rustic, with open rough-hewn beams and native Haida Indian art on the pine furniture. The acrid smell of smoke commingled with the salt air, and the mixture was somehow pleasant.

"We have a problem," Edward Brand said.

"So I gathered from your message," Stevens said, brushing an errant drop of water off his trouser leg.

"We have a leak in New York."

"Who?" Stevens asked, leaning forward.

Brand took a small sip of tea and asked, "You want a beer?"

Stevens nodded. "Sure."

Brand disappeared into the kitchen and returned a minute later with two beers. "Canadian. Much better than most of our American beer. Five percent alcohol as well. Only takes a few before you start to feel them."

"I like Canadian beer," Stevens said, accepting the bottle from Brand. He wanted to know what was going on in New York but waited. Edward Brand would offer the information when he was ready.

"I have a source inside the Bureau," Brand said. "I've had this person on the payroll for six years now. To date it's been nothing but a monthly output of cash with nothing to show in return. But that just changed. They've given me the name of the FBI agent who managed to worm her way into your organization."

Tony Stevens felt a trickle of sweat run down his side. The room was warm, but not overly so. "Who is it, Edward?"

"What worries me more than who it is, is how did she get inside? That definitely worries me, Tony."

"I can see why," Stevens said, now sweating profusely. Where was Brand going with this? He had been in charge of the New York operation, and it had come off without a hitch. And the longer Brand continued to be elusive, the more worried Tony was getting. "You going to tell me who it is?"

"Sure," Brand said, taking a long drink of beer and

running his free hand through his dark hair. "It's Alicia Walker."

Tony was mute. He had allowed Alicia to get close to the operation, although he had been careful to keep some distance between her and the day-to-day setup. In retrospect it wasn't that difficult to believe she was FBI. Her appearance at just the right time, her interest in how he spent his days, and more than anything else, her elusive nature when he tried to find out who she was and what made her tick. Stevens rubbed the back of his neck and frowned. Edward Brand was staring at the fireplace, but Tony knew the man's mind was focused on the problem. Brand was not a man you wanted to piss off. He had personally seen the results of Edward Brand's anger once, and didn't care to go there again. The man had barely resembled a human being when Brand was finished with him. Alive, but for what? Broken beyond repair. Tony briefly wondered if the guy who had crossed Brand was still alive. He doubted it.

Tony swallowed and said, "Where do we go from here, Edward?"

Brand was silent for the better part of a minute, then said, "Tony, this is a major problem. Not just with this Walker person. I'm not at all happy with you. The rules are very clear. Nobody gets in once the con is on. Nobody sees inside our operation or inside our heads once we're up and moving. Nobody." He slowly turned his head and faced his visitor, his gray eyes cold and penetrating. "Where do we go? Good question."

"Jesus, Edward, it was a one-time thing. It'll never happen again. I swear." He was shaking now and concentrated on keeping his beer steady. He swallowed heavily, his throat dry.

"You're a good guy, Tony, but business is business," Edward said. He remained motionless, and the room was absolutely quiet. A log shifted slightly in the fireplace and a few sparks shot up the flue. "I tell you what," Brand finally said. "I'll make you a deal."

"What sort of deal?"

"We need to take care of the problem we've got in New York. She's a very real threat to our safety. You take care of her, and everything's fine."

"Kill her?" Tony asked.

"Seems almost barbaric when you just come right out and say it," Brand said, finishing his beer. "Another beer?"

Tony shook his head. "I didn't sign on to kill people."

"I didn't sign you on to do stupid things," Brand shot back, his voice threatening. "My offer is non-negotiable. Take care of her, Tony, and you're off the hook."

Tony Stevens leaned back in his chair and took a deep breath. The room was warm, the fireplace soothing, the mountains outside almost ethereal, shrouded in mist. A beautiful day in a beautiful city. He felt cold and sick to his stomach.

"Okay," he said, his voice just a wisp. "Okay, Edward. I'll take care of it."

"Good choice, Tony," Brand said, a hint of a smile on his lips. "Very good choice."

CHAPTER TEN

Jamie Holland was a good kid who'd made a couple of dumb choices. Since he was old enough to tap out a few strokes on a keyboard, he had been working with computers in one form or another. Unfortunately for him, he'd made the mistake of getting caught while poking into a handful of restricted corporate and government mainframes. In the last year, he had been cutting code for the San Francisco police while working off his community-service hours for hacking into the Department of Defense's computer. In addition to writing programs, he had been Sam Morel's best asset in pulling information off computer hard drives that had been wiped clean.

Sam Morel had called him late Friday night and asked if he could come in over the weekend and spend a few hours working on a handful of systems that had just come on the black market. Sam suspected the computers had been used by a company called NewPro before it had abruptly disappeared, taking a lot of investors' money. Sam had the six computers and one server set up in a small room down the hall from his office in Central

District. Weekends were good for him, and Jamie had agreed to come in.

Jamie arrived at the police precinct at just after ten Saturday morning. He found Sam in his office, drinking coffee and scouring the contents of a thick red file. Sam grinned when Jamie arrived.

"You're up early," he said. "Didn't expect you until noon."

"Police work comes before sleep," Jamie said with a smirk. He dropped into the chair facing Sam and propped his feet on the cop's desk. Jamie's relationship with Sam was more like father-son than anything else, and he was probably the only person on the planet who could do that and get away with it. Jamie had bright, eager eyes and long hair that hung just past his shoulders. He was thin, skinny almost, and wore baggy clothes that made him look a bit like a walking laundry line. He hadn't shaved for a week and a scraggly goatee was starting to show.

"What's with the fuzz?" Sam said, rubbing his own freshly shaven chin.

"That's not fuzz," Jamie said. "It's a chick magnet. Girls love it."

"Sure. You ready to have a look at these computers?"

"Yeah. Where are they?"

"A few doors down. Close to the coffee station," Sam said, getting up and heading for the door. Jamie was only twenty-two, but he liked his caffeine. "One of my guys on the street got these six in and shipped them over. Like I told you on the phone, he thinks they came from NewPro."

"The company that folded and stole all that money. I read about it in the newspaper a couple of weeks ago."

"Two weeks almost to the day. Tough to keep the lid on a multimillion-dollar swindle," Sam said, unlocking the door and switching on the light. Sitting on a table inside the small windowless room were six desktop computers, one monitor, a laser printer and a single server. Cables and USB plugs were piled neatly on one edge of the table. "They're all yours."

Jamie didn't answer. He sat in the solitary swivel chair and attached the power cords to the first system and hooked it into the monitor and printer. Windows XP appeared on the screen, and once the operating system had finished loading, he got to work.

The hard drives inside the Pentium-based systems are simply a stack of discs, separated from each other by scant millimeters. While they spin at ten thousand revolutions a minute, an arm similar to that on a record player records files on the disc. These files are recorded to the disc in clusters, which might be located anywhere on the drive. The system then indexes the clusters so it can locate them later when the user requests that file. If the last portion of a file being saved doesn't take up all the space in a cluster, some slack space is left over. To a forensic specialist, that slack space is like gold, waiting to be mined.

Jamie knew that while the File Allocation Table, or FAT as it's often referred to, keeps track of exactly where the clusters are found on the drive, it ignores the slack space. He also knew that wiping a drive clean or overwriting files does not actually delete the previous data from the drive, but simply writes new data overtop of the old. While overwriting the data on a hard drive appears to erase it, that is not the way it works. Portions of the data still exist, a detail most users don't realize. That happens because the computer automatically archives the files while the user is working on them. It writes that information to the slack space on the drive. Those two simple details, archiving files and writing them to the slack space, are unknown to ninety-nine percent of computer users. That is where a forensic specialist can trip the criminal up every time. Jamie Holland knew how to exploit those details.

Jamie had encryption-cracking software with him, but that process was long and arduous. In fact, depending on the encryption level, cracking the code on the files was almost impossible. Rather than scanning the surface of the disc for remnants of encrypted files, he dug into the slack space, looking for chunks of the same files that had been dumped before being encrypted. He found them. He downloaded piece after piece, amazed at the incompetence of whoever had erased the hard drives. They had run three separate overwrites, the first a series of zeros, the second a series of ones, and the final overwrite a random selection of numbers from two to nine. All well and good, but not good enough.

The data began to materialize. Hidden inside the chunks of data were numerous references to Mexico, the Mexican banking system and a series of numbers. He had no idea if they were account numbers, but given the scope of the con, he suspected they were. The guys running the scam needed somewhere to dump the money. He spent the better part of four hours on the computers, then shut the power off and went in search of Sam Morel. Jamie found him hunched over his computer. Morel looked up as Jamie entered.

"Well?" he asked, leaning back in his chair and rubbing his eyes.

"It's definitely NewPro. I found their name on lots of documents. There was quite a bit of data left on the discs," Jamie said, handing Morel a CD and about fifteen pages of paper. Ninety-eight percent is boring— ordering paper and files for the office and paying the telephone bills, but the other two percent is more than a little interesting."

"What?" Morel asked leaning forward.

"Mexico is mentioned more than a few times. And three Mexican banks."

"Which ones?"

Jamie glanced at a sheet of paper. "Banco de Mexicali,

Union Federali and Mexico Uno," he said. "All based out of Mexico City."

"Anything else. Like any way of linking the numbers to the banks?"

Jamie shook his head. "If you're looking for the name of a bank followed by a transit number and the account, no. Nothing even remotely close. Look here, I'll show you." He flipped one of the pages around so Sam was looking at it right side up. "This starts halfway through a sentence. '. . . *need to ensure funds are in place at Banco Mexicali for further expansion of the eastern* . . .' That's typical. There isn't one place where the name of a bank and a series of numbers are together."

Sam scrutinized the page, top to bottom. When he was finished he took off his reading glasses and set them on the desk. "At least we know the banks they were using," he said. "We can try talking with them."

Jamie stashed his gear in a small nylon backpack. "That's everything on the hard drives, Sam," he said. "Thanks for letting me work off some of my community service on that. It was kind of fun."

"Useful too," Sam said, smiling. "Now get out of here. It's Saturday. Go out and chase some girls."

Jamie grinned. "Excellent idea. I'll tell them the cops said it was okay." He slung the backpack over his shoulder and disappeared into the hallway.

Sam Morel leaned back in his chair and closed his eyes. Mexico. Why Mexico? The days of Mexico being a country where an American on the run could find safe passage were long gone. The two governments cooperated on almost all levels, and the Mexican banks were not the place to deposit millions of dollars in ill-gotten funds. They tended to listen to the American authorities and seize assets. They did it quickly and with great zeal. Especially since they got to keep the money. No, something wasn't right. Even with the White Collar Crime Investigation Team, or WCCIT, in place and functioning at a high level in the Caribbean, that was still the best place to launder money. Europe was easy to hide money once it was legitimate, but depositing two hundred million American dollars without the proper paper trail was impossible. What were Edward Brand and his crew up to? Sam Morel didn't have an answer.

The money was out there somewhere. Two hundred million dollars. So was Edward Brand. What was his real name? Where was he from, and how did he manage to assemble the team to pull off such a caper? Who had financed the eight million in upfront money? Where were Brand and his co-conspirators now?

So many questions. So few answers.

He wished the answers would start to come. To date the FBI had been either reluctant to dole out information, or they didn't have much. He suspected the latter. He had spoken with Hawkins and Abrams five times since they had visited Alan and Taylor on the fifteenth. Five times in eight days. Each time it was the same story. They had squat. Edward Brand was not his real name, and they had absolutely no idea who he was. Their computers were chock-a-block full of names and faces, but they had yet to find a match. The same with Brand's two accomplices from San Francisco who had helped him run the office and set up the scam. One thing Hawkins and Abrams had been able to do was ascertain that the three men were the key players and the rest of the office staff were innocent dupes who signed on to work a few months for a company destined to disappear.

The corporate papers for NewPro were registered with a lawyer's office in San Mateo. The name searches were properly filed, the name duly registered with the State of California, complete with the board of directors' signatures. Every *t* crossed. Every *i* dotted. Every piece of information in the lawyer's files was falsified. The local agents were convinced the lawyer was just another pawn Brand had played in the con. Although the lawyer hadn't invested directly in NewPro, he was owed over eighty thousand dollars in legal fees. Money that would never be paid.

As cons went, or corporate fraud for that matter, the NewPro scam was incredible. It was larger than any single scam he had ever seen, and they had been smart to target private investors instead of banks and major corporations. Getting semi-rich people mad was bad, but pissing off a bank or a large corporation was downright stupid. They had teeth. If their teeth weren't big enough they bought bigger teeth. They often operated below the radar. That was something they didn't tell their shareholders at the AGMs. But the people Brand had targeted with his NewPro scam weren't in a position to go after him. Every one of them had invested in one of two ways—a couple of million, which was pocket change and not worth chasing, or everything they owned, which meant they had no resources left to use in the hunt.

Brilliant. Simply brilliant. But those weren't the words he'd use to describe it to Alan Bestwick and Taylor Simons. He picked up the phone and dialed the number for the local Bureau office. Hawkins and Abrams would be interested in what Jamie had dredged up off the computers. Keeping the FBI in the loop was a good idea.

Because they had teeth. Really big teeth. And he didn't need them taking a chunk out of his ass.

CHAPTER ELEVEN

Sunday morning.

Taylor woke at six and headed to the kitchen. She brewed some coffee and pureed a fistful of frozen fruit in the blender before mixing it with fresh orange juice. The concoction was thick, like a milkshake, and loaded with vitamins. She drank it, then sat down at the table with a cup of coffee and the morning newspaper. Most of the half hour she spent with the paper was divided between world news and the business section. She finished with the paper and poured another cup of coffee. It was quarter to seven when she sat on the window seat in the living room overlooking the street. It was a beautiful late September day, and the neighborhood was already alive with dog-walkers and joggers. She glanced at the SOLD sticker on the FOR SALE sign and smiled.

She was back. Back from the edge of the abyss of depression that had gripped her for almost two weeks. Moping about and feeling sorry for herself was something Taylor was unaccustomed to. She had taken her share of hits over the course of thirty-seven years and this was simply one more. G-cubed was her creation, built from the ground up. If she could do it once, she could do it again. The steely resolve that had given her direction and tenacity through the tough times in her life was ebbing back into her cells. She could feel the strength returning. She was physically stronger and mentally much more aware of what was happening. Strangely enough, she credited Alan's job loss as the catalyst she had needed to wake up.

His unemployment was a sign that they had bottomed out. The business, the house, and now their last source of income—all gone. There was no place to go but up. Starting from scratch at almost forty years old wasn't her idea of success, but at least she and Alan were tackling it together. To her, that was the key. There was something about two people attacking a problem together that diminished the size of the mountain. Maybe the mountain was crumbling a bit.

Sam Morel had called Saturday night while she and Alan were working through the offer on the house with their Realtor. His computer wizard had managed to pull something off a hard drive from one of Brand's computers. Something about Mexico. Nothing definite, but the drive had contained the names of a few banks and possibly even an account number or two. Just the fact that he had something was a boost. Whether that would ever translate to them getting all or part of their money back was another story. She wasn't holding her breath.

There was a low sound from the hall, and she glanced away from the street scene. Alan was leaning on the door jamb between the hall and the living room. He wore a white housecoat and the hint of a smile.

"Thinking?" he asked. His voice carried in the quiet house.

She nodded. "Thinking how lucky I am," she said, locking eyes with him. He didn't show surprise.

"It's good to have you back," he said, making his way into the room and sitting beside her so their hips were touching. He rubbed her calf and looked out the window. "You okay with the price we got for the house?"

"Sure," she said. "It was exactly what the Realtor thought. No surprises. I like that."

He gently squeezed her calf. "You look great."

"That's because I've already had two cups of coffee. You want some?"

"I'll get it," he said. "You want some more?"

She nodded and handed him her cup. He disappeared into the kitchen for a minute then returned with two steaming mugs. They drank the coffee and watched the activity outside their window for a few minutes. Then he said, "What do you think of Sam Morel's new information?"

She took a moment before answering. "I'm not getting my hopes up, but I like it. Any news is good news. The fact that they uncovered something about banks is probably the best we could hope for."

"He said it was unusual that they would use Mexican banks," Alan said. "One of the Caribbean countries was more likely." He sipped his coffee. "I wonder why they did that. I mean, they think about every detail, leave no paper trail that would lead back to them, then use a bank in a country with strong ties to the United States. It doesn't make sense."

Taylor was thoughtful. "No, it doesn't. Maybe the money's not there. Maybe it's a decoy."

It was Alan's turn to ponder. "Maybe," he said slowly, "but I don't know. Without Sam Morel's connections, the computers would have come on the market and been sold without anyone the wiser. The information they retrieved was on hard drives that had been wiped clean. That's a lot of hoops to jump through for planted information."

"I suppose. They would have made it easier to find the ties to the banks if that's what they wanted. That means the information Sam has is probably legit."

"That's good," Alan said, running his hand up her thigh. She smiled. "You know, we can always hope."

"That and get out there and earn some more money."

"You got something on the go?" he asked.

"Nick Adams offered me a senior position. I think I'll take it."

Alan raised an eyebrow. "You never said anything."

She gave him a quick grin. "I didn't want you to get all excited in case I turned him down. We've been competitors for quite a few years now."

Alan finished the last of his coffee. "Well, it doesn't surprise me that he'd make you an offer. He knows your abilities."

She nodded. "It's a good offer." She grasped his hand. "We're taking almost seven hundred thousand out of the house sale, and he's offering me one-eighty a year plus bonuses. We're going to be okay."

He saw the spark in her eyes and knew that his wife had returned. "Yeah," he said slowly. "We're going to be okay."

Chapter Twelve

New York was unseasonably cold for the last week of September and a few of the trees in Central Park were showing color. Alicia Walker loved autumn but detested winter. The advent of fall stirred up a conundrum of mixed emotions and left her emotionally confused, sometimes almost exhausted. The slight chill in the air was invigorating, but her mind often skittered ahead to scenes of snow blanketing the trees and pathways that ran through the park's rolling hills. It was a vexing time of year.

Alicia unhooked the shoulder strap and let her briefcase drop on the park bench. She unzipped the side compartment and pulled out a blue file folder. Inside were eight pages of typed text, single spaced in twelve-point font. Her new assignment. She skimmed over the first two pages, mostly background material she was already familiar with, then concentrated on the material that was new to her.

The assignment was a bit of a step outside the box for the Bureau. It was a joint effort with the Department of Homeland Security, which had insisted on retaining control of the operation. Alicia was surprised her superiors had agreed to lend her out on the conditions DHS was imposing. But given the scope of the sting, she could see their willingness to cooperate. Ahmed al-Jawahari was an American citizen of Iranian descent with questionable ties to al-Qaeda. DHS suspected him of being a major fundraiser for a handful of terrorist cells operating inside the United States. But al-Jawahari was also a well-respected citizen and prominent New York lawyer. Bashing down his front door and riffling through his files was not the way to bring him down. They needed someone on the inside. And that's where Alicia Walker figured in.

Al-Jawahari had one extra large skeleton in his closet. He was into bondage and sado-masochism. No sex, just the kinky stuff that involved leather outfits, whips and handcuffs. He often invited the women who indulged his fantasies back to his office for a quick session on the couch. Alicia Walker was being planted in the agency's inventory—her specialty being bondage without sex. It was inevitable she would end up in al-Jawahari's office. Which meant she needed to have a completely new background. A life totally different from her own. That information, and a condensed version of her target's life, were inside the blue file folder.

She spent an hour reviewing the details, then closed the file and slipped it back in her briefcase. The sun was just setting, another Monday drawing to a close. She exited the park at East Fifty-ninth and flagged a cab. She was hungry and had the cabbie drop her at The Red Cat, a trendy restaurant surrounded by art galleries that was only a few blocks from her townhouse. She ordered the roast chicken and flipped through a well-used copy of the *Times*. The meal was excellent, and she left the restaurant feeling full and a bit sleepy. A hot bath was foremost on her mind when she slipped the key in her lock and opened her front door. Her townhouse was peaceful and quiet after the constant noise and congestion of the city streets. She headed to the bathroom and turned on the water. Steam rose from the tub as it filled. She closed the door to keep the warmth in and undressed.

She pulled her hair into a ponytail and secured it with a scrunchy, then lowered herself into the water. Her gun was on the floor next to the tub, and she reached over and slid it out of its holster, then set it in the wall cavity next to the tub. She closed her eyes and slid her bottom down the tub, bending her knees and letting the water cover her shoulders. The warmth felt good after the September chill. A slight noise from just outside the bathroom startled her, and her eyes flicked open. She pushed her feet against the end of the tub, her shoulders and chest rising quickly above the water. A second later the door crashed open. Tony Stevens was framed in the doorway. In his right hand was a Colt revolver. The hammer was cocked, the gun ready to fire. For a second there was complete silence.

"What the hell do you think you're doing?" Alicia said, her arms and hands resting on the edge of the tub. Her left hand was inches from her gun, hidden behind the shower curtain. She made no attempt to cover herself.

"Don't move," Tony said, taking two steps into the room. "Don't move a fucking muscle."

"Tony, what the hell are you doing in here? This is my house. My bathroom. You have no right to be here. And what's with the gun?" Her mind was racing, thinking of some way to distract him. Anything to get her hand on her Glock.

"You bitch. You goddamn bitch. You're FBI." The gun was leveled at her chest, his hand shaking slightly from the weight.

She had to make a decision. There were two ways to play this out. One was to deny his accusations, the other to admit she was with the Bureau and play the 'shoot a cop and you're in a lot of shit' card. Her decision was quick.

"You don't want to do this, Tony. The guys I work with at the Bureau won't stop until they've tracked you down. They will not stop. Ever."

Sweat trickled down his forehead, and he used his free hand to wipe it away before it dripped in his eyes. "You have no idea who I am. You can't find a ghost."

"Are you kidding?" she said, sitting up a bit, the water lapping on the edge of the tub as she moved. She saw his finger tighten on the trigger. "Right now you and your buddies are wanted for stealing money from rich people. I'm not saying that what you've done is okay, but the resources the Bureau is going to put on that is absolutely nothing compared to what will happen if you pull that trigger. You can't kill an FBI agent and expect to get away with it. There's not a chance in hell, Tony."

"I don't have a choice," he said, his hand shaking more now. He sounded unsure.

"Edward Brand?" she asked. He didn't answer, but his eyes told her what she needed to know. "We can protect you, Tony. You work with us and we'll put Brand away for life. He'll never be able to touch you."

"I'm going to jail no matter what," Stevens said. "You can't stop that. Even if I rat him out I'm still going to prison."

He was right, and she knew it. "We have resources you can't even imagine," she said, shifting again in the water. He didn't react to her movement this time. Next time her hand was going for her gun.

"Do you have the ability to kill him?" Tony asked. "Because that's the only way you're going to keep Edward Brand from finding me and killing me."

"We can get you into the Witness Protection Program, Tony. We can drop you so deep in some remote corner of the country that he'll never find you. Never. And you get to live out your life in some quaint little town while he rots in jail. We've got that kind of power, Tony."

He shook his head slightly, a glazed look in his eyes.

"No, it won't work. He'll get me. I know this man. He's absolutely ruthless. You don't know him, Alicia." His eyes locked with hers. "Jesus Christ, why did you have to get involved?"

She knew the moment. The guy with the gun who doesn't want to pull the trigger but knows he has to. She was down to her last few seconds of life. She shifted again, this time her left hand grasping the Glock. She bent her wrist, the barrel of the gun now protruding from the cavity. Decision time. And only milliseconds to make it. She angled the gun upward and pulled the trigger.

Both guns fired at exactly the same moment, deafening roars in the small room. Her bullet tore into his chest, deflecting slightly off one of his ribs but smashing into his heart and tearing the left ventricle apart. He spun back into the wall and dropped in a heap on the floor.

His bullet hit Alicia in the upper neck, ripping through her muscle and severing the carotid artery. Blood spurted from the wound and she dropped her gun and clutched at the gaping hole. She tried to rise from the water but the trauma was too great. She felt her strength ebbing quickly as she bled out. Her hands slowly dropped from her neck into the water. She needed a phone. She needed to call for help. Now.

She could feel the water on her lips and closed her mouth, breathing through her nose. The water rose as her legs bent and she slid further down in the tub. She willed her knees to lock and keep her head above the water, but even the simplest commands weren't getting through. The water crested her nose and washed into her lungs. Her eyes were still open as they slowly slid beneath the surface of the water. She had one last thought before darkness enveloped her.

What a strange way to die.

CHAPTER THIRTEEN

Taylor and Alan received the call from Special Agent
Brent Hawkins at eight o'clock Tuesday morning. Their
presence was required at the San Francisco district office.
Immediately. They traveled together in Taylor's Audi,
arriving at just after nine. The receptionist took their
names, had them sign in and placed a call. Hawkins's
partner, John Abrams, came out to meet them. He didn't
offer his hand, just gave them a curt "good morning"
and pointed to the door he had entered from. They followed him down a carpeted hallway that was like the
spine of a fish carcass with a myriad of other halls,
branching off it. They reached one of the halls, and
Abrams turned, opening the first door on the left. He
waved them in.

Brent Hawkins and two other men dressed in dark
suits sat at a long table ringed with leather chairs.
Hawkins didn't rise when they entered, just said,
"Please have a seat." When they were sitting he said,
"This is Special Agent Smith and Special Agent Hob-
son." The two men nodded but didn't say a word.

"What's going on?" Alan asked Hawkins, who seemed to be the most senior agent in the room.

"Something has happened in New York," Hawkins replied. "One of our agents who was involved with the NewPro scam has been killed."

Taylor sucked in a breath. "That's terrible."

"We need to go back over your entire involvement with Edward Brand," the agent named Hobson said. He purposely neglected to mention that Alicia Walker had killed the man who shot her. Simply a need-to-know issue. Taylor Simons didn't need to know.

"We've already told the FBI and the San Francisco police everything we know," Alan said. "I don't see how we can help any further."

"We're looking for idiosyncrasies that might give us an idea who Brand really is and where he's from. Inflections in his speech, certain words he may have used that might give a clue to his background."

Both Alan and Taylor shrugged. Taylor said, "He talked about falling when he was skiing once and hurting his back. Said it bothered him when the weather changed."

Smith made a note on his pad. "Lots of cold-weather climates around," he said.

"It doesn't narrow things down much," Hawkins agreed. "Did he ever mention which sports teams he followed, a street name, a neighborhood, a time zone, anything like that?"

"He said he liked football, but never talked about one specific team," Alan said.

Taylor said, "The football thing. I remember that conversation. He said Joe Montana was the best quarterback to ever play. Maybe he was a Forty-niners fan."

"That's right," Alan concurred. "He knew a lot of Montana's stats. Loved the guy."

"Maybe," Hawkins said. "But he was handling the con

in San Francisco. He may have wanted to come off like he was a local guy."

"Hey," Alan said, leaning into the table. "That thing about speech you mentioned. Inflections. He did have a habit of saying 'eh' after some of his sentences."

"Give us an example," Abrams said.

"Looks like it's going to rain, eh," Alan said. "Simple sentences. He added it mostly when he was talking casually. When he was pitching us on the investment end of NewPro, his words were always very carefully chosen. He never did it then."

"That's right," Taylor said.

Hobson glanced around the table. "Only in casual speech. When his guard's down. A little bit of the real person coming out?"

"Canadian," Hawkins said. "Cold weather. Mountains. Skiing." He turned to Abrams. "John, get a list of ski resorts in Canada. The middle section of the country is pretty flat, but the Rocky Mountains are to the west side, and there are a few smaller ranges in the East." He turned back to Taylor and Alan. "Did you ever detect a hint of a French accent?"

Both were thoughtful. "No, I don't think so," Taylor said.

"Let's look at everything, but concentrate more on the west coast. Alberta and British Columbia both have ski resorts. Vancouver has a huge resort just north of the city where the 2010 Olympics are slated for."

"Whistler," Abrams said, jotting the name in his notebook.

They talked for another hour but nothing of any substance came to light. Brent Hawkins thanked Taylor and Alan for coming in and Hawkins himself walked them to the door and shook their hands. He assured them the Bureau was working overtime on the case. But Edward Brand was a careful man, covering every step he took with lies and deception. He was like an onion—peel the skin back and you were faced with multiple layers, the man himself hidden beneath the multitude of lies. Faceless, nameless, a ghost who appeared from nowhere and returned there when the con had run its course.

But something had happened, and Brand had pushed things too far. An FBI agent was dead and the Bureau was in a rage, like an anthill after an errant footstep. The scale of the investigation had just moved up a number of notches.

Edward Brand had made his first mistake.

CHAPTER FOURTEEN

The news of what had happened in New York on Monday evening was relayed to Edward Brand first thing Tuesday morning. Brand listened as his contact inside the FBI gave him the crime scene details. Tony Stevens had taken one bullet in the center of his chest, and death was instantaneous. Alicia Walker was hit in the neck, but her cause of death was asphyxiation. She had drowned after severe blood loss had rendered her incapable of hauling herself out of the bathtub. Death was inevitable, as the bullet had pierced her carotid artery and without immediate medical attention, she would have bled to death. Best guess from the CSI crew was that Stevens and Walker had fired at exactly the same time. Brand thanked his contact and hung up.

Tony Stevens had fucked up. He'd fucked up big time. First off he'd allowed an FBI agent to get inside the scam. Then he'd gotten himself killed while taking her out. Edward Brand heard a cracking noise and glanced down at his hand. His cell phone had snapped in half at the hinge. He relaxed his grip on the phone. It was ruined. He dumped it in a garbage can and headed for the bedroom.

Time to pack and get out of Vancouver. He'd planned on staying another day or two, but the FBI was going to ratchet up the NewPro investigation now, and he'd have to move faster than he had expected. The borders would get tighter. And quickly.

He called Air Canada and booked a flight to Hong Kong, departing Vancouver International at one-forty. Four hours. Plenty of time to pack and get to the airport. Brand didn't care where the flight went, he just needed to get out of Canada. He opened the door to the walk-in bedroom closet and knelt in front of a line of shoes neatly tucked in a line of small wooden niches. He pushed a piece of wood and a section of the compartmentalized shelving popped out an inch. He gripped it and pulled. It slid out, shoes still intact. Behind the false front was a wall safe. Brand spun the dial three times and pushed the handle down. The safe opened. Inside were a number of Canadian passports bundled together with an elastic. He rifed through them until he found one he liked. Reginald Brewer. A native of Vancouver who traveled extensively on business. Half the passport pages were filled with stamps from various countries. They were as false as the passport itself. He withdrew a few thousand dollars in American twenties and fifties then closed the safe and replaced the shoes.

The picture inside the passport was his face, but with a mustache and glasses. The same fake mustache and glasses he had worn for the picture were in a drawer in the bathroom. He affixed the mustache with spirit gum and donned the glasses. A small toiletry bag sat on the vanity, and he filled it with the necessities, then returned to the bedroom and packed a suitcase. A quick call to a cab company and he was on his way to the airport.

Edward Brand was a chameleon. He could change his face in minutes and had a complete set of identification for each person he could become. It had been years since he had used his real name. Robert Zindler. Jesus, the name sounded foreign even to him. That was probably a good thing. He wondered if the FBI would manage to tie him back to his origins on this one. They would be looking really hard now that Alicia Walker was dead. He knew that would happen when he sent Tony Stevens to kill her. But risks were all to be measured and then taken if the upside outweighed the downside. Locking Tony Stevens in for life by having him kill Alicia Walker had been worth the price. He liked Tony and respected the man's abilities as a con artist. But that whole end of things was gone. Tony was dead.

That was where things got dicey. Tony's body gave the FBI some tangible evidence to work with. They had his fingerprints, his DNA, his clothes and his gun. When you give an organization like the FBI that much to work with, they're going to come up with something. Still, tying Tony back to him was impossible. Every precaution had been taken to keep their lives completely separate. On this scam, Tony was New York. He was San Francisco. Brand was the man behind the entire operation, but once the con was under way, the cities were individual entities. No overlap. That way, if one operation went down, the others would still be viable long enough for them to get out before the cops came down on them. The only common factor was the name NewPro, and that was a necessity. Since NewPro wasn't a public company, the different centers were all functioning below the radar. Anything less than a simultaneous raid on all cities would be fruitless. Well thought out. Well executed.

Two hundred and twelve million dollars worth of well executed.

His taxi arrived, and he watched Vancouver slip past his window on his trip to the airport. North of the Fraser River, where the mountains touched down to the water, the land was heavily wooded with estate homes tucked into quiet cul-de-sacs. West, across Georgia Strait and Vancouver Island, was the Pacific Ocean. The water this far north was cold, not good for swimming, but perfect for fishing. He liked Vancouver. It was one of the most beautiful cities in the world. Too bad he wouldn't be back for a while. Maybe never. But that was the price you had to pay. Nothing without a price.

Despite the glitch caused by Tony's incompetence at such a simple thing as killing one person, everything was fine. In fact, it was perfect. Everything moving along as it should.

Because the con was never over until it was over.

CHAPTER FIFTEEN

Sam Morel ran his hands through his hair and sighed. It had been one very long day. Brent Hawkins had called at ten in the morning and filled him in on the death of Alicia Walker in New York and the possible Canadian connection to Edward Brand. Sam didn't know Alicia Walker from Adam, but any time a law enforcement person died it was a black day. With one of their agents on a slab in a morgue, the FBI was going to be taking a much more proactive approach to the NewPro case. That was probably a good thing.

He wondered about the Canadian angle. It seemed strange that Edward Brand would be so careful about every detail, then let something like that slip. Canadians were known for adding 'eh' on the end of sentences, turning a comment into a rhetorical question, but someone wishing to remain an unknown would be careful of slips like that. No, something didn't sit right with him on that one.

The Mexican angle was equally as confusing. The Mexican government didn't play ball with fraud artists. They kicked them out of the country. There had been an

Internet fraud run out of Costa Rica from 1999 to 2001 under the name Tri-West that had defrauded investors of about ninety million dollars. When the pyramid scheme had collapsed, the two key players had fled to Mexico and set up new lives in Puerto Vallarta. Both men had been expelled from Mexico and sent back to the United States, where they had received jail sentences for their complicity in the scam. Mexico was not the place to hide. Something wasn't right, but he couldn't put his finger on it.

He dialed Alan and Taylor's number from memory. Alan answered. "I heard you were visiting with Hawkins and Abrams today," he said after they had exchanged hellos.

"They called this morning. Wanted us to come down right away. One of their New York agents was killed last night. They were pretty hot."

"I can imagine. But getting a body along with hers gives them something to work with."

"What?" Alan asked. "What are you talking about?"

"They never told you that Walker managed to kill the guy who shot her?"

"No," Alan said. "They didn't say a word about that."

"Doesn't surprise me," Sam said. "I think it makes the feds feel smug when they know something you don't."

"Who was the guy? Was he involved in stealing our money?"

"They're not sure. He had no identification on him, and they didn't get a match on his fingerprints. They're submitting a DNA sample, but don't hold your breath on that. The DNA database in the States is nothing compared to the one in the UK. We're a little behind the times over here."

"Was this Alicia Walker woman working on the New-Pro case?" Alan asked.

"From what I understand—yes. She had met a guy about six weeks ago who called himself Tony Stevens, and she suspected he was planning some sort of scam with NewPro. The district office in New York didn't have any undercover work for her at that time and gave her the okay to follow up on it. And it was Tony Stevens who killed her. The connection's there all right."

"It's not good news that an agent is dead, but maybe this is a bit of a break." Alan heard a clicking sound as Taylor picked up the extension.

"Let's keep our fingers crossed," Sam said. He ran his fingers across the glass that covered a picture of him posing with his family. All four of them were smiling. Days long gone. "Hey, Hawkins told me you and Taylor may have given them something to work with."

"The Canadian thing?"

"Yeah. They're expanding the search to include Canada. Personally, I think they should be looking internationally on this one, but they seem convinced Brand and his accomplices are American."

"What about the tie to Mexico you found on the computers?" Alan asked.

"In their minds that's even more evidence pointing to them being from the States. They're definitely not Mexican or South American, so that just leaves the United States and Canada in close proximity to Mexico. None of them spoke with any kind of an accent, so they've mostly ruled out Europe as well. I think the real reason they're not looking outside the States or Canada is that once they do, they lose control. The FBI doesn't have jurisdiction outside the country's borders. They don't in Canada either, but our country and theirs are so tightly linked, the Bureau can operate there and get away with it. In a clandestine manner, of course."

"Maybe they're right about Brand and his guys being American. None of them had accents."

"You mean Brand and his two VPs here in San Francisco?" Morel asked.

"Yes. Roger Tate and Ben Wright. I don't imagine anything came up when they ran those names?" Alan asked.

Morel shook his head. "Nothing. Names mean nothing to these guys. They pick a name, use it for the duration of the con, then chuck it. Investigators refer to the name they were using just so we can keep track of who we're talking about."

Taylor nodded. "We understand. We discussed that." She was quiet for a minute, then asked, "What now? Where does it go from here?"

"There are a lot of people at the Bureau mighty pissed off right now, and that could help us. There's the possible Canadian connection, and we can always hope they match the DNA on the body they found in the bathroom with Alicia Walker. Other than that, we don't have a lot."

"Ghosts," Alan said. "These guys are ghosts. How is that possible with today's technology?"

"Sometimes I think technology makes things easier for the bad guys," Morel said. "If someone's got money and a bit of savvy, they can disappear quite easily. If you keep yourself clean and never get fingerprinted or have your DNA stored on a police database, you can just blend into the crowd. There are a lot of crowds out there these days."

"Six billion people on the planet. That's a pretty big haystack," Taylor said.

Alan's voice was grim. "And we need to find one."

CHAPTER SIXTEEN

Three weeks.

Twenty-one days had passed since they had first learned of Alicia Walker's death. Alan and Taylor had fielded nine calls from Sam Morel telling them that neither the San Francisco police nor the FBI had anything new. Trying to dredge up Tony Stevens's real identity had slowly drawn to a dead end. The Bureau had circulated his picture across the United States and to Interpol. No hits. There were no boats registered to a Tony Stevens anywhere in the Bahamas. DNA profiling had come up empty. Nothing on the cadaver's fingerprints either. Tony Stevens was a John Doe.

The Canadian angle had died a slow death as well. Edward Brand may have injected Canadian expressions in his speech, but the man wasn't on the Canadian radar. Hawkins and Abrams had linked up with the Royal Canadian Mounted Police and ran searches through their extensive database. Not even the slightest glitch. The entire investigation was slowly grinding to a halt.

Taylor glanced up from her desk at the sound of a

quiet knock on her door. Kelly Kramer was leaning against the door jamb. She jumped up, rounded the desk and gave him a hug. Both wore smiles.

"What are you doing here?" she asked as they sat on the couch against one of the walls without windows. Taylor's corner office at Ad-dicted, her new employer, was spacious and tastefully furnished. Dry-mounted posters of previous ad campaigns hung on the walls, and soft music played through the ceiling-mounted speakers. Her view was north to the bay, where a gentle October mist trailed across the water.

"I missed you," Kelly said, his handsome face still smiling. "Wanted to make sure they were treating you okay over here."

She let her eyes drift around the room. "I don't mind it as much as I thought I would. Nick's got a great team in place. No wonder we were always fighting with him for the best clients. He runs Ad-dicted much like G-cubed." She grinned. "And he's paying me very well. I'm already on track for a most generous bonus."

"We miss you," Kelly said. "Everyone at G-cubed misses you a lot."

"How is it over there?" she asked, not really wanting him to answer.

"It's good. Pretty much business as usual. The new owners were smart enough to realize they didn't need to reinvent the wheel. The groups are intact, and we've managed to retain all our clients. But we've noticed your boss is spending time on the golf course with some of those clients."

"Yeah, I noticed as well. But that's business, Kelly. If the tables were reversed I'd be all over them."

"I suppose." There was a short silence, and he thoughtfully stroked his goatee. "I'm quitting."

Taylor didn't show surprise. "What are you going to do?"

"I figure it's time to use that Master's degree in Crime

Investigation I spent five years getting. I threw my résumé out on the market and had three offers. Two in Washington and one in Dallas."

"Washington? D.C. or state?"

"D.C."

"You going to be a spy?" Taylor asked. Again the grin.

He returned the smile but shook his head. "Can't talk about it. But it's with the government."

"Ooh, it's true. I'm going to know a spy," Taylor said.

"That's a good line. If it helps to pick up women, I'll go with it." Kelly grinned. The last thing he needed was help picking up women.

"Be careful," she said.

He nodded. "Anything new on what happened?"

She shook her head. "Sam Morel over at Central District still keeps Alan and me in the loop, but there's not much new to report. We thought they had something a couple of times, but none of the leads worked out. One of them was kind of up your alley."

"How's that?"

"Sam managed to track down six of the computers NewPro used while their San Francisco office was up and running. He had some computer whiz scan the drives, and even though they'd been wiped clean, he still got some data off them. It pointed to Mexico, but the trail just dried up."

"Where are the computers now?"

"The FBI had them for a week, but they had trouble even duplicating what Sam's guy got off them. I think they sent the computers back to Sam's office. Why?"

He shrugged. "I could take a look. You never know."

"Sure. I'll call Sam and see if he could arrange it. You don't mind?"

"Mind?" He reached out and took her hand. "Taylor, there's not a day goes by when I don't think about what happened to you and Alan. If there's any way I can help, I want to."

"Okay. That's really sweet of you." She squeezed his hand. "I'll call Sam."

"Thanks."

They slowly unhooked hands. "Have you made a decision on which offer you'll take?"

"I have. Washington. It's closer to Baltimore, actually."

She smiled. "National Security Agency? Their main complex is somewhere between Baltimore and D.C."

He didn't nod or shake his head, just sat impassively. It confirmed her guess. "I've got to be going," he said, standing. She stood, and they hugged again. "Call me when you get the okay on the computers from your cop buddy."

"Will do," she said.

Kelly rounded the corner and disappeared from sight. Taylor returned to her desk and dropped into her chair. She swiveled about and stared out over the bay. The view was stunning. She loved San Francisco and the eclectic intensity that made the city so different from anywhere else she had visited or lived. It pulsed with originality and energy. The good news was that she didn't have to leave the city. They had found a rental not far from their current house, and although the monthly lease was steep, it allowed them to stay in the city itself and not have to venture into the surrounding communities. It was strange to think of renting after owning houses for so many years, but going that route allowed them to bank the proceeds from the sale and wait until they were in a position to buy something they really wanted, not just an interim house. Alan was at home packing up the last few things. The moving truck was coming tomorrow. Their possession date wasn't for another two weeks, but the movers had given them a huge break on the price for moving on a Wednesday in the middle of the month rather than waiting until the end of October when they were swamped.

Things had gone well at G-cubed. The new owners

had honored the company's commitment to the children's hospital, and she was seeing evidence of their work springing up all over the city. The billboards were designed to tug on the heartstrings, with pictures of small children with a parent and captions like, *You give me strength.* It was a brilliant twist, and it gave her some reassurance that she had sold her company to the right people. She turned away from the view and touched her mouse. The computer screen came back to life.

She returned to work, her mind split between the campaign she was overseeing and her personal situation. Her life had changed, and she had accepted the change. Maybe Kelly would find something on the computers, maybe not. She realized that she didn't really care. The money was gone, and it was time to rebuild. Alan and she were solid, they had come through the ordeal even more committed to each other than before, when their lives were so predictable. That was what really mattered.

Her computer beeped, reminding her of an eleven o'clock meeting with her clients. She packed up the latest drawings for the print ads on product line and tucked them under her arm. Close the deal, make Nick Adams a half million dollars in fees. Collect her salary and go home.

God, how her life had changed.

CHAPTER SEVENTEEN

Kelly Kramer locked the room behind him and went in search of Detective Sam Morel. Central District was quiet, the clock just ticking up to midnight. Thursday, October 19, dropped into the history books as the minute hand crossed twelve. A couple of minutes later Kelly found Morel sitting in the coffee room with his feet on the table. He had a steaming cup in his hand and waved to the empty chairs. Kelly sat opposite him at the table.

"Well, did you find anything on the computers?" he asked, cautiously sipping the hot liquid. When Brent Hawkins returned the six computers to SFPD, Morel had set up a time for Taylor's computer expert to have a look at the hard drives. Kelly Kramer had started working on the computers at five o'clock and hadn't left the room for seven hours except once to use the washroom.

Kelly had two sets of typed pages with him, and he laid them side-by-side on the table. One stack of papers was a compilation of the forensic investigations by both the San Francisco police and the FBI. They were almost identical. But his was two pages thicker, and he had highlighted the differences.

"I've dug up some stuff that your guy and the FBI both missed," he said. "It was hidden pretty well, and it doesn't surprise me that neither of you found it."

"Why's that?"

"One of the computers was encrypted at its most fundamental level—the basic input output system, or BIOS as it's usually called. It's almost impossible to decrypt a computer with that level of encryption, as the BIOS is directly linked to every component. Without the password you can't access any peripherals linked to the computer, including the hard drive."

"Jamie and the guys at the FBI never said they had trouble with any of the computers," Sam said.

"Again, no surprises there. Unless they dismantled the systems, they wouldn't have noticed the second hard drive. It operated like a computer within a computer, with its own BIOS. And that was the one with the high-level encryption."

"So how did you bypass it?"

"It's complicated, but I'll keep it simple. I used a shorting jumper, then removed the power supply to the memory on the motherboard. Once I had wiped its memory clean I input my own password and reconnected the power supply. It's a little more complicated than it sounds."

"Okay. What did you find?"

He flipped the page over so Sam was looking at it right side up and pointed to the highlighted entries. "The drive was wiped clean, just like the others, and I had to get what I could out of the slack space. It looks like this might jibe with the Mexican connection. I think it's an invoice for some sort of antique. It was ordered specifically by Edward Brand."

"Negretti and Zambra telescope, Antigüedades

Coloniart," Sam read the line aloud. "Could be. Antigüedades is Spanish for antique, I think. Should be pretty easy to find the shop."

Kelly nodded. "I think so." His finger ran down the page. "There's no address, but it says Zona Rosa down a little further in the text. And I know for sure that Zona Rosa is in Mexico City."

Sam raised an eyebrow. "You know computers, you know Mexico City. What don't you know?"

Kelly laughed. "That's an easy one. Zona Rosa is quite famous. I've only been to Mexico City once, about fifteen years ago, but it was a cool place to visit even back then."

Sam scratched his head and leaned back in his chair. "First the banks and now this. The Mexican connection is really entrenched in these computers. But so far, the FBI has nothing, not even a hint of where the money is, if it really is in one of the three Mexican banks we found earlier. You find anything else of interest?"

"There's a few other words spread about the disc, but it's mostly junk. I've highlighted it for you."

Sam glanced at his watch and stood. "Thanks for coming in on short notice," he said, extending his hand.

Kelly said, "Taylor's one of the best people I've ever met in my life. I'd do anything for her. Glad I could help."

"I'll see you out," Sam said.

They walked down the hall and Kelly asked, "Realistically, what are the chances?"

"Police work," Sam responded, their footsteps echoing through the hallway, "is just connecting the dots. Criminals inevitably leave clues, and those clues are like singular dots. String them together and a pattern will begin to emerge. This might be the break we need to get the investigation on track. Maybe, but there are no for-sures in this business. At least it's something for Taylor and Alan."

"They could use some good news."

"Yeah, I think so. Every new bit of information is a bit of hope. They're quickly running out of that. It's been five weeks, give or take, since Brand disappeared with their money, and both of them are starting to think the trail is too cold to ever heat up again."

"That's the feeling I get," Kelly agreed. "They're resigned to the fact that the money is gone."

"I'll call them in the morning and let them know what we found."

They reached the front door to the precinct, and the night clerk hit a button and opened the door. Sam thanked Kelly again for his help, then returned to the fourth floor. He arranged the printouts on his desk and spent another hour going over them, comparing Jamie's work to Kelly's. The two sets of data were almost identical except for the new scraps Kelly had found on the encrypted hard drive. He stared at what he suspected was the name of the antique shop. Antigüedades Coloniart. Was that the key? Was it the one detail Brand had missed?

CHAPTER EIGHTEEN

Hong Kong was starting to cool with the approach of autumn. The peak summer temperatures were gone, and an October chill was in the air. That wasn't a bad thing, considering the relentless heat and congestion of the city. To Edward Brand, standing on the eleventh hole of the Hong Kong Golf Club in prestigious Deep Water Bay, the changing weather didn't matter. Eight more holes of golf, and he was heading for Costa Rica. Hong Kong's usefulness as a city where one could easily disappear into a crowd was drawing to a close. His flight was departing Chek Lap Kok in six hours.

The foursome ahead of him moved off the green, and he swung an easy five wood, the ball traveling the two hundred and twenty yards and landing on the green, thirty feet from the pin. His golfing companions, all natives of Hong Kong and casual acquaintances, applauded the shot. He smiled and bowed slightly. He loved this game.

As he walked back to the golf cart he let his mind drift back over the last few months. The NewPro scam had gone off without a hitch. The FBI was dead in the water, unable to connect Tony Stevens back to him. They had nothing concrete to work with from any of the cities where they had run the con. Every detail had been carefully covered, nothing to chance. Still, mistakes can slip through, and the first few weeks after the con is run are the most crucial. That's when you find out if you really did cover all the bases.

He reached the cart and slipped into the passenger's seat. Losing Tony Stevens was akin to a boxer taking a hard punch to the solar plexus, but it hadn't knocked him down. The operation was in place and running smoothly. Only a few more loose ends to tie up, and they would be done. All nonessential players had been paid and were finished. Only three people remained in the know. Soon that would be down to two. Each cog in the wheel slowly dropping off until there were none left, and the gears that had driven the machine were stripped clean.

Two hundred and twelve million dollars. What a scam. Less than a year to set it up, up-front expenses of just over eight million and payouts to the key players in the range of sixty million. A lot of very happy people. And unhappy ones. He chuckled at that. It all depended on which side of the con you were on. Sometimes crime does pay—and when it does, it pays very well. His own take was somewhere between one hundred and fifty and one hundred and sixty million dollars. Not bad for forty months of his life and limited risk. The only downside to the scam was that his face was well known in the United States now, and he would have to steer clear of the country for a few years. Not a problem, he preferred Europe and Mexico anyway.

His partner pulled up by the green, and they walked onto the manicured grass, putters in hand. He waited for his turn, then read the green and tapped the ball. It broke hard right to left and rimmed the cup. Everyone groaned. He tapped in for a par and gave his buddies a grin. They were all rich, and shitty golfers. Common for Hong Kong. Lots of money, no time to get out for more than a couple of rounds a year. Brand slid back into the cart, and they headed for the next hole.

He had given the police and the FBI the Canadian connection, the computers and the tie to Mexico. And they had done exactly what he expected them to. Follow up, looking specifically for him. But Edward Brand didn't exist. Nothing about him existed. They were hunting for a ghost, and that's exactly what they would get. A mist that dissipated every time they got close. Nothing of substance. Nothing—ever. He smiled. Leading the police was so simple. They took the bait and ran about like lemmings until they finally headed for the cliff and the inevitable sea. The only real threat the authorities represented was that he might eventually get sloppy simply because they were so easy to manipulate. That was the only true danger.

They reached the tee box for the twelfth hole. He had the honors and hit first, his drive straight down the middle, two hundred and eighty yards. Again, the appreciative clapping. Jesus, golfing with these guys was an ego-booster. He smiled and retook his seat on the cart. He returned the polite clap when one of the others in the foursome hit a good shot. They started down the fairway, the breeze cool and invigorating.

One more detail and the con was wrapped up. One more. This should be fairly simple. It involved planning and execution, but then, what didn't? He glanced at the surrounding hills, home to the extremely wealthy and privileged of Hong Kong's society. Li Ka-shing, the reclusive real estate billionaire and Hong Kong's richest man, lived in those hills. What a life. But then, why did anyone really need more than a hundred and fifty million dollars. He could buy houses wherever he wanted and live out the rest of his life in luxury on the money the NewPro scam had generated. Whether he would or not was debatable. The lure of taking other people's money from them was too great. He had been wealthy before the NewPro job, but had still taken the time and risk to pull it off.

The truth was—he loved the risk. The adrenaline rush of knowing you had taken somebody completely by surprise and stolen something of great value. Because aside from children and family, nobody cared about anything as much as they cared about their money. They were all like Scrooge McDuck, alone in his money fortress, dancing on piles of coins and dollar bills. The silly fools.

Dance on. And enjoy it while it's there. Because you never know when someone might come along and take it.

And then what?

He grinned. That was a question only people like Alan Bestwick and Taylor Simons had an answer to. He was fine not knowing the answer to that question.

CHAPTER NINETEEN

The Federal Bureau of Investigation in Washington, D.C., made the decision. It was up to Special Agent Brent Hawkins, as the senior agent in charge of the NewPro case in San Francisco, to convey the results of that decision to Taylor Simons and Alan Bestwick. He phoned Sam Morel and asked him to be present as well. They met at Taylor and Alan's new house on Pierce Street at seven on Friday, October 20. The sun had dropped into the choppy ocean and a stiff breeze blew in off the water. It was cold when the three police officials walked from their cars to the front door.

Alan answered and welcomed them into a maze of piled boxes. The house smelled of stale smoke, from the previous tenants, and a couple of windows were open in an attempt to air out the rooms. Taylor was dressed in sweats while unpacking one of the larger crates in the living room, her long red hair pulled back in a ponytail. She glanced up as they entered and pointed to where the couch and loveseat sat facing each other in the center of the room.

"I'm not even going to start apologizing for this

mess," she said, sitting on the loveseat. Alan joined her, and the two FBI agents sat on the couch. Sam Morel found a solid box beside the couch and leaned on it. "What's so important that you had to see us on a Friday night?" she asked, her voice tinged with optimism.

Hawkins cleared his throat. "The D.C. office has reviewed the evidence Kelly Kramer found on the NewPro computers," he started.

Taylor leaned back into the couch, her body language speaking clearly. The moment the FBI agent passed off the blame on Washington, she knew they had nixed following up on what Kelly had found. Nobody started off positive news by pointing the finger at someone else.

"We just don't think there's enough concrete evidence to follow up on."

"What?" Alan said, outraged. "This is the first real lead you've had. Edward Brand purchased that antique himself. You've got the address of the antique shop in Mexico City."

"It's sketchy at best."

"Christ Almighty," Alan said, slamming his fist down on the armrest. "This is bullshit. We have to bring in our own guy, and when he finds something your people should have dug out of those hard drives, you back off." He stopped, then wagged his finger at both the FBI men. "That's it, isn't it? You're pissed off that we found something you didn't."

"It doesn't work that way, Mr. Bestwick," Hawkins countered. "We simply can't allocate resources to follow up on every clue we get. This one involves the purchase of an antique in Mexico City, which is out of our jurisdiction."

"Someone involved with this whole thing killed one of your agents," Alan said sharply. "I'd think you'd want to find these guys."

"We do," Hawkins shot back in a heated voice. "I knew Alicia Walker personally. This isn't any fun for us either. We want these guys as badly as you do."

"I doubt it," Alan said. "They didn't destroy your life."

"They destroyed Alicia's," Hawkins snapped. Then he took a couple of deep breaths and continued calmly. "None of us are happy that these guys are still out there."

"Right," Alan said, rising from the couch. "Is that it? That's all the news you have for us today?"

"That's it," Abrams said, also rising. Hawkins followed suit. They walked to the front door and let themselves out. The sound of the door clicking shut reached the living room.

Taylor slouched back into the throw pillows on the couch. "I don't believe this. We finally get a break, and nothing comes of it."

Sam Morel had stayed in the living room. "I never thought they'd disregard what Kelly found," he said. "It wasn't the reaction I expected. I thought they'd be all over this, especially with Alicia Walker in the ground."

"They're going to get away with it," Alan said, his voice shaking with fury. "Bastards."

Taylor was quiet for a minute. Then she said, "Alan, we've got the address to the antique shop. We could check it out."

"What?" Alan said. "What do you mean?"

Taylor sat forward. "Brand bought an antique from a shop in Mexico City. There's a chance that the owner of the shop may know where he is. Or who he is."

"You're talking about flying to Mexico and seeing this guy face to face?"

"Why not? He owns an antique store. How dangerous can he be?" There was a light in her eyes, one that Alan hadn't seen in weeks. A vibrancy to her body as she leaned toward him.

"Mexico can be dangerous," Morel said. "Even antique shops."

"This is the one clue we've got to work with right now," Taylor insisted. "If we leave this and let it die, we might as well just roll up in a ball and admit that they've beaten us."

"I don't know . . ." Alan said. "You've just started a new job, and we don't have a lot of money."

"Money we *do* have," Taylor said. "We're sitting on a few hundred thousand dollars from the sale of the house. I can get time off if I want. Nick's happy to have me. He'll give me as much time as I want."

"I wouldn't advise it," Sam said. "You could be getting in over your heads. I've known some pretty street-savvy guys who got into trouble in Mexico when they poked their noses in the wrong places. One of them came back in a body bag."

Quiet descended on the room, and Taylor and Sam looked at Alan. The decision rested with him. He rose and walked to the window, staring out. The streetlamps were on, bright yellow against the darkening sky. Taylor watched his face in the reflected glow, knowing the man and getting inside his head. Alan was a person who believed acting on opportunity was the only way. Anything less was a cop-out. But his decision would be made by weighing the risk against the possible outcome. The upside was that they may get some of their money back. The downside was that he could be putting them in harm's way. She knew it would be a difficult decision for him and readied herself to accept his decision—whichever way it went.

Alan turned away from the window and shook his head. "My head's telling me to stay here and play it safe." He sat on the couch beside Taylor. No one spoke for a minute. A clock ticked and the sound of a motorcycle driving past the house drifted in, then dissipated. Finally he said, "But I don't think this is a time to listen to logic. I think there are times in life when you've got to walk out on the branch and listen for the cracking sound."

"If there's anything I can do from this end . . ." Morel said.

"We'll call," Taylor said. She leaned over and kissed Alan on the cheek. Everything had just changed. They were no longer sitting back and waiting for the police or the FBI to solve the case. They were going on the offensive.

CHAPTER TWENTY

Taylor and Alan landed at Aeropuerto Internacional Benito Juárez at three in the afternoon on Wednesday, October 25. They found the airport that served Mexico City to be utterly confusing. The floor plan was an endless maze of departure and arrival gates jutting into the central corridors, making any sort of movement somewhere between difficult and impossible. It was beyond their comprehension how the Mexican airport authorities managed to keep people moving and flights on schedule.

Conversely, the taxi queue was short, and it only took a couple of minutes to get through the line. They gave the driver the name of the hotel and settled in the backseat, watching the city flash past. Barrios and ugly concrete commercial buildings lined the roads near the airport, but as they drove deeper into the congestion, the houses and businesses gradually changed from ill- to well-kept. When they crossed Avenida Ninos Héroes the architecture changed again, to renovated 1920 and 30s houses and buildings, colorful with trendy cafés and shops lining the main street. *Taquerías*, small stands on some of the corners of the tree-lined roads, were busy as the street vendors wrapped up the last of *comida*, the filling midday meal. Their driver pulled onto Paseo de la Reforma, slowed and stopped in front of the Marquis Reforma Hotel. The hotel's facade was stunning pink with graceful sections of curved glass, an art nouveau masterpiece in a tropical setting.

Alan paid the driver and a bellman jumped to take their luggage, delivering it to the front desk, where a pleasant man welcomed them in English. They had booked a suite on the seventh floor with a view of Castillo de Chapultepec, and the reception clerk had their electronic keys in seconds. Two front-end staff helped with the bags, and within a couple of minutes they were checking out the series of rooms that comprised their suite. The bellmen left with a few extra pesos, and Taylor and Alan were alone. Alone in a city of twenty-six million people. Taylor stood at the window staring over the huge expanse of green that was the Bosque de Chapultepec, the park where the castle rested on Grasshopper Hill. Dating back to Aztec times, the castle was the scene of the native Mexicans' last battle with the Spaniards. In 1940 the castle was modified into one of Mexico City's finest museums, the Museo Nacional de Historia. Taylor stared at the historical building and its tranquil surroundings, her mind alive with the possibilities of what they might find in Mexico City.

Had Edward Brand visited the city and picked out the antique in person, arranging payment later through the corporation he knew was destined to fail? Would the owner of the shop recognize the FBI sketch of Brand they had brought with them? If he did, what then? Would Brand have been sloppy enough to leave an address or phone number other than that of NewPro? Probably not. Even if he did make a mistake and leave a trail of some sort, what would they do with the information? The questions were inexhaustible, and there were no answers. She felt Alan's hands on her waist, smiled and turned toward him.

"When do you want to visit the antique shop?" he asked.

The sun was still above the hills and trees of the park, and the city was in the doldrums between *comida* and the advent of night, when the discos and nightclubs came alive. To Taylor there was a vibrancy in the air, a sort of adrenaline rush that had yet to happen. She shuddered slightly, perhaps as the air-conditioning touched her, perhaps from the anticipation.

"Does it say what time the shop is open until?"

Alan checked the page they had printed from the Internet. "Nine o'clock," he said. "We could try tonight if you want."

"Why not," Taylor said. "Give me fifteen minutes to freshen up."

"Sure." He wandered about the main room of the suite, picking through the magazines and tourist brochures he found laying about. They were in Spanish and English. He leafed through them, mostly disinterested in the content. Merchants trying to entice travelers to their shops to spend money. Money. It was always about money. Sometimes he hated the stuff. But mostly when he had none.

Taylor reappeared dressed in faded jeans and a tight shirt. Her hair was down and fell past her shoulders, the red hue almost luminescent in the growing shadows. She had a touch of makeup on her eyes and cheeks, and a pale sand-colored lipstick on her full lips. Alan caught his breath at the sight of her standing in the bathroom doorway. Christ, she was beautiful. And she was his wife. He crossed the room and slipped his hand around her waist and pulled her close. Her body was warm. She draped her arms over his shoulders.

"We have an antique shop to visit," she said softly. "I think if we don't get going soon, we may not make it tonight."

"Yeah, I think you're right," he said, kissing her on her forehead and loosening his grip. She slipped out of his arms.

"You think I'm dressed all right?" she asked.

"I think you're going to turn a lot of heads. If that's okay, then you're dressed fine."

She grinned. "Who knows, maybe the shop owner will be a middle-age guy with a thing for redheads."

"We should be so lucky."

They took the elevator to the lobby, a mixture of art deco meets terra cotta, and stood near one wall discussing their options. Taylor was worried that if they caught a cab to the antique shop and the driver left, they would be on their own to find one for the return trip. Taking just any cab off the street in Mexico City could be dangerous. The other option was to find a driver for the evening, but they were unsure of how to do so. After a couple of minutes, they opted to ask the concierge.

The concierge, whose name was Miguel, immediately advised them against one of the waiting taxis. He insisted upon arranging for a driver for the evening rather than having them take the next cab in the queue. Cab drivers who were allowed to work the hotel were government registered, with an orange or green stripe on the bottom of their license plate. But once they were away from the hotel, there was no guarantee whatever cab they got into would be safe. Having a private driver was the best—the safest. It took almost half an hour for the man to arrive, but when he did they were glad they had waited. His name was Ricardo and in addition to being very friendly and speaking fluent English, he drove a newer-model private Mercedes.

"Where to?" he asked after they had introduced themselves and settled into the backseat.

"Antigüedades Coloniart," Alan said. "It's on Estocolmo, in Zona Rosa."

Ricardo turned and glanced at Alan. "I know it. You're

shopping for antiques tonight? You look like you should be going out for dinner and dancing. This is Mexico City—alive with the world's best restaurants and many wonderful nightclubs."

"Maybe after the antique shop," Taylor said. "We'll see."

"Well, you've got me all night. So whatever you want is where I take you."

"Thanks," Alan said.

The streets were crowded now, the sidewalks filled with smartly dressed *Chilangos*, as natives to Mexico City were known. It was almost eight o'clock, and the restaurants were just beginning to fill. Ricardo kept his window rolled down and the evening air, thick with smog and cigarette smoke, filtered in along with the pounding music from passing cars and brightly lit discos. At least once every block someone would honk and wave at Ricardo, and he would grin back, sometimes yelling across the road at a pretty woman. They were obviously in Ricardo's section of town. After a few instances, he stopped at a red light and leaned back over the seat.

"I live a block over to the right. And I own a restaurant-supply business that keeps most of these places stocked up on fresh seafood and steaks. That's why I know so many people. Get me a few blocks from here and I'm another face in the crowd."

"So you don't drive for a living?" Taylor asked, looking at him a little closer now that he had given them a snippet of his life. He was about her age and very well-kept. His nails were manicured and his hair freshly cut. His teeth were white and straight, and he was impeccably dressed.

Ricardo laughed. "A couple of times a year. But tonight, Miguel, the concierge at your hotel, asked me for a favor. He doesn't ask often, so I said yes."

"A favor?"

The light turned green, but he didn't move. "Miguel is

a very savvy kind of guy. He's street smart. He grew up in one of the barrios on the edge of town and worked very hard to get his position with the hotel. He said he saw something in your eyes that worried him. He wanted me to drive you and to make sure you're okay." The honking behind the car was increasing in intensity and he turned back to the road. "Like I said, he's a smart guy."

Taylor sucked in a deep breath. They weren't even out of their five-star hotel and people were clueing in that they weren't just Jane and John Tourist. Was it that obvious? She ran her hands through her hair as Ricardo pulled up in front of the antique store. It was almost baroque in its architecture, with light gray stone batons bordering the portico and windows completely encased by ornate metal bars. Lights shone out from inside the store and Taylor could see a handful of people milling about. Ricardo slipped the car into park and switched off the ignition.

"Want me to come in with you?" he asked.

"No, I think we'll be okay," Alan said. "If we need someone to translate I'll come out and get you."

Ricardo laughed. "You won't need a translator. You have money, they speak English."

They opened the door and entered the shop, immediately leaving the cacophony of street noise behind them. The store was a couple of thousand square feet, with numerous antiques and works of art tastefully displayed. It was not crowded or junky, but leaning more toward quality than quantity. The lighting was muted, almost seductive, and much of the wall space was taken by old paintings and tapestries. A closer look showed the room to be divided up by sections of false walls, giving the vendor more display space. Each section contained a certain type of collectible. Old bicycles were near the back, and next to them was sports memorabilia, then handbags, corkscrews, and two full sections of plates and ewers. The science and technology area was about midway to the back and stocked with numerous telescopes and microscopes, weigh scales and ancient typewriters and cash registers. Interspersed throughout the well-organized showroom was a strong presence of Aztec and early Mexican history. Prices were not shown on any of the display pieces. A well-dressed man in his early thirties approached them and said good evening in both Spanish and English.

"Hello," Alan said.

"Visiting Mexico City?" the man asked.

"Yes."

"And looking for something special to take home?"

"Perhaps," Alan said. "Are you the manager?"

"No, that would be the gentleman at the desk. He is the owner actually. Would you like to speak with him?"

"Please."

The man bowed ever so slightly and moved away. A moment later the man at the desk joined them and introduced himself. He was in his late fifties with deep brown skin and jet-black hair, parted on one side and swept back from his serious face. "I am Fernando Domínguez. How can I help you this evening?" He was impeccably dressed in what appeared to be Armani with a subtle blue silk tie. His black shoes gleamed from polish, even in the low light.

"A friend of ours found a telescope in your shop and had it shipped back to the United States. When we saw it we asked where he had found it. He gave us your address."

"And you would like a telescope?" Domínguez asked.

"Yes," Taylor answered. "The same kind, if possible. It was lacquered brass—by Negretti, I think."

Domínguez smiled. "Yes, of course. A nineteenth-century piece by Negretti and Zambra." His correction of her error was very tasteful. "We had six telescopes, but three pieces have been sold, so our selection is somewhat limited. Do you remember exactly what the telescope looked like? The three we have are all a bit different." He led Alan and Taylor to where three brass telescopes sat on old-looking wooden legs.

Alan surveyed the scopes, then said, "I'm not sure. Perhaps you could pull the invoice from the sale and look at the model number."

"An excellent idea," Domínguez said. "What was the man's name?"

"Brand. Edward Brand," Alan said, his voice even and clear. "If it's not under his personal name, it might be under his company. NewPro." Alan spelled it.

"I'll have a look through our files. They're computerized, so it should only take a moment." He walked back to the desk, leaving Taylor and Alan alone with the menagerie of ancient scientific instruments.

"Good so far," Alan said quietly. "Let's hope he finds Brand's name in his computer."

"And an address," Taylor added.

They milled about for a couple of minutes until the store owner returned. He shook his head as he approached. "Nothing under either of those names. Sorry. Perhaps we could look closely at the telescopes, and maybe you will remember which one it is. Or maybe you'll just see one you like."

Taylor nodded, and they spent the next few minutes feigning interest over the three ancient telescopes and the fitted wooden cases that accompanied them. After a few minutes Alan shook his head.

"I don't know. I'm just not sure." Then he snapped his fingers. "Taylor, you've got a picture of Edward with you. Why don't you show it to Senor Domínguez. Perhaps he'll recognize him and will be able to place which piece Edward bought."

"Good idea," she said, digging through the small handbag she'd brought with her. She withdrew the sketch and unfolded it. "We all had these done by an artist at a country fair near our houses. Edward didn't like his so I kept it." She held it out so Domínguez could see the face.

For the briefest moment Domínguez's eyes opened slightly and his lips parted, sucking in a tiny breath. Then his features immediately returned to the stoic but accommodating man who was trying to sell them a telescope. "No, I'm sorry. I don't recognize the man."

"Perhaps one of your staff," Alan said.

"Perhaps," Domínguez said, his lips tighter now, any hint of a smile gone. "I will take the sketch and make a photocopy, then ask my staff tomorrow if anyone sold this man a telescope. If you leave me your name and your hotel, I will forward the results on to you."

"We'll call you tomorrow afternoon," Alan said before Taylor could answer.

"That would be fine," Domínguez said. "I'll make the photocopy." He went through a door behind the desk, was gone for the better part of a minute, then reappeared with the original in one hand and a copy in the other. "That worked well. I'll make sure and ask around tomorrow morning." He handed Taylor the sketch. "About the telescope . . ."

"Let's wait and see if we can figure out which one it is first," Taylor said. "Maybe one of your staff will remember selling Edward the piece. Then we can pull the invoice."

"As you wish," he said. "Good evening and thank you for coming in."

They returned to the sidewalk and to the early evening warmth. The shop had been mildly air conditioned and the air outside was warm and close. Ricardo saw them exit the shop and waved. They walked slowly to the car.

"Did you catch his reaction when he saw the picture?" Taylor asked.

"Oh, yeah. He knows who Brand is. No doubt about it."

"Why would he snap shut like that? He sold Brand an antique. Why not just tell us about the sale?"

Alan lightly grasped her arm, and they stopped on the sidewalk, out of earshot of the car. "Think about it, Taylor. If this guy really knows who Edward Brand is, then he knows that Brand is a criminal. And keep in mind Alicia Walker. She stuck her nose in the works, and she's dead. And she's an FBI agent. If Brand had that Tony Stevens guy kill Alicia Walker, he wouldn't think twice about getting someone to knock off some antique shop owner. No wonder he's scared."

Taylor was thoughtful. "So what now?"

Alan took a few seconds to answer, then said, "Now we get creative."

CHAPTER TWENTY-ONE

Fernando Domínguez switched off the lights and set the alarm. A low glow emanated from the night-lights positioned at sporadic intervals throughout the antique store. He exited and locked the door before the sixty-second delay on the alarm kicked in. The sidewalks were filled with young *Chilangos*, dressed for the night. He kept close to the front of his building, then cut down a narrow passageway between the building and the one to the west. There was no lighting and the old cobblestones provided little grip for his dress shoes. He almost slipped once, but caught the rough edge of the brick building and steadied himself. Domínguez disliked cutting through the narrow gap, but it beat a three-block walk to get from the front of his business to the rear, where his car was parked. And thanks to Mexico City's lax building codes in the 1980s and early 1990s, another building owner had erected a wall between the rear exit of his business and where he parked his car. So every night he slipped through the hole in the wall, wondering if this was the time a young street punk would be wait-

ing for him. He touched the leather holster under his
arm and felt the cold steel of his pistol. It was reassuring.

He reached the far end and pulled his keys from his
pocket, thumbing the key fob—the parking light blink-
ing twice in the dark. The Lexus was warm from sitting
all day, and he cranked up the air-conditioning. He
pulled out of the alley onto Avenida Chapultepec, heading west toward Lomas de Chapultepec, the wealthy
enclave of estate homes where he lived. His antique
store was busy and his markups almost criminal, giving him a quality of living that surpassed most doctors
and lawyers. And he was his own boss—had been for
twenty years.

He steered off the busy boulevard and onto one of the
quiet side streets leading to his house, his mind briefly
touching on the visit from the two Americans who had
visited his shop. They had been very focused on what
they wanted, and it wasn't a Negretti and Zambra telescope. Edward Brand. He knew the man. And Brand
himself had told him not to be surprised if someone came
looking for him. Brand himself had described tonight's
event as inevitable. That someone in fact *would* show, asking for him. But a fat bonus on top of the already marked-
up price on the telescope had sealed his lips. One thing
he had learned many years ago was that two kinds of
people kept secrets—smart ones and dead ones.

He saw himself as smart.

A long sloping drive appeared on the right side of the
road, and he touched a button on the upper visor. The
wrought-iron gates parted, then opened fully, and he
drove into the walled estate. The gates closed automatically behind him. He rounded two curves, and the house
came into view. It was colonial style with four pillars jux-
taposed against the broad but flat facade. He pulled the
Lexus up to the edge of the circular driveway fronting
the house and stepped out.

The air was warm and the night sky clear. What a

night. What a life. Everything felt right, even the slight breeze that stole gently through the surrounding trees. But even though he was in tune with what surrounded him, there was one thing that Fernando Domínguez was not aware of as he opened the door to his house. The late-model Mercedes that had followed him along Avenida Chapultepec and through the winding streets. The Mercedes that was parked outside the gates leading to the house. Inside the car, three people stared at the walled estate.

"We know where he works and where he lives," Taylor said, sitting in the Mercedes. "What now?"

Alan continued to stare at the closed gates. "I'd like to ask him a few more questions. Like where Edward Brand is. That guy knows more than what he's saying."

"I think so too," Taylor agreed, "but what can we do? We can't beat the information out of him."

"He owns an antique shop," Alan said. "Do you think there's a law in place that makes dealers in antiquities register every sale. If there is, then he would have a record of Brand's purchase. And maybe a sales receipt with an address or phone number."

Taylor nodded. "I wonder why he lied. Do you think he's really that scared of Brand?"

"Absolutely," Alan said. "The proof's in what we saw a couple of hours ago. He's willing to lie to cover up the fact that he knows him. Who would do that unless they were worried about the guy coming back looking for who snitched on him?"

Taylor was quiet for a few moments. After about thirty seconds, Ricardo said, "Are we finished here?"

"Sure," Alan said. "Could you take us back to La Condesa? Maybe we'll have a couple of drinks and dance a bit." La Condesa was the trendiest of the colonias bordering Zona Rosa, filled with dance clubs and discos.

"Now you're talking," Ricardo said. "What kind of club do you want?"

"Not too loud, but with good dancing music," Alan said, slipping his arm around Taylor and drawing her close. He whispered in her ear. "Enough following around after suspicious people for one night. Let's have a little fun."

She couldn't help but smile. "Okay. Fun it is."

Chapter Twenty-two

The electronic key sliding through the reader on the hotel door partially wakened her. The muffled sound of the door opening caused her to sit bolt upright in bed. Taylor glanced next to her for Alan—he was gone. The bed was empty. Her heart was racing as she glanced at the clock on the night table. Just after four in the morning. They had returned from the nightclub after midnight, made love, then drifted off to sleep. She pulled the covers up to her chin to hide her naked body as a figure entered the bedroom. It was a man's figure, Alan's size, but he was moving unsteadily. Then, just inside the door, the man collapsed.

"Taylor."

It was Alan's voice, but faint and filled with pain. She shot out of bed, wrapping a sheet around her as she moved quickly to where he lay on the plush carpet. He was groaning slightly and cradling his right arm. She flicked on the light and gasped. Her husband was curled on the floor, his entire right side covered with blood.

"Oh, my God," she exclaimed. "Alan, what happened?" She bent down, her eyes scanning his body, trying to determine the extent of his injuries. His right hand was bloodied, as was his forearm. His shirt was soaked with blood, but not torn. She couldn't tell whether the blood had run down from his hand and arm or if he had been shot or stabbed. His face was unmarked, but his eyes were filled with pain.

"I'm okay," he said. "Just shaken up a bit."

She stroked his hair back off his forehead. "You're not shot?"

"No. Nothing like that. It probably looks worse than it is." He uncurled slightly and then lay stretched out on his back. "I'll be all right. I was unsure on my feet when I got here. I think I just need to clean up."

"I'll get a towel," she said. "Don't move." Taylor scurried to the bathroom and grabbed one of the bath towels, wet it under the shower, then snatched another dry towel and hurried back to the bedroom. Alan had propped himself up against the foot of the bed. She took the wet towel and began dabbing at the bloodied areas. He grimaced in pain when she touched his hand.

"Where were you? What happened?"

"I went back to the antique shop," he said in a raspy voice.

"You did what?"

"The antique shop. I went back after you fell asleep to have a look at Domínguez's computer files."

"Just a minute," she said, disappearing back into the bathroom and reappearing with a glass of water. He drank it slowly. "That better?"

"Much. Thanks."

"Why would you do that?" Taylor asked, wiping at the blood on his hand and arm. He was scraped and had a few cuts, but nothing that would require stitches.

Alan's voice was stronger now. "I was lying in bed, just thinking. I couldn't sleep. The one thing that kept running through my mind was that Fernando Domínguez was our only connection to Edward Brand. And that he probably knew more than he let on when we were in his store. Instead of just lying around all night, I thought I'd have a look inside his files. See if Brand's name and address were in there somewhere."

"Are you crazy? Look at what happened to you. You could have been killed."

He shifted a bit, trying to get comfortable. "It's not that bad."

"Here," she said, lifting him under the left arm and directing him to the bed. "Lie down." She unbuttoned his shirt and slipped it off. The right side of his chest and stomach were covered with splotches of blood. When she had him resting on the bed, his head propped up on a pillow, she took a towel and gently dabbed at the blood. As she worked, she asked, "Tell me what happened."

"I caught a cab outside the hotel and the driver dropped me off about two blocks from Domínguez's place. I asked him to wait for me, which turned out to be a good thing. I had to go in through the front door, but getting in was simple. The door locks were single tumblers. Takes less than ten seconds to pick those. Disabling the security system was easy—it's a variation of the ones I installed in San Francisco."

"Easy for some people, maybe. What happened once you were inside?"

"Aside from a couple of night-lights, the store was dark, and I had to remember my way through without knocking anything over. That was probably the toughest part. There was hardly any light coming in off the street. When I found the back room, I closed the door behind me and switched on a light. There were three computers on the desks. I powered them up and looked through their client base."

"And . . ."

"I found a listing for Edward Brand."

"You're kidding."

"Nope. Brand has a house in Cabo San Lucas. Somewhere in the Cabo del Sol development. That's where he lives some of the time."

"Did you get an address?"

"No, he has invoices and shipments sent through the area developer. Note on the file said it was in case he wasn't at his villa. But Cabo del Sol is a single development. I would suspect it's not that big. It shouldn't be too hard to find him. We just narrowed the entire world down to one subdivision."

"Crazy," Taylor said, "but well done. That's obviously not the end of the story. Otherwise you wouldn't be all scraped up."

Alan glanced down at the right side of his body. "I was just coming out of the shop when this guy came around the corner and yelled at me in Spanish. I've got no idea if he was a mugger or a plainclothes cop or someone who knew I shouldn't be in the shop. I cut through a narrow gap between the antique shop and the next building, but the ground was uneven and I lost my balance and fell into the stucco wall. It had a rough finish. That's what scraped me up so badly."

"Was he still following you?"

"Yeah, but he was having trouble with his footing as well. It was dark and getting any sort of good grip on the rocks was almost impossible."

"How did you get away?" Taylor asked.

"Ran. Ran like hell. There was a wall at the end of the alley and I was in front of him. I hopped over. Straight down the road to where the cab was waiting and back here. Paid the driver really well on top of the initial hundred." He rolled over a touch so he could see her face. "I did okay?"

"Yeah, you did okay. Just don't do it again."

"Promise," he said, raising himself up on his elbows. "I think we're done here."

"Mexico City?"

He nodded.

"Cabo San Lucas?"

"That's where Edward Brand is."

"And when we find him?" Taylor asked.

"We get our money back."

"And if he doesn't want to give it?"

Alan was quiet, but his eyes told a story. The story of a man who had been wronged. A man who was fed up with being taken advantage of. An angry man. A dangerous man. When he finally answered her question, his voice was intense. More intense than she had ever heard.

"I'll kill him," was all he said.

CHAPTER TWENTY-THREE

Cabo San Lucas evolved since the Guaycura tribes first settled the cape and subsisted on fruit and whatever small game they could bring down with their blowguns. The Spaniards, under Conquistador Hernán Cortés and fresh from their European victory over the Moors, trampled across the Aztec empire and by 1565 were firmly in control of the archipelago. But the Spanish failed to realize the potential of the region, their maps even showing California and Baja California as islands. They neglected the area, and when Mexico finally achieved independence from Spain in 1821 after eleven years of intense fighting, the Baja was part of the deal.

The temperate climate and world-class deep-sea fishing transformed the cape from sleepy Mexican villages to tourist hotspot. Restaurants and night clubs flung open their doors. Even rock singer Sammy Hagar, the front-man for Van Halen, discovered Cabo San Lucas and opened Cabo Wabo, a restaurant that catered to the young rock crowd. The notoriety that followed designated Cabo San Lucas as a party town for college students on spring break. Or any other time of the year.

Students don't care when, so long as the tequila is flowing and the sun is baking the beaches.

And somewhere in the winding, insanely crowded streets of Cabo San Lucas was one man. Edward Brand.

Taylor and Alan flew into Los Cabos International Airport, just outside San José del Cabo, the sleepy sister of the more boisterous Cabo San Lucas. They caught a cab into Cabo and went directly to Playa Grande, a massive resort set into the rocks west of the marina. The lobby was circular, a hundred feet or more in diameter, with marble floors and twenty-foot pillars framing the long, half-round reception desk. The reservations Taylor had made from Mexico City were in the computer, and after they had checked out their room, Alan arranged for a rental car. They asked the concierge if he knew where the development of Cabo del Sol was located. He nodded and pulled out a well-worn map.

"Cabo del Sol is a new residential and golf community just east of Cabo," he said, his English almost unaccented. "Take the main road toward San José del Cabo. About three miles out you'll see a sign that says *returno*, and a rock cairn with Cabo del Sol on it. Take the off ramp, and at the top of the hill, turn right. Just follow the road past the security checkpoint, and you're in. They're building a lot of houses right now, so expect some construction."

"How do we get through the security?" Taylor asked.

"You're *gringos*," the concierge said with a wry smile. "Just look white."

"Thanks," Alan said, the irony of Caucasians breezing through checkpoints while Mexicans were stopped and questioned not lost on him.

Alan took the wheel of the rental, getting twisted around twice in the maze of one-way streets before finding the main boulevard and skirting the marina. Avenida Lazaro Cardenas led to the eastern edge of Cabo, then out of the city and into the arid scrublands that once claimed the entire southern edge of the cape. Mega-hotels, most of them timeshares, were built along the coast, rising amidst the cactus and arroyos, colorful but foreign against the rugged beauty of the coastline. After a ten-minute drive they reached the turnoff for Cabo del Sol, and Alan steered the car up the hill and took the right turn. The paved road curved alongside one of the golfing fairways as it dipped toward the ocean. At the end of the sweeping curve, a security station came into view. It was tucked under a massive set of brick arches. Alan glanced at Taylor.

"Here goes," he said, pulling up to the roadblock.

A uniformed guard glanced into the vehicle as they rolled to a stop, then smiled, wished them a good afternoon and raised the arm. They drove through into the upscale community of Cabo del Sol. The roads were smooth and winding and bordered by long sandy beds filled with organ pipe cactus and desert succulents. A few palm trees lined the streets, mostly planted around the perimeters of the stucco and stone estate houses set into the rocky hills. A number of new homes were under construction, the cinder-block skeletons in stark contrast to the impeccable finishing on the existing villas. They drove through the maze of streets for about fifteen minutes before coming to a realization. Finding Edward Brand was not going to be easy.

"This place is huge," Taylor said as they pulled up to the golf clubhouse. "He could be anywhere. And if he's in one of these houses and doesn't come out, we'll never find him."

Alan switched off the car and shook his head. "If he's even here. Damn it. This isn't going to be easy."

"You said the computer at the antique shop gave the developer's address, in case he wasn't at his villa. We could check there."

"Good idea," he said, starting the car and backing it out of the stall. "There was a place on the left side of the road on the way in."

"I saw it. The house with all the flags, like they put out at show-homes in new neighborhoods."

"Yeah, let's try it."

It took less than ten minutes to find the show suite, park and ask the saleswoman working the desk if she had an address for Edward Brand. They were down from the States and wanted to visit. The woman checked her files, but there was no record of a sale to anyone by that name. There were hundreds of names on the list. The chances of figuring out what name he had registered under were zero. They returned to the golf clubhouse and parked in the shade.

They checked out the clubhouse, a hub of activity as many of the day's golfers were just finishing their rounds and coming in for something to drink. Alan asked one of the pros for a scorecard and perused it, taking in the lay of the land. The course was actually two full tracts of eighteen holes. The ocean course led west from the clubhouse toward the water, while the desert course ran through the undulating hills along the northern edge of the development. They walked through the pro shop into the restaurant and onto the outdoor patio. The view from the south-facing balcony was the last few thousand yards of land sloping to the water, then the deep blue of the Pacific Ocean. A little to the west, a rocky hill with a solitary, white lighthouse jutted above the coastline. Taylor and Alan sat at one of the tables and ordered a drink.

"Maybe he likes to golf," Alan said.

"So?"

"Rather than running all over the place looking for him, why don't we let Brand come to us?" The drinks arrived, and Alan sipped his Corona. "We could set up shop in the development, see if we can find a rental villa that overlooks the clubhouse. One that gives us a good view of the restaurant and the finishing hole on the desert course. That way, if he's a golfer, we'll see him as he's putting on eighteen. Or if he comes in for lunch. Works both ways. And we'll see him teeing off on the first hole if he's playing the ocean course."

Taylor thought about the idea. "That would mean staying in Cabo for a while. Days, maybe weeks."

Alan leaned back in his chair, taking in the view. "And that's a bad thing?"

Villa Anterra was a four-room, very private resort set between the eighteenth hole of the desert course and the first tee box of the ocean links. Four separate rooms, each complete with its own balcony and luxury bath, tied into a wide hall that led to the central meeting rooms, comprised of a kitchen, games area and media room. Imported Italian tile graced the bath and shower walls in addition to the floors inside the rooms. The numerous outdoor decks were constructed of perfectly interlocked rough-hewn sandstone. The exterior finish was smooth cream stucco and red tile on the roof. Pillars delineated the different spaces, their soft lines melding well with the background desert scene.

Edward Brand sat in one of the chaise lounges overlooking the infinity pool and felt the warm Mexican sun on his skin. Beyond the pool was a sea of cactus poking out of the sandy soil, and on the horizon the azure blue of the Pacific Ocean. White-naped brush finches flittered about the prickly pear cacti, landing and alighting, the same scene played out countless times a day. A few hundred yards between the villa and the ocean was the clubhouse for the two golf courses, a majestic building ringed by mature royal palms. An occasional golf cart wheeled by, but mostly it was peaceful. Brand finished his beer and set the empty bottle on the table next to his chair.

Everything had gone according to plan. With one small glitch. Tony Stevens should never have involved Alicia Walker in his life, something that had proved fatal for both him and the FBI agent. Stupid. That was the only word Edward Brand had to describe the entire fiasco. But even with the unexpected problem, they had still managed to stay invisible to the police. Neither he nor any of his key players had criminal records, and without something for the police to work with, their job was like finding a needle in a haystack. And the world was one very big haystack. Especially Mexico.

Even with all the trade agreements and bilateral cooperation between the United States, Canada and Mexico that had developed over the past few years, it was still extremely easy for a *gringo* to meld into Mexican society. Having money helped. It was surprising how quickly people accepted you into their community when you paid cash. The police were polite and understanding that the new foreigner required his privacy. In return, numerous high-ranking officials in the Cabo detachment were driving newer cars. Things were so simple with money. And money was one thing Edward Brand had a lot of.

The final figures were in. Two hundred and twelve million dollars. Less expenses, they had netted one hundred and eighty-nine million. After he had paid everyone else, his take was one-fifty-six. A hundred and fifty-six million dollars. Not bad for forty months of work. He had always known that NewPro would work, but he had needed to wait until he had the resources, both money and key personnel, to run the con. It was elaborate, but with precise execution it was also very simple.

He felt the wind start to pick up, and he glanced at his watch. Almost five o'clock. Omar, the Mexican man who ran the villa for him, would be calling him for dinner soon. He rose from the lounger and stretched, scanning the horizon. A couple of golf carts whizzed past, and he glanced over at the clubhouse. Maybe a round of golf would be nice. Something to break up the day. Maybe tomorrow. Then again, he thought, maybe not.

God it was nice to have options. That was one thing having an excess of money gave him. It was something he would never have to give up.

Being rich was fun. Especially with other people's money.

CHAPTER TWENTY-FOUR

It was almost three o'clock on Friday, November 3. Taylor and Alan had found a timeshare unit with a view of the golf clubhouse from the small patio off the kitchen, and spent the daylight hours watching the golfers on the first tee and coming off the course at eighteen. Every day they walked over to the dining room in the clubhouse at Cabo del Sol for lunch and watched the tee on the ocean course and the eighteenth green of the desert course from the restaurant balcony. After lunch they spent the afternoon relaxing on their patio, then headed back to the clubhouse for dinner. By Friday evening, they had tried most of the entrees on the menu.

"This is crazy," Taylor said. "We came up with this idea a week ago, and we've got nothing to show for it."

"He's here somewhere," Alan said. "He'll show up."

"Do you have any idea how many times you've said that? I think we've got to reconsider what we're doing."

Alan sipped his drink, a local beer. He allowed himself one a day, the rest of the time sticking to soda or Perrier water. "Maybe you're right."

"Quit after today?" Taylor asked.

He nodded. "Okay. Today is the last day watching the golf course."

He excused himself to use the bathroom, and Taylor looked over the room. She was so tired of sitting here doing nothing. Edward Brand had stolen everything they had, and although they suspected they were within a square mile of where he was living, they still couldn't find him. It was crazy. Alan returned and they talked for a few minutes, finished their drinks and paid the tab. They walked out toward the parking lot, and Taylor froze.

"Alan," she said quietly. "Look over there, where they take the clubs off the carts. It's him. It's Edward Brand."

Alan looked where she indicated. Taylor was right. It was definitely Brand. He was just picking up his clubs from one of the young men who cleaned and stored the members' golf bags. They watched as Brand slung them over his shoulder and headed for the parking lot. He reached a dark blue Ford Explorer and threw the clubs in the back, then jumped in the driver's seat and backed out of his parking spot. Taylor and Alan raced across the lot to their car and pulled in behind the Explorer. Brand drove slowly through the winding streets of Cabo del Sol, then pulled out onto the highway.

Brand opened the Explorer up when he hit the main road between Cabo San Lucas and San José del Cabo, the speedometer quickly topping ninety miles an hour. The traffic was as varied as it was insane—beaters trying to make it up the steep hills and delivery trucks with drivers who thought they were in the Baja 1000 mixed in with tourists who had absolutely no idea where they were going. Driving on the southern tip of the Baja peninsula was crazy at the speed limit, and insanely dangerous at almost double it. Alan tried to keep close to Brand, but not so close that he would see them in his rearview mirror. They reached the outskirts of San José del Cabo, and Alan tightened up the distance between them.

"He's going to see you," Taylor said as he slid in just two cars back.

"I've got to keep him close. This place is a goddamn maze. If he gets out of sight and turns a corner, we've lost him."

Taylor hung on as they took a fast corner, staying about eighty feet behind the tail of the Explorer. "Where do you think he's going?" The side window was open halfway, and her long red hair whipped about. She grabbed it and held it in a makeshift ponytail with her free hand.

"I've got no idea, but I sure hope he gets there soon. He drives like an asshole. This is not fun."

The target vehicle kept on the main road that serviced the major resorts, then turned toward town at the first traffic circle. Brand slowed as he approached the central part of town. At the point where the street narrowed to a single lane in both directions and tiny shops appeared on each side, he turned right and took the road to Laguna Hills. It bypassed the main commercial section of San José del Cabo and swung toward the coastline. Tiny cinder-block houses lined the left side of the road, their yards filled with stripped cars and broken appliances. The road was deteriorating quickly, the pavement pockmarked with potholes and ruts. Homemade speed bumps, embedded in the roadway by locals to slow speeding cars, rattled their teeth as they flew over them, trying to keep the Explorer in sight. At the second traffic circle, Brand turned away from the marina and headed northwest, inland but paralleling the coast.

The small decrepit homes lining the street thinned out and eventually disappeared. The road became a twisting thread of asphalt, cutting through the rugged Baja scrubland. The pavement was newer but without any shoulders, the road was dangerous at high speeds. There was no room for error. Cacti and large boulders flew past as they navigated the serpentine stretch of highway at close to breakneck speeds. Still, the Explorer stayed well ahead of them. Only on occasion did the landscape open enough for them to see the vehicle they were following, and Alan edged his speed up even more, trying to close the gap between the two vehicles.

They crested yet another ridge and rounded a corner. Alan hit the brakes and the car slid to a stop. In front of them was a T-intersection. To the right was an incline down to a waterless valley, or arroyo, and across the far side was a small village. A sign indicated it was La Laguna. To the left was a dirt road, heading north along the coast of the East Cape. A small dust plume was just settling at the base of the hill leading to La Laguna. Alan inched forward until he could see into the arroyo. The Explorer was parked in front of a building rimmed by an old wood fence. A sign hung over the entrance. The picture was a cartoon drawing of a vulture carrying a surfboard. The printing was barely visible from where they were parked. Buzzards Bar & Grill.

Alan looked over at Taylor. "What now?"

She thought for a minute, then said, "Pull down the hill. Just try to keep out of sight as best you can. Maybe we can spot him and watch what he's up to."

"Okay." Alan eased the rental down the stretch of road leading to the bottom of the dry riverbed. The road mutated from pavement to sand and dry clay as he reached the low point in the small valley. To the left of the car, toward the ocean, they could see an outdoor restaurant, the plastic tables covered by bright orange and pink tablecloths. It was protected from the late afternoon sun by a thatched roof, and was surprisingly busy. Sitting in one of the chairs with his back to them was Edward Brand.

Alan was livid, staring at the man who had stolen their money. "Why don't we sneak up behind him and smack him over the head. Knock him out and tie him up. When he comes to we'll beat the shit out of him until he tells us where our money is."

Taylor shook her head. "Look at the place. It's too crowded. Nobody is going to let you just whack him over the head and carry him out. We have to wait until he's alone somewhere."

"What if he's got a gun? Then what?"

She shrugged. "I don't know. I just know that now is not the time."

"I'm losing my patience with this game," Alan said testily.

They waited while Brand ate dinner. He had two beers with his meal, then made a phone call on the house phone, paid the tab and headed back to the Explorer. Taylor and Alan ducked below the dash until he had pulled out and retreated back up the access road. Alan gunned the engine and followed.

Brand didn't turn back onto the paved road, but continued up the dirt road that ran parallel to the coastline. It was a rough track, gutted with ruts, and white dust churned up behind the vehicles, coating everything with a fine grit. The Explorer kicked up a dust trail as it bumped along the road, which allowed Alan to back off to a few hundred yards with no risk of losing Brand. Inland, the earth was arid, punctuated with cacti and prickly shrubs, and useless for anything productive. To the right was the beach, light brown sand commingled with white rocks that thrust from the sand like outstretched fingers. Waves slammed against the craggy formations. To the west, the sun approached the distant horizon.

"A couple of hours until it gets dark," Taylor said as they bounced over the uneven roadway.

"I know," Alan said.

The approaching darkness was not a good thing. Right now they could keep Brand in sight, but once the sun dipped below the mountains, it would be impossible to track him. After about two miles, the road turned inland. The going was slow, Brand averaging about fifteen to twenty miles an hour, and Alan matching that pace. The ocean was out of sight for a mile. Then the road twisted about and angled back to the east. A massive tangle of rocks rose a couple of hundred feet and jutted out to the coast. In the dwindling sunlight they could see the road snaking around the formation, about halfway up. Brand's vehicle climbed up the narrow road and disappeared around the corner. Alan hit the bottom of the hill and gave the car some gas. As they drove, the ocean quickly dropped away. The road was barely wide enough for two cars, and there was no guard rail. Beneath them was a sheer drop to the ocean, where the waves were at high tide and crashing into the base of the rocks. They rounded the corner and before they could stop they were face to face with Edward Brand. He had parked the Explorer at the edge of the cliff and was standing next to the driver's door looking out over the ocean.

"What the fuck?" Brand yelled as they almost hit him. All three stared at each other for a second, then Brand grabbed the door handle and pulled. He jumped into the vehicle, which was parked in a small section of the road where it was wide enough for two cars to pass and one to park. It was sitting precariously close to the edge.

"Hold on," Alan screamed and floored the car. It shot forward and smashed into the side of the Explorer, pushing it toward the cliff. The rear passenger's tire hung on the edge. Brand started the truck and hit the gas. The differential rear axle sent power to the wheel with the least resistance and the one hanging over the edge began to spin. Brand slammed on the brakes, stopping the tire from spinning and reached for the button to kick in the four wheel drive.

Alan slammed the rental into reverse and backed up a few feet. He saw what Brand was doing and knew he had a few seconds before the Explorer would be back on the

road. He grabbed the clasp on Taylor's seat belt and unhooked it, reached across and pulled on her door handle.

"Out," he yelled. "Get out."

"No, Alan."

She tried to shut the door but he pushed her and she
tumbled from the passenger's seat onto the dusty road.
She stumbled to her feet just in time to see him ram the
car into drive. He gave her a quick look as he hit the gas.

"He's dead, Taylor," he said loud enough for her to
hear over the two motors. A split second later the car
shot ahead.

Edward Brand floored the SUV at precisely the same
time. The all-wheel drive sent power to the front tires as
well as the rear and the vehicle leapt ahead. Alan
couldn't react fast enough. He pulled his foot off the gas
and hit the brake but it was too late. The car missed the
Explorer and careened off the cliff, floating, suspended
in midair for a few seconds, then smashing into the sea.
A huge spray shot up and a large wave hit the car, sending it tumbling on its side before it dropped below the
surface and disappeared.

Brand spun the Explorer about and shot past Taylor,
heading north on the dirt road. He was laughing. She
rushed over to the edge of the cliff and looked down. The
ocean was over a hundred feet below, waves relentlessly
crashing into the rocks. There was no sign of the car—or
of Alan. She fell to the ground, her lungs heaving but her
breath barely coming. She stared at the sheer rock wall
rising above the road, at her hands covered with the fine
white dust, then at the darkening sky. But her mind
could only process one image.

The look of horror in Alan's eyes as he plunged over
the cliff.

CHAPTER TWENTY-FIVE

Taylor sat in the hard wooden chair, oblivious to the chaos about her. She was in the San José del Cabo *policia* station, a drab and depressing building near the center of town. The police had driven her to their precinct from the accident scene after determining she was involved in the crash. The interior of the precinct was rather decrepit, the painted stucco walls peeling and most desks and chairs in disrepair. She had decided very quickly that telling the Mexican police that Alan was trying to kill someone when he drove over the cliff was a bad idea to the nth degree, and had instead woven a story that included both truth and conjecture. So far they seemed to be buying it. One of the more senior officers, who spoke passable English, returned to where she sat and positioned himself beside her. His name was Manuel Ortega.

"Ms. Simons, you are sure your husband drove farther up the road after he dropped you at the viewpoint?" Ortega asked.

"Yes, I'm sure," she replied in a soft voice. She was a mess, her eyes black from the mascara running and red from crying. She sat with her shoulders hunched over, staring at the floor.

Ortega's eyes were steady on her. "There are houses just up the road, and no one living in those houses saw your husband drive by. One of the women was outside in her yard hanging her laundry to dry. I think she would remember seeing a tourist in a rental car. There is not much traffic on this road." His tone was interesting, almost inviting her to tell the truth.

"My husband wanted to see what was ahead on the road. I wished to stay at the lookout and enjoy the view. When he returned he was traveling too fast and went over the cliff." She looked up and stared straight into his eyes, unblinking. "My husband is dead, Senor Ortega. Please try to respect that fact."

He nodded, barely and very slowly. "I just find it a little strange that no one saw him drive up the road, and that the tracks from his car appear to go straight off the cliff, not on an angle, like they would if the car was coming around the corner at a high speed."

Taylor was quiet. It was very obvious this man was not a Mexican police officer who didn't care what happened to the *gringos* except to take their bribes. He knew something was askew, now it was a question of whether he wanted to pursue it.

"When will you be returning to the United States?" he asked.

"Soon. I have no reason to stay in Mexico."

He nodded again. This time with a little more conviction. He looked down at the file on his lap and opened it. "I see," he said, flipping through a few pages. He was quiet, scanning the contents of each page. Finally he closed the file. "The divers are searching for your husband's body, but it will be difficult. The tides and the waves in that area of the coastline are very dangerous."

"I can imagine," Taylor said.

"Yes, I'm sure you can." He tapped the file against his knee a few times, then said, "Is there anything else you want to tell me, Ms. Simons? Anything at all?" Ortega's eyes told her that he knew there was more to this than what she was telling.

Her eyes teared up again and she dabbed at them with a tissue. It came away stained with mascara. "I loved my husband, Senor Ortega. And sometimes things happen that are beyond your own control."

"Do you wish to discuss these things?"

She shook her head. "They're private. My husband and I had a very good marriage. We loved each other, and neither of us would cause harm to the other. For that to happen, it would take outside influences."

"These outside influences, they would be private."

"Yes."

He scratched his cheek lightly, then rubbed his clean-shaven chin. His dark eyes were thoughtful. He rose from his chair and said, "I'm sorry about your husband, Ms. Simons. It was a tragic accident. Please accept my condolences. You are free to go."

"Thank you," she said, rising and shaking his hand.

"Would you like a ride back to your hotel?"

She shook her head. "No, I'll find a cab. I need some time alone right now."

"I understand," Ortega said.

Taylor left the police station. The streets outside were almost deserted, the hour late. She walked slowly along the uneven cement, oblivious to the shopkeepers trying to lure in the last tourist of the day. She was alone in Mexico, alone in the world. Her parents were gone, she had no brothers or sisters, and now her husband was dead. G-cubed was gone—in the hands of a competitor, and although the loss of the business seemed trite in comparison to what had just happened on the rugged cliffs of the East Baja Cape, it was still a loss. She had suffered enough loss for one lifetime. She leaned against the rough concrete walls of a small silver store and closed her eyes. The night breeze was chilly. She tugged her thin coat about her waist and pulled up the zipper. The street was quiet, save for an occasional car or moped driving by.

Things could be worse. She could be in a Mexican prison cell waiting for Manuel Ortega to decide what to do with her. Alan had tried to kill Edward Brand by pushing the Ford Explorer over the cliff. It had backfired, and Alan had died instead. But if the police were to find out what his intentions were, she could be held as an accessory. Then a disturbing thought occurred to her. Edward Brand seemed quite at home in Mexico. First Mexico City, now the Baja peninsula. If he were as well connected as he appeared to be, what were the chances he might go to the police himself and tell them what happened? Perhaps he knew the local police well enough. Perhaps.

She looked up and down the street. Dim streetlights lit the roadway at uneven intervals and an old mangy dog lay on the sidewalk a few feet from her, disinterested now that he was sure she had no food. A set of headlights appeared, and a car pulled up to the curb. It was a cab. The driver leaned over and rolled down the passenger window.

"Taxi?" he said. He was a young man with an eager dark-skinned face. His eyes were hopeful. Perhaps he had a fare.

Taylor stared at his eyes, seeing the hope. That was the key. Hope. She had to keep hope alive in her spirit. Hope and belief. Belief that there was a reason for what happens, and that the world was not just a giant ball of random events all jumbled together to form the lives of those who got up every day and went about their various routines. She needed to believe there was a purpose to what happened. She broke off the eye contact and took a deep breath. The taxi was an older car, but well maintained. And it was the start of her new life without Alan. The moment she slipped into the backseat of that car, she was starting the long and arduous process of rebuilding her life. It was one step closer to whatever normalcy she could find.

She smiled at the young man. It was a sad smile, with sad eyes. And sad eyes never lie.

"Yes," she said quietly. "Yes. I'd like to start the journey right now."

He jumped from the driver's seat and opened the rear passenger door. She slid in, knowing the importance of the moment, but also knowing the enormity of the hill in front of her. But somehow, just taking the first step felt good.

"Where to, señorita?" he asked, leaning over the seat.

"Playa Grande, Cabo San Lucas," she said, but she knew this journey was longer.

Much longer.

CHAPTER TWENTY-SIX

Taylor loved the Japanese Tea Garden. She always had. It was her favorite spot not only in Golden Gate Park, but in all of San Francisco. She sat in the Tea House sipping herbal tea, her jacket buttoned against the late November chill. The waterfalls still flowed and the humpback bridges and pagodas were as unique as always, but the beauty of spring, when the cherry blossoms were at their peak, was sadly missing. The lack of color didn't bother her. In fact, it suited her mood.

Twenty-six days had passed since the car had slipped over the cliff taking her husband to his death. Twenty-six nights sleeping alone. Twenty-six times dragging herself out of bed in the morning and trying to make some sense out of what had happened. The horrified look on his face as the car plunged toward the sea was forever etched into her brain. His eyes, so alive, so vulnerable. Then gone.

She sipped her tea, the warm liquid pleasing to her senses. Sometimes she seemed impervious to the cold; other days she couldn't get warm even after a steaming hot bath. Her body was trying to tell her something, but she didn't know what. But what was happening with her mind was clear. She was depressed. That was something she had never known. She had been furious when Edward Brand had stolen their money, and for a few days she had felt the long tentacles of depression reaching out for her, but she had not given in to the darkness.

This was different. A dark cloud covered her life, and although she tried to strip it away and let normalcy return, it was absolute and omnipresent. For the first time in her life she understood what depression was and why it was so ugly. Her heart went out to every person who suffered from the disease. To her this was new and horrific; to many others it was a life sentence. She wondered if she was now a member of that group. She closed her eyes and said a silent prayer. When she opened her eyes, she saw a man in a suit, carrying a briefcase enter the garden. He looked to where she sat, and they briefly locked eyes. She tried to smile, but ended up just nodding. He started toward her.

The Mexican police had recovered the twisted remains of the car, but Alan's body had been washed away by the currents. All of his body except his right hand, which had been torn off by the impact of the vehicle crashing into the surf. The divers who worked the crash scene had found his hand caught in the steering column, his fingers crushed between the column and the dash. But in one way that awful indignity had been a blessing. The doctors had run a DNA profile from the hand that had matched perfectly with Alan's DNA on file at his doctor's office. That identification allowed the insurance company to close the file on Alan's death. The man who was now within a few feet of Taylor's small table was the insurance company's representative. In the briefcase was a check.

"Ms. Simons," he said as he came within earshot.

"Hello, Greg," she said. She had spoken with him numerous times in the past three weeks and had found him to be very professional and caring.

He sat in the chair beside her. "Nice place to meet," he said, glancing about.

"I like it here," she said, a sudden chill sweeping through her. She tried to pull her coat tighter against her throat, but it was already snug. "It's peaceful."

He was quiet for a minute, both of them watching a small group of tourists as they made their way slowly through the garden, stopping on one of the humpback bridges for a picture. Finally he said, "You're very fortunate that you and Mr. Bestwick decided to have some of his sperm frozen. Without a body, the company probably would have balked at paying out the claim. But the positive DNA identification allowed us to move quickly. And to print this." He handed her a check for just over a million dollars. "There's a couple of thousand dollars interest on top of the policy amount. It's paid retroactive to the day when Mr. Bestwick died."

Taylor didn't take the check, so the insurance rep tucked it under her teacup. It fluttered slightly in the wind. She could see the amount. It brought tears to her eyes. Was that the value of Alan's life? It seemed so cold. So cut and dried. When the tears subsided, she said, "We had thought that maybe we'd try to have a child. But Alan had a very low sperm count, and the chances of me getting pregnant were slim. That's why we opted to have some of his sperm frozen. Just in case."

Greg nodded. "The guys at the lab had no problem getting a definite match. If it's any consolation, Ms. Simons, lots of people aren't adequately insured and have a very difficult time after their partner passes away. At least you were wise enough to make sure you had insurance."

She gave him a weak smile. "I'd like to take credit, Greg, but it was Alan's idea." She was quiet for a minute, then said, "What should I do with my policy? I've got the same amount, a million dollars, in term life. But there's no one to give it to now."

"No family?" he asked.

She shook her head. "My parents passed away about three years ago. They were a bit older when I was born, and I was an only child. Dad was eighty-one and Mom was seventy-seven. Mom only lasted six months after Dad died." This time she managed a smile. "I guess that's true love. She couldn't live without him."

"Why don't you give it a few months before you make a decision. Term life is cheap. You can always change your will and give the money to a good cause. A lot of people leave money to charity. There are plenty of very worthwhile causes."

She nodded, a slow, almost indistinguishable motion. "I'll think about it."

"Okay," he said, shutting the clasp on his briefcase. "I'm so sorry, Ms. Simons."

She looked in his eyes and saw real emotion. And for a moment she felt for him, always meeting with people awash in tragedy. Feeling their pain. She reached out and took his hand and simply held it for a minute. "You're a wonderful person, Greg. Enjoy every day you have with those you love."

"I will," he said. He waited until she released his hand, then slowly stood and gave her a final nod. "You take care, Ms. Simons."

"Thanks." She watched him walk through the garden and out of the front gates into the park. Her tea was tepid, and she sipped it quicker now. When she finished, she took one last tour through the garden, spending a half hour in one of the pagodas. Then she returned to her car and drove home. The check was sitting on the passenger's seat and when she was stopped at a red light she glanced down and read the numbers. A million dollars. In addition to the money left over from the sale of their house, she had well over one-point-five million in cash.

Enough to buy a small house somewhere well outside San Francisco, where the property values were easier on the pocketbook, and still have the better part of a million dollars in the bank. The light turned green, and she looked back to the road.

A million dollars wasn't a lot by today's standards, but with no expenses for housing or a car, she could easily manage on five thousand a month, give or take. And the interest on a million dollars, wisely invested, would about cover that. If she were careful, she wouldn't need to work again. But was that what she wanted? To sit at home in her little bungalow letting the world slip past? Maybe right now, but what about the future? She didn't know.

Taylor pulled up in front of her house, collected the check off the car seat and went inside. It was dark, the curtains and blinds all pulled shut. She forced herself to open the window coverings and let in the November sun. It hurt her eyes, but that was crazy—she had just been outside without sunglasses. God, the mind was truly a powerful thing. She slid the check under the spine of a book on the fireplace. Another book caught her eye and she pulled it off the mantle. Picasso. She turned to page 108 and stared at the picture of Alan. With shaking hands she removed it, slid the book back into its slot and sat on the couch. God, she loved this picture of him. Every part of the man was laughing—his eyes, his mouth, his whole body. What had he found so funny, so wonderful, that he would be so happy.

If she could only rewind time.

She held the photo for a long while, the minutes melding together and slipping by without consequence. She gently kissed the picture and held it close to her cheek. Where was he when the picture was taken? Where, on this sometimes very large planet was he at that precise moment? She set the picture on the coffee table and stared at it. She had always thought that the buildings behind him looked European. But where in Europe?

There was a sign of some sort on one of the buildings, but it was too small and blurred to make out the print. God, she wanted to know where he had stood at the precise moment someone had snapped the picture. She rose from the couch and walked over to the phone. The number she dialed was prefixed with a Washington, D.C., area code. When a voice answered, it was Kelly Kramer.

"Hi, Taylor," he said. "How are you today?"

"I'm okay, Kelly. I went to the Japanese Tea Garden today. It was good to get out."

"It's November, Taylor. You dressing for the weather?"

"Of course," she said. "Stop worrying about me so much. I'm all right."

"You sure everything's okay?"

"Yes, everything's fine. Actually, I've got something I'd like you to do for me."

"Anything. What is it?"

"I have a picture of Alan, but I don't know where it was taken. I'd like to know. There's writing on one of the buildings in the background, but I can't read it. I thought you might have a computer program that could enhance it. Every movie I've seen with spies in it has that sort of technology."

"We probably do," he said, laughing. "I'm still too new to know what we've got. You want to mail me the photo?"

"No," she said. "I'll bring it myself."

"You're coming to Washington?" he asked, surprise in his voice.

"I think so. I'll call you and let you know when I'm in and where I'll be staying."

"No way. You're not staying at a hotel. I've got lots of room at my house. You need to be with friends right now, not in some hotel."

She thought about the offer for a minute, then said, "Okay, Kelly. Thanks."

"Call me when you confirm your flight," he said.

"Okay."

She hung up and stared at the phone. Why had she said she was coming to Washington? Where had that come from? She had no idea. Maybe it was because she didn't want to distance herself from the picture by putting it in the mail. Maybe. Maybe she needed a friend right now. And Kelly was a friend—the one guy who had always been there for her. She trusted him more than anyone she knew. Maybe that was it.

CHAPTER TWENTY-SEVEN

Taylor saw Kelly Kramer the second she exited the arrival gate at Baltimore-Washington International. He was standing against the posts that delineated the arriving passengers from those waiting. He looked taller than she remembered. He smiled as she approached, his teeth white against the natural pigments in his skin. His hair was longer, almost to his shoulders, and he still sported the goatee. He looked good.

"Hi," she said, dropping her carry-on and hugging him, a simple act repeated countless times every day in every airport.

"You okay?" he asked when they broke off the embrace. "You look great."

"I'm doing a bit better," she said. They walked toward the baggage carousel. "I'm really trying to fight off this depression. It's tough."

The warning light flashed and a siren sounded for a few seconds, and then the carousel chugged to life. The first bag to drop onto the stainless steel track was hers. "Now that's never happened before," she said.

Kelly plucked the bag off and set it on its wheels. "A

sign, that's what it is. A good sign. You're supposed to be here."

"That the way these things work?" she asked as they headed for the parking lot. He just grinned.

They took 295 South, the Friday afternoon traffic thick but moving well, and Taylor watched the mileage signs as they neared Washington. When they were only a few miles out, she said, "I thought your place was in Baltimore."

He shook his head. "Nope. I'm in D.C."

"You should have told me. I'd have flown into Dulles or Reagan."

"Don't worry about it," he said, concentrating on the road.

"The National Security Agency is about halfway between the two cities, isn't it?"

"Pretty close," he said as they passed Cheverly, on the outskirts of the city. Kelly took 50 West and cut north of Anacostia Park, following the main thoroughfare past Mount Vernon Square. The traffic was heavy but moving as they rounded Dupont Circle, the massive trees ghosts of their summer selves. A light layer of fresh snow covered the ground, bright white against the starkness of the barren trees. "You want to get an early dinner?" he asked.

"Sure. What do you have in mind?"

"There's a great little Italian place near my condo. And they don't take reservations."

"That's a good thing?" she asked.

"Friday night in D.C. without a reservation and you'll starve. The only places we'll get in now are the ones who don't book in advance. And it's a wonderful little restaurant, if you like pasta."

"Love pasta," she said. "Let's try it."

Kelly navigated through the rush-hour traffic jamming the circle, then cut north on Connecticut Avenue to Columbia. He found a parking space a few doors from the bistro and they walked briskly down the block. The wind had come up, and the snow was beginning to fall again. Taylor buttoned her coat and held the lapels tight to her neck. She detested cold weather and found driving in snow about the most confusing and dangerous thing in the world. Her view of people who lived in cold climates was mixed—admiration for living with the adversity and wonderment at why they would choose to do it. After all, there was always California. Warm, and by the looks of rush hour, the traffic wasn't any worse. They pushed on the door, and a blast of warm air hit them.

"I'll stay here," she said, standing between the inner and outer doors where the heat vent aimed a steady stream of hot air at the new arrivals.

Kelly shook his head. "California girl," he said. More customers were a few feet from the door, and he pulled her in by the elbow. "Come on. Let's get a table."

The interior of Pasta Mia was very crowded and very Italian, with brightly colored red-checkered tablecloths adorning the tightly packed tables. They found a table, one of the last empty ones and settled in, draping their coats on the backs of their chairs. The waiter was by a few seconds after they sat down, with menus and to take their drink order. Taylor scanned the selection of twenty-five or more pastas.

"What's good?"

"The spinach fettuccine is out of this world. It's done in a porcini-mushroom sauce. And the bread is baked fresh in the kitchen."

"The food looks really good," she said, watching the waiter go past with two steaming plates of pasta.

"It is." He changed the subject. "Anything more on what the Mexican police found at the scene?"

"Not really. Nothing of any significance."

"Did they find any more of him—I mean, more than just his hand?" He swallowed hard, realizing how insensitive that must have sounded to Taylor.

She reached over and touched his hand lightly, to let him know the gaffe was okay. "I think the Mexican police tried to find his body. There was no way. Not with the currents at the end of the cape. And there are so many fish. Big fish." She didn't bother describing any more of what had happened to Alan's body.

"Where's this photo that you didn't want to part with?"

Taylor dug in her inside pocket and pulled it out. She handed it across to him. "I suppose I should have asked Alan where this picture was taken, but this was my little piece of him that he didn't know I had."

"How's that?" Kelly asked, taking the photo. "Not sure I know what you mean."

Taylor waited as the waiter dropped off their drinks and took their order, then said, "You remember how every now and then I'd get roped into going to one of those horrible golf tournaments with clients?" she asked.

Kelly rolled his eyes back in his head. "Remember? You'd make all our lives hell for about three days every time that happened. You hated those tournaments."

"Loathed them," she said. "Anyway, I had one and I checked my golf bag—no balls, no tees. So I poked through Alan's bag. Found what I was looking for, but also found this picture. It was in one of the side pockets of his bag. I thought about telling him, but tucked it away in a book instead. It was my little piece of him that was just mine. I've always treasured it."

"He sure looks happy," Kelly said. "I wonder what got him laughing like that."

"It's a great picture."

Kelly scrutinized it closely. "I see the writing you were talking about. I can't make it out either."

"Do you think somebody at your office could enlarge it, maybe sharpen it up?"

"Probably. I think I know who to ask. She's a real whiz at stuff like this."

"Thanks."

Their food arrived, and they ate and talked mostly about his new life in Washington. Taylor was interested and asked a lot of questions, some of which Kelly was very vague answering. After he had danced about a few replies, she set her fork on her plate and leaned back in the chair.

"Sorry, Kelly, I know you too well. There's something you're not telling me. I'm okay if you want to keep certain things private—just tell me to stop asking questions. I'll live."

Kelly played with his food for a minute or two. Finally, he set his fork down and took a drink of beer. "Because of who I work for, there are some things I can tell you and some things I can't. I'm sure you understand that." She nodded and he continued. "What I'm going to tell you is not classified, but it's stretching the limits of what they would want me to say. And all this stays at this table."

"Of course."

He took another drink of beer. "Before I came to work for G-cubed, I was with the agency."

Taylor's face registered shock. "But your résumé, your work history. I checked out your references before hiring you. There was no tie-in to the National Security Agency."

He shook his head. "They're very good at manufacturing past identities to mask where their former employees have worked. For some reason, they like to wipe that slate clean when you leave." He set the beer glass on the checkered cloth. "And there's one other thing. Not all my time is spent at NSA."

She furrowed her brow. "What? Then where do you . . ." She let the sentence trail off. Finally, she said, "You work for the CIA. That's why you live in D.C."

He nodded. "National Security Agency loans me out to the guys over at Langley. I'm not a spy or anything like that. I work in the Science and Technology Directorate. Computer forensics. Nothing devious. And technically speaking, I'm employed by NSA."

"How long did you work there before you came to San Francisco?" she asked, her mind spinning.

"About five years. I was getting burned out. I needed a change, and we agreed on an extended leave of absence. It was a good idea to put a lot of mileage between myself and both agencies, so something on the West Coast was perfect. They created a work history for me, and I applied for the job at G-cubed. Everything from there on is exactly as you know it. I wasn't involved in any clandestine activities while I was working for you. What you saw is what you got. With the exception of my work history."

Taylor was quiet. The news was simply unbelievable. Was nothing in her life normal anymore? The one person she had reached out to when all else seemed surreal wasn't who he seemed. Kelly Kramer's life was a lie. She stared at her pasta, her appetite gone. She saw her hand reaching for her wineglass, wondering if she was telling it to do that. Her fingers closed around the stem and she took a sip, the fruity taste of the chardonnay pleasing to her palate. She repeated the action, this time tilting the glass back and drinking heartily. She set the empty glass on the table.

Kelly hadn't deceived her without good reason. He was bound by whatever contract he had signed when he first entered the top-secret world of the National Security Agency. They had manufactured the work history for him and insisted he use it on his résumé. She had done her due diligence and phoned the references he had provided. The answers to her questions concerning his work ethic had been predetermined by the agency.

She made a decision.

Taylor let her hand slide across the table and rest on top of Kelly's. "Okay, I can live with this. I think I understand."

He didn't move his hand, just left it sitting under hers.

"All right then, let's see if we can't find a silver lining in this cloud. After all, we've got some pretty high-tech government resources at our fingertips."

"Tomorrow," she said, smiling. It felt good to smile. "Tomorrow we find out what we can about that photo."

He returned the smile and turned his hand over, gripping hers. "Tomorrow."

CHAPTER TWENTY-EIGHT

Taylor woke and rolled over on her side, the pillow soft on her cheek. The room was dark except for the low red glow from the alarm clock. 6:35. She closed her eyes and let her mind drift.

Kelly and she had spent another hour in the restaurant, sipping wine and talking. The more she listened to him talk, the more she realized Kelly was exactly the person she thought he was. The National Security Agency recruited him after he graduated Missouri Southern State University, wooing him with a substantial salary and the promise that he would be contributing to the betterment of his country. But it didn't take long for him to understand the intelligence community was fighting a losing battle. Every time they decoded a covert message or uncovered a terrorist plot, another one popped up on the radar. And the scientists working the cutting-edge technology at NSA knew they were just touching the tip of a very large iceberg. Decipher a communiqué, forward the information to the SEAL teams and watch the real-time satellite images of the commandos destroying a lab or a clandestine terrorist camp, knowing the entire time that the monster was a Hydra—cut off one head and two more appear. And after seeing a handful of missions go sideways, watching the live satellite feed of American and British soldiers dying in distant sand-swept lands, he had needed to get out. Just for a while. A break. Something different. Anything.

He ended up on her doorstep in San Francisco. A man looking to escape a horror many suspected was real, but few admitted existed. Kelly Kramer had operated in the dark corners of the nation's back alleys. The information he dredged out of secret messages had seen many terrorists killed, but had also sent good men to their deaths. His desire was to close that door and open a new one, where light filtered in and life flourished. And by offering him employment at G-cubed, Taylor had given him that chance. That made her feel good.

She opened her eyes and glanced about his guest room. It was well-furnished, the maple headboard matching the night stands and the credenza, the wall color a muted ochre. She burrowed into the pillow, soft against the nape of her neck. It struck her that it was the first night since Alan had died that she had slept right through. She reluctantly pulled herself out of bed and padded into the attached bathroom. The shower had a pulsating head, and the water prickled her skin. It was invigorating, and after ten minutes she reluctantly shut off the water. She toweled dry, refreshed and ready for whatever Kelly had planned. When she reached the main floor of the condo, Kelly was sitting at the kitchen table drinking coffee and reading the newspaper.

"Sleep okay?" he asked.

"Great. I feel really good. Rejuvenated, sort of," she said, sitting at the table.

He poured her a coffee and set it in front of her. The cream and sugar were already on the table, and she added a bit of each. She glanced around the condo, noting the designer touches—black vases and bric-a-brac a solid contrast against the soft color of the maple. The floors were slate, the kitchen countertop dark granite. It worked, and it worked well.

"You have an interior designer in here?"

"Nope. Did it myself. You like it?"

"Very much," she said, sipping her coffee. "You're a man of many talents, Mr. Kramer."

He just smiled. "You ready for a trip to Crypto-City?"

"Absolutely." She set her cup on the table. "You won't get in any trouble for this, will you?"

He shook his head. "I cleared it with my boss. It's all above board. I'm coming in on my own time and so is Renita."

"Who's Renita?" Taylor asked.

"Renita Gallant. She's our resident genius at stuff like this. Her specialty is recovering data from grainy photos and blurry videotape. It's mostly a matter of filtering out the garbage and enhancing the right pixels. Sounds easy, but it's not."

"I can imagine. You sure she doesn't mind coming in on the weekend?"

"Positive. In fact, she's got two kids and her husband is taking them to a movie. She'd rather come in and do this than go to the flick. Called it boys-time-out."

"When are we meeting her?"

Kelly checked his watch. "Noon."

They finished their coffee, snugged into their coats, and Kelly pulled his Subaru around the block and picked Taylor up in front of the condo. The car was cold from sitting outside all night, but it warmed up quickly. After a couple of minutes, she started to fidget in her seat.

"Are these heated seats?" she asked.

He laughed. "You really are a California girl. Yes, they're heated."

"Oh, thank God, I thought I was starting to have hot flashes."

Washington was white, blanketed under an inch of

fresh snow. The roads were mostly clear, but the boulevards and trees sparkled like gemstones as the sun refracted off the snow. The evening storm had passed—the sky was blue and the air still. Taylor watched the monuments and squares flash past as they drove. The nation's capital, a city of pride and history. The dome of the Library of Congress was briefly visible to the south, the pinnacle of the world's largest library. They passed Capitol Hill, the Supreme Court and Union Station on their route out of the city.

The surrounding countryside was covered with virgin snow. Kelly took a right onto Route 32 after the Patuxent Wildlife Reserve. Ahead of them, a group of buildings loomed above the snow, their reflective windows showcasing the brilliant white popcorn clouds against the deep blue December sky. The road inclined a bit, then crested and began dropping toward the buildings. Taylor caught her breath. Laid out before her was the entrance to the National Security Agency. Cameras were everywhere, following the progress of the car as it approached the main gates. Huge concrete pylons punctuated the road, forcing them to reduce their speed as they pulled up to the barbed-wire fence. It took the better part of five minutes to get a visitor's pass for Taylor and go through the security checkpoint. Once they were in, Kelly took the main road to National Business Park-1, the building where he worked, and used his parking pass to access the underground lot. He drove directly to P6 and slipped into stall 874.

"Even on a Saturday, you don't park in anyone else's spot. That's one thing around here—we're all pretty anal about our assigned parking."

"That's universal," she said, following him to the elevator. They rode it to the twelfth floor. The halls were dimly lit, only the emergency sconces throwing shards of yellow on the walls. They walked abreast through a maze of cubicles, and Kelly pointed to a bank of darkly tinted glass with one security door. It was impossible to see what was behind the glass. Kelly entered a code, and the door swung open. He waved Taylor through, and she sucked in a breath as she entered.

The room was very large with no walls to delineate the space, which was taken up by banks of networked computers and workstations. The lighting was low, most of the visible wavelengths coming from the computer screens. Against the far wall was a large, blank white screen. A solitary woman was in the room, working on one of the computers. She looked up and smiled when Kelly entered behind Taylor.

Kelly steered Taylor to where the woman sat. She was mid-thirties with straight blond hair just past her shoulders. She had a quick smile and lively, blue eyes. Taylor liked her before she said hello. Kelly made the introductions, and the two women shook hands.

"Thanks for coming in today," Taylor said as they sat around the work station.

"Not a problem. Don's got the kids. Even with working all week, I still need breaks. This is a nice one." She waved her hands about the room. "No one in but me. I can actually get some work done."

Kelly handed her the photograph. "What do you think?"

Renita slipped it under a desk lamp and flipped the switch. She studied it for a minute, then said, "It's pretty blurred. The photographer had the f-stop wide open, probably 2.8. It wiped out a lot of the background, but I might be able to get it back. The architecture looks very European, the stone baton work on the corner of this building and the wrought iron covering this arched window." She pointed to a jumble of colors and shapes behind Alan.

Taylor stared at the photo. "You can see all that?"

"That and a bit more. Wait until I sharpen it up. Make yourselves comfy, it'll take an hour or so."

Renita scanned the photo into her computer and alternated between the cordless mouse and the keyboard. She talked as she worked and explained what she was doing. She used a series of filters to break the picture down into its various color components. Each color represented a change in the way the light reflected off the surface of the stone buildings. As she worked, the edges of the batons began to sharpen, and a darker image on the wall mutated into what appeared to be a street sign mounted to the stone. Light lettering was cut into the sign, a rectangle with a small half-round on top. The photo began to take on more dimension as well, and what had appeared to be one building was actually two, the structure on the right side farther away and on a different angle from the nearest building. Lettering appeared just under the wrought iron fronting the domed window.

"Now here's the fun part," Renita said, her fingers flying across the keyboard. "This is my own program. It recognizes letters from almost every known alphabet and about a million common shapes as well. Then it ignores all the superfluous stuff and sharpens what it considers to be the image. Here goes." She hit Enter, and the screen went blank for about a second, then flashed back on. Clearly written on the road sign was *Rue Mazarine*. The letters under the window were *FRE* and what appeared to be the first half of an *E* or a *B*, cut off by the edge of the picture. To everyone's surprise, the program also found six more letters on the upper left corner. KTAILS. Renita clicked on the print icon and the laser printer hummed. A moment later it spit out a high-quality picture of the image on the screen. She laid it on the table, under the light.

"Rue Mazarine," she said, looking closely at the lettering. "An entire street name. That should be easy to find." She exited the sharpening program and started another application. It took a few seconds and three entries popped up on the screen. "Israel, and two in France. One in Paris." She glanced again at the picture, scrutinizing the architecture. She tapped in a couple of commands and leaned back in her chair, a slow smile creasing her lips. "Rue Mazarine," she said, pointing.

"Where is it?" Taylor asked, in shock at the ease which Renita had pulled the hidden information from the picture, then identified its exact location.

"This is a partial map of Paris. It covers the Latin Quarter and St. Germain-des-Pres, just south of Île de la Cité."

"That's the island where Notre Dame is," Taylor said excitedly. "I know it. I've been there."

"And this architecture is exactly right for that part of Paris. No guarantees, but I would say that this picture was taken at the corner of Rue Mazarine and Rue Dauphine." She used her pen tip to identify an intersection on the map. "See the way Dauphine cuts off at a forty-five degree angle. That would explain the difference in light levels coming off the buildings."

"Paris," Taylor said, staring at the back-lit map in the darkened room.

"I would say."

Taylor sat back in her chair and exhaled deeply. "Thank you so much." She ran her fingers over the smooth surface of the photo. Then she said, "Are you curious why I wanted to know where this photo was taken?"

Renita shook her head. "We learn not to ask."

"Alan, the man in the picture, was my husband. He died recently. This is my favorite picture of him. But it was taken before we were married, and I never knew where. Now I do."

Renita just nodded.

They packed up and left the room, then the building and the complex. The snow had started again, and the roads were slick. The all-wheel drive component on the Subaru kept the car from skidding or spinning out on the ice. Still, the drive back into the city took more than twice as long as the drive out. When they got back to the condo, Kelly brewed some coffee, and they sat on the floor by the fire, drinking it slowly and warming up. The wind outside was brisk, and both of them were chilled through. Taylor finished hers, and Kelly poured her another.

"I can't believe the technology," Taylor said. "She had an answer just like that."

"Renita's the best I know," Kelly said, adjusting his throw pillow against the side of the couch and leaning into it. "There aren't a lot of people who could have done that."

"I appreciate it."

"I know you do." Kelly ran his finger around the top of his mug. "So what now?"

Taylor was quiet. She stared into the fire, her eyes somewhere else. Finally, she said, "I want to stand on that corner. I want to be at that precise spot on the planet. I want to be exactly where he was when he was that happy."

"You're going to Paris?" he asked.

It took a minute for her to respond, but when she did it was with an almost imperceptible nod of her head. "Yes," she said so quietly her voice was barely audible over the crackle of the fire. "Yes, I'm going to Paris."

CHAPTER TWENTY-NINE

Taylor had been to Paris three times in her life. Every trip she made to the city, she fell a little more in love with it. To her, Paris was an eclectic mixture of class and avant garde, of love and youth, of the world's finest architecture and simple cobblestone streets. And there was an energy to the city—it pulsed, like a vein carrying blood from the heart. She felt it even as she deplaned at Charles de Gaulle.

The airport was crowded with business travelers and an occasional family. It was Monday, early December, and most children were in school. The pace throughout the airport was fast, and she purposefully moved slowly, watching the men and women rush to their flight or to grab a taxi, oblivious of their surroundings. No one smiled, no time for that—the business world moved at the speed of life, and that was quick. Taylor wheeled her suitcase to the curb and waited in the queue for a taxi. She slipped into the backseat and gave the driver the name of her hotel, Edouard VII, which she had booked Sunday morning from Kelly's condo in Washington. It was on the Avenue de l'Opéra, a short distance to the

Louvre and also the Left Bank, where the Latin Quarter was located. And tucked away inconspicuously in the Latin Quarter was the intersection of Rue Mazarin and Rue Dauphine.

The hotel was classic Parisian, with a massive arch and a coat of arms above the main doors. Inside the lobby was a hand-carved wooden centerpiece, modern in its sweeping design but at home under the elegant crystal chandelier. The front desk clerk had her key in seconds, and she was shown to her room, a junior suite with a partial view of the Opera. The décor was tasteful gold with original oils on the walls and plush rugs underfoot. The clock in her room showed just after two in the afternoon as she tipped the bellman and dropped onto the edge of the bed. She lay on her back and stared at the ceiling. What was she doing here? What moment of insanity had resulted in her flying halfway across the world to stand on a street corner? She had no idea.

Taylor drew a hot bath and dipped under the water, trying to warm her bones. Paris was cold in December, and her thin California blood didn't do well in colder climates. She had nearly frozen in Washington, and this wasn't much better. After a half hour she wrestled herself from the tub and dressed. She slipped into a sweater and pulled her coat over top, feeling about the size of an NFL linebacker with all the heavy clothes. She tucked a thick tam in her pocket and headed for the lobby. The bellman whistled for a cab, and she sat in the front seat with the driver so she would have a better view of the city. He spoke passable English, and she asked him to just drive about for a while. He nodded and smiled. A nice American lady, pretty and in no rush. Just his kind of passenger.

Notre Dame, the gothic giant that took 212 years to build, towered above the bare trees and medieval houses as they crossed Pont D'Arcole. He slowed as they passed the church. No matter how many times Taylor had seen the building, it still took her breath away. The three portals dominating the west facade reared up, with the Last Judgment—Christ and the celestial court—prominent in the central one. She craned her neck, watching the building slowly slide from view. They crossed the southern bridge and entered the Latin Quarter.

"Could you drive to where Rue Mazarin and Rue Dauphine meet?" she asked.

"Of course, mademoiselle."

The cobblestone and asphalt streets were narrow and congested, and the three- and four-story buildings on each side blocked any view of the city. Small cafés and bistros lined the roads, but the outdoor terraces were gone for the winter, and they looked lonely. A few brave souls, dressed against the weather, walked the streets, but most people were relying on their cars to get about. The snow began as they steered onto Boulevard St-Germain. The driver switched on his wipers, and the rhythmic tapping seemed to suit the mood of the day. He made one turn off St-Germain, drove a full block and pulled over to the east curb. Ahead of them, the road they were on split in two, each going off at about forty-five-degree angles.

"This is it," he said. "Rue Mazarin is on the left, Rue Dauphine on the right.

Taylor sat in the front seat, unable to move. Her legs were like leaden weights, immobilizing her. She stared ahead at the intersection. The angle they were on was different from the photo, and it was impossible to tell if she was at the right spot. She glanced to the left side of the road. If Rue Mazarin was on that side, then whoever had taken the photo would have had to be over there or the street sign on the building wouldn't be in the picture. She sucked in a deep breath.

"Could you wait for me please?" she asked.

"Yes, of course."

Taylor pulled on her tam and tucked her hair under

the hat, then opened the door and stood on shaky legs. She walked across to the west side of the street and looked back at the intersection. From this angle, the corner was exactly as the photo had shown. The street sign was firmly anchored to the corner of the building, Rue Mazarin clearly printed on the rectangular plaque. She walked a little farther and stopped. Just to the left of the building corner, with the batons and the road sign, was another bit of signage.

COCKTAILS. Across Rue Dauphine the first three letters of the business sign were also very visible. FRE. Everything fit. She leaned against the rough stone building and cried. This was it. Alan had stood on this exact street corner. He had laughed at some unknown joke, and that moment had been preserved forever on one tiny piece of film. She pulled the photo from her pocket and stared at it, shielding its glossy surface from the snow as a mother would cover a newborn baby.

For ten minutes she stood on the corner, envisioning Alan at that moment. Why was he so happy? Who had snapped the photo? When was it taken? Questions she would never know the answers to. Why did he have to die? Why did they go after Edward Brand? Questions she *did* have the answers to. Answers that now made no sense.

She was shivering almost uncontrollably when she returned to the cab. The driver asked if she was okay, and she told him she was fine. He turned up the heat, and she could feel the warm air on her face as it blew from the windshield vents. They sat for a minute, then she asked him to take her back to the hotel. They drove through the ancient streets in silence, he concentrating on the thick traffic, she on the memories of her husband. She watched a couple walking arm in arm toward them on the sidewalk. Together. Lucky people. The traffic in front of the cab slowed to a stop, and they sat unmoving on the cobblestones. She stared at the man and woman, her mind still a haze.

Then, in a split second she realized she knew the man. It was Alan. She stared through the windshield as they came within twenty feet, walking quickly into the wind. The windshield wiper cleared the drops of melted snow from the glass just as they passed, and she saw the face, the eyes, the mouth.

It was definitely Alan. He was alive.

She reached for the door handle and pushed down, the door opening and a second later her foot hit the pavement. Then she stopped, frozen in her tracks. She watched them walk down the road and around the corner, out of view. She sat on the seat with her right foot on the road, staring at the empty sidewalk, her heart beating like a strobe light.

What had just happened? Was it really him? Yes, she was sure of that. It was Alan. He was alive. Why didn't she run after him? Her initial instinct was to hesitate. What had held her back?

Shock? That certainly could be part of it. She had watched Alan plunge over a cliff in Mexico—had seen the car swallowed by waves crashing violently on the rocks far below the cliff. Alan had died on that desolate stretch of road. There was no chance he could have survived the crash. Or was there? What she had seen seconds before was a testament to the fact that he had not died. Taylor remained motionless, her mind a kaleidoscope of whirling thoughts. Slowly, a band of clarity pushed through the jumble, and she began to see with some degree of order. The picture wasn't pretty. If Alan were alive and he wasn't with her in San Francisco, then it was because he wanted it that way. This was no accident. He had staged his death. There was no other answer. The anger began to swell, replacing the initial shock and disbelief.

Slowly, in response to the blaring of horns behind them and the driver's insistence, she pulled her foot back into the cab and shut the door. "Could you drive around the block please?" she asked. "Turn right at the corner."

"You know those people?" the driver asked. "You want to see if we can find them?"

"Yes, please," she answered.

They spent the next twenty minutes trolling up and down the streets bordering Rue Mazarin, but to no avail. Alan, and whomever he was with, had disappeared, probably into one of the many shops or restaurants, or perhaps into an apartment. A city like Paris can swallow someone up very quickly. And it had. It was just after six when the cabbie dropped Taylor at her hotel. She paid the fare, then doubled it for the tip. The man smiled, but it was forced. He looked concerned.

"You are okay?" he asked her.

She nodded. "I'll be fine. But thank you for asking."

She walked through the lobby and took the elevator to her room, every footstep an out-of-body experience. The door closed behind her, and she walked through the darkness to a chair near the window. She sat in the silence, her mind now focused and sharp. He had betrayed her. He had set her up. Nothing else made sense. She had never seen the one-point-six million dollars of Alan's money physically change hands. If Alan didn't have a cent invested in NewPro, then it had been all her money—the cash, the loan levered against her company. No risk to him. And then there was his degree. There had never been any alumni mail to their house from Stanford. The degree must be a fake as well. His job with Angus Strang at the corporate security company. All fake?

She rolled over on her back and grabbed her head. It was pounding from the stress. She closed her eyes and the pressure diminished slightly. Things kept flooding in, her memory uncovering the magnitude of how he had deceived her. That night in Mexico City. When Alan had broken into Fernando Dominguez's antique shop and rifled through the computers. When he had learned that Edward Brand had a villa in Cabo San Lucas. The superficial scrapes on his arm and hand. All part of the setup.

But Cabo San Lucas. He had gone over the cliff in the car, crashing into the violent sea at the base of the rocks. How had he survived? And the hand that the police had found in the car, ripped from his arm. When she had seen him on the street earlier he still had both hands. How? She racked her brain. Why had they left the hand in the car? If it wasn't Alan's, it didn't make sense. The DNA had matched perfectly. It proved to the police and the insurance company that Alan was dead. And then it hit her. That was exactly what they had wanted.

A million-dollar policy, payable to her, would ensure she was financially okay. It would keep her from delving into his death any further, trying to prove to the insurance company that he had actually died. She would take the money, shut up and go away. It had been Alan's idea to visit the sperm bank. Her insurance rep had said Alan's sperm count was fine, not as low as he had professed. So the real reason Alan had insisted on depositing the sperm was so his DNA would be accessible. That meant someone in Mexico had altered the DNA sample taken from the hand in the car. Not surprising. Police could be bribed. And the hand. The one caught in the dash of the destroyed car. The police had shown her a photo of it, and now she was positive that it wasn't Alan's. The nails were chewed almost to the quick. Alan filed his nails and never bit them.

It was all adding up. The "chance" meeting, when they saw Brand at the golf course. What a fool she had been. Right after they had agreed it was their last day at the course, Alan had excused himself to use the bathroom. He must have used the opportunity to call Brand and let him know it was time for him to make an appearance.

Nothing left to chance. Nothing but her poking through his golf bag one day and taking out a picture. A picture he didn't know she had. A picture that had led her to Paris, where Alan was quite obviously at home. He must have an apartment close to the intersection she had sought out. That was the only answer. Seeing him there was too much of a coincidence for any other explanation.

He had inadvertently left her one clue. The photo. And now she knew.

He had deceived her. He had courted her, married her and made love to her all to get her money. His very being was a lie. Nothing about the man was real. Nothing. She raised her hand to her eyes to wipe away the tears, but her eyes were dry. She stood and walked into the bathroom and stood in front of the mirror. The tiny bit of makeup she wore was smudged, but that wasn't what she noticed. It was her eyes. She stared into her pupils, amazed at the intensity of her own gaze. These were not the eyes of a woman ready to lie down and die. They were the eyes of a woman who had been used. Used in the most unthinkable way.

Used by her husband.

She returned to the main room and picked up the telephone, dialing a number from memory. A man answered.

"Kelly, it's Taylor. I'm coming back to Washington in a day or two. And I'm going to need a bit more help if that's okay."

CHAPTER THIRTY

Paris had lost its luster. What had always been the most beautiful city in the world to Taylor was now just a jumble of crowded streets and muddy sidewalks, bordered by imposing stone buildings. Perspective was everything. People were rude, prices were ridiculous, and the cold cut through to her bones. The only time she felt any semblance of warmth was when she was sequestered in the bathtub at her hotel. By Wednesday evening, she gave up on the idea of finding Alan and booked a Thursday afternoon flight back to Dulles.

Taylor wheeled her bag to the lobby three hours before her flight was to depart, and the bellman called a cab. She tipped him and slid in the backseat, wanting to be alone with her thoughts from the past two days.

First thing Tuesday morning she had rented a car and spent the daylight hours driving the streets of the East Bank, concentrating mostly on the vicinity of Rue Mazarin and Rue Dauphine, where she had seen Alan on the sidewalk the day before. Her flaming red hair was tucked up inside the tam, as it had been when she had seen him. Lucky thing, she thought, as Alan probably would have caught the color flash and recognized her. Women with striking red hair were not that common.

He was there somewhere, amidst the tangle of ancient cobblestone roads and historic buildings. He lived there, of that she was now certain. Anything else was just too coincidental. That meant he was either French by birth or had relocated to Paris later in life. She leaned toward the latter, as he had absolutely no trace of a French accent, nor did he drop his h's when he spoke. At dinner, he switched the fork to his left hand to slice through the meat, then back to his right hand to eat. A North American trait not practiced in Europe. There were other details as well, all leading to the same conclusion—Alan was an American living in Paris. But where?

She wasn't ready to spend any more time on what was a long shot. She had been very lucky to see him on the street Monday, but the chances of a repeat performance were slim to nil, and the longer she trolled the streets, the more she was convinced counting on sheer luck twice was not the answer. There were other ways to attack this problem. And to Taylor, that was exactly what this had now become. A problem. Something to be solved. She had always excelled at circumstances that involved logistics and creativity. And what could be more apt than trying to piece together exactly how Alan Bestwick and Edward Brand had worked together to pull off the scam. They had taken her for a lot of money, but Alan had taken something far more valuable. He had reached inside her soul and stolen her trust. The money she could live without, but the deception was too much. There was one word that summed up what she wanted. It wasn't a pretty word, but it was the one.

Revenge.

How to get it was another story. She wasn't sure. But she felt that the first step toward that goal was to involve Kelly Kramer. Whether he could empower the resources of the NSA was doubtful, but Kelly was an intelligent man who thought outside the box. The kind of person she needed on her side right now. On her side. What a way to think. Almost as if it were a battle. Or a war for that matter. But in some ways, it was. Alan had infiltrated her life, wooed her, married her and lived with her as her husband for almost three years. All of it, every minute, a lie. She felt the anger rising again, as it had so often over the past forty-eight hours.

Her driver pulled into the airport and stopped in front of the Delta entrance. She paid him, wheeled her bag to the counter, checked in and immediately went through the gate to the waiting area. It was cold in the airport, and she kept her jacket on, shivering as she sat alone in the crowded terminal. They announced the boarding for her flight, and she waited until most of the passengers had checked through before getting on. The plane departed about six minutes off schedule, and once it reached cruising altitude, she pulled a blanket over her, tucked her head into the pillow and slept. When she woke they were about an hour from landing at D.C. It was the best sleep she'd since bedding down in Kelly's guest room.

He was waiting for her when the plane arrived, just after six on Thursday afternoon. She had departed Paris at four in the afternoon, and the time change had almost wiped out the flying time. Since she hadn't eaten on the plane, she was hungry.

"Perfect," Kelly said when she told him she needed to eat. "I thought you'd be hungry so I made reservations at the Dupont Grille. You'll like it. Great atmosphere, very good food."

"Need both right now," she said, staring out the window at the snow as Kelly drove. A low-pressure front had passed through, dumping about six inches of snow on the city. Plows were out, and the main streets were clear, but the side streets were a mess, with cars sitting under huge mounds of ice and snow, useless until the plows made it through. "My God, look at this. It's like the North Pole."

He laughed. "This is nothing. Boston is at a complete standstill."

They made it to Dupont Circle and through some stroke of incredibly good luck found a parking spot less than a block down Nineteenth Street. The snow had been cleared from the sidewalk and walking was easy. They reached Jurys Washington Hotel and cut in the Nineteenth Street entrance to the restaurant, which was part of the main floor of the hotel. Inside, the décor was colorful and invigorating. Pumpkin-hued booths were framed by large blocks of white, black and yellow painted on the walls. The sidewalk café was long closed, but the bar occupying the rear wall of the restaurant was jammed with the after-work crowd. Their table was ready and the hostess escorted them in.

"So what's going on? You said you might need my help with something," Kelly said as the drinks arrived.

Taylor tried the merlot she had ordered and nodded in approval. It seemed almost trite that it was French. "I've been scammed like you would not believe."

"I know." His tone was understanding.

"No, you don't know," Taylor said. "There's a lot more to what happened with NewPro than first appeared on the radar. A lot."

"What do you mean?" Kelly said, leaning into the table.

"Alan is alive."

There was a full fifteen seconds of silence. Then Kelly said, "What do you mean, Alan's alive? That's impossible."

She wanted to laugh at the conviction with which he said those words. The same conviction she would have used only days before. When she answered, her voice was rife with sarcasm. "Oh, he's alive all right. Alive and living in Paris. I saw him on the street, walking hand in hand with another woman. He had both his hands by the way."

"Oh, my God," Kelly said as what she was telling him sunk in. "Don't tell me . . ."

She just nodded. Then after a minute and another drink of wine she said, "It was him, Kelly. I know it was him. There is absolutely no doubt in my mind that my husband is alive. And I'm equally as sure that he was involved in the NewPro scam from minute one."

She went on to tell him about the cash Alan had never invested in the company and his antics in Mexico City. It just kept coming—the fake job working for Angus Strang, the severed hand with the chewed fingernails, the million-dollar insurance policy to keep her from digging into his death in desperation, and the sperm Alan had insisted on depositing in case they wanted to have children.

"Children," she said. "The bastard. He had no intention of staying with me one minute longer than he had to. Get the money and run. And that's exactly what he did." The tears wanted to come, but she wouldn't acquiesce. Not now. Not over him. "I lived with him as his wife for almost three years, Kelly. Do you know how that makes me feel?"

He was silent. He shook his head.

"Like some sort of trailer trash."

"You're too good for that," Kelly said softly.

Taylor stared at him for a second, then smiled. She took another drink of wine. "This food is wonderful."

"Told you." They ate in silence for a minute, then Kelly asked, "What now? What are you going to do?"

She shrugged, her mouth full. When she finished chewing, she said, "I'm not sure. I thought you might have some ideas. You're the spy."

"I told you, I'm not a spy. I'm a cubicle rat who works on computers."

"Well, cubicle rats always have ideas in the movies. Remember *Three Days of the Condor* with Robert Redford. He was totally out of his element, but he used his CIA connections to figure out what was going on."

"Good movie," Kelly said. "Wasn't Faye Dunaway the woman he grabbed out of the store?"

She nodded, spearing a piece of grilled waluu on her fork. "I love this fish." She finished chewing and leaned forward, her elbows on the table. "I want to get him, Kelly. He used me in the most horrific way a person can be used. I want . . ." She was reluctant to use the word. He waited, and finally she said, "I want revenge."

Kelly looked down at the half-eaten food on his plate. Taylor Simons was a real person. She had given him a job, trained him, allowed him to grow and mature in one of the most fascinating businesses he had ever seen, and all the while she had been his friend. Taylor was real because she put people first, everything else second. When she was committed to someone, it was for the duration. She didn't discard people. Ever. That wasn't her way. But now *she* had been discarded. By the one person she felt she could trust no matter what happened. She had taken Alan into her life and had dropped every veil of secrecy. She had let him, and only him, see the real her. In return he had stolen her money and disappeared. He had abused the trust she had bestowed on him. Kelly could only begin to imagine how deeply she was hurt.

He made a decision. "Let's go back over everything. Right from the start. There's got to be some way to find Alan and Edward Brand."

She reached out and grabbed his hand. "Thanks."

CHAPTER THIRTY-ONE

Three days of digging. All for naught.

One thing became very clear very quickly: Edward Brand and his cronies had left no visible trail for their pursuers to follow. Every possible lead ended up in a dead end. Sam Morel and the SFPD had nothing new, and a call to the FBI district office in San Francisco gave them no more satisfaction. Brent Hawkins and John Abrams, still heading up the Western investigation into the NewPro scam were dead in the water. Even with the considerable resources of the Bureau at their fingertips, neither they nor their New York counterparts had managed to garner one clue from Alicia Walker's murder that led back to who Tony Stevens or Edward Brand really were.

Taylor hung up from speaking with Brent Hawkins and set the cordless phone on the kitchen table beside her tea. It was lukewarm and she took a small sip, then dumped the last of it down the sink drain. She and Kelly Kramer were in his condo, where they had spent the last four hours going over everything she could remember of her life with Alan that could be tied back to the scam.

There was precious little, save for the photograph that had connected Alan to his life in Paris. Alan and Edward Brand had been meticulous in their planning and execution, and that caution was now paying off.

Taylor plunked down on the kitchen chair and said, "Why didn't you want me to tell Sam Morel or the FBI guys about Alan? That might help them in their search."

"I don't know, just a feeling. Sometimes it's better to keep a little information just to yourself." He leaned back in his chair and ran his hands through his hair. "And the whole thing with the computers is still bugging me a bit."

"What do you mean?"

"The hard drive I found the information on was tough to find but not impossible. If Sam Morel's computer guy was even reasonably good, he should have found it."

She was hesitant. "But that's not what you said earlier. You led everyone to believe it was quite probable he would have missed it."

Kelly grinned. "Like I said, always keep a little something under wraps."

Taylor was puzzled. "I don't understand."

"How well do you know Sam Morel? Or either of the FBI agents working the case?"

"I'd never met any of them until this happened."

"So what if they're not who they seem?"

"Sam's a cop. Hawkins and Abrams are FBI. Who else would they be?" Taylor was shocked at the direction of Kelly's thoughts.

Kelly pulled himself out of his chair, picked up the kettle, filled it with water and set it on the stove. He turned on the element and leaned against the granite edge of the counter. "I find something on a computer that another expert missed. Alicia Walker gets shot in her bathtub. One coincidence I can live with—two, I start to get suspicious."

"Are you insinuating that one of those three is working with Brand?"

Kelly shrugged. "I'm not insinuating anything. I'm just being careful. What were they like to you? Overly friendly? Helpful? Businesslike? Curt?"

"Well, Hawkins and Abrams were very standoffish. Typical FBI, I think. I'm guessing really. I've never had to deal with the FBI before so I don't have a benchmark. But Sam Morel was very accommodating. He kept us in the loop throughout the investigation." She caught herself and said, "Us," her voice dripping with sarcasm. She and Alan—what a joke.

Kelly nodded. "So what have we got? Right now you and I are the only ones who know Alan Bestwick is alive. Except, of course, for Edward Brand and Alan himself and whoever helped him survive that car crash. If, and that's a big if, there's a leak somewhere and one of these guys is on Brand's payroll, we're only going to expose ourselves by letting them know what we know." The kettle whistled, and he turned off the stove. He poured two fresh teas and delivered them to the table. He sat opposite her, poking his tea bag with a spoon until the water had turned a light brown, then removed the bag. "They think you've taken the bait, Taylor. You've got a million-dollar life insurance policy that paid out on Alan's death. You have no financial worries. You're grieving, but getting on with your life. As long as you're doing exactly what they expect, they won't bother watching you too closely. But if you walk into FBI headquarters and tell them you suspect Alan is still alive, and one of them is in bed with Edward Brand, you're a dead woman." He took a sip of tea, made a face and set it back on the table. "Wow, that's hot."

Taylor just stared at him, mouth open. "You're kidding me, right?"

He didn't smile. "No, I'm not."

Taylor touched the side of the teacup and felt the warmth transfer to her finger. What had happened to her normal life? Four months ago, she had been a successful businesswoman with a great husband and a life that ninety-nine percent of the world's population would want. But everything had changed. Her marriage was a sham, her business gone, and if what Kelly was saying were true, her very life could be in danger.

"What do I do?" she asked. She briefly thought about the million-dollar check still sitting in her house, tucked under the book on her fireplace.

"We," he corrected her.

"What?"

"We, not just you. We're in this together, Taylor. I'm not the kind of guy who deserts his friends when they need him. If it's okay with you, I'd like to help."

She nodded, her mouth suddenly dry. The tea was still steaming, but she took a sip. "That would be great."

"What do we do?" Kelly said rhetorically. "That's the question. I think I've got an answer. Edward Brand and his crew were highly visible during the scam, and they had to know that once they pulled the plug, everything they did to rip off their marks would come under the microscope. They left no clues. What about the one thing they never thought we'd figure out? Maybe they weren't quite as careful there."

"What's the one thing?" Taylor asked, intrigued.

"The crash."

"When Alan went over the cliff?"

"Exactly." Kelly stroked his goatee as he spoke. "Brand counted on everyone accepting the fact that Alan had died in the crash. They bought off a Mexican official and planted the DNA so it would match the sperm sample Alan had on file in San Francisco. Finding that official is impossible, I'll tell you that right now. What Brand didn't consider, was that someone would find out Alan was alive and know the crash was a setup. That the same someone would take a really close look at the accident."

"What do you think we'll find?" Taylor asked.

He shook his head. "Maybe nothing, but to me that looks to be the weak point in their plan. And weak spots should always be exploited."

"How?"

Kelly pursed his lips, looking serious. "I don't know if I can get my hands on them, but NSA has satellite surveillance tapes that cover almost every inch of the earth. They're downloaded to the mainframe at Crypto-City every twelve hours and filed by time and GPS location. If I could get the okay to retrieve the data the satellite picked up at that precise time, we may have something."

"Can you do that?" she asked.

"I don't know. I can try. The worst that will happen is someone will say no."

"You're willing to try?"

"Yeah, Taylor, I am. Brand's theft was bad enough, but what Alan did to you is unbelievable."

Taylor sat at the table, her hands cupped around the tepid teacup. Where one person had deceived her, another was now standing up and saying 'enough.' She had a true friend in Kelly Kramer and to deny him an opportunity to help would be a slap in the face. That was something she would not do. Not to a friend. Couple that loyalty with the fact that the man worked for the country's premier intelligence-gathering agency, telling him she didn't want his help would be more than a slap in the face. It would be stupid.

CHAPTER THIRTY-TWO

Richard Tolman headed the arm of the National Security Agency where both Renita Gallant and Kelly Kramer worked. He was a career bureaucrat, a family man and a fair man. Still, he didn't like the idea of Kelly and Renita using government data for what was, in effect, a private investigation into Alan Bestwick's disappearance. His arms were crossed and his jaw set as Kelly made his pitch. If body language were any indicator, they were out of luck.

Taylor sat in Tolman's office, listening and watching as Kelly presented his case for why they should have access to the satellite imagery. Kelly was convincing, playing to Tolman's sense of right versus wrong. While Kramer portrayed Taylor Simons as a woman who had been more than just slightly wronged, he barely touched on what Alan had done to her emotionally—NSA didn't base its decisions on emotion. Rather, he gave Tolman every detail on the crime. How Brand and Alan had stolen millions of dollars from her. When Kelly finished speaking, the room was silent.

Tolman uncrossed his arms and set his hands on his

desk in front of him. He was a gangly man with thinning hair and wire-rimmed spectacles and would have looked right at home at a CPA convention. There was a wedding ring on his left hand. He glanced at all three of them, then locked eyes with Taylor.

"Was there ever any indication that Alan Bestwick wasn't who he seemed to be?" Tolman asked.

The question surprised her. "Never. Alan and I were married and lived a very normal life as husband and wife. He worked, I owned a business, we came home every day and had dinner together and took vacations a couple of times a year. That's why Alan's involvement in this is so devastating. I trusted him—as my husband."

Tolman's eyes didn't flicker. His gaze bored into her, stripping off the layers and searching for the truth. Under that stare, Taylor realized that while this man may appear to be an accountant, he most certainly wasn't.

"It is within my authority to grant access to the satellite imagery you want, Ms. Simons," he said, his voice even but not monotone. "I'm reluctant. This almost appears to be vigilante action. I do not want to be party to anything even remotely resembling that."

Taylor returned the gaze, not threatening or pleading, just eye to eye. "I need to put this to rest."

"And if you find he *is* alive? Then what? Do you go after him? Do you use Mr. Kramer's connections inside the intelligence community to find someone to kill Alan Bestwick?"

Taylor was shocked at the words. "Of course not."

Tolman nodded slightly and held up one hand in a stopping motion. "Don't get upset, Ms. Simons. You have to understand where this could go. You can imagine my position if it were traced back to this office that I had assisted you in finding a man who subsequently died. I'm not sure I want to do that much paperwork. Or retire early."

"I want to know," Taylor said.

Tolman broke off his eye contact with Taylor and turned to face Kelly. "Give me your word you won't involve your contacts at Langley in this."

Kelly shifted slightly. "That's difficult, Richard. I may need logistical help that I can't get here. I'd hate to say for certain I won't ask anyone at the CIA for help. At some point I may need to."

"You know what I mean, Kelly. I don't care if you ask them to run a license plate number. I care if you sanction Mr. Bestwick. If you have him killed."

"That I can promise you. No harm will come to Alan Bestwick. At least, nothing will happen to him because of what *we* do."

Tolman was thoughtful. Finally, he said, "I'll authorize you to access the satellite data we have stored on the hard drive for the southernmost thirty miles of the Cabo region for two hours on either side of when the car went over the cliff. That's it. No more."

"Thank you," Kelly said. Taylor nodded and smiled.

"Don't make me regret this decision, Kelly," Tolman said as they all rose.

"I won't, Richard."

They shook hands and left the office, closing the door behind them. They walked down the hall to the elevator in silence. Kelly's and Renita's offices were two floors below Tolman's, and they punched the appropriate button. It wasn't until they were in Renita's office that they spoke.

"I can't believe it," Taylor said. "I never thought we'd get the okay."

Kelly grinned. "Richard Tolman and I go back a long time. He was my boss before I took the leave of absence and worked for you at G-cubed. We've got a mutual respect for each other. He trusts me. That's why his final decision was made on my promise that we wouldn't remove Alan if we found him."

"Remove Alan," Taylor said. "Christ, do you have any

idea what you sound like when you say that? You talk about killing people like you're ordering breakfast at a Holiday Inn."

Kelly was quiet for a minute, then said, "Taylor, this is a different world than the one most people live in. We deal in national security. When it comes to the nation's well-being, individual people are expendable. It's that simple. Cross the line and there's a good chance you will not live. When you've got those kinds of resources at your fingertips, you've got to be careful how you use them. That was Tolman's concern. Alan Bestwick is not a threat to national security, and other than analyzing the satellite data, we leave him alone."

"I know what Tolman was saying," Taylor said. "I'm just a bit shocked at the offhand way you and he refer to killing someone. That's all."

"I've never been involved in anything like that," Kelly said. "I never want to be." He turned to Renita, who had been mute for the entire meeting. "When can you start analyzing the download from the hard drive?"

She shrugged, brushing her hair behind her ears. "Anytime. I've got a hundred things to do, but nothing on the front burner. As soon as the authorization comes through, I can start working on it."

Kelly smiled. "It's already through. I know Tolman. The moment we stepped out of his office he was on his computer setting up the access codes."

Renita checked her watch. "I'm going to grab some lunch. Meet you in the situation room on twelve in an hour?"

Sixty minutes later they met up with Renita Gallant outside the darkened computer room on the twelfth floor. She punched in her code, and they entered. Taylor sat in a chair near a bank of computer terminals facing the large screen on one of the walls. Renita took the seat at the center console and began typing on the keyboard. After a couple of minutes, she leaned back and smiled.

"Up and running. I've got a four-hour chunk of satellite data from November third, between three-thirty and seven-thirty. The GPS coordinates cover the tip of the Baja Peninsula, to about thirty miles up from Land's End." She worked the keyboard for a minute, and an image flashed on the large screen. It was the exact stretch of land she had just mentioned and the surrounding water, the Sea of Cortez to the east and the Pacific Ocean to the west and south. "Okay, point to where the car went over the cliff."

Taylor walked up to the screen and traced the road from San José del Cabo northward along the coast. She asked Renita to enlarge the area so she could see the details better. The screen changed, now showing the east coast from San José del Cabo and a few miles north. Taylor ran her finger along the road, pausing at a tiny dot she thought might be Buzzard's Bar.

"Can you zoom in on this?" she asked. The image changed again, this time gaining great detail as Renita zoomed in on the precise location. With eleven million pixels in each frame the satellite recorded, the quality of the picture didn't diminish in the least. "Okay, that's Buzzard's. Alan went over the cliff about four miles up this road."

She waited while Renita recalculated the distance into GPS positioning, then realigned the image. When the new picture flashed on the screen, the section of road where the car had plunged over the cliff was near the top. Taylor put her finger on the corner.

"This is it. He went over right here." Again the image shifted, sharpened up.

"Okay, when did it happen?" Renita asked.

"Five-ten," Taylor replied. "Give or take about five minutes."

There was a pause, then a slight blip and the time in the lower right hand corner changed by one hour and fifty-two minutes. They watched the section of road and coast in real time, the individual stones on the road surface clearly visible. Waves crashed into the base of the cliff and the image was so clear they could see the spray from the surf. Then Taylor sucked in her breath. The cars had just come into view.

She watched as Brand parked the Explorer and slipped out the driver's side of the vehicle. He stood by the door, but he was not looking out over the ocean. He was watching the road—waiting for her and Alan to arrive. A minute later their rental car rounded the corner and came to an abrupt stop. Brand jumped back into the Explorer and a second later their car rammed the SUV, driving the rear tire over the edge of the cliff. The car backed up, and Taylor watched as she tumbled out of the car onto the road. The car roared ahead, kicking up dust in its wake. The Explorer surged forward just as the car reached the edge of the cliff. A few milliseconds later it was airborne. Then it hit the surf, sending up a plume of water. Moments later the car disappeared beneath the choppy waves.

"Good God," Renita said, staring at the screen. "No wonder you thought he was dead. That was one hell of a convincing crash."

Taylor's eyes followed Edward Brand's car as it careened back onto the road and headed north. A few seconds and it was out of view. Then she watched herself as she ran to the edge of the cliff and looked down. She saw herself fall on the ground. And she relived every second of what she had thought was her husband dying. But this time there were no tears. Just anger.

Renita concentrated on Brand's vehicle as it headed northward along the coastline. "We're almost at the end of our coverage to the north. If he goes any farther, we're going to lose him," she said after a few minutes of tracking his SUV as it moved up the coast. They got a short distance farther, and the screen froze. It wouldn't move any more. They had reached the north end of the data Tolman had authorized. The Explorer disappeared. "That's it. We've lost him."

"We need more," Taylor said. "We need to know where Brand went."

Kelly shook his head. "Not going to happen. Tolman authorized us to find out what happened to Alan, not Edward Brand. He's not going to give us any more of the satellite data than what we have here."

"Now what?" Taylor asked, frustrated.

The image on the screen rewound until it was centered on the crash. Then it shifted ever so slightly so the section of water where the car impacted was dead center on the screen. Renita positioned the time to precisely when the car went over, and they all watched again as it tumbled over the cliff and hit the water. She let the video run for about three seconds, then froze the picture.

"I'm going to try applying a polarizing filter to the data," she explained as she worked on the keyboard.

"What's that?" Taylor asked.

"It's really a very simple filter. Photographers use it all the time when they're shooting something under the surface of a body of water. Say for example you're on the side of a lake and you see a large trout sunning himself next to a log. He's maybe six to ten feet underwater. You pull out your 35mm camera and snap the shot. When you get it processed, all you see is the surface of the water and whatever reflection is on it. But put a polarizing filter on the lens and turn it until the filter aligns with the light reflecting off the water's surface and suddenly the fish is visible on the picture."

"So you're going to adjust this filter so we can see beneath the surface?" Taylor asked.

"Exactly."

Renita worked for a minute or two. The image began to mutate. The tops of the waves disappeared and the entire sea took on a homogenous blue tone. She let the video run, the underwater picture now visible and undulating with the flow as the waves hit the rocks and the undertow forced the water back from the rocky shore. The impact from the car hitting the water dissipated, but they could see the distinct outline of the vehicle as it sunk beneath the waves. Then something appeared from the left side of the screen—from under the rocks at the shore's edge. Two figures, moving quickly toward the car, towing a bag behind them. Scuba divers.

"Oh, my God," Taylor said. "Look. Divers."

Renita pulled the image in a little closer and sharpened it. The car, still sinking to the bottom, was dead in the center of the screen. Bubbles poured from the driver's window as the air inside the vehicle escaped. The divers reached the car, and one of them pulled on the driver's door while the other dug in the bag they had brought with them. Because Alan had cracked the window, the pressure between the sea and the inside of the car was equalized, and the door opened easily. Alan appeared, and in a flash the second diver had a scuba regulator in his mouth. A steady stream of air bubbles floated upward as Alan began rhythmic breathing. One of the divers fitted him into a buoyancy control device, weights, flippers and a mask; the other worked on attaching the severed hand to the dash. Then, when Alan was in complete scuba gear, the three figures began to move. They swam south from the wreck, paralleling the shore.

"Son of a bitch," Taylor said as they sat watching the divers round a set of rocks. Renita kept the image focused on them as they swam, slowly moving the positioning so the divers stayed in the center of the screen. Since they were moving south, there was no chance the NSA computers would run out of data before the divers had to surface. They swam underwater for the better part of an hour, covering well over a mile before surfacing. Moments after they broke the surface, a twenty-foot speedboat appeared from off the screen. The divers pulled themselves and their gear into the boat. The smile on Alan's face was not lost on Taylor.

"You bastard," she hissed as she watched the speedboat take off toward San José del Cabo. Another boat appeared as Renita followed the first one. Moored just offshore, the yacht was waiting for the smaller boat to arrive. As it pulled up alongside, Taylor sucked in her breath. Standing on the deck, waiting, was Edward Brand. He must have doubled back on an inland road, driven into San José del Cabo, then taken a shuttle boat to the yacht. As Alan climbed up the ladder and onto the yacht, Brand walked to the top of the stairway. When they met, they shook hands, both men all smiles. Then they disappeared inside the vessel.

Taylor sat staring at the screen. She was in complete shock. Even though she had known in her heart that Alan was involved in the scam, the definitive proof was overwhelming. But again, there were no tears. Her emotions were in overdrive, but empathy or understanding weren't part of them. Loathing and anger topped the list. She continued to stare at the screen as Renita further adjusted the sharpness and zoomed in on the stern of the yacht. There was lettering and it was clearly visible.

Mary Dyer.

Edward Brand had just left them an opening. Taylor glanced over at Kelly and he nodded.

"Got him," he said quietly. There was a hint of a smile on his face.

CHAPTER THIRTY-THREE

The Mexican sun was intense against a backdrop of pale blue sky. Its rays reflected off the tips of the small waves, making the water shimmer and dance as the boat sliced through the cool blue of the gulf. Ahead, gracing the Mexican shoreline was Puerto Vallarta, the once sleepy village that grew to a major tourist destination. Aboard the deck of the seventy-two-foot Viking Sport Cruiser was a solitary man. He cupped a mug of coffee in his hands and watched the approaching shoreline with a touch of trepidation.

Edward Brand didn't like Puerto Vallarta. On at least two occasions, the local police had extradited high-level con artists who used Mexico as their base of operations. The highest profile arrest was Alyn Waage, the Internet scam artist who had run a ninety million-dollar con out of Puerto Vallarta and Costa Rica until he ended up in a Guadalajara prison. His abrupt crash from luxury hillside living to a squalid jail cell came about when Mexican customs agents found four-point-five million dollars in money orders on board a chartered Learjet at the Puerto Vallarta airport. Brand could envision the scene in his mind—Waage trying desperately to buy off the customs agents, knowing that he was facing a pivotal moment in his life. But for some reason he had failed to convince the agents to let him go. And that lack of cooperation by the Mexican authorities worried Brand.

But trying to conceal a seventy-two-foot yacht in a smaller center was impossible. And keeping a low profile was one of the keys to staying out of jail. The *Mary Dyer* was a beautiful ship, and it blended in well in an upscale marina. But the Cabo region was too hot now that they had faked Alan Bestwick's death on the cliffs at La Laguna. Taylor Simons was a resourceful woman, and although Brand doubted she would stay on in Cabo San Lucas, he wasn't about to take foolish risks. She had a million dollars from Alan's death—a detail they had built into the scam to keep the grieving widow from digging too deeply into her husband's death. But he was more than just a little aware that it could also backfire. The million dollars gave Taylor the resources to stay on in Mexico and search for him. If she decided to go that route and he stayed in Cabo, she would eventually find him. Other than Puerto Vallarta, that left ports in Manzinillo, Mazatlan and Acapulco on the Pacific coast. None of which truly thrilled him.

He figured the risk to be the least in Puerto Vallarta. His yacht just another one in the pack, moored in a slip and surrounded by like boats. The captain slowed as they approached the final leg into the marina. One of the crew members appeared from the salon, a phone in his hand. He passed it across to Brand and disappeared back into the boat. The wind was almost nonexistent and the line clear of static. The voice on the other end came through as though the man was in the next room.

"I'm still waiting for the final installment," he said once they had traded greetings.

"It's coming," Brand said. "Give it another week or two, just to make sure your end of things is under control."

"Everything is fine here," the man snapped back. "Just get me my money."

Edward Brand watched the harbor lights slip past as the boat neared the marina entrance. Brand knew the man on the other end of the line had the potential to be very dangerous to his freedom. But only in the United States. Right now he was in Mexico, where he planned to stay for quite some time. Which put him in a favorable position for negotiating and also for how much crap he had to take. He decided today wasn't a good day to take any.

"You'll get your money when I decide to send it," he said coolly. "That will be when I know for certain all loose ends on NewPro are tied down. Including Taylor Simons."

"The woman is not a threat. She's wandering around like a lost puppy right now."

"What do you mean?" Brand asked.

"She flew to Paris and stayed for a few days. Now she's in Washington, D.C., visiting a friend. Following her movements is simple—she's using credit cards everywhere she goes. She's dragging an electronic trail behind her like a comet's tail."

Brand stiffened at the mention of France. "When did she go to Paris?"

"Monday, December fourth. Why?"

"How long did she stay?" Brand asked, ignoring the man's question.

"Three days. She flew back to Washington on the seventh."

"What else do you know?" Brand asked, sitting forward in the chair as the boat passed the final marker and entered the marina.

"Not much. We weren't very interested, so we didn't watch her too closely. We know from her credit card purchases that she stayed at Edouard VII. It's an upscale hotel on Avenue de l'Opéra."

"Shit," Brand said. He knew Paris and he knew where Alan's flat was located. Too close for coincidence? He didn't know. "Get me everything you can on what she did, where she went," he said.

"Let's back up a bit," the voice said. "This conversation started with me wondering where my money was. I don't recall asking for more work."

"Your money is coming. It's safe. But it won't be if I'm in jail. I need to know what Taylor Simons was up to in Paris. I'll pay you an additional fifty large to find out."

"Okay, but I want this wrapped up quickly. I feel like my ass is hanging out of my shorts, and I don't like it."

"Like I said, you'll get your money." Brand clicked the end button on the phone and set it on the table next to his coffee mug. The *Mary Dyer* was barely moving now, the captain keeping the wake in check as he navigated the narrow channel between the docked boats. Brand leaned on the railing and watched the people watch him—wondering who this man was. If only they knew.

Taylor Simons's trip to Paris was probably just a strange coincidence. She was probably still in some sort of shock over Alan's death. Grieving at least. But there would be no benefit to Taylor having a chance run-in with her husband, who lived in a second-floor apartment in the Latin Quarter. Brand checked the time, calculated the difference to Paris, then realized he didn't care. He dialed Alan's number.

"Bonjour." The voice that answered was tired but coherent. It was Alan Bestwick.

"Alan, it's Edward," Brand said.

"Yes," Alan said hesitantly, switching to English. "I thought you weren't going to call here."

"Unless the situation warrants it. Right now this is one of those situations."

"Is everything all right?" Alan asked, wide awake, concern creeping into his tone.

"Yes, fine. Taylor was in Paris recently. Did you see her?"

"No." Now there was anxiety in his voice. "What was she doing in Paris?"

"I thought you might know."

"Taylor thinks I'm dead. There's no reason for her to be in Paris looking for me."

"I hope not," Brand said. "You're positive that you didn't leave something that would tie you to France?"

There was a long pause as Alan Bestwick went back over things in his mind. Finally he said, "No. Taylor had nothing that could lead her to Paris. Nothing. I'm sure of it."

"Okay. Just keep a low profile. I'm going to have someone watch her. I'll let you know if she comes anywhere near you."

"Maybe I should take off for a while," Alan said. "Head south. Lie on a beach somewhere."

Brand mulled over the idea. "No, I don't think so. All that does is introduce another variable. With you in Paris, I know where you are and whether she's close to you. If you're on a beach somewhere, my guy may know where Taylor is, but we won't know where you are. It's definitely better if you just stay put. And if she returns to Paris, we'll know something's up."

"Okay."

"Just keep on your toes."

"I'll do that." The international line clicked over to a dial tone.

The *Mary Dyer* scraped the edge of the dock slightly as the captain backed her into her assigned spot in the marina. The yachts on each side were comparable in size and finishing, giving Brand the anonymity he was hoping for. He had purchased the boat through one of his dummy corporations three years earlier with the take from another scam, and had registered it out of the Seychelles Islands. Boats were a wonderful way to stay incognito, especially if you were smart enough to leave little or no paper trail back to your real identity. They were highly mobile, traveled in international waters and could disappear from the radar in hours if necessary. He was quite pleased with his decision to live on the boat, all the while giving the police clues that led nowhere.

The FBI had spun their wheels on the Canadian connection. Brand had learned early in the game that the police always wanted to find something to put in their files. If they had a blank file folder, they got embarrassed and angry. They had a basic need that had to be filled, and they kept looking until they had enough reports to make it appear they had given the bad guy a real run for his money. For that reason, he had given them enough to find the condo in Vancouver if they were on their game, but even that hadn't happened. Now, close to ninety days had passed since he had emptied out the NewPro offices and disappeared. After ninety days the trail was growing cold, the file gathering dust. That suited him just fine.

Two hundred and twelve million dollars. God, what a scam. Every individual piece of the puzzle had fallen into place without a hitch. The only possible problem right now was Taylor Simons, and her impromptu trip to Paris. The more he thought about it, the more he was convinced that it was simply a coincidence. Alan Bestwick was fastidious in his attention to detail, and if Alan was sure he had left no clues for Taylor to follow, then that was the way it was. Still, he would keep tabs on Taylor Simons for a while. It was simply a matter of due diligence.

The engines slowed to an idle, then stopped. A young Mexican boy in white pants and shirt, one of the many wharf rats who worked the marina, secured the lines and clamped the gangplank in place. Two uniformed Mexicans from the port authority marched down the long wooden wharf. Edward Brand leaned back in his chair and motioned for one of his crew to refill his coffee mug. The Mexicans could come to him. Unlike Alyn Waage, who was dumb enough to carry millions of dollars with him, Brand never traveled with more than nine thousand five hundred US dollars. Never. There were banks in Grand Cayman with managers who didn't ask too many questions as long as they were sure the money wasn't coming from the sale of drugs, and there were bank machines in every port. There was no reason to invite a trip to a Mexican jail. He heard the heavy clumping of boots on the deck and smiled. They would check him out and clear him for unlimited entry to Mexico. And Mexico was where he would stay.

Things were so simple, if you didn't complicate them.

CHAPTER THIRTY-FOUR

They left Renita Gallant in the situation room at the National Security Agency and drove back to Kelly's condo in D.C. It was suppertime on Monday and three hours since they had learned how Alan had survived the crash into the ocean. Kelly moved about the kitchen with an amazing degree of alacrity and in less than an hour whipped up an authentic paella, complete with chicken and seafood and flavored with saffron. Taylor picked the wine, uncorked it and poured for both of them. She tried the paella and gave him a slight nod.

"This is excellent," she said. "I didn't know we had a gourmet cook working at G-cubed. You never volunteered to cook lunch for the staff."

He speared a piece of chicken and grinned. "Once people know you can cook, they expect it. Keep them in the dark. It's a good rule of thumb."

"Now that I know, you're in trouble."

They finished their meal, talking about everything from politics to hot lunches for underprivileged school kids. When they were both done, Taylor cleared the dishes and Kelly poured more wine. They sat on comfortable leather couches in the living room, Michael Jones playing on the sound system, every note crystal clear. Kelly flipped a switch and the gas fireplace threw a dim flickering light through the room.

"So what now?" Taylor asked. "We know the son of a bitch is alive, but what can we do with it?"

Kelly gently swished the wine about in the glass. He took a small sip and rested the glass in his lap. "We've got a couple of things to follow up on. First off is the boat. That's our best course of action right now. The *Mary Dyer* has to be registered—all boats have to be registered somewhere. We find out where and what name it's under. Brand probably has no idea that we know about the yacht. It could be a rental, but it could also be his."

Taylor managed a small smile. "That's good thinking. What else? You said there were a couple of things."

"Maybe. When you were telling me what happened before Alan went over the cliff, you said Brand stopped and had lunch at a bar a few miles before the cliff."

"Yes. So?"

"You said he used the house phone to make a call. You were specific on that—the house phone, not a cell phone."

Taylor nodded vigorously. "Yes. He used the restaurant's phone. Why?"

"Phone logs," Kelly said. "The Mexican phone company will have a record of the number he dialed."

"Jesus, you're smart. I would never have thought of that."

"Guess what that gives us?"

She shook her head. "I have absolutely no idea."

"You're sure," he said. "Think about it. Who was he calling?"

She stared at her wineglass, trying to figure out who Brand would have needed to speak with. It had to be logical or Kelly wouldn't have figured it out. There had been no one but Brand on the road when they had arrived at the point where Alan had gone over, so there was no reason to call ahead to have someone block the road or pretend to be injured so they would stop. Meeting Brand on the curve had been more than enough to guarantee that. So what else was there? Then it hit her. She gave Kelly a smile.

"Got it. Scuba divers can only stay underwater for a certain length of time. He called ahead to let them know he was coming so they could get in position."

"Very, very good," Kelly said, giving her a small clap. "Whoever was on the other end of that line is a possible connection back to Edward Brand."

"Two avenues to figuring out who he is and maybe even where he is."

"That's the idea." Kelly drained the last of his wine and headed to the kitchen to put on some water for tea. He returned a few minutes later with a teapot and cups on a tray. He left it on the coffee table, giving the tea time to steep.

"You know," he said, "checking out the yacht registry and the phone call isn't going to take a lot of time. Guess what else we could look into?"

"What Alan's real name is? I'm damn sure it's not Bestwick."

"That's one. There's one more."

"What?"

"I still think one of the cops is dirty," Kelly said, pouring the tea and handing her a cup. "That stuff on the computer didn't get there by accident. We could dig around a little bit and see what we come up with."

"Then it would have to be one of the FBI agents— either Brent Hawkins or John Abrams. It couldn't be Sam Morel. He didn't have time to rig the computers."

Kelly shook his head. "Sure he did. The computers were sitting in the room when I got there. They were plugged in and ready to go. Detective Morel easily could have generated that invoice from the antique shop in Mexico City, then powered the systems down and locked the door. And remember, you said Morel went out of his way to keep you and Alan in the know. He was your ears and eyes to what was happening with the FBI's investigation."

Taylor didn't answer. Sam Morel was a nice man who had tried to help her and Alan when their lives had come crashing down around them. He had been assigned by the San Francisco Police Department as their liaison between the victims and the District Attorney's office. What possible upside was there for Sam Morel to be feeding information back to Edward Brand? Except money, of course. Brand had just ripped them off for almost fourteen million—two million less than originally thought once she subtracted Alan's million and a half that had never been part of the equation. That amount of money could sway people to do things that they may not otherwise do. Kelly was right, Sam Morel was as much a suspect as a conspirator as were the two FBI agents.

"Here's a question for you: how do we manage to dredge up all the information we need on three cops— two of them federal agents?"

"I have some connections," Kelly said.

"Ones you can use?"

He shrugged. "It all goes back to asking and seeing what they say. The worst is no."

Taylor set her empty tea cup on the table and grabbed the sides of her head. "This is hard on the brain. We've got too many things on the go."

"Never too many," Kelly said. "It gets bleak when your options are limited. Right now we've got lots of options. That's a good thing."

She smiled and dropped her hands back on her lap. "Okay, you're the expert. I've never done anything like this before. Checking out federal agents who might be working with the bad guy, looking at phone records, tracking down who owns a luxury yacht—this is all out of a suspense novel."

"The bad news is I've never done it before either. But I think it's just a matter of logic. We have a few problems, and we need solutions. We deal with each angle individually and then take the results and throw them in the collective pot. If we can find the right information, everything is going to lead back to Edward Brand. And eventually to Alan."

"Okay, back to my original question—what now?"

"I've got to work this week. I haven't been back long enough to have accrued any holidays. Maybe it's better if you head back to San Francisco."

"Is that important?"

Kelly shrugged. "We're trying to find out who Brand is, but keep in mind that he knows who you are, where you live and just about every detail in your life. It's easy for him to keep tabs on you. If I were him, that's exactly what I'd be doing. If he does have someone on the inside, every time you use your debit card or one of your credit cards he'll know exactly when and where. Brand can track where you are at any given time and what you're doing. He probably already knows you were in Paris."

"Then it's already too late. He'll know I was in Paris looking for Alan."

"But you weren't. You originally went to Paris just to stand on a street corner. You could have been there for any number of reasons. I wouldn't panic about it."

"I suppose you're right. That's assuming he's watching me."

"If I were him, I'd watch all my marks for signs that they're getting on with their lives. The best thing you can do is give the appearance that you're resigned to the fact you lost your money. Get back to what he will think is your normal life. That way if he has someone watching you, the red flags don't go up."

Taylor slowly nodded. She hardly liked being referred to as a mark, but that was exactly how Edward Brand viewed her. She had been chosen because she was a woman with money. No other reason was necessary. Then they had methodically removed the money from her life and discarded her. Kelly's choice of words was accurate. She had been a mark. It wasn't a nice thought. Now she had to go back to San Francisco and try to live a normal life. It wasn't going to be easy, sitting on her butt knowing that Alan was wandering around somewhere with a smug grin and millions of her money. Still, Kelly was right.

"What about the check from the insurance company?" she asked.

"Cash it," he said without hesitation.

"But I know Alan's alive. That's fraud."

"Not cashing the check is an absolute giveaway that you suspect something. You have to do it. You can always give the money back later."

"Okay, but make a note that I'm doing this under duress. I don't like it. The first chance I have, that money goes back to the insurance company."

He laughed. "You and your morals. They're incorruptible. Most people couldn't cash the check fast enough." He finished the last of his tea. "I'll do what I can from this end, Taylor. I've got some pretty good resources to draw on. You try to keep it together in San Francisco."

"Why are you doing this, Kelly?" she asked. "I know you're climbing out on a limb a bit at work. You could lose your job."

He laughed again and shook his head. "Maybe, but I doubt it. I'm not pushing the limits. Getting the satellite data was tough. Running some personnel checks on a couple of FBI agents isn't going to raise any eyebrows. Checking the registry on the *Mary Dyer* is nothing. I can submit the search at nine and have an answer back by noon. Same thing with the phone logs for that restaurant near San José del Cabo. Buzzards. That's it. Nothing to it, Taylor. Don't worry."

"Thanks," she said.

Michael Jones played on, his piano soft and relaxing. Taylor settled back into the cushions, relaxed and warm. The flame in the fireplace was mesmerizing. She watched it for a few minutes, alternating between wondering what had happened to her life and marveling at her own tenacity. It was amazing what the human spirit could endure. Now, instead of just rolling up in a ball and fading away, she and Kelly were going on the offensive. They were looking for Edward Brand, the mastermind of the scam and the key to finding Alan. And through some grace of God, with Kelly working for the NSA, they had connections she would never have thought possible. In that moment, tucked between the cushions watching the fire, she felt for the first time that they might find him.

CHAPTER THIRTY-FIVE

Kelly keyed in the request to pull the personnel files on Brent Hawkins and John Abrams, then studied what he had on Sam Morel. Getting Morel's information was going to be a bit trickier than the two Federal agents. The National Security Agency and the FBI were linked in many ways, one of them being the sharing of information at a nonclassified level. But the agency had no such working relationship with the San Francisco Police Department. That posed a problem.

He pulled the hierarchy for the SFPD, looking for any names he might know from the years he spent in the city working with G-cubed. The best he could do was a lieutenant from the Tenderloin District. A beer-league-baseball and drinking buddy. Not the greatest resource, but it would have to do. He printed the page and set it on the side of his desk. It was still too early on the West Coast to call.

He switched to the registration for the *Mary Dyer*. It took almost an hour, but he found the yacht registered through OCRA worldwide, a yacht and ship registration company out of Mauritius. The ship itself was registered in the Seychelles, a group of forty-one islands lying a few hundred miles off the east coast of Africa. The owner of the *Mary Dyer* was a corporation called Atolls Are Fun, which had provided the necessary builder's certificate with technical details, proof of ownership and a radio license. The corporation was registered in the Seychelles under the International Corporate Service Providers Act 2003, which granted special offshore regulated privileges. Low tax status was first on that list, followed immediately by treaty access and trustee services for administering the corporation. Through all the smoke and mirrors, Kelly was able to dig deep enough to bypass the trustees, who were just bankers charging a fee to keep Atolls Are Fun in tune with the laws of the country, and find the owner. There was only one name.

Robert Zindler.

He jotted the name on a separate sheet of paper and stared at it for a minute. Was that Brand? It well could be. Edward Brand had no reason to think anyone would ever key in on his yacht. Even if they did, there was nothing to tie Robert Zindler to Edward Brand or to the New-Pro scam. The fact that the two men were so distinct in their lives lent Kelly to think he may have found the link. If nothing else, it was one more dot, and every dot counted.

Kelly set Taylor's stuff aside for a couple of hours and concentrated on work the NSA paid him to do. A SEAL unit had intercepted coded communications between two al-Qaeda terrorist cells operating out of remote regions of northern Algeria. The problem with the data was two-fold. Straight off the top it was in Arabic, which was only a minor inconvenience as they had Arabic-speaking persons on staff at both NSA and CIA. But it was the encryption the terrorists had used on the data that was stumping the experts at Langley. When that happened, the first place they turned to was the National Security Agency—the code breakers.

After four hours of uninterrupted work, Kelly set the SEAL data aside and ran his hands through his hair, rubbing his scalp and stimulating his brain. He loved the work, but it was mentally draining. He made a quick trip to the coffee station and returned with a cup of fresh java. The phone number for Buzzards Bar & Grill on the East Cape near San José del Cabo was on a slip of paper on the side of his desk and he keyed it into his computer. He then ran a global search program to find the service provider for that phone number. It was a medium-size Mexican company, and Kelly had little trouble bringing up a screen with the phone logs. The calls were sorted daily, then by increasing time during each twenty-four-hour period. He found the calls for November 3.

Kelly did the math in his head. Taylor said Alan had gone over the cliff around ten after five in the evening. The section of cliff where the accident had occurred was four miles north of Buzzards, and on rugged potholed roads that distance would take about fifteen minutes. He calculated sometime between four-fifty and five o'clock. There was one outgoing call inside the ten-minute time span—at 4:53. It was the only call for fifteen minutes either side. Whoever owned that number had spoken with Edward Brand just before Alan went over the cliff.

He typed in the phone number listed and hit Enter. The response was back in less than six seconds. Carlos Valendez. Address was noted as 417 Matamoros Street, Cabo San Lucas. It meant nothing to him, but somehow Senor Valendez was tied in with Edward Brand, and it was another dot that needed connecting. If there were enough dots, the trail would eventually lead back to Brand. Then to Alan. But Kelly was smart enough to know that Brand was the target. Alan Bestwick was simply another cog in the very efficient wheel Edward Brand had assembled to pull off the con. Find Brand and the wheel would crumble. In the rubble would be Alan Bestwick.

It was time to call his contact in the SFPD. He placed the call and waited for someone to pick up. When they did he asked for Lieutenant Barry Gilmore. The line rang again, and a man answered. His voice was a deep baritone.

"Barry, it's Kelly Kramer."

"Kelly." Gilmore's voice changed slightly—took on a friendly tone. "Where the hell are you? I tried your number last week. It's disconnected."

"I'm in D.C." Kelly said. "Took a job out here a while back. Had enough of your crazy up-and-down streets. My brakes kept wearing out."

"You're really in Washington?"

"Yup."

"Holy shit. We sure don't miss you on the diamond, but we do miss you down at the bar. You bought a lot of rounds to make up for all your errors in the field and strikeouts at the plate. You ever coming back for a visit?"

"Maybe. But right now I've got something else on my mind."

"What's that?"

"Do you know a guy named Sam Morel?"

"Yeah, of course. I know Sam real well. He's over at Central Station. He's good people. What do you need to know?"

"Everything." Kelly said. "I need his personnel file."

There was a small silence, then, "What for, Kelly? Why would an advertising guy need a file on a police inspector?"

Kelly had a choice. He could try to bullshit his way around Gilmore, or he could give him the goods and hope for some level of cooperation. It was actually a pretty easy decision. Straight off the top, he told the lieutenant what agency he worked for. That in itself lent some credibility to his request. After he had filled Gilmore in with what had happened to Taylor Simons, with the exception of knowing her husband was alive, he shut his mouth and waited.

"You think Sam might be in bed with this Edward Brand guy?" he asked.

"Don't know. Personally, I think it's one of the FBI guys. But you never know. I'm just covering all the bases."

"So what are you looking for?"

"Somewhere along the line, Brand has got his hooks into one of these three guys. And whoever it is, is feeding him information. I've run the personnel records on both Abrams and Hawkins, and I'm waiting for the results. Somewhere in all this there is an arrest that went sideways, or something like that. Somewhere that Brand began his relationship with the dirty cop. I just need to find it."

"What if Sam's the guilty one? What then? I can't be giving up one of my own guys."

"This is just for me, Barry. I'm trying to figure out who Brand really is and how to find him. This has nothing to do with taking down a dirty cop."

Again, the silence. "All right, Kelly. I'll do this for you. I'll pull Sam's file and look at it myself. If I see any sign he might have linked up with someone in return for cash, I'll give it to you. But it's my call. My decision as to what I release. His file is confidential."

"Not a problem, Barry. That works for me. Thanks."

"Okay. Hey, how did you ever get a job at the National Security Agency? That's spy shit, right?"

Kelly laughed. "Sort of. I'm just a computer geek."

"You said it, not me."

They said good-bye, and both men hung up. Kelly returned to his work on the Algerian communiqué, spending almost three hours working on the coded transmission before finally shutting down the file and securing it in his computer. He opened his e-mail server and checked to see if there was any information back on Hawkins and Abrams. There was a return e-mail from the search engine. Inside were two separate files—one for each agent. He was just starting on John Abrams's file when his phone rang. He checked the caller ID. It was Barry Gilmore in San Francisco.

"Hey, Barry," he said.

"Jesus, you weren't kidding. You really do work for NSA. I called the main switchboard and they put me through."

Kelly laughed. "I told you, I just work on computer stuff. I'm a cubicle rat."

"Okay, cubicle rat, I've got something for you."

"What?" Kelly replied, leaning forward with his pen poised over a pad on his desk.

"There was one glitch in Sam's file. I had to look long and hard to find it. He had a run-in with senior brass on a file about six years ago. He was working a major-crimes case with ties to organized crime. It started when an upscale drug dealer got shot execution style in his mansion. Looked to be a turf war between two rival dealers, but then it took some interesting twists."

"How so?"

"There was a lot of money laundering going on. The guy who was murdered had a bank manager on his payroll, and he was pumping a lot of dirty money through the Bahamas—tens of millions of dollars a year. So there was tons of money at stake when the dealer got popped. Everyone wanted in. According to Sam Morel, the guy the police had fingered for the murder wasn't the shooter. He was being framed, and the real killers were part of the dead guy's staff and had worked the deal from the inside."

"So what's wrong with that? Maybe Sam was right. How did he piss off the senior guys in the force?"

"They wanted the collar to stick. It was an easy sell to the DA. One drug dealer killing another one. Nobody gives a shit, even if the dead guy is rich. Because of Sam, the case fell apart. They never got the shooters. He got his transfer out of major crimes about two months later."

"The guy he got off, what was his name?" Kelly asked, holding his breath. Maybe Morel was the one.

"Armand DeGaussier. Why?"

"Just wondering. You think that's his real name?"

"That's what's in the file."

"You have a picture of this DeGaussier fellow?"

There was the sound of Gilmore striking keys on his computer; then he said, "Yeah, I've got a picture. You want me to e-mail it to you?"

"Sure," Kelly said, giving Barry Gilmore his e-mail address. "Nothing else on Morel?"

"That's it. He's a straight shooter, Kelly. A good cop."

"Okay, thanks."

Kelly hung up and watched his computer screen. A couple of minutes later the machine beeped, and a new e-mail with an attachment appeared. He opened the e-mail and read the quick message from Gilmore. Then he opened the attachment and took a deep breath. Was it Edward Brand? Nothing happened for a few seconds; then a photo of a man appeared on the screen. He was olive-skinned with jet-black hair and piercing gray eyes. He had gaunt cheeks and a full forehead, out of proportion with the rest of his face. One thing was quickly certain. It wasn't Edward Brand.

Kelly closed the attachment and the e-mail. He reopened the file on John Abrams and printed it. Then he did the same with Brent Hawkins. His briefcase was on the floor by his desk, and he deposited the two personnel files in one of the compartments and zipped it. Then he shut down his computer, hoisted the briefcase and turned out the lights. It was almost eight o'clock and he'd been in since seven-thirty that morning. That made for a long day. Taylor had booked a flight back to San Francisco and had departed Washington at eleven in the morning. She would be safely back in her house by now, probably staring at the million-dollar check and hating that she had to deposit it.

He slid his security pass through the reader and the doors to the parking area opened automatically. He trudged to his car, feeling a little depressed. It had been nice when Taylor was visiting, but now the condo was empty. Friends like Taylor Simons didn't come around every day. A sadness settled over him as he started his car. He was going to miss her.

CHAPTER THIRTY-SIX

The clock had just ticked past ten on Wednesday morning when the phone rang. Taylor left the Internet page on her computer screen and checked her call display. It was Kelly.

"Hi," she said. "How are things?"

"Pretty good, but your voice is all muffled. You having a problem with your home phone?"

"No, why?"

"I can hardly hear you. Could you do me a favor and find a pay phone and call me back? You've got the number."

"I'll try my cell phone. That might be better."

"No. Try a pay phone. You can find one if you drive a mile or so."

Taylor was silent, thinking about what Kelly was saying. There was nothing wrong with her home phone, she could hear him fine, and he didn't want her on a cell. At least, not on a cell phone that might be being monitored. She understood. Someone could be listening.

"Sure. I need to go out for groceries anyway. I'll call you." She hung up and headed for the front door. Then she paused for a second, returned to the computer, printed the page and left the house with it folded in her pocket. The December winds off the bay were cold and she was shivering by the time she got to her car. She started the Audi and pulled into traffic. Kelly Kramer was not a man who spooked easily. She had seen him rock solid in the boardroom, unflinching when millions of dollars were resting on a single word. He worked for the NSA and the CIA as well. The man was intelligent and focused. If he thought it was a good idea for her to call from an untraceable phone, then she agreed. She pulled up around the corner from a coffee shop that she knew had a pay phone hanging on the wall just inside the front door. The clerk smiled when she entered, and she ordered a small medium roast before making her way to the phone and swiping her calling card. She dialed Kelly's direct line. He answered on the second ring.

"You're on a safe phone?" he asked.

"Yes. I'm in a coffee shop near where Alan and I used to live. I wanted to go someplace indoors. It's cold outside."

"Here too. And snowing." He took a breath. "I've got something for you."

"What?"

"The good news is that Sam Morel isn't our guy. Aside from a run-in with some piece-of-shit drug dealer that looked like it might go sideways, he's clean. In fact, from what I heard from a buddy who works in the Tenderloin District, Sam's a good guy to have on our side. He's honest and ethical."

"That's good news. I like Sam. But what else did you find?"

"I pulled the personnel records for Brent Hawkins and John Abrams, right back to when they were students at Quantico. John Abrams is squeaky clean. He's probably never gone to the bathroom without disinfecting his hands after. But Hawkins is a little different. He looks good on the surface, but when I started digging I found some interesting stuff."

"Like what?" Taylor asked, sipping the coffee and watching the street for suspicious-looking vehicles. She wasn't sure whether she was getting paranoid or cautious. The two were delineated by a very fine line.

"Hawkins was running a sting operation in New Orleans about six years ago. They were trying to entrap a man they suspected was running a series of cons on elderly people who had recently lost their spouses. They were looking seriously at one person. Robert Zindler. Mere hours before they were ready to move in, the case fell apart. Zindler disappeared, almost as if he had been warned. They wrapped things up, assuming that Zindler had gotten wise or scared, and went on to their next case. But that wasn't what happened."

"Zindler was warned."

"I'm pretty sure he was. Because after digging through all the smoke and mirrors, guess who owns the *Mary Dyer*?"

"Robert Zindler."

"Exactly."

"Edward Brand is really Robert Zindler."

"Yes. So I stuck Robert Zindler in the computer and guess what I got?"

"Very little," Taylor said.

"Try nothing. He's American, born in Chicago. Both parents deceased for over a decade. The man has never been convicted of any offense. Last known address was San Diego, eighteen years ago. He dropped off the face of the earth since then. Probably using different aliases for each of his scams and never went back to using his real name."

"Smart guy. I'm sure he's pissed off a lot of people over the years."

"Take someone's money and they're going to be mad

all right. Since he seems to take on the new identity for whatever con he's running, I think we should still refer to him as Edward Brand. Less confusing."

"Sure. It's all semantics. Edward Brand it is." Taylor watched a dark four-door sedan cruise past. The windows were tinted. She turned away from the road and spoke softly. "Well, the man has a bit of a sense of humor."

"What do you mean?"

Taylor pulled the sheet of paper she had printed from her pocket. "I checked the name *Mary Dyer* on the Internet. It was a sailing ship back in the early 1800s. In fact, it was the ship that transported the Treasure of Lima from the Peruvian capitol when it appeared the city was going to fall to invaders. One small problem. The captain of the ship absconded with the treasure. It's never been found."

"You're kidding."

"Nope. Edward Brand has a rather dry sense of humor."

"He does. Listen, I've got something else as well."

"What?

"The phone number Brand dialed when he used the house phone at Buzzards belongs to some guy named Carlos Valendez. He's tied in with Brand somehow. Probably who we figured—the contact man for the scuba divers who pulled Alan out of the car."

"What can we do with that information?"

"No idea. Maybe it'll come in handy at some point. It's better to have more info than less."

"I suppose so." Taylor watched as the same car with the tinted windows drove by for a second time. Were they watching her, or was it someone trolling for a parking spot? "You know what bugs me, Kelly?"

"What?"

"If *we* can find out who Brand is, why can't the FBI? They've got pretty much the same resources you have."

"They don't have the tie to the *Mary Dyer*. It was getting the name off Brand's yacht that started the process. Without a starting point, you're often dead in the water.

That, and the fact that Brent Hawkins isn't going to be pointing the investigation in the right direction."

"What do we do with this? We know who he is, but have no idea where he is."

"The *Mary Dyer* will have to dock somewhere eventually, unless he owns waterfront property with a large enough berth for a seventy-two-foot yacht. When he does, I'll see him. I've got a search engine up and running, scanning all the marinas where yachts that size can be moored. He'll show up at some point."

"Okay, then we know who he is and where he is. That still doesn't get me what I want."

"Your money?"

"That and Alan."

"Don't worry about Alan right now. We concentrate on Edward Brand. We get him, we'll get Alan."

"Okay. Still, it pisses me off that Alan's out there somewhere."

"I understand. Hey, one more thing. Watch where you use your credit cards. Hawkins is probably watching you electronically. Try to keep your purchases mainstream. Don't go running ownership profiles on yachts and stuff like that. We need Hawkins reporting back to Brand that you're settling in to your new life without your husband."

"All right."

"Did you deposit the check?"

"This morning, about an hour before you called. Boy, did that raise a couple of eyebrows at the bank."

Kelly laughed. "I would think so." There was a short break, and then he said, "I'll call you when I've got a hit on the yacht. You'll have to go to a pay phone. Don't ever use the same one twice."

"Tell you what, I'll check my caller ID. If I see your name come up I'll just head for a phone and call you. I won't even pick up."

"Okay, but I'll only call you from the office. They could

tap my home phone, but there's absolutely no chance they can put any sort of listening device on this one. Security's too tight here. So if you return my call, always use my office number."

"Okay. And thanks again, Kelly."

"My pleasure."

Taylor returned to the street and glanced up and down the narrow roadway, concentrating on the parked cars. She couldn't see the sedan with the tinted windows. Probably just a local trying to find a parking space close to home. She tucked a handful of red hair up in her tam and snugged it down over her ears. God, it was cold. Mid-December and no sign of spring. It was depressing outside. Low cloud cover and a very real threat of rain. Cold rain. Not like the warm rains that fall in the Caribbean—short cloudbursts that replenish the air with ozone and green up the vegetation, then pass on to the next island.

As she walked down the sidewalk in that gray world, she wondered which route her life was destined to travel. Was she on an island in the midst of a short-lived squall? Or was she trapped in a world of depressing gray, with a constant drizzle that sucked the spirit from the soul?

CHAPTER THIRTY-SEVEN

Foot traffic on the Malecon was normal for a Thursday. In fact, it was normal for any day in December in Puerto Vallarta. The popular walkway, paralleling the beach and just on the fringe of the city center, was a curious mix of already-brown and still-browning tourists. The only Mexicans on the stroll were the timeshare sales people, a dwindling breed in a resort town where fractional ownership had peaked years back, and street vendors hawking beads and blankets. Edward Brand, dressed in khaki shorts and a loose-fitting white shirt, blended right in.

He passed the scuba shop just as a group of divers exited, heading across the beach to a waiting skiff. A dive boat was anchored a few hundred feet offshore. Brand sat on the bench overlooking the still waters of the Pacific and lit a cigarette. He sucked in the smoke and exhaled, watching the divers board the small craft. He thought it was funny that they would try to get in the boat without getting their feet wet. A dark-skinned Mestizo pulled the string on the motor, and it coughed to life, spewing blue smoke into the fresh ocean air. The motor revved, and then the craft was on its way, a small wake spreading through the gentle surf. Brand finished his cigarette and stepped on the embers. A moment later, his cell phone rang. He checked the caller ID and answered.

"Yes?" was all he said.

"Just calling in to report on the woman in San Francisco," the voice said. It belonged to Brent Hawkins, and he was referring to Taylor Simons.

"And . . ."

"Her trip to Paris seems to be coincidental. She toured about a bit, some of the time in the Latin Quarter, but that's normal. It's a popular part of town for tourists."

"It's also a dangerous part of town for her to be wandering around in."

"I know. But I don't think she was there to look for our guy. I had a careful look at her credit card authorizations, and most were for meals and taxis. Some of the meals were close to his apartment, but probably more coincidental than anything else."

Brand weighed his response, then said, "All right, so much for Paris. What is she up to now?"

"She was in Washington for a bit, but she's back at home now. I'm keeping an eye on her the best I can. After she got back to San Francisco, she took a call from the friend she visited when she was in D.C., but it was a bad connection and they ended up talking on a pay phone. I had a directional mike in the car and made a couple of sweeps by the building she was in when she made the call, but there was too much ambient noise. I had no way to record the conversation. I'm not sure what they talked about."

"Is this a problem?" Brand asked, watching the divers climb from the smaller craft onto the dive boat. One of the women slipped and would have tumbled into the water if a crew member hadn't caught her.

"No, I don't think so. But Kelly Kramer, her friend, works at the National Security Agency."

Brand sucked in a sharp breath. The odor from a

nearby sewage outlet stung his nose and lungs. "What did you say?"

"NSA. Kelly Kramer works for the National Security Agency."

"Jesus Christ. You call to tell me Taylor Simons is talking with a guy who works for NSA and you don't think this is a problem. Are you fucking nuts?"

"It's okay, Edward. Her relationship with Kramer goes back to G-cubed. He worked there as her Web-design expert. He just took the NSA job and moved to Washington. Kramer's a newbie at the agency. He's no threat."

"Don't tell me that someone working inside an agency like the NSA isn't a threat," Brand shot back. "These guys have access to information no one else does."

"That's crap," Hawkins said crisply. "They're not any better connected than we are. I checked out his application and his work history. He's simply a computer forensics expert they've hired to work on information they get from the field operatives. On a scale of one to ten in the agency's hierarchy, he's belly-button lint. Nothing."

"Christ, you had better be right. That kind of shit scares me."

"Don't let it. From what I can see, Kramer and Simons were pretty tight at G-cubed. They were more like friends than employer-employee. It fits that she'd visit him, given what happened. He's out of San Fran, and he's safe. She's still grieving. She hops a plane and visits a friend in a different city where she isn't reminded of her husband every time she turns around. It makes sense."

"I want you to watch him. Watch him closely."

"He's NSA, Edward. You don't watch these guys too closely without getting caught. I'll keep tabs on Taylor. She's the easy one to watch. I've got a bug on her home phone. I can try to track her cell phone, but that's much more difficult, especially without the office sanctioning it."

"Okay," Brand said. There was a brief silence where

neither man spoke. The deep throaty sound of diesel engines skimmed over the water as the dive boat weighed anchor and turned toward the open ocean. It quickly diminished in size as it left the protected area near the beach and headed for Los Arcos, the local dive site near Mismaloya Beach.

"How are things going with the money?" Hawkins asked.

"I'll transfer the funds this afternoon. The money should be in your account by six o'clock tonight."

"That's fast for a Mexican bank."

"What do you mean?"

"It's no secret that you've been using Mexican banks, out of Mexico City. And they're notoriously slow. I'm impressed they can get the money across so fast."

"I don't use Mexican banks," Brand said. "Seven of our marks were given scraps of information so they could find the antique shop in Mexico City. That's why those accounts were set up. I transferred a bit of money to them, but nothing substantial. Your money will be coming from a Caribbean account. That's all you need to know."

"I don't care if a stork drops it, so long as I get it."

"It's coming. This afternoon. Including the fifty large for checking out the woman's trip to Paris."

"Good. I'll be waiting." Hawkins hung up.

Edward Brand lit another cigarette and watched the smoke curl up and slowly dissipate into the warm Mexican air. He stared out at the ocean, the water's surface a series of gentle sine waves as the surf touched the shore. There was no sign that a boat had just passed that way. If he hadn't been sitting in that chair, watching the dive boat leave the harbor, he would never have known. It struck him that the world was filled with two kinds of people. There were those who blazed trails across the landscape leaving indelible marks on the terrain of their lives. Others floated on water leaving no trail to show where they had been or what they had done.

And for the first time in his life, he felt a tinge of sadness. Perhaps that he was wasting his life, leaving no mark. He had no children, no career that he could point to and say, *This is what I did with my life.* Not unless he wanted to highlight the trail of misery and anger he left in his wake. But they were choices made many years ago and those choices had led him to where he was now. And that included being very wealthy. That it was other people's money was merely a technicality. Money didn't care who owned it.

He smiled and crushed out the cigarette. An inkling of a conscience. Now that was a first.

CHAPTER THIRTY-EIGHT

Taylor glanced at the phone and saw Kelly's ID. She ignored it, slipped into a heavy coat and drove her Audi to the local grocery store. Inside, she wheeled her cart to the rear of the store and dialed his direct line from the pay phone. He answered immediately.

"Where are you?" he asked.

"Grocery store. Pay phone. What's up?"

"I found the *Mary Dyer*."

Taylor felt her pulse surge. Edward Brand, within their grasp. "Where?"

"It's docked in the marina at Puerto Vallarta."

"I know Puerto Vallarta. I've been there three or four times. So he's still in Mexico."

"He is—and that's unfortunate for us. It's tough to get any sort of police force or government agency to try to extradite a criminal unless it's been proven beyond the wildest glimmer of doubt that he's guilty. Guilty of something pretty substantial. I'm not sure the scam he pulled with NewPro would fall inside those guidelines. Two hundred million dollars is a lot of money, but it's probably too complicated to find him, drag him back to the States and convict him in a court of law. So my guess is that he's safe—for now at least. No wonder he likes it down there so much."

"Yeah, that and the weather," Taylor said cynically. She didn't want to dwell on the thought that they may know where Brand was but that there would be no help forthcoming from the cops. "So what can we do? I mean, we know who he is and where he is. There must be something we can do with what we know."

"Maybe. I'm not sure what."

There was a long, silent pause. Taylor had been toying with something, and she figured this was as good a time as ever to mention it. "Listen, Kelly, Brand being in Mexico might not be a bad thing."

"Why?"

"I've got an idea. It's kind of been banging around in my head the last couple of weeks, and I've done a lot of poking around on the Internet and in a few research books. I think I might have something."

"I don't understand. What are you talking about?"

It was complicated and she decided that face-to-face would be the best way to let Kelly know what she was thinking about. "Not on the phone. Let's get together."

"Where?"

"Is it okay if I come back to your place?"

"Of course. I'd like that."

"Thanks, Kelly," she said. The sincerity in his voice wasn't lost on her. "I don't think it's a good idea if I fly direct to Washington. I might be getting paranoid, but I think I'm being followed."

"Dark four-door cars? Tinted windows?"

"Exactly."

"Could be our friend at the FBI. What are you thinking?"

"I've got a friend in Houston. I fly down to see her, then continue on to Washington. But I leave her my credit card, and she goes out every day or two and buys dinner or a piece of clothing. That way, if they're watching me electronically, like you think they might be, they'll think I'm still in Houston."

"You're starting to think like a spook. That's kind of scary."

"What do you think?"

"It's a good idea. Will your friend go for it?"

"Sure. She'll just buy the clothes to fit her, not me."

"Okay. How do you plan on getting to D.C. from Houston."

"I'll probably have to take the bus. You need ID to fly."

There was a silence, then Kelly said, "I doubt if Hawkins would risk tracking your passport. That requires an entirely different level of clearance than just watching your credit cards. You're probably fine to fly from Houston to Washington. Just make sure you pay cash for your flight."

"You can do that?" she asked.

"Sure. Just go to a travel agent in Houston and pay cash. So long as you have ID, they'll sell you a ticket.

"Okay, I'll get to Houston and link up with my friend. Once I know when the flight arrives in D.C. I'll call you at the office."

"That'll work fine."

Taylor hung up and left the grocery store. She went back home, called her travel agent and had her book a flight from San Francisco to Houston, returning in twenty days. She had no intention of using the return portion of the ticket, but if Brent Hawkins was watching her he would think she was planted in Texas for a while and maybe get lazy. If her friend didn't mind signing her Visa card and picking up some free clothes, Taylor had the perfect cover. Hawkins would think she was in Houston, and that worked for her. Because she had an idea that might relieve Edward Brand of some of the money he had stolen.

Taylor had always been fascinated by tales of treasure.

Treasure of any sort—buried, entombed, plundered—it didn't matter. The thought that great wealth was just sitting there, ready for the taking, was powerful. She had read *Treasure Island* three times, always wondering why Robert Louis Stevenson never let his infamous Captain Silver find at least a taste of what lay buried under the sand. The National Geographic channel was one of her favorites, and she never missed a special on the Egyptian tombs or any archeological dig that may unearth objects of value. She read extensively on the subject, and that's how she first heard of the treasure of Oaxaca.

The state of Oaxaca, which she learned was pronounced wa-HA-ka, was a perfect setting for lost treasure. Over a seven hundred-year period, no fewer than fifteen different Indian tribes had settled in the fertile valleys nestled between the mountain ranges of the Sierra Madre del Sur and the Sierra Madre de Oaxaca. Their level of advancement rivaled or exceeded that of twelfth-century Europe, with intricate pyramids and temples rising above the virgin cloud forests that blanketed the region. The Zapotec people devised a primitive alphabet and began using the 365-day calendar. They also built a city they called Monte Alban.

As Taylor dug into the history of the area, she found that throughout the rule of the Zapotec tribe, the city grew in wealth and prosperity. When the Aztecs finally arrived in the 1400s, there was already an incredible base of wealth, measured in gold and jewels. The Aztecs simply added to that trove. The result was one of the most substantial treasures ever amassed.

But what intrigued Taylor was that the treasure the Spaniards looted when they overthrew the Aztecs was not even close to what had been recorded by the Zapotec tribes. Something was missing. That fact had not gone unnoticed. In the last two decades, a couple of top-level treasure hunters had put together expeditions and tried to find the remaining cache of gold and precious stones.

Despite a logical and exacting approach to the problem, the undiscovered treasure had eluded them. Then, in 1999, there was a major earthquake that had essentially sealed the abandoned city of Monte Alban. The Mexican government put a moratorium on hunting for treasure anywhere in the region, and that meant the treasure was still there. Sitting, waiting to be found.

That treasure, buried somewhere in the ancient city of Monte Alban, was her bait.

Edward Brand was a cautious man who dotted every *i* and crossed every *t*. He was also a greedy man who liked wealth and what it could buy. She knew a bit about Edward Brand, having met him and having seen the scope of his con. This was not a man who thought small. If she and Kelly could somehow get Brand to believe they had the key to the Monte Alban treasure, maybe they could retrieve some of the money he had stolen.

Maybe. It was a long shot.

She packed and headed to bed early, her flight leaving at just after ten in the morning. Sleep didn't come for a while, and she lay in bed staring around her bedroom thinking of what Alan was doing that very moment. Paris was six hours ahead of the West Coast of the United States, which meant it was almost six in the morning in the Latin Quarter. Was he waking up next to another woman? Did she know who he was? Did she care? Alan was wealthy, having taken her for millions of dollars. There were a lot of women in the world who didn't care where the money came from—so long as it was there. Somehow she doubted he was sleeping alone. Her mind finally slowed, and she drifted off. But just before darkness slipped over her, she had one last vision.

Alan and Edward Brand, on the street and penniless.

CHAPTER THIRTY-NINE

Flying into Houston on Saturday, just nine days before Christmas, was crazy. The airport was packed with holiday travelers, and it took Taylor a few minutes to find Linda Frederick, one of her closest and longest friends. They hugged, oblivious to the mayhem around them, then went in search of Taylor's bags. Once they had her suitcase, they pushed their way through to the parking lot. The quiet inside Linda's car was a welcome break.

"What the heck is going on?" Linda asked as she drove. She was a natural blonde with widely spaced eyes, high cheekbones and a quick smile. She had a habit of going google-eyed whenever someone made a comment she considered interesting. She was five-ten and medium-boned, but in excellent shape and wore stylish clothes that accented her figure. Linda Frederick was a woman who turned heads.

"Oh, you wouldn't believe me if I told you," Taylor said, cracking the window and enjoying the warm Texas air. It was a pleasant change from the cold winds coming in off the bay.

"Try me." Linda grinned, and her face lit up. Always

happened. You just couldn't dislike someone who glowed every time she smiled.

Taylor spent the entire drive to Linda's house recounting what had happened. Her friend simply drove and kept her mouth shut, listening. When Taylor finished, the car was completely silent for a minute. Linda pulled into her driveway and switched off the ignition. She unclipped her seatbelt and shifted in her seat so she was facing Taylor.

"You're heading for Mexico to try to find this Edward Brand guy who stole thirteen million dollars from you?"

"You got it."

"And Alan is in on this?"

"Yes." Taylor could feel her eyes start to tear, but as quickly as it started, it stopped. "There's no doubt about it. Everything pointed to him being part of the scam, but when I saw the divers pull him out of the car, I knew for sure."

"Taylor, this whole thing is just unbelievable!"

"Tell me about it. I've spent the last three years of my life married to a man whose only connection to me was my money. You want to talk about feeling slightly used." This time the tears spilled down her cheeks.

Linda reached over and took her hand. "Okay, God, you poor woman. What can I do for you? Anything. Just name it, I'm there for you."

Taylor managed a partial smile. "It's not so bad, what I need you to do. In fact, you'll probably like it."

"What?" Linda asked, ready to burst.

"I need you to use my credit card every day or two so the FBI agent in cahoots with Brand thinks I'm in Houston. You'll be spending my money on new clothes and dinners at fancy restaurants."

Linda really glowed when she smiled. "*That*, is no problem."

"Didn't think so."

* * *

Taylor spent Saturday and Sunday with Linda and her husband, John, before flying out to Washington. They hugged again at the airport, and Linda looked her right in the eyes.

"Be careful, Taylor. It's only money. Don't do anything that could get you hurt or killed. It's not worth it."

"You're probably right. But the way I'm feeling right now, I want revenge. I want to destroy both Alan and Edward Brand. I want them to suffer."

"Vindictive little bitch, aren't you?" Linda said. "Didn't know you had that side in you."

"Oh, yeah, it's there. It's coming out more and more each day. I'm really focused on this. I think I've got a way to get Edward Brand."

"Be careful."

"Promise."

Taylor headed through the security check and into her gate area. The flight was on time, and Kelly was waiting at Dulles. They walked together to his car, and he drove straight to his condo. It was three in the afternoon when they arrived, and he unloaded her suitcase in the spare bedroom. Taylor freshened up, and when she came into the kitchen the unmistakable aroma of freshly baked muffins greeted her. Kelly put two muffins on a plate and set them and the butter in front of her.

"I feel spoiled," she said, spreading the butter and biting in.

"You should. It took me all day to bake those."

"Liar," Taylor said. "But nice try."

Kelly poured tea for both of them and sat across the table from her. "What's up?" he asked.

"I think I might have a way to get Edward Brand back for what he did."

"Not Alan?" Kelly asked, sipping his tea.

"Not right now. Like you said, concentrate on Edward Brand and Alan's turn will come in time."

"Revenge with a schedule," Kelly said. "So how does it work?"

"There's a region in southern Mexico called Oaxaca. It's been inhabited by native tribes since about 200 AD. Three of the tribes that were influential were the Zapotecs, the Mixtecs and the Aztecs. Guess what that means?"

"Well, the Aztecs were well known for working with gold. So I'd have to guess that you're thinking about treasure of some sort."

"Absolutely." Taylor spent fifteen minutes filling Kelly in on the ancient city of Monte Alban, high above the cloud forests of central Mexico. About the possible existence of treasure hidden somewhere in the ruins. And about the earthquake in 1999 that had closed down any treasure hunting and placed Monte Alban strictly off limits.

"So how does the hidden treasure relate to Edward Brand?"

"We set him up," Taylor said. "We get him to believe that we've found the treasure and once he's at Monte Alban, we call the Mexican police. They arrest him and throw him in jail. He spends the next twenty years rotting in a Mexican prison."

Kelly was thoughtful. Finally, he said, "I like the idea, but not the ending. I don't think it'll work."

"Why not?"

"Brand's got too much money. He can buy his way out of something as inconsequential as looking for artifacts in a banned area. If we could nail him for murder or something more substantial, that might work. But not for entering an archeological dig that's been deemed unsafe because of an earthquake. He'll walk."

Taylor leaned back in her chair and asked, "You said you liked the idea. Got any ideas for a different ending?"

"Not sure." He thought for a minute, then asked her a couple of questions. "What do you know about Monte Alban? How the missing treasure got there? Where it might be?"

She finished her tea and set the empty mug on the table. "The Zapotec tribe built Monte Alban, but they abandoned it sometime around 1000 AD. After that the Mixtec tribe came along and revitalized it. They also built hundreds of tombs and burial sites—more than two hundred tombs and three hundred burial sites have already been opened and pillaged. One of them, Tumba Seven, was an absolute gold mine. Inside were over five thousand objects, priceless works by the Mixtecs. You name it, it was in there. Precious stones, gold, ivory, jade, pearl—the value of the find was in the hundreds of millions of dollars. And that's not counting what the Aztecs left on the site."

"You're kidding."

"Nope. Here's the great part of the story. The experts agree that only about ten percent of the city has been uncovered."

"So there's the possibility of finding more treasure somewhere on the site," Kelly said thoughtfully. He could see the logic behind Taylor's idea.

"That's what I was hoping Brand would think. If we could entice him to the ruins, we could set him up."

"I don't think trying to get the Mexican police to throw him in prison is the best plan. But I've got something that might work." There was a sparkle in his eyes. "Another ending, so to speak."

"What?" she asked, leaning forward against the table.

"Rather than putting Brand in a Mexican jail, we hit him where it really hurts. We take his money."

"How?"

"It'll take a lot of planning, but here's the idea. We find someone in Mexico we can trust. A native Mexican who could be associated with Monte Alban and not raise any red flags. Then we have him approach Edward Brand with a story of found treasure. But the man who knows where the treasure is can't get at it. He needs help. He needs financing before he can attempt to move the gold and jewels. There are officials to be bribed, palms to be greased, supplies to be purchased. He gets Brand interested. Once we get Brand on the hook, we clean him out."

Taylor's eyes gleamed at the thought. "We can do that?"

"Maybe. Like I said, it'll take a lot of planning and perfect execution. We'd be conning a con man. We need him to believe there is treasure inside the tombs and that we've got the means to get that treasure out. Once we've done that, we reel him in. We get him to advance the bribe money. That gives us access to his bank accounts."

"Jesus, Kelly. You think we can fool him? He's probably one of the smoothest con men on the planet."

Kelly smiled. "Maybe. It's a challenge. But I know you, Taylor. You're never one to back down from an opportunity."

"What about Alan?"

"Alan's turn will come. Right now we work on Edward Brand."

Taylor held up her mug. Kelly clinked his mug against hers. "To getting even," she said.

"To heck with getting even," Kelly said. "Here's to getting it all."

Chapter Forty

They flew to Mexico City three days later, on December 21. Kelly took the allotted time off for the Christmas holidays, and Richard Tolman had signed off on six additional days, giving Kelly until January 3 to return. It was just approaching the supper hour when they checked in at the Marquis Reforma Hotel and Miguel, the concierge who had introduced Taylor and Alan to Ricardo, recognized her the moment she walked into the lobby. He smiled and bowed slightly as he approached.

"You are back, Senora Simons," he said, tastefully not acknowledging that she was with a different man. "Welcome."

"Thank you, Miguel." She turned to Kelly. "This is Kelly Kramer. He's a good friend of mine from Washington, D.C."

"A senator? Congressman, perhaps?" Miguel said, shaking his hand.

"Nonpolitical. Sorry."

Miguel shrugged. "I always ask. I once had a famous author stay here and didn't find out until after he left who he was. I think it's nice to take an interest in people, especially what they do for a living."

"Of course," Kelly said, not offering what his job was.

"We'll need separate rooms," Taylor said.

"I'll arrange it. Why don't you and Mr. Kramer sit in the lounge and have a drink. I'll have the rooms assigned and your luggage delivered. Would you like the rooms next to each other?"

"Yes, please," Taylor said.

They left their bags in the lobby and headed for the bar. Kelly and Taylor had decided they would approach Ricardo, the driver who had taken her and Alan to the antique shop that night, to help them. When she and Alan had traveled to Mexico City, Taylor had made all the arrangements, including the hotel. There was absolutely no chance that Miguel or Ricardo could possibly have known Alan prior to their arrival. That meant Edward Brand did not know Ricardo. It was impossible for Kelly or Taylor to be involved in meeting with Brand, as he knew who they were. Ricardo would make for the perfect front man—providing he wanted to take the risk.

The bar was well appointed, with rich teak woodwork on the tables and booths, and original oil paintings of rural Mexican scenes on the walls. Soft music was playing, but otherwise the space was quiet. Kelly ordered a beer and Taylor a glass of red wine. They had been flying for almost six hours, and both were tired. At the high altitude the alcohol hit them quick, and Taylor felt giddy. She cupped her hands around the glass and stared at the deep red wine. It reminded her of blood.

"You think this Ricardo fellow will go for it?" Kelly asked.

She shrugged. "No idea. But what are our options? We need a native Mexican to work the Monte Alban angle. Someone who can convince Brand that he knows where the treasure is and how to get it out. From what I saw when Ricardo was driving us around the city, he's the guy. He's connected, articulate and smooth. We just need to convince him to do it."

"How do we contact him?"

"Miguel, the concierge. He knows how to find Ricardo."

Kelly took a long draught on his beer and set the empty on the table. "This too crazy for you? I mean, going after Brand like this."

She shook her head, her long hair moving with the motion. "No. It's exactly what I need right now. The bastard deserves whatever he gets. I had a vision of him and Alan on the streets, destitute and homeless." Her eyes had a hard edge to them. "I liked it."

"That's not like you," Kelly said.

"There's a line, Kelly. When you cross it, you burn all the bridges you spent years building. It takes a lot for someone to cross my line, but when they do, watch out. 'An eye for an eye' just doesn't cut it. I want more. I want to put these men in the gutter. I want to destroy them."

Kelly pursed his lips and swallowed. "Okay. Fair enough. But if I ever start edging up to that line, let me know."

She laughed, and the softness returned to her eyes. "Sure. I'll do that."

Miguel entered the bar and approached their table. "Your rooms are ready," he said.

"Thanks, Miguel," she said, waving to the waiter for the check. "Miguel, do you remember Ricardo? He was the man you had drive Alan and me around last time we were in Mexico City."

"Of course. Why?"

"I wonder if you could arrange for us to meet with him."

Miguel looked confused for a moment, but then his smile returned and he said, "That shouldn't be a problem. When would you like the meeting to happen?"

"Quickly."

"I'll phone him." He glanced at his watch. "The best time to see Ricardo is in the evening, as he's quite busy with his restaurant-supply business during the day. I could see if he's available for this evening."

"That would be great," Taylor said. "Say, in about two hours?"

"Ten o'clock. I'll call your room and let you know."

"Thanks."

Taylor and Kelly retreated to their rooms, and Taylor drew a hot bath. The phone rang before she could lower herself into the steaming water. It was Miguel. The meeting was on for ten o'clock. She hung up the phone, dialed Kelly's room and told him, then slid into the bath. Evenings in late December in Mexico City weren't exactly tropical, and she had a chill through her bones. She lay in the water, adding more hot every few minutes, until her fingers started to prune. Reluctantly, she pulled herself out of the tub and rubbed her skin with the soft towel. After she was dried, she put on new makeup and dried the ends of her hair that had dipped in the water. Then she dressed and checked her watch. Time to meet Ricardo. She knocked on Kelly's door, and they took the elevator down together. It was ten to ten, but Ricardo had already arrived and was sitting in one of the corner booths. He caught her eye and gave her a subtle wave. When they reached the table, she did the introductions. The two men shook hands, and they all slipped into the booth.

"Miguel said you wanted to speak with me," Ricardo said. He was as Taylor remembered him, tall and light skinned, with penetrating brown eyes and well-groomed black hair just off his shoulders. His smile was brilliant white and his nails freshly manicured. He was dressed in a pressed white shirt and black trousers.

"I did, but not until we've had a drink. I'm parched." Taylor wanted to get an idea of what Ricardo was like— whether he was a risk taker or a stay-at-home kind of guy. She had her suspicions, and they leaned toward him being the more adventurous type. After twenty minutes of animated, and often very funny conversation with him, she had her answer. Ricardo was exactly who she had hoped. He skydived on occasion and drove a racing car on weekends at one of the local tracks. He was single and dated regularly, but seldom the same woman. And he was smart and funny. He had a quick mind, which would be a definite asset if he were to meet Edward Brand face-to-face at some point. It was pressing eleven o'clock when the talk drifted around to why they were at the table together.

"Do you remember my husband, Alan?" she asked Ricardo.

"Yes. Not vividly, but I do remember his face."

"Well, it turned out that Alan wasn't who I thought he was. I've got a bit of a story to tell you if you have the time."

"I'm yours for the evening," Ricardo said, motioning to the waitress for another round. "Please continue."

Taylor spent the next fifteen minutes detailing what Edward Brand and Alan Bestwick had done. Every detail, including how Alan had faked his death by plunging over the cliff at La Laguna. She told him of her trip to Paris and how she had seen him on the street in the Latin Quarter. When she was finished, she sipped her drink, her throat dry from talking so much. Ricardo was quiet, his face serious.

"Your husband deceived you quite badly," he said. His voice was soft, but there was an edge to it. "That is cowardly. In Mexico, many men fool around on their wives and bed other women, but it is few and far between that a man would do something like this. Your husband is a snake."

"Good description," Taylor said.

Ricardo rubbed his closely shaved chin. "How do I figure into all this?"

"Kelly, maybe you should take over here," Taylor said.

"Sure," Kelly said. "We think there may be an opportunity to get Taylor's money back from Edward Brand. But we need help."

"What sort of help?" Ricardo asked, reclining back into the soft leather.

"There's a series of ruins about five miles northwest of Oaxaca City. Monte Alban. Have you heard of them?"

He nodded. "Yes, of course. In school we take classes in Mexican history and Monte Alban is one of the more interesting parts. If I remember correctly, the Zapotec Indians built the city in about 200 or 300 AD. And one of the tombs they found was full of priceless works of art. It was quite the find."

"That's the place."

"But the government has closed down any archeological work because of an earthquake. It was back in 1999 or 2000, I think."

"1999. And that's what makes this the perfect bait for Edward Brand," Kelly said. "The place has the potential to yield millions of dollars in treasure, but no one can get at it. But what if someone *could* get in? And what if they found a bunch of treasure? But for some reason, they were unable to get it out. Say, an official who needed his palm greased before he would turn a blind eye. And if the person who knew where the treasure was didn't have that money, then the gold and jewels would just sit there until someone else discovered them."

"Unless this person could find someone with money to pay off the corrupt officials," Ricardo said. "I understand."

"So that's where you come in. You have to hook Brand—get him to believe that you have access to hundreds of millions of dollars in ancient Aztec and Mixtec treasure. And once you have him believing, you need him to wire money from his account to one of these officials."

"And you take the money," Ricardo said.

"Sort of," Taylor interjected. "We'll only ask him for half a million dollars, and since that money will be traceable, we don't really want it. But that gives us access to his account numbers. Once we have those, plus the passwords, we can empty the accounts. That's where the real money is."

"How much?" Ricardo asked.

Taylor thought for a minute. Brand took over two hundred million dollars out of the scam, but he would have had serious expenses. Even if he kept twenty-five percent of the total, that amount was still substantial. "Fifty million, give or take," she said.

Ricardo whistled, a low monotone note that carried through the smoky air. "Fifty million?"

Taylor and Kelly both nodded. "At least," she said.

"That's a lot of money." Ricardo was very thoughtful. He sipped his drink, then waved at the waitress for another one. He waited until she had dropped off the rye and coke before continuing. "What is my share?" he finally asked.

"Depends on what we get," Kelly said. "But we'll guarantee you one hundred thousand dollars, even if we don't get a single peso. Paid up front."

"And if we get a peso, how much of that peso will I get?" he asked.

Taylor could read the interest in his eyes. It was extremely high. "Ten percent," she said. "Capped at five million, even if we take in more than fifty."

"Ten percent," Ricardo repeated. "That seems low."

She shook her head. "Ninety-nine percent of this con is knowing who has the money and what kind of person he is. The final one percent is pulling it off. You're well paid at ten percent."

Ricardo did the math for each increment up to fifty. If they were anywhere near the fifty million, the amount was staggering. "Is he dangerous?" he asked.

"Extremely. He's already had one of his men kill an FBI agent. You don't want to blow your cover. The chances are good he'd kill you on the spot," Kelly said.

Ricardo arched one eyebrow. "Now that's an honest

answer." He was silent, thoughtful. When he spoke his voice was distant. "I've had a good life. One filled with nice clothes, fast cars and lots of women. I've built a thriving business in a city where it is very difficult to succeed. Now is the time of my life to enjoy this success." He paused to finish his drink. "But there has always been something missing. A piece of the puzzle that wasn't there. I never knew what it was. Not until tonight. But now I know. Although Mexico City can be dangerous, I have never been in a life-or-death situation. I've never had to rely on my abilities to think fast and say the right things to stay alive. And that is what is missing."

"And . . ." Taylor said.

"And tonight, you have presented me with a very unique opportunity. Perhaps one that could fill that void."

"You'll help us?" she asked, then held her breath.

He smiled, but his eyes were serious. "Yes, I'll help you."

It was Taylor's turn to smile. She reached over and shook his hand. "Then we're a team of three."

"A team of three," Ricardo said. "I like that. It's got a—how do you say it in English?—a certain ring to it."

CHAPTER FORTY-ONE

They met again the next day at La Jolla restaurant, the upscale dining room in the Marquis Reforma Hotel. The décor was understated elegance, an extension of the hotel, which consistently made the coveted Leading Hotels of the World list. Ricardo was dressed casually, in khakis and a soft beige shirt while Kelly and Taylor both had on jeans and T-shirts. They fit the image of tourists having a late breakfast with a Mexican friend.

"Your English is impeccable," Kelly said as they settled in. "Where did you learn?"

"My parents are upper-middle class. My father is a lawyer, and my mother is an interior designer for commercial buildings. They sent me to an English-immersion school. All my studies, from grade one right through to graduation were in English. I was very fortunate."

"No kidding. I wish I had a second language."

The waiter came by and they ordered coffee and breakfast. They waited until he left the table before talking about Monte Alban.

"I spent some time on the Internet going over the layout of Monte Alban, but I think we need to visit the site," Ricardo said. "We have to be very informed on the area."

Kelly nodded. "That's what we thought. We've already checked on flights. Aeroméxico has daily flights directly to Oaxaca City. Getting there is not a problem. Hotels are mostly basic, but there's one that looks good. Camino Real Oaxaca. We had Miguel phone and check availability, and there are rooms available. It seems most people leave the city at Christmas time."

"Probably visiting relatives in Mexico City," Ricardo said. "It can be tough to find a good hotel room here at this time of year." He sipped his coffee and asked, "Do you have any sort of plan?"

"A basic idea of how things could work," Taylor said. "But setting anything in stone before we visit Monte Alban to see exactly what we're up against is impossible. We need to visit and get a lay of the land."

"Can you get away?" Kelly asked Ricardo.

"I'd like to stay in Mexico City for Christmas. That's only three days from now. After that I can fly down and meet you there."

Taylor glanced at Kelly. "Works for me. How about you?"

Kelly nodded and spoke directly to Ricardo. "Better than we could have hoped for. Twenty-four hours ago your life was normal. Then we drop in from nowhere and dump this on your lap. You're being very accommodating."

Ricardo smiled, his olive skin crinkling into soft laugh lines around his mouth. "You enticed me with a lot of money. It's not often a man gets an opportunity to earn anywhere between a hundred thousand and five million dollars. No, that's not something that comes around every day. I can be most accommodating with that sort of incentive."

"Good," Taylor said. "We may need a couple more people to help us. Who do you know that's trustworthy?"

"What would they be doing?" Ricardo asked.

"We'll need someone to play the part of a government official," Taylor said. "Someone high-ranking in whatever department handles antiquities and treasure."

"Of course. They will be at Monte Alban to convince the person you are relieving of his money that the treasure is real." Ricardo nodded at the logic.

"I think so, but we'll need to use the actual name of someone inside the department, because our man will check."

"I can get a name," Ricardo said. "I know a man who could forge an ID badge."

"Good," Kelly said. "Whoever you get should be light on his feet and able to think fast, because he might be in the line of fire if Brand realizes he's been taken."

"Brand? That's the man's name?"

"That's not his real name, but it's the one he's been living under for some time now. The most recent seems the best to use," Taylor replied.

Ricardo leaned back in his chair, a serious look on his face. He crossed his arms over his chest, the first time his body language had taken a defensive stance. "You realize how dangerous this is. You're trying to take money from a man who has grown very rich from doing exactly the same thing to other people. He's going to be savvy to all the tricks, know all the angles. He'll know something is wrong the second you make the smallest mistake. From what you've said, he can be violent. If you corner a man like this, he'll strike back. You know all these things." It was a statement, not a question.

"Edward Brand stole almost fourteen million dollars from me," Taylor said. "He inserted a man into my life who became my husband. He humiliated me."

"I know this," Ricardo said. "That wasn't the point I was making."

"I know what your point is," Taylor said. "Brand is all that and more. He's dangerous. Extremely dangerous. And he's smart. But we've got three things going for us that might give us what we need to pull this off. Straight off the top, Brand doesn't know we've tracked him down and that we know where he is and who he is. He thinks I'm visiting a friend in Houston. To him, I'm a nonentity. That complacency works well for us. It makes me invisible, and if I'm invisible, so is Kelly."

"All right. He doesn't know you're setting him up. He'll still be suspicious of any opportunity that's dropped in his lap."

"True, but what happens if we don't drop it directly in Brand's lap?"

"What do you mean?"

"Before Alan went over the cliff at La Laguna, Brand made a phone call from a restaurant just down the road. We suspect he was calling someone to make sure the scuba divers were in place. We tracked the number to its owner. The man's name is Carlos Valendez, and he lives in Cabo San Lucas. He's our connection to Edward Brand."

"So that's the person I'll be approaching," Ricardo said.

"Yes."

Ricardo nodded and raised an eyebrow. "That's good. Then once I've pitched the idea to Carlos, he goes to Brand and sells him on it. That's very good."

"Thanks," Taylor said.

"Okay, you've removed us one layer from Brand and you know a lot more about him than he is aware of. That's one thing. You said there were three things—what are the other two?"

"Brand has an FBI agent on his payroll. Brent Hawkins is the guy. He's based out of San Francisco, and he's probably the resource Brand is using to watch me. But they have no idea we've managed to link the two."

"You know for sure this Hawkins fellow is dirty?" Ricardo asked.

"Positive. Because they don't know that we know, we can manipulate him."

Ricardo's arms uncrossed, and he leaned forward. "How do you manipulate an FBI agent?"

Kelly answered. "By giving him classified information on the Monte Alban excavation that no one else is privy to. Details of the American government's discovery of unrecorded ruins at the site—ruins that are still overgrown with dense jungle. Satellite information showing new formations, gravity and magnetic studies pinpointing exactly where these ruins are. Then a report by a clandestine CIA operation showing exactly where an undiscovered tomb is located and what is inside."

"And what *is* inside?" Ricardo asked. "A wonderful cache of gold and gems?"

"Precisely."

Ricardo shook his head. "Is what you're saying true? Is there such information on the American computers?"

"No."

"Then this doesn't work. It's impossible."

"Not really," Kelly said.

"Why?"

"Because of the third little trick up our sleeve. I work at the National Security Agency."

A slow smile spread across the handsome Mexican's face. His gaze flickered back and forth between Taylor and Kelly. Finally he said, "You can make this data appear on the CIA database?"

Kelly nodded.

Again, the smile. He picked up his coffee cup and drained the last of the dark roast. He leaned forward, his elbows on the table. "Then maybe what you are planning is possible."

"Maybe," Taylor said. "Keep in mind one more thing."

"What's that?" Ricardo asked.

"Determination. Getting this guy is high on my list."

"Motivation is important." Ricardo pursed his lips and tilted his head ever so slightly to the side. "Yes, motivation is very important."

Taylor stared straight into his eyes. "I won't be denied, Ricardo. I'll get this son of a bitch."

"Perhaps," Ricardo said slowly. "That remains to be seen."

CHAPTER FORTY-TWO

Taylor and Kelly flew Aeroméxico from Mexico City to Oaxaca City on Saturday, December 23. They found a taxi near the front door and gave the driver the name of the hotel, marveling at the drive through Oaxaca City. The pale green stone used in the construction of most buildings, including the cathedral, reflected the midday light, giving the street scenes a surreal feel. Colonnades lined *zócalo*, the main square, which was busy with locals shopping at the colorful kiosks, most set up under large acacia trees that provided shade from the hot sun. Mariachis played on the street corners. The people were dark skinned and mainly of Indian heritage—Zapotec and Mixtec the dominant ancestry. Tributes to Benito Juárez, the Oaxaca native who was the first full-blooded Indian to achieve the presidency of the republic, were everywhere. Restaurants were just gearing up for *comida corrida*, the traditional midday meal, and children excited by the prospect of Christ's upcoming birthday skipped over the cobblestones. It was a series of scenes out of a glossy tourist brochure.

Their driver deposited them at the Camino Real

Oaxaca, which was at one time the Convento de Santa Catalina de Siena, and which still retained the original charm and simplicity of the convent. They checked in using Kelly's credit card. The front desk clerk was a dapper man in his late sixties who spoke passable English. He had one of the warmest smiles Taylor had ever seen. When they requested separate rooms, he gave them a look that was easily interpreted as *youth is wasted on young people*. He had a young boy, no more than twelve, carry their bags to their rooms. After they washed up and finished lunch in the attached restaurant, they flagged down a passing taxi and told him they wished to visit Monte Alban.

The road to the site of the ancient Zapotec ruins was narrow and winding, rising to a plateau overlooking the Oaxaca Valley, where Yagul and Mitla, two other archeological digs from the second century, were situated a few miles to the south. The view from atop the 5,000-plus-foot plateau was stunning, the arid valley floor snaking between the mountain ranges to the far horizon. They drove past the museum and into the parking lot at the north end of the excavation, and their driver parked in a spot reserved for taxis. Kelly asked the man to wait, and he simply nodded, switched off the ignition and pulled his hat down over his eyes. He was asleep before they were out of the parking lot.

They stopped in the museum and picked up a couple of glossy books, one of which gave an accurate plot plan of the known ruins. They followed a well-worn path to the north mound, close to where the sealed tomb of Tumba 7 was located. To their right was a series of four buildings called the north palaces, and stretching in front of them to the south was the central plaza. Sketchy grass eked out an existence on the hard, rocky ground, and a solitary tree grew opposite the Juego de Pelota, or Ball Court, where the ancient tribes had held a game in which the losers were sacrificed to the gods. The Zapotecs had built the complex following an orderly north-south axis. Remnants of the buildings, most of them pyramids of stone with inlaid stairs, covered a rectangular area about six hundred and fifty yards long and three hundred wide. Under the barren rock, almost devoid of topsoil, was a series of intricate tunnels, linking the different buildings and giving access to many of the subterranean tombs. The majority of the tunnels had yet to be excavated. The most celebrated building, the Galería de las Danzantes, or the Dancer's Gallery, was two-thirds of the distance to the south, close to the massive south platform that dominated the excavation. The walls of the gallery were engraved with hundreds of figures, their faces twisted in grotesque agony—tortured captives of the Zapotecs. The ones used for the ritual human sacrifices.

Taylor and Kelly walked the site, taking their time to get the lay of the land. Small stones crunched under their boots as they strolled across the same sacred grounds that had felt bare Zapotec and Mixtec feet some two thousand years ago. The complexity of the construction and its ability to weather the elements for so many centuries wasn't lost on either of them. Monte Alban was an amazing testament to the ancient tribes who had cut the stones and painstakingly placed them atop each other.

"What do you think?" Kelly asked as they finished touring the entire site and stood again at the north end. "Where's the best place to put our newly discovered tomb?"

"I don't know. It's so wide open. It's going to be difficult to hide what we're doing. The guards will see us."

"There are a couple of things we know for sure," Kelly said, looking back over the complex. "Tumba Seven was the most prolific tomb discovered on the site, and it's here, at the far north end. It would make sense to pick a location somewhere close to that. The only problem is that the north end of the complex is the busiest." He pointed to the parking lot and the museum, which were a short distance from the closed tomb. "Lots of people about."

"True, but when we have Brand show up to remove the treasure, we'll do it at night. So we don't have to worry about tourists milling around. Just the guards."

"I wonder how well patrolled this place is at night," Kelly said.

"My guess would be one or two men. I mean, it's not like they're guarding a stack of gold. All that's here is a bunch of ruins. Anything of value is inside the museum, and it'll be locked up tight at night. There is no gold or jewels in the museum, just masks and stone artifacts."

Kelly nodded. "So it should be fairly easy to distract the guards. We arrange for some sort of commotion at the far south end of the complex. They hustle down there, which gives us at least ten minutes by the time they get to the far end and back."

"A fire?" Taylor offered. "There's some sagebrush and dry twigs down at that end that could burn if we gave it a little incentive."

"That's a good idea. So the guards are gone, down at the other end of the complex. Then what?"

"We need to know exactly where we want the fake tomb to be. We need to have the electronic gear in place to track his account numbers when he makes the call to transfer the money to the Mexican official."

"Ricardo will supply the official," Kelly said. At their meeting in Mexico City, Ricardo had indicated he had two men who could help work the scam. One would watch the *Mary Dyer* in its berth in Puerto Vallarta; another would pose as the Mexican official who needed to be bribed in order to get the treasure out of the tomb. Ricardo had dug into the personnel files of the Department of Antiquities in Mexico City and determined which name to use. It was Manuel Sanchez, Director of Antiquities for the Mexican government. Sanchez was out of the office for the first week of January, not uncommon as many employees were off on holidays over the Christmas break. That worked well for them. Ricardo had also begun the procedure of getting the false identity card in Sanchez's name. In return for assuring these two men, Taylor and Kelly had bumped Ricardo's guaranteed dollar amount to a quarter million. Ricardo himself would work the Cabo San Lucas angle and hook Carlos Valendez. Then, with Valendez vouching for him, Ricardo would meet Edward Brand in person. At that point, the success of the con rested entirely on Ricardo's shoulders.

Taylor pointed to the north edge of the plateau. "All the houses where the population lived and most of the tombs were dug into the sides of the mesa. Let's have a look over there and see if that would work." As they walked, she said, "What do you think of Ricardo? You think he's trustworthy?"

Kelly shrugged. "We need him, or someone like him. He's the only guy we know. He's well connected, very suave and likes the idea of pulling a few million dollars out of this. I don't think we're going to do any better."

"So you're saying you think he's a good choice."

"I am. I like him. I think I trust him. Remember, he has to trust us as well. If we manage to get Brand's account number and his password, we've got the money. We're nowhere in sight. He and two of his men are the ones with their asses on the line. We could just leave them hanging and take off with the money."

"We'd never do that," Taylor said, as they reached the edge of the plateau, the valley stretching northward beneath them.

"We know that, but he doesn't. He's trusting us more than we're trusting him. Keep in mind that he has to meet Brand face-to-face and sell him on the idea. As I see it, we've got the good end of the deal here. Ricardo's the one who stands to lose the most."

"You thinking that Brand might kill him?" Taylor asked.

"In a second. If Edward Brand thinks he's getting screwed, he'll react. He won't think twice about killing Ricardo and everyone working with him. Think back, Taylor. We both know Edward Brand. We've both sat across the table from him. We've looked into his eyes. He's not a nice man."

"He's ruthless," Taylor agreed. "His eyes are cold."

"Ice," Kelly said.

They peered over the edge. There were a few well-worn but treacherous trails leading down the mountainside. They started down, careful with their footing. The stone stairs were carved into the solid rock and grooved from the impact of millions of feet over the centuries. Zapotec mothers and fathers and children returning to their hillside homes after visiting the sacred plateau. Centuries ago. A people now long dead, only their architecture remaining to tell the world of their culture. Taylor led the way, clutching the rock wall on her left where possible. A tumble over the edge would be painful, bouncing off a few rocks before becoming embedded in one of the many crags lining the hillside, possibly even fatal. Caution was the word of the day.

They crisscrossed the rocky slope for an hour, amazed at the complexity of the caves and tombs embedded in the stone. Many had been pried open and excavated, but there were sections of the mountainside that could easily hold hidden entrances to undiscovered tombs. Selling Edward Brand on the existence of a tomb laden with treasure somewhere on this site was no long shot. In fact, if it were not for the moratorium placed on further excavations by the Mexican government, Monte Alban would most likely be a busy place. The treasure removed from Tumba 7 was legendary, and the monetary value of the artifacts in the tens of millions of dollars. For their purposes, Monte Alban was perfect.

"What about this?" Taylor said, standing on an ex-

ceedingly narrow stretch of smooth rock. Next to her was
what appeared to be a huge boulder fitted into an opening in the stone wall. At the foot of the boulder was a
small hole, just large enough for a person to crawl
through. Kelly peered in through the hole. It was too
dark to see much, but there appeared to be a cave of
some sort in the cliff. Lying parallel to the sheer wall, he
dropped to his belly and slithered through the opening
and into the cave. Taylor waited on the ledge.

"Can you see anything?" she called into the hole.

"A bit," came the muffled reply. "There's some light
filtering through the opening. I'm just waiting for my
eyes to adjust." A minute later, he continued. "It's a cave,
about twenty feet deep by eight feet high. And it seems to
go farther back into the mountainside. I'm going to have
a look."

There was a few minutes of silence. Then Kelly's head
poked out of the hole, and he dragged the rest of his
body through, careful to stay on the ledge. He pulled
himself up on his feet and brushed the dust off his
clothes.

"We've got a winner. The first chamber is pretty big,
but in behind it is a smaller series of rooms. We could set
up a few gold-painted artifacts in one of the narrow entrances to the smaller chambers, then cover the rocks
with tarps, and it would look like the room was jammed
with treasure. We just need to be sure Brand can't see too
well when he's inside, and that Ricardo gets him in and
out really fast. In to see the treasure, out to make the call
to transfer the money to the Mexican official's account. I
doubt if a satellite phone could get a dial tone that deep
inside the rock, so he'll have to come back out. Once he's
made the call, it's just a matter of getting Ricardo and his
men out before Brand catches on."

"If he goes back in after he's made the call, can we trap
him somehow?"

"Maybe. If we had some sort of metal bar we could

wedge into the ground and secure from this side, he would be stuck. We'll have to get Ricardo down here to see what he thinks."

"Christ, Kelly, this is scary," Taylor said, glancing about. The location was dangerous, set on the side of an unforgiving mountainside, and their prey was wary and intelligent. Timing would be tight, almost to the second. Kelly would have to intercept the phone call to Brand's bank, record the account number and the password, then make another call to the bank to transfer the remaining funds to their account. That transfer and account would have to be completely untraceable. The odds of pulling it off, even if they *were* to get Edward Brand to the cave entrance, were marginal. The degree of difficulty staggering.

"I think scary is a mild word," Kelly said. "Insane might be a bit closer."

CHAPTER FORTY-THREE

Ricardo Allende was completely focused on his task. He needed two men he could trust to work the con with the Americans. He needed the con to work. He had not been entirely honest with Kelly and Taylor about his motivation. Dangerous was good, and he was looking forward to pulling off the con. But his real motivation was money. Pure and simple. He desperately needed money. His business was floundering, due to a steady flow of cash going to his bookie every Friday. He had made a few bad choices on the horses, then compounded that with a disastrous series of bets on a handful of Mexican soccer teams. The tab was at three hundred thousand American dollars and rising quickly as the interest accrued. The hole was deep and getting deeper.

Then divine providence had dropped Taylor Simons and Kelly Kramer in his lap. How or why, he had no idea. He had learned many years ago to trust the Lord when He chose to smile on His loyal subjects. Although Ricardo knew he wasn't the most loyal—he hadn't graced the inside of a cathedral for almost ten years—he felt he was still in God's good books. What else could explain two Americans showing up with a crazy scheme that might just work, right when he needed it.

It was Saturday afternoon, and Taylor and Kelly would be in Oaxaca by now. He was far from his usual stomping ground of Zona Rosa, in one of the many low- to middle-class districts that make up the congested maze of Mexico City. He crossed Héroes de Granaditas heading north and made two quick right turns, pulling up in front of a four-story colonial-style apartment building. He locked his car and skipped up the stairs to the third floor and knocked on the second door on the right. There were no markings on the door. A moment later there was the sound of the latch sliding back, and the door swung open. The man was expecting him.

"*Hola*, Ricardo," he said. He was fair skinned, about fifty-five and clean cut. Reading glasses hung on a cord about his neck. His body and face were lean but not muscular, the mark of a man with either a high metabolism or a perpetual lack of pesos to buy fattening items at the local supermarket. His name was Adolfo and his metabolism was normal.

"Good morning, Adolfo," Ricardo replied. He followed the older man into the apartment. It was small and very basic—a kitchen table with two chairs and a solitary couch facing an older RCA color television. The set was turned off, and the room was quiet except for the neighbors fighting next door. The woman's voice was shrill and carried through the wall like it didn't exist.

"They don't like each other much," Adolfo said, sitting on the couch and pointing for his guest to follow suit. Adolfo's space was small, but it was clean.

Ricardo sat. "How are things? I haven't seen you for, what, a month or more?"

"Almost two months," Adolfo said, crossing his legs and smoothing his dark pants. His clothes were as clean as his apartment and well pressed. "You didn't sound like this was a social visit when you called. What can I help you with?"

Ricardo cleared his throat. "This is going to sound a little off the wall, but I need you to help me relieve an American of some money."

Adolfo grinned. "You always know how to make me smile."

"Got any coffee?"

"Of course. Give me a minute to brew some." He disappeared into the tiny kitchen and returned a few minutes later with two cups of freshly ground dark roast.

"Thanks," Ricardo said. His friend made the best coffee in Mexico City. He sipped the liquid, the taste sweet on his tongue. "I've got a proposition for you. It might be dangerous, but it could also be very profitable."

"I'm listening."

"I'll skip the preamble, but the gist is that I've worked a deal with two Americans who want to take another *gringo* for a substantial amount of money. They're offering a modest amount just for trying, whether they get any money or not. But the payday goes up quite a bit if they're successful."

"What sort of money are we talking about?" Adolfo said, lighting a cigarette and offering one to Ricardo.

Ricardo waved away the cigarette. "I quit." He sipped the coffee and smiled. "Christ, you make excellent coffee." Another sip, then, "Two thousand American dollars just to say yes. Fifty thousand dollars if they hit the mother lode."

Adolfo's eyes grew considerably. "Fifty thousand?"

"Fifty thousand. Minimum. Could be more."

Sweat beaded on his brow and he dabbed at it with a neatly pressed handkerchief. "What is it that I have to do?"

"I need someone to pose as a high-ranking government official. A man who wants money for turning his head when some artifacts go missing from the Monte Alban ruins near Oaxaca City."

"That's it?"

"That's it, but it could be dangerous."

"How dangerous?"

"The American they're trying to scam is a violent man. If he smells a rat, we could be in big trouble."

"We? You're there as well."

"I would think so, yes. My job is to get the *gringo* to Monte Alban to meet with you. Then you demand a certain amount of money for turning a blind eye. He pays you electronically by transferring the cash to an offshore account. You disappear. Quickly. Then so do I before he realizes what has happened."

"And we keep the money."

Ricardo nodded. No sense muddying the waters with the absolute truth. And if Adolfo knew that the half million dollars that was being wired was simply fodder, he may want to try and keep it. That would leave a trail back to him. Ultimately back to all of them. No, it was better if Adolfo thought the half million dollars was the goal. It kept things simple.

"When do you need me?"

"The Americans I'm working with are in Monte Alban now. I think they want to move quickly. Perhaps just into the new year."

"For fifty thousand dollars, I can be very flexible."

"Like a gymnast."

"Yes," Adolfo said, grinning. "More coffee?"

"Yes, please."

Ricardo leaned back into the couch and looked around the tiny room. There were a few pieces of bric-a-brac, none of it worth more than a few pesos. It was depressing. But what wasn't depressing was that he had the first of the two men he needed to work the con. And the most important. He had seen Adolfo in action many times over the years. The man was a natural liar. Not that that was a bad thing—there was just a time and a place for such things. This was an ideal time. None better.

He had one of the two, one more to go. The second man would be easy—the one to watch Edward Brand on his yacht in Puerto Vallarta. Things would come together quickly. He needed them to. Or he'd be facing his bookie with no money in his hands. A dangerous thing to do, especially in Mexico City.

Adolfo returned with fresh coffee, and they talked about the details. Ricardo watched his friend get more and more animated as they discussed what was involved, and he realized that although it was dangerous, it was possible. One thought ran through Ricardo's mind again and again as they talked.

Ten percent of fifty million.

CHAPTER FORTY-FOUR

The thirteenth floor of 450 Golden Gate Avenue was quiet on Sunday morning, one day before Christmas. Only one man was in the San Francisco offices of the FBI, and he was hunched over a computer watching the results of his request to the Bureau's mainframe. A series of characters scrolled across the screen, and he smiled. Taylor Simons was still in Houston. In the last twenty-four hours she had used her credit card twice. Once at a women's boutique, the total damage just over three hundred dollars. There was a charge for eighty-seven dollars at Charley's 517, a popular Houston steak and seafood restaurant on Louisiana Street.

Brent Hawkins killed the screen and initiated another program. The logo for a Cayman Islands bank appeared. He clicked on Internet banking and input his account number and password, then held his breath as the system pulled up his balances. A slow smile spread across his face as he read the numbers. Edward Brand had finally deposited the eight hundred and fifty thousand dollars they had agreed on. Those funds brought his balance to just over one-point-five million. Not bad for a government employee. Then the image of Alicia Walker, dead in her bathtub, flashed through his mind. It wiped the smile from his face. He closed the link to the bank and signed off.

Outside the FBI offices, the December air coming off the bay was cold. He buttoned his coat against the chill and walked briskly to his car. Once he was out of the wind, he placed a call to Edward Brand's cell phone. It rang a few times, and then Brand's distinctive voice came over the line.

"Simons is still in Houston," he said after they had exchanged hellos.

"Good. I don't trust that woman. Keep watching her."

"That's not a problem." There was a brief silence. "Thanks for sending the money."

"You earned it," Brand said.

Again, the image of Alicia Walker's bloated face, floating in her bathtub flashed through his mind. "Sure. I earned it."

"Kelly Kramer, Taylor's friend in Washington. What's he up to?"

"No idea. I'm only watching her credit cards."

"Maybe we should keep an eye on him as well."

"I told you, Edward. That's dangerous. You mess with anyone tied in with the NSA or the CIA and you've got problems. These guys have resources you can only dream about. You start putting tracers on them or their lives, and they find out. And once they know you're watching them, they want to know why. Watching Kelly Kramer is a very bad idea."

"Okay," Brand said. "But I don't like that Taylor Simons is tied in with him."

"He worked for her. That's it. They were friends. You met Kramer when you were setting Taylor up. You know what he's like. He's a geek. A numbers guy. Harmless."

"Don't ever label people as harmless, Brent. Because

that's how you get bit in the ass. No one who works for the NSA is harmless."

"All right. I get what you're saying, but you've got to believe me when I tell you that spying on this guy in any manner is really bad business. We leave him alone unless we see him and Taylor linking up again."

There was a total silence, and Brent Hawkins swallowed heavily as he realized he had just told Edward Brand what to do. That wasn't something that rested well with Brand. He was a man who made decisions, not took orders. He was wealthy and ruthless. Rich enough and crazy enough to give some faceless person a lump of money and a picture of an FBI agent in San Francisco who had stepped over the line. Hawkins thought seriously about retracting the last statement, but didn't. Brand hated weak people almost as much as he hated being told what to do. Dealing with Edward Brand was like walking down the center line on a busy highway.

"If you think leaving Kelly Kramer alone is the best thing to do, then that's what we'll do," Brand finally said. His voice was curt.

"I do, Edward," Hawkins said, perhaps just a bit too quickly.

"Don't lose track of Taylor Simons."

"I won't."

"Good-bye."

The line died, and Brent Hawkins closed his cell phone. Jesus, how could he be so stupid? Pissing off Edward Brand was beyond dumb. It was suicidal. He started his car and pulled away from the curb. Home to no one. No wife, no kids, no life. Maybe he should retire, buy a little place down south, somewhere in the Caribbean. Live the quiet life. Walk to the local bar each day and sip Coronas in the shade, watching the waves come in and talking with the locals about nothing. Maybe. He'd give it some thought.

Right now he had a commitment that couldn't be set

aside. Edward Brand was wary of Taylor Simons. He considered her to be a threat. Although he didn't agree with Brand, he didn't want to piss the man off any more than he already had. So until Brand decided that everything was copasetic, his job was to keep tabs on the woman.

Not a problem.

CHAPTER FORTY-FIVE

Christmas day dawned with little celebration for Taylor and Kelly. They were thousands of miles from family and friends, in a foreign country where the language and customs were different. Breakfast was surprisingly depressing. Despite having each other's company, they both felt alone and disassociated. After they had eaten, they ventured into the city, and their day quickly changed.

The streets were alive with natives in traditional garb celebrating the birth of Christ. The oldest street market, *Central de Abastos*, was a mecca of activity and bargains. Multicolored chilies were the preferred vegetable of the day, and tropical fruit was piled high in many of the stalls. Poor-quality audio tapes, obviously bootlegs, were blasting as each vendor tried to attract the festive shoppers. Tastefully painted and fired pottery, glossy black and shimmering green, was plentiful. And throughout the market the mood was one of love and acceptance. Every person they ran into, every street vendor they spoke halting English with, all wished them a wonderful day. An hour into their foray onto the cobblestone streets, Taylor and Kelly felt at home in the strange city.

By eight that evening, when they finally poured themselves back into the lobby of their hotel, they both agreed on one thing. It was the most interesting and fun Christmas either of them had ever had.

They settled into the bar, tucked away in a grassy alcove that was once the convent's courtyard. The waiter brought drinks and wished them a merry Christmas. He offered them a menu, but they waved it off, having eaten more than enough over the course of the day. Kelly pushed the slice of lime through the thin neck of the bottle and tipped back his Corona. He drained almost half of the beer and set the bottle on the table.

"Now that was fun," he said.

"A Christmas we'll never forget," Taylor agreed. "I don't think I've ever met nicer people."

"Mexicans get a bad rap," Kelly said. "Most of them are wonderful people. You get a few bad apples that really screw it up for the rest. I suppose that's true of almost any culture."

There was a minute or two of silence as they both looked about the courtyard and listened to the gurgling sound of the water as it trickled down the fountain that dominated the small space. The rough stone walls were mostly covered with creeping plants, their leaves vibrant green in the pale moonlight. The setting was peaceful after a hectic day.

"I wonder how Ricardo is doing," Taylor said.

Kelly shrugged. "He'll be here tomorrow. We'll find out then."

"I hope he's trustworthy."

"So do I. If we've decided he's our guy, then we have to trust him. We can't jump halfway in the water. We're either in or out."

"We're in," Taylor said. "I just hope we're in with the right guy."

"You're just second-guessing yourself. When we first decided we needed someone of Mexican descent to hook Edward Brand, you had no qualms about contacting him."

She smiled. "Yeah, you're right. Look where thinking things over can get you. Paranoid."

They spent another two hours sitting in the quiet garden, talking and sipping on Coronas and cognac before retiring for the night. When they rose the next morning and headed down for breakfast, the polite man who worked the front desk had a message for them. It was from Ricardo Allende. He would be arriving in Oaxaca City at four-fifteen that afternoon.

They spent the day reviewing their plan and revisited Monte Alban, walking the site one more time. Clouds had moved in from the neighboring valleys and the plateau was engulfed in wet mist. With no warmth from the sun and at such a high altitude, it was bone-chilling cold atop the mountain. They drove back about three and had the taxi take them to the airport. At four-thirty-five Ricardo appeared at the main doorway leading from the arrivals area. He saw Kelly leaning against the cab and waved.

"*Amigo*," Ricardo said as he reached the taxi. He shook Kelly's hand and they slipped in the car as the driver loaded the luggage. The conversation was generic during the drive, talking about Christmas and family, but it changed quickly when they reached the hotel and settled into the private gardens of the courtyard. The trickling water helped mute their conversation, although that was hardly necessary as they were the only guests in the area.

"I've arranged for the other two men we need," Ricardo said. "I have a man who is perfect for the government official. His name is Adolfo, and he's in his mid-fifties, very conservative looking and quite formal. He is also a very good actor. I've seen him talk his way through lots of circumstances. On occasion, dangerous circumstances."

"Excellent," Taylor said, her feelings of distrust in Ricardo waning quickly. "And the other man?"

"A barrio rat from Mexico City who can blend in to almost any background. He is absolutely trustworthy—when money is on the table. He is on his way to Puerto Vallarta today and when he finds the *Mary Dyer* he'll call me on a cell phone I gave him. I bought him a new set of clothes for the plane flight and arranged for him to stay at Posada de Roger, a low-end hotel just a few blocks from Playa los Muertos. He'll have to take a bus to the marina every day, but that's not a problem. Once he's there, he'll change back into his street clothes, which will allow him to blend in totally at the marina. There are plenty of wharf rats about. He'll just be another one."

"He'll watch the *Mary Dyer* and report back to you?" Kelly asked.

"That's his job. For what I'm paying him, he'll be there eighteen to twenty hours a day. To him the daily rate I'm paying is like hitting the lottery. He's never stayed at a hotel in his life. Even a modest one like the Posada de Roger is a real thrill."

"So we've got eyes watching Edward Brand as of this afternoon," Taylor said. "Good."

Ricardo nodded. "Yes."

"We've been up to Monte Alban twice," Kelly said, "and I think we've found the right location to place the treasure." He pulled out the glossy tourist book and opened it to a page showing the layout of the ancient Zapotec ruins. He pointed to the north end of the site, close to where Tumba 7 had been discovered. "This is the area where most of the real treasure was found. The entire mountaintop is a labyrinth of underground tunnels and caves, most of which have never been explored. We've found one here, just over the edge of the plateau. It's accessible through a tiny hole in the side of the mountain, just large enough to crawl through. It shouldn't be hard to find a stone that will fit the opening. We can jam it in just before Brand shows up. That way the find looks authentic."

"What's inside the cave?"

"We thought that we'd make up a few fake artifacts, paint them gold and stick them in the back of the cave. There's absolutely no light inside, and when you take Brand to the site, you only have a low-voltage flashlight with you. That way he doesn't get a really good look at the loot."

"Let's see if I've got this right," Ricardo said, setting his tea on the table. "I hook Brand, get him to the site where we meet with the government official who needs to be bribed. Brand takes a quick look inside the sealed chamber, sees the treasure and makes the call to transfer the money to the official's account. That about it?"

"In a nutshell," Kelly said.

"What?" Ricardo. "What's with the nutshell?"

"Figure of speech, Ricardo. Your English is so good I sometimes forget your mother tongue is Spanish. It means a shortened version of the story—small enough to fit in a nutshell. You got it."

"Ah, I see. In a nutshell. I'll have to remember that one." He took a sip of tea, then refilled his cup from the teapot. "What happens to the money once it's transferred?"

"I intercept it," Kelly said.

"From Monte Alban?" Ricardo asked, surprised.

"No, from Washington. I'll need the resources at the National Security Agency to do my end of things. I'll be in the United States, at my desk at the NSA."

Ricardo was silent. Then he looked at Taylor and said, "Where will you be?"

"Oaxaca City. Mexico City. Washington. I don't think it matters where I am. It's Kelly who has to be at his computer. At the point where Edward Brand is looking in the tomb and initiating the transfer of money, my end of things is covered."

Ricardo gave Taylor a wry smile. "It would be nice if you were close by. Just in case."

"Just in case?" Taylor asked.

Ricardo stirred a touch of cream in his tea and tasted it. "It occurs to me that I'm putting a lot of trust in you two. Kelly is safe in Washington with the money. I am only a few feet from the man who has just been ripped off. I have to get myself and Adolfo out of Monte Alban before Brand discovers he's been tricked. If I don't, chances are there will be violence. Someone could get shot. I would be very upset if that someone was me. Maybe so upset that I would be dead."

He stopped and looked long and hard at both Taylor and Kelly. "My ass is on the line," he continued. "I would feel much more comfortable with the situation if Ms. Simons was to remain in Mexico. In Oaxaca City to be precise. There would be a feeling of comfort knowing one of you is on the front line with Adolfo and me."

Taylor accepted his condition before Kelly could object. "Agreed. I understand where you're coming from. Most of the risk is falling on your shoulders. I don't mind staying close by."

Ricardo smiled and nodded. "Fine. Then I feel comfortable with the arrangements. Now, when are we going to have a look at Monte Alban? At the cave you have picked for our treasure."

"Tomorrow okay?" Taylor asked. "In the daylight. That's probably best."

"Tomorrow is fine."

The waiter dropped by and Ricardo ordered a round of Coronas. When the beers arrived, he held his up. "To our success," he said.

They clinked bottles and drank.

CHAPTER FORTY-SIX

The clouds refused to clear, and December 27 was wet and cold atop the mountain. The ruins of Monte Alban were shrouded in heavy mist, and the wind was biting as it cut through jackets and jeans. Taylor tucked her long hair up into her hat and pulled it down over her ears. Hardly the same Mexico she knew from lying on warm sandy beaches at the coastal resorts.

They walked abreast across the long open stretch of anemic grass and rocky outcrops, past the ancient structures built to appease the gods through human sacrifice. As an occasional whisper of wind sliced through the narrow cracks in the rocks, Taylor envisioned dying men and women, their voices crying for mercy as their captors disemboweled them on the cold slabs. Mercy that never came. Just death. The ruins took on a very different look when one actually thought about the horrors inflicted on helpless victims so many hundreds of years ago. Perhaps their spirits still clung to the rocks. Perhaps not.

The trio reached the massive South Platform at the far end of the complex. They peered over the edge of the plateau toward the valley floor. The mountainside was rugged, with giant slabs of stone jutting from the steep embankment. There were many places where a wrongly placed footstep would result in a tumble down the cliff side and certain death. Even in daylight it was treacherous. At night, with only moonlight to guide a person foolhardy enough to walk the edge of the cliff, it would be almost suicidal.

Ricardo sat on one of the exposed rocks and pointed at the edge. "That's a nasty drop."

"Fatal," Kelly agreed.

"And this is where you want to light the fire to distract the guards," he said.

"Yes. It has to be down at this end of the plateau. That will give us five or ten minutes to give Brand a quick look in the cave and for him to make the call."

"Who is going to light the fire?" Ricardo asked. "Adolfo will be with Edward Brand and I at the cave. My other man will still be in Puerto Vallarta. He needs to stay until Brand is on the airplane to Oaxaca. And, Kelly, you'll be at your desk in Washington. That leaves us one person short."

"I'll still be in Oaxaca," Taylor said. "I can light it."

Kelly shook his head immediately. "No way. It's too dangerous. Once you light it, you'll have to duck over the edge and make your way back to the north end by skirting the plateau. The side of the mountain is covered with rocks, and lots of them are loose. If you miss one foothold you'll die."

"Who else do we have?" Taylor said. "Ricardo is already here, not in Mexico City. He doesn't know anyone in Oaxaca City well enough to bring them in. Unless we want to put things off by a week or two, I'll have to light the fire. And every delay we have is more time for Brand to pull anchor and sail out of the marina at Puerto Vallarta. I don't want to risk losing him."

Kelly was silent. Ricardo said, "Taylor's right. She's

the only one we've got if we want to stay on any sort of schedule."

"Keeps her close to you as well," Kelly said to Ricardo.

"Anywhere in Oaxaca is fine with me," Ricardo replied evenly. "She doesn't need to be at the ruins. But this makes sense."

Kelly shook his head. "I don't like it."

Ricardo was silent, giving Kelly's last statement the consideration it deserved. Then he said, "Is there cell phone service up here?"

Taylor shook her head. "No. We already thought of that and asked at the local phone provider. The only way to take a call or place a call from on top of the plateau is by satellite phone."

"Do you have one?" Ricardo asked.

Taylor nodded. "We had them set up an account."

"I'll need the number," Ricardo said.

Taylor nodded and started walking north, toward where she and Kelly had found the hole in the side of the mountain. "Let's have a look at the cave."

They walked the six hundred yards from one end of the excavation to the other in relative silence, alone with their thoughts. This was where it would play out. This was the place they had chosen to go up against Edward Brand. The plan was fraught with danger, especially considering Brand's tendency to violence. An FBI agent had stood in his way and he'd had her murdered—shot to death in her own bathtub. Killing a couple of people who were trying to rip him off would be nothing to this man. And he would probably be armed. Brand was coming into Oaxaca from Puerto Vallarta, and that meant he didn't have to cross an international border. Whatever weapons he had aboard the *Mary Dyer* would undoubtedly be with him. Nothing about the upcoming venture was very comforting.

They reached the far end of the plateau and skirted the museum and Tumba 7 before making their way to the edge of the cliff. Kelly led the way along the thin path carved into the mountainside by countless bare feet over thousands of years. Moving in single file, they reached the section of the cliff where Kelly and Taylor had found the hidden cave. Kelly got down on his belly and crawled into the dark space, Ricardo immediately behind him. Kelly flipped on the flashlight he had brought, as did Ricardo, the beams of yellow light playing off the walls and the floors. It was rugged inside the cave, the walls jagged with exposed rocks that hadn't been worn smooth by water or wind. The floor was slippery and uneven, treacherous footing even with the flashlights. Ricardo nodded his approval as they moved from the main cave into the smaller ones deeper in the mountain.

"This is perfect," he said. "Very believable. We just need to put a few pieces of treasure in here and cover the opening." He allowed himself a small smile. "This might work."

"It better," Taylor said, venom in her words. "He's a prick. He deserves this."

Kelly shone his light into the smaller spaces to the rear. "This one is good," he said. "The opening is tiny. It'll be difficult for Brand to get inside and have a good look at the treasure. But your government official has got to get him in and out of here fast. Very fast. If he has any length of time to look things over, he'll know he's being scammed."

"Adolfo will keep things under control. I trust his abilities."

"Good," Kelly said. "Have you seen enough?"

"I'm fine. Let's get a rock to cover that hole. Then we need to pick up some Zapotec and Mixtec masks and goblets that we can gold plate."

"You don't think we could just paint them?" Taylor asked.

Ricardo shook his head. "No way. If you paint directly on top of ceramic and he touches one of those pieces he'll know. If it's gold plated, it'll feel real."

"Where the hell do we get something gold plated?" Kelly asked.

Ricardo smiled. "This is Mexico, *amigo*. With the right connections, anything is possible."

"You have the right connections?"

"Of course."

They crawled back through the tiny opening and went in search of a stone to jam in the hole. It took the better part of two hours to find one that fit, but once it was in place it was almost impossible to see anything but a slight fissure in the rocks. They tried prying it out once to see how long it would take. Six minutes, just to get the stone out and rolled a few feet down the path. They replaced the rock and returned to the parking lot. Their driver was asleep, the windows rolled down to keep some air moving through the parked car. Ricardo rattled off some staccato Spanish, and the man jerked awake and started the car. The first few turns down the windy mountain road were interesting as he continued to wake up. They reached Oaxaca City without incident and split up. Ricardo went in search of a local craftsman to take care of the gold plating, and Kelly and Taylor scoured the local shops for pieces of Zapotec art.

Time was moving ahead, closing in on the day when Edward Brand would arrive at Monte Alban. With each passing hour, the tension was mounting. They could still back off, let the man go. But to Taylor Simons, that wasn't an option. Edward Brand was going down. She was willing to risk her life on that. Her involvement in the scam had just gone from one of observer to that of active participant. Her role was not only crucial, it was dangerous. She felt a shiver of anticipation creep down her spine as she picked up a Mixtec mask and felt its coarse texture against her skin.

CHAPTER FORTY-SEVEN

Juan Morena had never led a fortunate or privileged life. He was thirty-one years old and had already lost seven teeth to advanced gingivitis. He had the dark skin of the working-class Mestizo, and his hair was matted to his scalp from sweating in the hot sun. His eyes were reluctant to meet a stranger's stare, and he shuffled his feet in worn sandals when he walked. Juan Morena blended in perfectly with the other wharf rats living on the edge of the upscale marina in Puerto Vallarta.

Juan fingered the digital camera through his rags. He had never been entrusted with such an expensive piece of equipment, and he constantly touched it to ensure it hadn't fallen from his pocket onto the dusty earth. Ricardo had paid for his plane fare and his hotel room and had given him the camera and a cellular telephone. All in return for watching a large boat docked in the marina. He had three hundred American dollars under his mattress in his small room in Mexico City. Juan allowed himself a small smile at the thought. Three hundred American dollars. Such a stash was unheard of. Ricardo had promised him another five hundred if he did a good job. Just watch the yacht and report back on any activity. Take pictures of everyone who boarded the boat. So far there had been no guests. But the digital camera came with a cord that attached to the computer back at the hotel, and the pictures could be sent to Ricardo through the computer. He would not do that. It was too complicated. The owner of the hotel would send the pictures, if there were any.

Juan touched the camera again. It was an expensive one, with a zoom lens. He felt a trickle of sweat run down his side, beneath his armpit, a nervous reaction to the thought of what might happen if he lost the camera. He wiped his brow with his right hand and swallowed. What if it was stolen? There were many other wharf rats about who would beat him and pull it from his neck if they knew he had it. He started to shake. Ricardo would be angry.

Juan watched a man walk up to the locked gate that serviced the pier where the *Mary Dyer* was anchored. He called someone on the intercom, and they buzzed him through. He was a *gringo*, with curly blond hair that hung to his shoulders. His shirt was loosened almost to his waist, and Juan could see the taut muscles on his chest and abs. His skin wasn't pasty, but it also was not tanned. He looked like a recent arrival to the sun. Juan stiffened slightly as the newcomer slowed as he approached the *Mary Dyer*. He reached the gangway and hoisted himself up the plank.

Juan fumbled with the camera but managed to get it out from under his rags as the man he knew to be Edward Brand came into view. Juan kept the camera concealed from any prying eyes near him by draping his loose, ragged sleeve over the body but leaving the lens to point at the boat. He kept pushing the button, the camera loading image after image of the two men as they met at the top of the gangplank. They stayed in sight for only a few seconds, then disappeared below the main deck.

Juan slipped the camera back inside his shirt and watched for a few minutes. When there was no further activity, he left the alcove where he hung out during the hot daylight hours and hurried to the main road. A bus pulled up inside five minutes, and he jumped on. The trip to his hotel took under ten minutes.

When he arrived, Juan gave the camera to the hotel manager and watched as the man downloaded the pictures into a file, then forwarded them to the e-mail Ricardo had given him. Juan knew Ricardo and the manager had an agreement in place, but had no idea how much money the man received for sending the pictures. He didn't care.

Once the pictures were in the system and sent ahead to Ricardo, Juan returned to the marina and retook his position next to the Dumpsters that lined the rear wall of the hotel closest to the water. He slid into his alcove and waited. From what he had seen on the computer screen, his shots had been very good. He had managed to get both men's faces on one or two of the shots, just as they were turning to go below to a lower deck. He hoped Ricardo would be pleased. Maybe there would be more money.

CHAPTER FORTY-EIGHT

The jpeg files appeared on Ricardo's laptop computer seconds after Juan sent them. The computer beeped to let the user know a new e-mail had arrived. Ricardo was in his hotel room, and he clicked on the server. The new file appeared and he opened one of the jpegs—and sucked in a sharp breath. He opened file after file, looking for the best shot of the two men on the luxury yacht. He found what he considered to be the sharpest image and printed it on his portable Canon I-70. Then he went in search of Taylor and Kelly. He found them sitting in the small garden, talking.

"My man in Puerto Vallarta sent me some pictures," he said, joining them at the table. The gardens were lush, and the sound of trickling water relaxing.

"And . . ." Kelly said.

"Edward Brand had a visitor," Ricardo said. He dropped the color image on the table.

Kelly slowly reached out and picked it up. Neither spoke for a moment. They just stared at the man's face. A face they both knew very well. It was Alan Bestwick.

"So the son of a bitch is in Mexico," Taylor said. Her voice was smothered with bitterness.

"When did he arrive?" Kelly asked.

Ricardo shrugged. "I would guess within the last couple of hours. I told Juan to get pictures of any visitors and send them to my e-mail immediately." He pointed at the picture. "Look at the shadows. They are almost nonexistent. The sun was directly overhead. That would put the time around noon. It's just a little after one right now. I'd say these are as close to real time as we're going to get."

"Why would Alan visit Edward Brand?" Taylor asked no one, shaking her head. "It doesn't make sense."

"They know each other. They were partners in the scam. Maybe they think enough time has passed that it's safe for them to get together. Who knows?" Kelly said. "The fact is, we've got a problem."

Ricardo nodded. "Brand might bring Alan with him to Monte Alban. He knows me. Remember back to Mexico City when I drove you and Alan to the antique shop. It will be much more difficult. Impossible perhaps. They will suspect something immediately."

"Maybe we should back off until Alan leaves."

Taylor shook her head. "No. If Brand pulls anchor and sails out of the marina, he's gone. Then we have to find him and start from scratch. Right now we're only a few days from making this happen. I say we stay on schedule."

Ricardo looked unsure. "I don't know, Taylor. Kelly's right. This is getting very dangerous."

"It was dangerous before Alan arrived," Kelly said, nodding emphatically. "Like Ricardo says, the problem we have now is that Alan knows who he is. If Alan is within eyesight when Ricardo and Edward Brand meet, the gig is up."

"I don't think Brand will involve Alan. He'd have to split the profits."

"Going ahead is dangerous, Taylor," Kelly said.

Ricardo checked his watch and stood. "I've got to pick up Adolfo at the airport. He's in at two-twenty. You two can figure out what you want to do. I'm okay if you want to go ahead. If anyone else shows up at the boat, we shut it down. Alan is a detail we can probably handle, but that's it. No more."

"That's fair. Did you take the artifacts we bought to the goldsmith?" Taylor asked. They had purchased nine pieces of Mixtec and Zapotec art and given them to Ricardo the previous day.

Ricardo nodded. "He'll have them done sometime tomorrow. He figured the cost to be around four thousand U.S. dollars. I told him we'd pay him when we picked them up."

"That's fine," Kelly said.

"Oh," Ricardo said, turning back to the table. "I was going to ask. Who is going to coordinate the information? I'll be in Cabo; Kelly, you'll be in Washington; and Taylor will be here. Before I can meet with Edward Brand, I'm going to need to know what story Kelly fed to that FBI agent. We need someone to pass information between us."

Kelly turned to Taylor. "Probably best if you do it. I don't want traceable calls coming into the NSA. I'd rather call you from my cell or my home phone. Then you let Ricardo know what Brent Hawkins will find in the computer."

Taylor agreed. "That works for me. I'll relay to you what's happening with Ricardo—when he's meeting with Brand and when he expects them to be in Oaxaca City."

"We'll use your cell phone," Ricardo said to Taylor. "Just make sure to keep it charged."

"Okay."

Ricardo left for the airport and Kelly ordered another Corona. "You're sure you want to finish this, Taylor?"

"Absolutely. The only way Edward Brand gets away is if he floats out of that harbor before we're ready. Today's the twenty-eighth. I think Ricardo can hook him and get him to Monte Alban by January second or third."

Kelly picked up a pen and made a few notes on a napkin. "We need to have the artifacts plated and in place. Adolfo already has his false identification, but he needs time to see the layout at the ruins. I have to get back to Washington and input the false data on the CIA computers. Ricardo needs to meet with Carlos Valendez, entice him to believe his story and deliver him to Edward Brand. They have to get from Puerto Vallarta to Oaxaca City. I think we're cutting the timing too close."

"You fly out tomorrow?" Taylor asked.

"Eight in the morning. But I've got to hub through Mexico City and Dallas. I don't get into D.C. until almost nine at night."

"You lose an entire day. That puts you at the office on Saturday, December thirtieth. How much time do you need?"

Kelly shrugged. "Not sure. I know how to access Langley's computers without being seen by any of their sniffing devices. Getting in isn't a problem. It's where to put it. I've got to create a file that shows the CIA had an operative at Monte Alban who discovered the cave, and Brent Hawkins, our rotten little FBI agent, has to be able to find it. So it has to be deep, but not too deep. That's going to be the problem."

"You can do it," Taylor said.

Kelly smiled. "Sure. I can do it."

Taylor brightened. "When you initiate the transfers, where does the money go?"

"Well, the first five hundred thousand will go to a charity of my choice. Probably the children's hospital in Washington. They can always use another half million dollars. I'm not sure where to send the bulk of the money. I'll figure it out."

"What sort of account do you need?" she asked.

"Somewhere in the Caribbean. An existing account would be best, but a new one will do in a pinch. I can probably set one up from D.C."

"I've got an account in the Bahamas," Taylor said. "I was thinking about buying a condo down there before I met Alan. When we got married I kind of forgot about it."

Kelly sat forward. "Is the account still active?"

"Sure. I've got about twenty thousand dollars in it. And they debit their administrative fees every year. Why? Do you think it would work?"

"It should. And it's a long-established account. That's a good thing. Do you have the number with you?"

She laughed. "You've got to be kidding. No. But it's on my computer back in San Francisco. I'll give you my IP address and password so you can log into my hard drive."

"Do you have some sort of remote access on your system? I'll need it to get in."

She nodded. "PC Anywhere, and it's hooked into the Internet. The account number and the access code are in an encrypted file."

"Smart girl. Did Alan know about the account?"

Taylor took some time to think. Finally she said, "No, I don't think I ever mentioned it. We never discussed buying a property in the Caribbean."

"Excellent. The file has always been encrypted?"

"Yes. The banker who set up the account recommended it, and I was scared that someone would hack into my computer and get the code, so I did it right away."

"Okay, jot down the file name and the password into your computer, and I'll pull it. That's where we'll send the bulk of the money."

"Won't he be able to trace it?" Taylor asked.

Kelly grinned. "Not a chance. I'm going to bounce the money off fifteen satellites and twenty banks before putting it in the account. There is absolutely no chance he'll be able to trace it."

Taylor took a deep breath. "Then we're almost there. Ricardo will get Adolfo up to speed, then head for Cabo San Lucas to meet Carlos Valendez. You're leaving for D.C., and I'm staying here to get the fake artifacts in place and light the fire. Everyone with a part to play."

"Cogs in the wheel. Just keep your fingers crossed that Alan doesn't see Ricardo in Puerto Vallarta."

Taylor played with her empty cup, the coffee long since drank. "When you leave tomorrow, I won't see you again until this is over. In fact, if it goes wrong I may never see you again."

Kelly tried to smile, but the reality of what she said hit him hard. It was true. If Edward Brand or Alan Bestwick smelled a rat or figured out the scam too quickly, people would die. Taylor was at risk. She would be on top of an unforgiving mountain in the heart of Mexico in the middle of the night. At least one person, probably armed, would be nearby. If that person learned they had been robbed, they would go ballistic. Taylor's life would be on the line.

"It'll be okay," he said. "We'll make this work."

She slowly nodded. "Just get the money. All of it. Ruin him."

"I'll get the money," Kelly said. "I promise."

CHAPTER FOURTY-NINE

Alan Bestwick played with the label on the beer bottle. He scraped one edge until it began to lift, then pulled. The label came off in one piece. He set it on the glossy wood tabletop and glanced about for the thirtieth time. The inside of the yacht was opulent, polished teak and chrome, with a wide-screen plasma television tucked against the bulkhead. The window coverings were drawn shut, and it was dark. The television was off, and there was no remote control in sight. He simply sat and waited as Edward Brand had told him to an hour ago when he arrived at the yacht. Brand was on the phone in another part of the boat, and Alan could pick up occasional snippets of the conversation when the man's voice rose. Brand wasn't happy about something.

The wall clock had just ticked past two o'clock when Brand pulled open the door to the salon and entered. He walked through the plush salon and into the galley. He took a beer from the fridge and twisted off the cap, then returned and sat opposite Alan on one of the soft leather chairs beside the television.

"What the hell are you doing here?" he asked.

Alan shrugged. "The weather in Paris is shitty. I felt like getting some sun."

"This isn't the only place on the planet with warm weather."

"It's been almost four months," Alan said. "The proverbial dust has settled. The job is over. We did it. You're just being overly cautious."

Alan's easygoing manner partially disarmed Brand. He sipped the beer. "Still, it's not a good idea. The less we're together the better."

"I wanted to find out what you were up to. To see if you had anything on the go."

Brand motioned to the room he had just left. "I'm trying to get something off the ground, but I'm dealing with idiots. I don't think it's going to work."

"What's wrong?"

"There's an industrialist in Germany who is looking for offshore investments. I've set up a shell company in St. Lucia and a great prospectus on a company about to be listed on the New York Stock Exchange, but the banker in St. Lucia is getting greedy. He wants twenty-five percent. The figures aren't working with him taking that kind of slice."

"What are you going to do?" Alan asked, rising and grabbing two more beers from the fridge. He set one in front of Brand and retook his seat.

"I've got a man on the island who is willing to take care of my problem."

"The banker?"

Brand nodded. "For ten large he's fish food. It's simply amazing what a small sum of money can buy."

Alan laughed. "I've always found that interesting. An absolute value on a human life. Ten grand. So that's what a Caribbean banker is worth."

"This particular piece of shit, yes. That leaves me with having to find a substitute. I'll be doing that while the police are poking about trying to figure out who killed the first one. It's a no-win situation."

"Go to a different island."

"A lot of the islands are starting to tighten up. The Caymans are still the best, but that's where the NewPro money is, and I'm not drawing any heat to that. There's too much money in that account to do something stupid."

"Yeah, I suppose."

Brand's face clouded over again. "I still don't like that you're here, Alan. It's a dumb idea."

"Okay, I'll stay a couple of days and then take off. Maybe go down the coast to Acapulco. Lots of nightlife there. Lots of women who like money."

"You get your share okay?" Brand asked.

"Fine. Thanks."

"You earned it. Good job with Taylor."

Alan's face changed. Emotion flooded into his eyes. "Taylor is an incredible woman. There were times when I wished this whole thing would collapse, and we would back off. I think I could have stayed married to her and been quite happy. She's beautiful and intelligent. Very intelligent. It probably sounds kind of strange, but I miss her."

"You were married for three years. It's normal. You've got to let it go."

"Yeah, I know." Alan paused, staring at the ground, then said, "You want to go out and get some dinner?"

Brand shook his head. "Something's not getting through that thick skull of yours, Alan. I don't want to be seen together. Not now, not ever, unless we're working and we know the marks. Doing stupid things is how people get caught."

Alan launched himself off the couch. "All right, but I'm going to have some fun. Maybe I'll stay in town. If I don't make it back, I'll be at the Sheraton."

Brand's eyes narrowed. "Don't make it back. Stay away, Alan. Your presence only complicates things. For no reason."

Alan gave him a grin as he headed up the stairs. "Nice boat, by the way."

"Thanks," Brand muttered under his breath to the empty room. "Idiot."

Edward Brand finished the beer and picked up the empties. It was almost New Year, just three days until the fireworks would usher in another January 1. This year had been very good to him. He wondered about what the next would hold. Perhaps he should quit while he was ahead. It was the safe thing to do. Even as he cleaned the galley and wiped down the countertops, he knew that wasn't going to happen. Conning people, taking their money, was like a drug. He thrived on it. Needed it, almost. No, no almost about it. He needed it. It was his habit, and he needed his fix.

He finished cleaning the galley and headed toward the aft of the boat. He was going stir crazy on the yacht. His crew was stripping one of the motors and retooling a drive shaft, and he wanted to see how things were coming. Patience, he told himself as he strode through the luxury craft. Patience. Something always came up. Never failed. The world was funny that way.

CHAPTER FIFTY

Ricardo and Kelly both left Oaxaca City on December 29—Kelly early in the morning and Ricardo two hours later, at ten. The flight into Cabo San Lucas was through Mexico City, but the layover was short, and Ricardo landed on the tip of the Baja Peninsula just after two in the afternoon. He slipped into one of the many cabs lining the road in front of the modest two-story airport and sat back for the ride along the stretch of highway commonly known as the corridor. Traffic was light on the twenty-two-mile strip, and he was in Cabo San Lucas by three-thirty. He paid the driver and exited at Puerto Paraiso, the ultra-modern three-story shopping mall adjacent to the marina.

Ricardo checked Carlos Valendez's address. 417 Matamoros Street. He glanced quickly at a sheet of paper with directions written in pencil while on the plane. He didn't look like a tourist, dressed in faded jeans and a casual plaid shirt, and the last thing he needed was to stand on a street corner studying a map like one of the countless *gringos* off the cruise ships. He stuffed the directions back in his pocket and hiked up the neighboring street.

The odor of tacos and refried beans lingered in the hot air as he passed strings of restaurants filled with tourists. Small shops selling silver and tacky ceramic iguanas lined the narrow roads. He found Matamoros and headed northwest toward the higher numbers. In the three hundreds, he slowed and began to saunter up the slight incline. He crossed a side street, concentrating now on the numbers. Four-seventeen was about halfway up the block and only two doors from a hole-in-the-wall bar catering more to locals than tourists. He settled into a chair near the open window and picked up a newspaper. When the bartender looked his way he ordered a Corona.

Now it was time to wait. To wait and hope Carlos Valendez, the man Edward Brand had relied on to let the scuba divers know he was on his way, was home. He nursed the Corona and read the paper. There were worse ways to pass the time.

Taylor stopped by the goldsmith's shop at four o'clock. He had promised the work would be finished and ready to be moved before sunset. She took a cab directly from the bank where she had used Kelly's debit card to withdraw the necessary four thousand dollars to pay for the service. The shop was a dingy space, with no windows save the one fronting onto the street, which was so caked with dirt and grime that the illumination from the sun reminded her more of moonlight. She set the package containing the money on the desk as the goldsmith, a wizened old man well into his seventies, carted the masks and other artifacts to the front of the shop. He spoke no English, and Taylor no Spanish, but communicating wasn't hard. He counted the money, and she checked the quality of his work. Both were fine. She carried the items out the front door in a large box and set them in the trunk of the cab. Ten minutes later, she was safely back in her hotel. After she had stashed the items in her room, she went in search of Adolfo. He was in his room and answered the door on the first knock. He smiled and waved her in.

"Did you bring your identification with you?" she asked.

"Yes," he replied in English. He wasn't fluent, but they could easily communicate. "This is it." He produced a single card with his picture in one corner and an official-looking stamp in the other. Beneath that was his name and title, in Spanish.

Taylor scrutinized it closely. The quality was outstanding. She didn't read or speak the language, but she got the drift. Adolfo was a high-ranking government official. One who needed his palm greased before the treasure could be released from the cave. Adolfo had brought the identification with him from Mexico City, where a skilled craftsman had worked magic with the forged document. And Edward Brand would be looking at the ID in poor light. It was fine.

"Tomorrow we will go to Monte Alban," she said. "In the morning."

"Yes. It is good. The morning. I will be ready."

"Good," she said. "See you tomorrow. Eight o'clock."

Taylor returned to her room. It was quiet now that Kelly and Ricardo were both gone. She could have dinner with Adolfo, but that would drag because of his limited English and right now what she needed was time to herself. Time to rest. Time to prepare.

Edward Brand. The man would be in Oaxaca City soon. And then it would begin.

Kelly arrived at Dulles at nine-eighteen on Friday night. The flight leg from Mexico City to Dallas was smooth, and he had slept for a portion. He felt somewhat rested and despite the late hour, he decided to stop at home and pick up his car, then head for Crypto-City. It was just after eleven when he swiped his ID badge through the card reader and drove up the winding roadway to the main building in the vast NSA complex. He cleared the required security checks and unlocked his office. He powered up his computer and took a few minutes to sift through his e-mails before getting started.

He was looking for legitimacy more than anything else. Brent Hawkins had to believe what he found about Monte Alban to be true. The story could not be outrageous, nor could it be without teeth. It had to draw his attention, then hook him. Once he was hooked, Hawkins had to relay the false information to Edward Brand and sell the man on it. Kelly needed to create all this inside one of the most carefully guarded computer systems in the world. Treacherous was a mild word for what he was attempting.

He started inside the NSA mainframe, where his user ID allowed him free rein of most files. He scanned the computer's hard drive for information on Monte Alban. There were numerous entries, most dealing with the positioning of the ruins and a few attempts to find embedded codes inside the pattern the Zapotec tribes had used to construct their temples. Typical NSA—always trying to find a hidden code. There were a few notes about the treasure that had been removed from Tumba 7. It was truly amazing. Hundreds of priceless Zapotec and Mixtec artifacts, most formed from gold and some encrusted with precious and semi-precious stones. The references to Tumba 7 were good, as it would reinforce the possibility of another large discovery.

Midnight rolled by, then one o'clock. At half past the hour he shut down the computer and headed home. He had stumbled on one possible angle. A cross-link to the CIA computers had a report of a covert operative who had been killed recently in Bolivia. The agency was being very tight-lipped about the details, but getting Brent Hawkins to draw a line between the dead agent and Monte Alban might be the way to go. He wanted to think about it, formulate some sort of plan in his mind before he went any further. That, and he was tired. Very tired.

The drive home was easy, the roads almost devoid of other cars. It gave him time to think. Taylor was the key to keeping everything moving. She was the hub. Whatever story he concocted and input into the computers had to be relayed through her to Ricardo, who needed that information before he got too tight with Carlos Valendez. Timing was crucial, and they were cutting it close. If they wanted to have Edward Brand at the ruins just after January 1, everything had to move with absolute precision.

Tomorrow. He would find some way to tie the death of the CIA agent to Monte Alban, create the file and download it to the CIA mainframe. Then he'd call Taylor.

Timing. It was all in the timing.

CHAPTER FIFTY-ONE

Nothing.

Ricardo had spent the entire night watching the front entry to 417 Matamoros Street with nothing to show for it. Not one person had entered or exited the modest two-story stucco house tucked between a souvenir shop and a decrepit-looking *pharmacia* promoting Viagra and a host of other prescription drugs available over the counter. A couple of older *gringos* had visited the drugstore and come away with small bags and a smile. It disgusted him. A man was a man—he didn't need that shit to get it up.

After a few hours' sleep, he was back in his favorite chair in the bar, the daily newspaper on the table along with an espresso. The sun began to heat the street, and he loosened his cuffs and rolled up his sleeves. It was going to be hot. Noon crawled by, and he ordered his first beer of the day. He'd had enough coffee. For the first time he wondered if this was going to work. They were relying on Carlos Valendez to open a back door to Edward Brand. But if Valendez didn't show, everything changed. Ricardo would have to fly to Puerto Vallarta

and try to get face to face with Brand without a middle-
man. Not easy and not without its pitfalls. Edward
Brand was a con man, and con men were suspicious by
nature. Selling him on Monte Alban without some sort of
a lead-in would be difficult, if not impossible.

The beer arrived, and he took a short swig. He'd
nursed six of them yesterday, but today was going to be
even longer. He'd have to pace himself. A pretty girl
walked by with a fat friend, and he smiled. She returned
the smile, and glanced back. He was just about to wave at
her and invite her in for a drink when the heavy wood
door at 417 opened and a man appeared. He turned back
to the door and locked it, then moved south on Matamoros toward the marina. Ricardo dropped some money
on the table and settled in about a half block behind the
man. That he had locked the door behind him was a
good sign. It might mean that he lived there alone, which
would mean that he was Valendez. Maybe, maybe not.
No one told him this would be easy.

The man he was following was a working-class Mexican
in his thirties. He wore ripped jeans and a white T-shirt
with a small stain on the front. His gait was reasonably
quick, and Ricardo hurried when the man reached
Avenida Lazaro Cárdenas and disappeared around the
corner. Ricardo picked him up again on the main street
that skirted the marina. His target was moving slower
now, eyeing the throngs of young college coeds that are
staples in Cabo San Lucas. He crossed the street and entered one of the many bars fronting onto the marina. Ricardo waited for a minute then followed him in.

The bar was about half full, and most of the patrons
were *gringos* in varying stages of sunburn. The décor was
tacky Mexican, which the tourists seemed to love, and
the menu was an entire list of high-cholesterol food. Valendez, if that was his name, was sitting at the bar talking
with the bartender. They appeared to know each other.
Ricardo moved through the bar slowly, as if deciding

where to sit. In his peripheral vision, he saw the bartender was watching him. He stopped and continued to look about. Then he moved toward the bar and took a seat two stools down from the man he had followed. The bartender sidled over and set a coaster on the bar.

"What can I get you?" he asked in Spanish.

"A few more Mexicans in the bar, less *gringos*," Ricardo said. That prompted a laugh from the bartender. "Corona." Sol and Corona had the lock on the Mexican beer market, but he preferred Corona hands down.

"You got it."

Ricardo glanced toward Valendez and caught the man's eye. They nodded at each other. The beer arrived and he took a long drink. He finished it quickly and ordered another. Ricardo kept his eyes off Valendez until he was halfway through the second beer. When he glanced over, they locked eyes again.

"Too many *gringos*," Ricardo said quietly, but loud enough for the man to hear. "The women are nice, but it's like we're giving them our country."

"*Gringos* bring money, *amigo*," the man said. His voice was throaty, deeper than Ricardo expected. "Lots of money."

"Yeah, and then they fuck you," Ricardo said. Again, only loud enough for his conversation partner to hear.

"That's a good thing, if it's a woman," the man joked. He smiled, and his teeth were crooked and stained from cigarettes and coffee. His eyes were dark brown, but cold. A small scar ran down the left side of his face, from the corner of his eye to halfway down his cheek. His hair was long and looked greasy.

Ricardo turned back to the bar. "I wish. It's nothing like that. I just got screwed, is all."

There was a break, then the man asked, "What happened?"

Ricardo looked at him out of the corner of his eye. "You wouldn't believe me if I told you."

The man shifted over one seat so he was next to Ricardo. Cigar smoke drifted up from the stub in the man's hand. "Try me."

"Ricardo." He offered his hand.

"Carlos."

Ricardo sipped his beer. Pay dirt. He had his man. "I had a deal of sorts. A good one. I needed some money to make it work. I had a *gringo* who lived in Texas and has one of those luxury villas down here interested in covering the up-front money for a percentage."

"He back out?"

Ricardo sneered into his beer. "Yeah, the chickenshit asshole. He realized it was more than just handing me a wad of cash and got scared. Now I'm fucked. Fucked beyond belief."

Carlos finished his beer and motioned to the bartender. Two Coronas appeared in record time. He puffed on a short, stubby cigar. "What sort of deal did you have on the go?"

Ricardo turned a bit and eyed Carlos up and down. "It's private," he said, turning back to his beer.

"Too bad. Maybe I know someone."

The Eagles played in the background—"Lyin' Eyes"—and a table of tourists laughed at an unheard joke. The bartender slowly polished a glass, watching the two men at his bar with interest. Finally, Ricardo swiveled about slightly and faced Carlos.

"I've been burned once," he said. "Don't need it to happen again."

Carlos shrugged. Both men were feeling each other out now—the game was on. "Right now you got nothing. The deal is dead."

"Yeah," Ricardo said quietly, turning back to the bar and working on his beer. "It's dead."

"Is it worth doing?" Carlos asked.

Ricardo stared straight ahead. "Would have set me up

for life," he said. "Could have had one of those fucking villas. Asshole fucked it all up."

"Big money," Carlos said. "That might be worth looking at."

Ricardo didn't look over. Just shook his head. "No time. The deal has to be done in a few days. It's done." He finished his beer and stuck his finger in the neck of the bottle and idly swung it around a few times before setting it on the bar. He glanced at Carlos. "Done, *amigo*. Gone. Millions of dollars. Gone."

"I'm not shitting you," Carlos said. "I've got a guy can make things happen. Quick if it's a good deal."

"So what's in it for you?" Ricardo asked. Another beer showed up.

"A finder's fee. My guy pays well if things work out."

Ricardo finally allowed himself a wry smile. "Oh, if this works out, you'd get the finder's fee of all times."

"Then let's talk," Carlos said.

Ricardo gave the man a long, hard look. "Okay," he said as the Eagles tune finished and Bob Seger started singing "Night Moves." "Let's talk."

CHAPTER FIFTY-TWO

Kelly pulled into the main NSA complex at ten on Saturday morning. The security guard recognized him and smiled. He still double-checked the picture ID. Nothing to chance at the nation's most clandestine spy agency. Kelly parked and made his way to his office, his mind already alive with some of the options he could use to build the file for Brent Hawkins.

The recent death of Brian Palmer, the CIA agent who had succumbed to a hail of bullets in an alley in La Paz, Bolivia, was a tragedy. It was one that he could use to their advantage. The Central Intelligence Agency was keeping the entire affair under wraps. Nothing had been released to the press, and according to the files he had managed to dredge up, Palmer's family was being paid to keep quiet. Kelly suspected the CIA had stuck their fingers in a politically incorrect pie, and now they were scrambling about trying to keep a lid on it. What they had done was a complete unknown, but that didn't matter. What *did* matter was that by using Brian Palmer as the source for the information on the undiscovered tomb at Monte Alban, he was using a source that could not be substantiated.

The space around his office was empty, the computer screens dark. Some departments of the NSA were nine-to-five on the weekdays, and his was one of them. Not a bad thing—it gave him privacy and a quiet space to work. He hit the power button on his computer, then headed to the coffee room and brewed a fresh pot of medium roast. When he returned to his office, his system had cleared the internal security checks and was online. He sat at the desk, sipping the coffee.

The first thing he did was check the status of Taylor's bank account in the Bahamas. With the account number and password, he was inside the bank's mainframe in under two minutes. Her account was active with a balance of just over twenty-three thousand dollars. That was good—it gave them a legitimate account to deposit the money into once they had transferred it out of Edward Brand's. He closed the link and returned to the NSA prompt. Kelly unlocked his drawer and pulled out a file. Inside was the information on Brian Palmer he had sent to the printer the previous evening. He reread the file.

Palmer had been stationed out of Mexico City for three years. He was single but dating another operative, a distinct no-no but something that the field office had chosen to overlook. Most of the time he had spent in the field was drug related—Bolivia, Columbia and Mexico. On three occasions, he had traveled to Oaxaca City. The most recent trip to the central Mexican city was six months ago, but Kelly figured he could work with that. He highlighted a few passages, got his dates straight, then started to type.

An hour later he printed the file and reviewed it. The format was standard for a field operative, but classified. Very few eyes would be privy to the contents. The gist of the report was that Palmer had met with a Mexican late at night on June 15, but the meet had gone wrong from minute one. The man had insisted he found a cache of treasure atop the plateau at Monte Alban. He wanted the CIA to get the treasure out and protect him from the Mexican authorities and an entire list of corrupt and violent locals who would want in on the find. Palmer had refused. The next night the man had been found in a field bordering the city with his throat sliced open and his eyes gouged out. That sparked Palmer to look at the validity of the man's claim.

He then visited Monte Alban and from what the Mexican had told him, managed to locate the cave. Inside were gold artifacts, many encrusted with precious stones. The find was just off the north end of the plateau, along a narrow and dangerous path. It was set into the side of the mountain, the entrance concealed by large rocks that appeared to be part of the natural landscape. Palmer had reported the find to his immediate superior, who had in turn taken the report directly to the deputy director of the CIA. In a two-hour meeting that involved only the three men, it had been decided that there was no upside to the agency getting involved. A Mexican citizen had been murdered, and any hint of CIA activity in the area would only end up in a lot of unnecessary finger pointing. The report was closed and buried in with the other dead case files. Six months later, Brian Palmer had been murdered in Bolivia. End of story.

Kelly reviewed the text a few times, correcting it so the writing wasn't too polished and ensuring it read like a real field file. Then he accessed the CIA database and looked for somewhere to plant it. Covert personnel were employed under the Directorate of Operations, so he immediately went to that section. His status with the NSA allowed him to bypass a couple of firewalls, but there were additional security measures in place that attempted to stop his progress as he ventured deeper into the system.

He skirted the secondary firewalls and found a spot he thought would work well. It was a section of the hard drive dedicated to reports by field operatives working Central and South America. Mexico was close enough. The file had Monte Alban as a keyword, and anyone searching for information on the Mexican ruins would find it. Even the FBI.

Kelly powered off the computer and leaned back in his chair. The bait was in place. He called Taylor and gave her the story he had concocted. And got the good news. Ricardo had checked in with her. He had found Carlos Valendez, and the doors to Edward Brand were beginning to open. Pieces of the puzzle were fitting together.

Taylor and Adolfo would be getting the treasure in place, and if things went well, Ricardo would be meeting with Edward Brand inside the next twenty-four to forty-eight hours. The bank account they needed for the transfer was verified and ready for the deposit. The satellite phone Brand would use to make the call from atop the mountain was operational. Because he and Taylor had set up the phone account, Kelly knew the number and the password. That enabled him to trace and monitor the call without being seen. Everything ready to go. The details taken care of. Now there were only two questions that remained to be answered.

Would Alan Bestwick be there when Ricardo met with Edward Brand?

And would Edward Brand take the bait?

CHAPTER FIFTY-THREE

Edward Brand listened intently as Carlos Valendez wrapped up the story of treasure on the side of Monte Alban. Brand had known the Mexican for about three years and had relied on him numerous times to cover the mundane tasks that made the scams go smoothly. He was from a working-class background, but of good intellect and absolute loyalty. Carlos had shown ingenuity on a con they had run in Buenos Aires, resulting in them raking in an additional six million dollars from one of the marks. To Brand, that was impressive. What really won Brand over was Valendez's lack of greed. Where most men would have been looking for a good chunk of the extra cash, Valendez had taken his original pay and returned home. Not a word about more money. What that bought with Edward Brand was respect. Respect and trust.

"The CIA agent who was killed in Bolivia—what was his name?" Brand asked.

"Brian Palmer," Valendez said.

Brand jotted down the name and underlined it. Above

the name were numerous points he had scrawled on the paper as Valendez had talked. *Monte Alban. Treasure—cave. Corrupt government official. Half million. January 3. Tumba 7. Millions.* The last word had a series of lines under it.

"What's this guy's name who gave you this?" Brand asked.

"Ricardo."

"Ricardo who?"

"Won't say. Just Ricardo."

"Where'd you meet him?"

"Here in Cabo. In a bar. He was bitching about how many *gringos* were in town, and we got talking. He seems okay."

"All right, leave it with me. Keep your phone on. I'll call you if things check out. If they do, I want you and this Ricardo fellow to fly down to Puerto Vallarta. I'd like to meet him."

"Okay." The line died.

Edward Brand dialed another number. Brent Hawkins picked up. "I want you to check on something for me," Brand said.

There was a rustling of paper. "Go ahead," Hawkins replied.

"There was a CIA agent got himself killed in Bolivia a little while back. Guy's name was Brian Palmer. See what you can find on him. Run Monte Alban through your computers."

"What the hell is Monte Alban?"

"Mexican ruins near Oaxaca City. Didn't you take social studies in school?"

"Like I'd know anything about some fucking Mexican ruins. When do you need it?"

"Quick. Real quick."

"Couple of hours okay?"

"Perfect."

Brand hung up and ventured onto the main deck. The sun was high overhead, a brilliant round inferno that superheated every object it touched. Brand was amazed by the intensity of the Mexican sun, especially in the middle of winter. He felt the warmth on his skin and smiled. It was his, all his. The yacht, the money, the lifestyle—he had risen to the top of his chosen profession and now the spoils were his to enjoy. Most of the people he had stolen from were ultra-rich. They didn't need the money to pay the mortgage. They cursed and fretted, then got on with their lives. It worked well for him.

He opened a beer and sat in one of the chairs on the aft deck, overlooking the entrance to the marina. This was an interesting one. A chance meeting had dropped it in his lap, and he was always suspicious of chance meetings. One never knew. If there was some validity to the story about the dead CIA agent, there may be some degree of truth to the entire tale. If the part about the treasure was true, he was definitely interested. Pay off some piece-of-shit government official and get access to millions of dollars in gold. Not a bad deal. No wonder no one wanted to touch the treasure without paying off the guy tied in with the government. The Mexicans didn't like people who stole from their sacred tombs. In fact, if you wanted to end up in the dirtiest and most dangerous Mexican prison, don't commit murder. Steal their heritage.

He cradled the beer in his lap and took an occasional sip. Time drifted past, slowly. When the phone finally rang, he answered it before the second ring. Hawkins's voice sounded distant and crackled slightly. He was most likely on his cell phone.

"How did you get this stuff?" Hawkins asked.

"Never mind that, what did you find out?"

"Brian Palmer died in Bolivia a short time ago. Prior to his death, he had been stationed in Mexico City and had visited Oaxaca City three times. That puts him within a few miles of Monte Alban. There wasn't much more in his personnel file, but I ran a search on the CIA computers using Monte Alban, and you'll never guess what I found."

"Don't fuck around," Brand said testily. "Just tell me."

"There's another file buried way back in the mainframe. It looks like Palmer had some sort of meeting with an unnamed source in Oaxaca City, and this guy told him about an undiscovered cave. The cave is stuffed with treasure. Right after this guy tells Palmer about the stash, someone kills him. When Palmer submits his report, the director of operations decides that going after the treasure, or even telling the Mexicans about it, is risky. All that will do is implicate them in the Mexican's death. They buried the file. Did nothing."

"What do you think?" Brand asked. "There any legitimacy to it?"

"I think so. I've read hundreds of files written by field operatives, and this one is pretty typical. The reasoning is good. The CIA takes enough hits without jumping into something where they know they're going to get pounded. I'd say it's probably legit."

"Okay, thanks."

He hung up and dialed Carlos Valendez's cell phone. "Carlos," he said. "I want you and your new friend here by tomorrow noon at the latest. Call me when you get into P.V."

"*Sí.*"

Brand hit End and dropped the phone on the table. "Son of a bitch," he said, a grin creeping across his face.

CHAPTER FIFTY-FOUR

Night had settled on the valley, the still air slowly cooling from being superheated during the day. Taylor slipped behind the wheel of the rental Jeep, and Adolfo climbed in beside her. She pulled out from the curb, the gold-plated artifacts jiggling about in the rear compartment as the Jeep bounced over the cobblestones. She could feel the air cool as they climbed the windy road toward Monte Alban. It was after midnight, and they were the only vehicle on the lonely road. The moon was bright in the sky, midway between first quarter and full.

Taylor reached a bend close to the top of the road and stopped. "You know what to do?" she asked Adolfo.

"*Sí.* I park, then go to the guards. I show them my papers. Manuel Sanchez, Director of Antiquities from Mexico City. Then I tell them I want to run the site."

"Walk, Adolfo. You want to walk the site with them."

"*Sí sí.* I know. I will not make such mistakes when speaking Spanish. Only English." He looked hurt that she had corrected him.

"*Lo siento,*" she said. "I'm sorry. Of course you'll do well."

"Yes. I'll do well. I walk with the guards for fifteen minutes. Then everything is fancy."

She didn't bother correcting him. "And how do you explain showing up so late at night?"

"That it is normal for me to check out the night security at archeological sites."

"Good. Okay, now you drive." She jumped in the back of the Jeep and pulled the tarp over her. It was dark and the tarp smelled of mold. When Adolfo pulled ahead and began the final leg to the ruins, she was thrown about like a marble in a can. She grabbed whatever she could that was welded to the frame and hung on. The drive was mercifully short, and once he had parked she let go of her handholds and adjusted the tarp so she could breathe fresh air. They had only been parked for a few moments when she heard voices. She felt the Jeep rock slightly as Adolfo got out to meet the men. There was an exchange, then silence. The next voice was Adolfo's, and there was a definite tone of authority to it. A couple of minutes later, the group moved away from the Jeep, their voices diminishing as the distance increased.

Taylor waited until she was sure they were down by the ball court and out of eyesight. She lifted the tarp and peeked out. Nothing. Just wide open sky, alive with stars. As she dragged the burlap bag containing the fake treasure from the back of the vehicle, it struck her that the scene she was looking at, with the exception of the parking lot and the museum, was the same as the Zapotec Indians would have seen two thousand years ago. It was an eerie feeling.

She hoisted the bag over her shoulder and trudged to the extreme north end of the complex. It was heavy, and she struggled under the weight. The path was a wavy narrow line in the light from the half-moon. Walking on the worn rocks was slower going than when the sun was out, and the cracks and loose pebbles were visible. It took far too long to reach the entrance to the cave. When she came to the spot, she was shaking from the stress of picking her way along what was a glorified goat path with an awkward burlap sack. She laid the sack on the ground and drank from the water bottle she had hooked onto her belt before leaving the hotel. The cool water felt good on her throat.

It took her a full six minutes, maybe more, to dislodge the small rock from the opening to the cave. Then, one piece at a time, she slid the artifacts into the darkness. She crawled through and pulled the flashlight from her back pocket. It was sufficient to light the room so she could see to walk. She moved the treasure into the small alcove at the back of the cave and positioned the pieces atop a jumble of loose rocks. Then she ripped the seam on the burlap bag and laid it around the pieces, giving the impression that the entire mound inside the enclosed space could be treasure. She shone the light over it from every angle possible at the opening, then made a few adjustments until she had it exactly as she wanted. One last look and she left, dragging the rock back into place and securing it so it was impossible to tell there was an opening. Then she hurried back to the Jeep.

She heard the voices before she reached the parking lot. Adolfo and the guards had already returned and were standing beside the Jeep. The first thing she noticed was that Adolfo had positioned himself so that he was facing her and the guard's backs were to her. She raised her head and shoulders above a boulder, partially exposed for a few moments. They were talking, but the moment she came into sight, he made a waving motion with his hand, as if gesturing to make a point. She got the idea. He wanted her to get moving down the mountain. She turned and skirted the farthest edge of the parking lot, then started down the road. After a couple of turns she stopped and slid behind a large rock. She didn't have long to wait. In less than five minutes, headlights appeared. The vehicle was moving very slowly, the driver scanning both sides of the road. It was Adolfo. She slipped out from behind the rock and he stopped.

"Good work," she said, grabbing his shoulder and then leaning over and giving him a quick kiss on the cheek. "Very good, Adolfo."

He grinned at the kiss. "Yes. Tonight, I am good. Everything is fine."

"Everything go okay with the guards?"

"Yes. To them, I am Manuel Sanchez, Director of Antiquities."

"Excellent."

They drove back to the hotel, Adolfo careful on the night roads. The streets in Oaxaca City were mostly deserted, save for an occasional stray dog padding down the dark streets, searching out anything edible. Adolfo pulled in by the hotel and locked the Jeep. The desk clerk stopped them as they passed through the lobby and handed Taylor a message. She thanked him and headed to her room. Once inside her room and behind the locked door, she unfolded the paper and read the contents. It was a phone message from Ricardo. *Sorry, can't meet you as planned. Had to fly out to Puerto Vallarta. Talk to you soon.* Taylor set the message on the worn wooden table next to the bed and lay on her back on top of the sheets.

Everything was working. Kelly was at his computer in D.C., creating the screenplay for his actors. Somehow, he had crafted a story believable enough for Ricardo to get the invite to Puerto Vallarta. Adolfo was proving his worth, distracting the guards while she snuck into the cave and arranged the fake treasure. He had kept the guards focused to the south, so when she appeared on the northern edge of the plateau, she was only visible to him. Smart fellow. If that were any indication of his abilities, she was confident he would hold his own when finally under Brand's scrutiny.

She was in Oaxaca City, poised and ready. She liked her

part in the game, coordinating everyone's movements—knowing every detail the moment it arose. She was more than ready to risk the treacherous mountainside and light the fire that would distract the guards. Anything to get the bastard.

Ricardo was on his way to meet with Edward Brand. That meeting was crucial. If Ricardo wasn't able to sell Brand on the deal, they were done. But if he could, Edward Brand would move into the trap. She stared at the ceiling, a lazy smile on her face.

Soon. Very soon.

CHAPTER FIFTY-FIVE

They met at Bianco, a hip bar-restaurant on Calle Insurgentes in the southern section of the old city of Puerto Vallarta. Edward Brand was seated at a table along the back wall, quiet and private. The colors on the walls and the soft upholstery were muted cinnamon. A painting of a woman, sitting, from midway up her calves to just below her eyes, dominated the wall next to the table. Brand liked Bianco, liked this table, and always wondered why the artist had cut the painting off without showing the viewer the woman's eyes. It was one of those things without an answer. The five-star restaurant was almost empty, the hour too early for serious diners. That suited Edward Brand just fine.

Brand watched as two men entered the restaurant and stood by the long, curved glass bar. Carlos spotted him and started over. The man with him followed. Brand's gaze was focused on Ricardo. The Mexican was dressed simply, in jeans and a white shirt. He wore no jewelry, kept his hair well groomed and walked with confidence. They reached the table, and Carlos sat next to Brand. Ricardo took the seat opposite, facing the two men.

"I'm Edward," he said simply. No offer to shake hands.
"Ricardo."

Brand waved for the waiter and ordered Coronas for
the table. "Carlos tells me you have an interesting proposition." Brand's eyes were unwavering.

"I think so," Ricardo said, meeting the stare, then
looking about. The last thing he wanted to do was challenge Edward Brand by continuing to meet his gaze. Yet,
not making eye contact was a mistake. Brand may think
he was lying.

"Want to tell me about it?"

"I already told Carlos," Ricardo said.

"I know. I want to hear it from you." The beers arrived,
and they waited while the server dropped coasters on
the table, then set the beers in front of each man. When
he had left, Brand said, "Just in case I misunderstood
something."

"Sure," Ricardo said, sipping his beer. "A friend of
mine, a very good friend of mine in fact, was visiting the
ruins at Monte Alban about eight months ago. He was
sitting against what he thought was a solid rock wall,
staring at the view of the valley, when the rock behind
him moved slightly. He pried at it and managed to pull it
out. The opening was just large enough for him to crawl
through. When he did, he found himself in a cave. He
was inside for the better part of an hour, but what he
found was quite amazing."

"Really," Brand said.

"The back portion of the cave was awash in treasure.
Gold. More gold than he had ever seen in his life. He re-
sealed the cave and returned the next day with a flashlight. What he had thought to be a good size cache of
Zapotec treasure was more than that. It was the mother
lode. Now he had a problem. Getting it out. The Mexican
government is extremely protective of its heritage, especially when it comes to valuable artifacts at ancient ruins.
He left it sitting for a bit while he tried to figure out what

to do. It was about a month later when he mentioned it to me. We both went back and had a look. He was right. He needed help getting the stuff out of there. I had an idea."

"What was that?" Brand asked.

"I knew a *gringo* who worked for the Central Intelligence Agency. His name was Brian. I met him in Mexico City when he was asking questions about illegal drugs in the neighborhood where I live. I don't like drugs or the men who sell them, so I agreed to help him. We got to know each other a bit. I asked him if he'd meet with my friend. He said yes. He traveled to Oaxaca City and listened to what my friend had to say. Brian said that the CIA wouldn't be able to help him. It was too risky, and there was no upside to the operation, as they would have to give the artifacts to the Mexican government. The meeting was a total failure. What was worse, someone must have overheard, because the next night my friend was found murdered just outside Oaxaca City. Whoever killed him tortured him first."

"Whoever killed your friend never found the treasure?"

"No. It's still there."

"What did this Brian fellow do?"

Ricardo looked puzzled. "I don't know. I haven't seen him since. Why?"

Brand studied the man intently. "He's dead."

Ricardo swallowed. "I didn't know."

Brand finished his beer and motioned to the waiter. When the man arrived, he ordered coffee. "Please continue."

"I wanted to get at the treasure, but I had the same problem my friend did. Trying to get it out was difficult, but attempting to sell it afterward was next to impossible. The gold would be worth a lot if the pieces were melted down, but only a small fraction of what they would be worth intact. I needed someone in the government. Someone in a position of authority. A man who could pave the way for removing the treasure and then ensuring I could sell it. It took quite a while, but I finally found such a man."

"Who is it?"

"His name is Manuel Sanchez. He's the Director of Antiquities in Mexico City. He agreed to help me get the treasure out by simply being there. If anything went wrong, he would take care of the guards. That would cost me five hundred thousand American dollars. Then he would take the list I gave him once I had cataloged the treasure and add that to the known inventory on the government's books. With the pieces already entered into inventory, I could resell them. That would cost me ten percent of whatever I managed to get on the open market."

"A lucrative deal for Senor Sanchez."

Ricardo shrugged. "Without him it was impossible. Even if I could get the treasure out of the cave, I'd have nowhere to sell it."

"Okay, you had the guy on the hook. What happened?"

"I didn't have the half million. I needed a backer to front the money. I found one—an American who was ready to front the half million. Things looked good. Sanchez insisted the transfer of funds occur at the site."

"At Monte Alban?" Brand asked.

"Yes. That's when this stupid asshole who had promised the up-front money backed out. He got scared. The thought of being on top of a Mexican mountain in the middle of the night with me and Sanchez was too much. He was worried for his health. The idiot. If we wanted to steal his money we certainly wouldn't do it on a remote mountain at night. God, I just got to wonder about the level of stupidity some people carry around with them." He stopped, then said, "Sorry, I get a little pissed off when I think about it."

"Why the rush?"

"Sanchez is running out of patience. He knows what he's doing is extremely risky and unless we get it done soon, he's going to announce the discovery and take credit for finding it."

"Why would he do that?" Brand asked. "He's potentially giving up millions of dollars."

"Perhaps. His position as Director of Antiquities would be secure for the rest of his life. He would get some sort of stipend from the government for his discovery. Senor Sanchez wouldn't be hurting too badly. He's in a win-win situation."

"What's the deadline?"

"January second. January third, tops. He's not prepared to wait any longer."

"That's only two or three days from now, counting today," Brand said. He was quiet, thoughtful. "What is my role in all this, Ricardo?"

"You provide the money."

"The five hundred thousand dollars."

"Yes."

"How?"

"By electronic transfer to Sanchez's bank account."

"Where's his account?"

Ricardo shrugged. "I have no idea."

Silence descended on the table. No one spoke as Edward Brand toyed with his coffee cup. Finally, he said, "What do you think would happen to you if you were trying to rip me off?"

Ricardo stared at Brand. "What? What do you mean?"

"What I mean is that if you're setting me up to steal a half million dollars of my money, then you had better think very seriously of leaving here while you still can."

Ricardo's eyes flashed anger. "Are you calling me a thief?" he said. His voice had changed. It was curt, almost vicious.

Brand remained relaxed. "Just letting you know that I will kill you if you try to steal from me."

"I am an honest man," Ricardo said.

"Honest?" Brand laughed. "You're taking Mexican artifacts out of a tomb on a protected archeological site. I don't think you're quite as honest as you make out to be, Ricardo."

Ricardo stared at Brand, his jaw firmly set. Then the edges of his lips curled slightly. He smiled. His voice returned to normal. "No, perhaps not. Please don't tell my mother." He finished his coffee and set the cup on the table.

Brand returned the smile. "Okay, Ricardo. Just so long as you understand what will happen if you try something stupid."

"You've made your point."

"What's in it for me? What percentage do I take out of this?"

"Ten percent of whatever I can sell the treasure for."

Brand laughed. He laughed out loud and Carlos snickered, although he wasn't sure why his boss had found the remark so amusing.

"No chance," Brand said when he had stopped. "Fifty percent."

"No fucking way," Ricardo said. "Not a chance in hell. This is my deal. I'm the one who knows where this treasure is and I've got Sanchez in my back pocket. You expect to take half of everything by providing a little up-front money. No way."

"Then make me an offer."

"Twenty percent. Final offer. You want more, I let the deal go sideways."

"Thirty."

"You're not listening," Ricardo said, leaning over the table. "Twenty is my top offer. Even that is too much."

Brand grinned. He turned to Carlos. "I think I like this guy." He looked back to Ricardo. "Twenty-five. That's my final offer."

Ricardo and Brand stared into each other's eyes. This time Ricardo wasn't looking away. This time he was challenging the American. This was Mexico, and in Mexico machismo ruled. The weak died broke, and they usually died early. Neither man flinched for the better part of a minute.

"Twenty-five," Ricardo hissed between his teeth. "You warned me not to steal from you. Now I'm warning you. Don't fuck with me."

"Fair enough," Brand said, extending his hand.

They shook.

Chapter Fifty-six

Taylor was in the secluded garden at the hotel when the call came through on her cell phone. It was Ricardo. He spoke quickly and kept his voice low. Although he didn't say it, she sensed he had little time to talk.

"We're on our way from Puerto Vallarta. Brand is chartering a Learjet for the flight. We'll be in Oaxaca City sometime tomorrow. New Year's Day."

"You did it," Taylor said excitedly. "Good work, Ricardo."

"Thanks. He's a scary guy. Came right out and told me he'd kill me if I tried to rip him off."

"That must have been a bit unsettling."

"What was unsettling is that I believe him. I think he'd do it."

"Don't give him a chance," Taylor said. "I take it there was no sign of Alan."

"None, thank God. But until we're out of Puerto Vallarta it could still happen. That's weighing on me as well. I've got to go. I'll call you again when we get to Oaxaca City. Just stay out of sight after tonight. Brand will recognize you from a block away just by seeing your hair. Not a lot of redheads in Mexico."

"Okay." She hung up.

One potential disaster was out of the way. Had Alan been present for the meeting, things would have gone very wrong, very quickly. Taylor could only imagine the scene—Ricardo feigning shock at seeing Alan, asking what *he* was doing there. Alan telling Brand that he knew Ricardo—and worse yet, that Ricardo knew Taylor. Brand taking the most obvious course of action. Breaking off the meeting and sending someone to take care of Ricardo. She put the thought out of her mind—it hadn't happened. Not yet at least.

The fact that Edward Brand was chartering a Lear wasn't the best news. Not unexpected, but worrisome. She knew the reason. On a domestic flight there was no chance of bringing a gun. On a Lear there was every chance of bringing one. Brand wanted to be armed. She didn't blame him. He had no idea what he was walking into. He probably would have balked if they had insisted the money transfer be in cash. And that worked well for them. They didn't want cash. The half million was nothing. It was the next transfer out of Brand's account that counted. She wondered how much he was sitting on. She was pretty sure it was substantial. Very substantial. Certainly worth all the work.

Taylor paid her bill for the tea and salad, and left the quiet garden. Noise from the street percolated in as she neared the front of the hotel. New Year's Eve revelers off to an early start. It wasn't even nine o'clock, and the city was starting to come to life. A sense of loneliness overwhelmed her as she walked down the short hallway to her room. It had been many years since she had celebrated the birth of a new year by herself. In fact, she couldn't remember any time in her life when she hadn't been with friends or family as the calendar switched over. She unlocked the door and let herself into the empty room.

Taylor drew a bath and settled into the hot water. It was soothing to both her body and mind. She wasn't a woman to feel stress, but right now the tension was rising, and she was beginning to wonder whether they could pull this off. Edward Brand was no fool. He was intelligent and would be suspicious of everything until he was off that mountain with the treasure. That, of course, would never happen. Alan posed a distinct threat. Kelly and Ricardo were right, they should probably back off until Alan was out of the picture. But that meant letting Brand go. All the planning. All for naught.

No way.

She ducked her head under the water, her long hair swaying gently with the ripples. She slicked it back and squeezed until most of the excess water was gone, then climbed out of the tub and towel dried. There was a full-length mirror on the back of the bathroom door, and she looked at her reflection. Nowhere to hide the extra pounds or the stretch marks when the clothes were off. She had neither. Her body was taut and lean, her long legs the reason many men glanced back when they passed her on the street. She slipped on the terry housecoat the hotel provided and padded back into the bedroom.

She placed a quick call to Adolfo's room. He answered immediately. "Adolfo, it's Taylor. I need you to pick up something for me."

"Yes. What?"

"Do you know what walkie-talkies are?"

"Yes, I know this. For two people to talk. Push the button, then let it go."

"Exactly. Could you find a pair and purchase them. I'll pay you whatever they cost. Make sure they have new batteries."

"*Sí*, I will do."

"Thanks."

"De nada."

Taylor replaced the phone in the cradle. They needed a way to communicate while at Monte Alban. If Adolfo taped down his talk button, she could hear the conversation and know exactly when to light the fire and distract the guards. It was crude, but it didn't have to be sophisticated to work. That's all that mattered—whether it worked or not. She switched her thoughts to Kelly Kramer. His story about the CIA being involved in Monte Alban must have made the grade. She checked the time and dialed his number. He was still at the office and picked up on the third ring.

"Hi," she said. "How are things in Washington?"

"Cold. It's miserable here. I think it's about eight degrees outside right now. There's snow everywhere. I can't remember a nastier winter."

"Well, it's nice down here. Sixty-five and holding."

"No kidding. It's Mexico. Is everything okay?"

"Perfect. Couldn't be better, in fact. Adolfo and I got the treasure in place. No problems that we couldn't handle. He's good, Kelly. He thinks quick on his feet. If anyone can sell Edward Brand that he's a corrupt government employee, it's Adolfo. It appears that Brent Hawkins swallowed your story about the CIA operative and then sold Brand on it."

"Good. Did Ricardo meet with them yet?"

"This afternoon. They're flying into Oaxaca City tomorrow." She paused, then added, "I think we should try to be ready to go on the second."

"Twenty-four to thirty hours after they arrive. That's fast, Taylor. Maybe too fast."

"I'm worried about Alan. If he shows up, he'll blow Ricardo's cover. Then it's over. Ricardo's dead. Brand made no bones about it—Ricardo tries to rip him off and he's a dead man. I didn't get him involved in this to get him killed."

"Of course not. I'm ready from this end. I've got what

I need to intercept the satellite call, and I've even isolated a decoding program in case he's encrypted his account number. The chances of that are minimal, but I'm just being careful. I don't want to be scrambling around trying to find a computer program when I've only got seconds to spare."

"You'll do fine," Taylor said. She lay on the bed, her wet hair on the pillow. "There's nothing else to do. I think that the longer we wait, the more we're inviting problems. Brand will be here tomorrow. We give him a day to settle in, then run the con the next night. That's January second. I think that's our timetable."

"Okay, Taylor, you're the one with your finger on the pulse. I'll be wired on caffeine and wide awake by ten at night on the second. Any time after that is fine." There was a break, then he said, "Hey, Happy New Year."

"Yeah, you too." Taylor took a deep breath. "We're going to do this, Kelly."

"Absolutely."

CHAPTER FIFTY-SEVEN

At Aeropuerto Internacional Gustavo Díaz Ordáz in Puerto Vallarta, the private jets melded into the takeoff queue with the same priority as the commercial airliners. At eleven minutes after noon, Edward Brand's chartered Learjet was fifth in the queue, but he refused to give the pilots permission to enter the line. The co-pilot left the cockpit and ventured back into the cabin. He did not look happy.

"Sir, the tower is demanding we move into the queue. We have to leave now."

"Tell the tower we'll take a later spot. I'm not ready yet." There was no mistaking the authority in Brand's voice.

"Mr. Brand, we were supposed to depart Puerto Vallarta over an hour ago. We've already shifted our position three times. The pilot will not do it again."

"I'm paying you," Brand shot back. "You'll wait if I tell you to."

"No, sir. I'm afraid it doesn't work that way. You chartered this plane to Oaxaca City, departing ten-thirty-seven. We booked a return flight with a paying customer based on that departure time. We can't bump our spot in the queue again. I'm sorry." He turned and headed toward the cabin.

Brand cursed and glanced out the window. Where the hell was Alan Bestwick? He had called Alan the previous evening and told him to be at the airport for ten-thirty. Alan had been partially inebriated, but forgetting a flight the next day? That was totally out of character. Where the hell was he?

"What's wrong?" Carlos asked. He was sitting in one of the plush leather chairs, a very satisfied look on his face. This was his first flight in a private jet.

"I'm waiting for someone," Brand snapped back. The plane wasn't moving yet, and he scanned the outside of the private terminal for Alan. Nothing. He glanced back inside the plane. Ricardo was reading a magazine, totally engrossed in the article. The man hadn't even noticed they weren't moving. Damn it. Once he decided on something, he wanted it to happen. And he had decided last night that having Alan along to Oaxaca City was a good idea. He was moving into unknown waters with only one other person he could trust. Two allies were far better than one. He knew the decision would cost him some money, but he was willing to take the hit. Safety in numbers.

He took another look out the small oval window. Heat waves rising from the black asphalt distorted the view, but what he was seeing was pretty clear. No Alan Bestwick. He felt a tiny shudder as the chocks were removed from the wheels and the pilots revved the engines slightly. Time was running out.

Ricardo Allende kept his eyes focused on the page. Keep them moving, line after line, pretend to read the text. Brand was watching. He had no idea what the article was about. None whatsoever. Not one word had sunk in except for what Edward Brand had said. *I'm waiting for someone.* Christ, he didn't have to have an IQ above that of a tree frog to know who Brand was waiting for.

Alan Bestwick.

And if Bestwick made it to the plane before they began to taxi, he was a dead man. Ricardo could feel a slight dampness in his armpits. He concentrated on not sweating. Relax, just keep calm. Bestwick wasn't here yet. Don't try to solve problems that don't exist. There was a slight motion and the plane began to move. He tried to keep his breathing even.

Get into the takeoff queue.

Once they were in, there was no turning back. Another private jet, a Gulfstream II, was immediately ahead of them. An Air Canada 707 was being pushed back from its gate. That was their spot, between the two planes. Seconds now, only seconds and he'd be okay.

"There he is," Brand said, staring out the window. He unbuckled his seat belt and hustled to cockpit. "The man we're waiting for, he's here."

There was a muffled response from the pilot, but Ricardo didn't need to hear what he had said. Brand's response told the story.

"He's standing right there," he yelled. "This is insane. Just stop and pick him up."

Again, the incoherent reply.

"Shit," Brand said, returning to his seat and snapping the seat belt in place. He was a blistering shade of red.

"What's wrong?" Carlos asked. "Why won't they stop?"

Brand didn't answer for a minute, and when he did it was very tight-lipped. "He said we'd lose our spot in the queue."

Ricardo didn't say a word. He looked up from his magazine and glanced out the window. Standing in front of the executive terminal watching the plane taxi onto the runway was Alan Bestwick. Ricardo could see Bestwick through the tinted window, but the man could not see in. No chance of recognition. Not now. But if Brand wanted Alan in Oaxaca City, then the chances were pretty good that Alan would be following on a commercial flight. Which meant they would have to move quickly. He hoped Taylor and Kelly would be ready. He settled back with the magazine and focused on the content of the article he'd been staring at for the last ten minutes. It was the latest issue of *Chatelaine*—"Ten Ways to be a Better Lover."

He closed the magazine and tucked it under a copy of *Sports Illustrated*.

Alan Bestwick stared at the Lear as it taxied onto the runway. He cursed under his breath at the Mexican police. Some minor fender-bender on the main road from the Sheraton to the airport and they'd completely shut down the highway. Idiots.

He made his way into the main terminal and waited in the long line at the Aeroméxico counter. When he finally reached the ticket agent she didn't speak English. An airline employee pulled him out of the line and when an English-speaking agent opened they slid him in.

"I need to get to Oaxaca City," Alan said.

"When would you like to fly, sir?" the woman asked.

"As soon as possible."

Her fingernails clicked on the keyboard as she searched the outgoing flights for availability. "It's very busy, sir, being New Year's Day."

"Yes, I'm sure it is. But it's important I get there quickly."

"I understand." She glanced at the series of lines snaking back from the counter. The meaning of the look wasn't lost on Alan. No one was standing in line for the fun of it. "The best I can do is tomorrow evening. Eight-fourteen departure."

"When does that arrive in Oaxaca?"

She checked the screen. "Eleven-twenty-one."

"Nothing today?" he asked and she shook her head. "Standby?"

"Already six people on the waiting list."

"Okay, I'll take it."

"I'll need to see your passport please."

Alan traded the cool air-conditioning of the airport for the hot streets of Puerto Vallarta. Taxis were doing a brisk business, ripping off the tourists by charging them double the usual rate. The heat was irritating and the stench of diesel hard on his throat and lungs. He slid into the backseat of the first taxi in line.

"Sheraton," he said, handing the man twelve dollars. The driver started to say something, but Alan just held up his hand and looked out the window. He'd already been screwed enough for one day, he wasn't going to let a cab driver nail him too.

CHAPTER FIFTY-EIGHT

Monday morning. New Year's Day.

The streets of Oaxaca City were quiet, most residents of the city sleeping late after a night of celebrating. Taylor had taken an early morning walk about the cobblestone streets, getting some fresh air. Once Edward Brand arrived in the Learjet from Puerto Vallarta, she would have to stay inside. Ricardo was right, her hair would be a dead giveaway in a country where almost one hundred percent of the people had black hair. If Brand were to spot her, he would know he was being set up.

There was a knock on the door. It was Adolfo. He had a set of compact walkie-talkies that he had somehow found in one of the many tiny shops tucked away in the city center. They were new, still in the box. Four nine-volt batteries were necessary to power them, and Adolfo had purchased those as well. Taylor looked over the gear and nodded.

"Good work, Adolfo," she said, slipping the batteries in the housing and clipping the plastic cover closed. "Let's try them out."

"*Sí*," he said, taking one and heading out the door. "I go to the street?"

"Yes, that's good. Maybe five hundred yards."

"*Sí*, I understand. Five hundred yards is same as five hundred meters."

"Yes. Five hundred meters. Give or take."

"What?" he asked, confused at the colloquialism.

"Nothing. Five hundred meters."

He closed the door and the room was silent for a few minutes. Then there was a slight crackle and his voice came through the walkie-talkie. It was very clear.

"That's fine, Adolfo. I can hear you okay. Can you hear me?"

"*Sí*. I hear you."

"Okay, come on back. They work well."

She turned off the small transmitter and set it on the bed. Everything was ready. Kelly in D.C., Ricardo working the inside track with Brand, Adolfo with his fake ID and walkie-talkie. The satellite phone was active and charged. Now she just needed the man himself.

Edward Brand.

The Learjet touched down on the steaming pavement at two-thirty-eight on January 1. The flight time was well under two hours at a cruising speed of four hundred and sixty miles an hour. The pilot had gained twenty-three minutes by opening the throttles a touch and with the assistance of a slight tailwind. If he could get the ground crews to refuel the plane quickly, he would be close enough to his schedule to keep his next client from complaining. He didn't bother talking to the client from this leg—he knew the man didn't give a shit.

A customs vehicle pulled up to the Lear once it had taxied to a stop, sat for a minute, then received the flight plan from the tower and backed off. The flight had originated inside Mexico and was outside their jurisdiction. Once the steps were lowered, Brand, Carlos and Ricardo exited. They waited for the co-pilot to unload their luggage and carried it through the terminal to the taxi queue. They had four rooms reserved at the Hacienda Los Laureles, a quiet hotel with temazcal steam baths and a fully functional spa on site. Brand didn't care about either, he just wanted to be out of Oaxaca City. The drive was about twenty minutes, and after they checked in he filled out the necessary paperwork to rent one of the four-wheel-drive Jeeps in the parking lot. The porters dropped their bags in their rooms, and the men met in the bar a half hour later.

"When can we meet Manuel Sanchez?" Brand asked over a small green bottle of San Pellegrino sparkling water.

"I'll call him. He's here in Oaxaca City somewhere. I've got his cell number. When did you want to meet?" Ricardo asked.

"Tonight."

"I'll see if that works for him," Ricardo said.

"Make it work," Brand said. It wasn't threatening or indecisive—simply a statement.

Ricardo finished his drink and went back to his room to get Sanchez's number and make the call. Edward Brand and Carlos stayed in the bar, a laidback affair with only a few tables and no music playing. The floors were ochre-colored adobe tiles, and voices tended to echo slightly in the room. Brand didn't like it. He preferred a space where what he said remained between himself and the person he was talking to. After Ricardo left, the only people in the bar were Brand, Carlos and the bartender. He made a call on his cell phone.

"I need you to check on someone for me," Brand said when Brent Hawkins answered.

"Who?" the FBI agent asked.

"His name is Manuel Sanchez. Mexican. Lives in Mexico City."

"Common name. Could be more than one. You got anything else on this guy."

"Just see what you come up with. Get their job descriptions if you can. I might be able to tell from that."

"Time frames?"

"Immediately."

"Okay."

Brand killed the line and shook his head. He should have called Hawkins the minute he got Sanchez's name from Ricardo in Puerto Vallarta. He wasn't thinking. Mistakes like that were inexcusable. He glanced up as Ricardo returned to the bar.

"He's on his way over," Ricardo said. "He figured about half an hour."

"We'll talk by the pool," Brand said. The area surrounding the swimming pool was far more secluded, with alcoves set back into the plants.

Ricardo nodded. "I'll meet him at the front desk and bring him around." He retook his seat and ordered a Corona. The three of them talked about nothing for twenty minutes, and then Ricardo excused himself and went to the lobby to wait for Sanchez. Brand and Carlos headed for the pool.

Almost to the minute on a half hour, Adolfo pulled up in front of the hotel in a taxi. He asked the driver to wait and met Ricardo at the front entrance. They shook hands and said polite hellos, but nothing that would indicate they knew each other any better than the relationship they had sold Edward Brand on. Nothing to chance. One set of ears in the wrong place could be fatal. When they reached the pool, Brand and Carlos were already settled in under a royal palm on the far side of the water. They walked around the edge of the pool and Ricardo did the introductions. Adolfo apologized for his English up front. Brand just waved it off as inconsequential.

"How can you help us, Senor Sanchez?" Brand asked when the newcomers were settled and non-alcoholic drinks had been served.

"With Monte Alban?"

"Yes. With the situation at Monte Alban."

"Ricardo has not told you?" Adolfo asked, looking to Ricardo.

"Yes, but I'd like to hear it from you."

"Is good. Yes. I can take care of the guards at Monte Alban. You take pictures of what you find with a digital camera and send that to me. Then I will write down the pieces you find in the cave. I will put them in the Mexican computers. Once they are in the computers you can sell them. Until I do that, you will not find the buyer."

"What does this cost?" Brand asked.

Again, Adolfo shot Ricardo a look. "Five hundred thousand American dollars."

"I have the cash," Brand said.

Adolfo shook his head violently. "No, no, I do not want cash. Cash I have to explain to the Mexican government. That is not good. I need the money sent to my account outside Mexico."

Brand nodded. "Yes, that's right. Ricardo *did* tell us that." He toyed with his glass for a minute, then asked, "When will this happen?"

"I do not want to stay in Oaxaca City long. My job is in Mexico City. I need to get back. Not today, but the next day. *Manana.* How is that in English?"

"Tomorrow," Brand said.

"Yes. Tomorrow. Tomorrow night at twelve. We meet at Monte Alban. You can see the treasure. Then the next night you can have it."

"Tomorrow night at midnight we finish the deal, but we can't move what we find until the next day?" Brand asked. "I don't think I like that."

Ricardo interjected. "Senor Sanchez does not wish to be nearby when you take the treasure. He wishes to be back in Mexico City."

Brand's eyes were on fire. "That was never part of the deal."

"The treasure has been there since the Zapotecs walked

about Monte Alban," Ricardo said. "I don't think it's going very far in the next day or two."

Edward Brand's jaw was locked tight. He stared at Adolfo for the better part of a minute. The diminutive Mexican looked about, occasionally meeting his gaze. He looked like he couldn't care less what Brand decided.

"Okay," Brand said. "I'll be watching the treasure until I can get it out."

"As you wish," Adolfo said. He rose and gave the three men at the table a curt bow. "Until tomorrow. Midnight. On the mountain."

"Tomorrow," Brand said. There was no emotion in his voice.

CHAPTER FIFTY-NINE

January 2 dawned clear, not a cloud marring the deep blue Mexican sky. Probably not the best, Taylor thought, envisioning the plateau at Monte Alban awash in moonlight. Cloud cover would have been better. Maybe the sky would change by midnight. Maybe, but probably not.

She sat in her small stone room, staring out the window of the convent-turned-hotel. How many nuns had sat in the exact same spot, staring at the same scene? Did they love their lives? Their devotion to Christ? Or did they wonder what the other side was like? A loving husband, a family, a life that allowed pleasure. Such devotion to what they believed was their calling. But what was hers? What was her calling in life? She had no children, no business, no career and was sixteen hours from perpetuating a massive fraud. True, it was on a man who deserved it, but it was illegal nonetheless.

A man rounded the corner and limped down the narrow road that bordered the hotel. He used a cane and found the footing on the uneven cobblestones difficult, stumbling many times as he walked past her window. His clothing was in tatters, and his face heavily creased from a tough life under too much sun. He glanced up as he passed and for a split second their eyes locked. They were sad eyes. Taylor watched him until he rounded the corner and disappeared from view. Gone from her life, but for him nothing had changed. He was still decrepit and poor, living a life no one would want. As she turned from the window back to the simple room that had once housed penitent nuns, she made her final decision.

She would not have that life. Not now, not ever. She deserved better. The opportunity to live a life of wealth was within her grasp. Only Edward Brand stood in her way. Tonight he would pay for what he had done.

He would pay beyond his wildest dreams.

Ricardo Allende sat beside the pool at Hacienda Los Laureles reading a Spanish mystery novel. He was on chapter eighteen, but had absolutely no idea what was going on in the book. Neither Edward Brand nor Carlos Valendez had shown their face yet, and it was almost three in the afternoon. Not seeing the men made him nervous. He waved to the pool waiter and ordered another sparkling water. The temperature had risen during the day, peaking at over eighty degrees. The air was still and the sky a homogenous palate of deep blue. He set the book on the small table beside his chaise lounge and dove in the pool. The water was refreshing.

Midnight was closing in quickly. Nine hours until he would be standing atop the plateau at Monte Alban. Nine hours until he would give the performance of his life. Perhaps *for* his life. If Taylor Simons were right about what was in Edward Brand's bank account, the payoff would be staggering. If she were wrong, the end result would be very different from what he had envisioned.

So many variables.

Ricardo pulled himself out of the pool, his athletic body glistening in the hot Mexican sun. A couple of women sunning themselves by the bar gave him an approving look. He smiled as he returned to his seat and his book. There would be plenty of time for that later. Many women who would desire the rich, attractive Mexican. Nine hours. The adage that time would tell could never be truer. Nine hours. A smile began to creep across his face, but it quickly disappeared as another thought raced through his mind.

Nine hours to live?

Alan Bestwick nursed his drink, cursing the airlines and anyone else who crossed his line of vision. It was still four and a half, almost five hours until his flight departed. Wasted time. Time he would never get back. Crucial time. Edward Brand had called two hours ago and told him the deal was on at midnight, a scant thirty-nine minutes after his flight was scheduled to arrive in Oaxaca City. He would travel with a carry-on, no checked bags and grab the first taxi in the queue. Straight to Monte Alban, but have the driver stop just shy of the plateau. Headlights showing up just as the guards were distracted to the far south end of the site was a bad idea.

Brand had checked with the local service provider and there was no cell service available on the mountain top. The best they could do was for Alan to stand on the easternmost of the four north palaces. Brand would watch for him and give one blink with his flashlight. That was it—one only. Miss that and miss the show. Brand had been adamant on that. He would not risk attracting the guards. He needed the meeting tonight to go without any complications as he couldn't move the treasure until the next night. Something he had not been pleased about.

Alan had spent twenty minutes on the hotel Internet searching for information on Monte Alban. He was surprised at how well documented the archeological site was. The Mexican government was high on it, confident that there were other undiscovered tombs atop the mountain.

It was just a matter of time before they were found. One of the Web sites had a layout of the site, and he had familiarized himself with the exact location of the north palaces. He would be where he should be when he should be.

God help anyone who got in his way.

Adolfo was a religious man. He was well aware that God was most likely looking down on him with a frown at this particular moment, but there was little he could do about that. Money was a necessary evil, and he had very little of it. Surely God would understand that He had not given this humble servant much in the way of riches to sustain a decent life. Many nights had seen him sleep with an empty belly. Adolfo was certain that God had not intended that.

He saw tonight as a gift. An opportunity to rise above the life he had lived, surviving one day to face another that was painfully the same as every other. An endless series of days spent wanting something more. To date, that something had never appeared. Not until now.

Tonight everything could change. He would have to be on his game. He was facing the greatest test of his life. Convincing Edward Brand that the treasure was real, that he could catalogue the items so they could be sold and that the money must be transferred immediately. Tonight he must be Manuel Sanchez, Director of Antiquities for the Mexican government.

Tonight he must be invincible.

Kelly Kramer pulled into the NSA complex at six o'clock, Tuesday, January 2. He parked and headed directly to his office, bypassing the coffee station. That would come later. He set up in his office, deflected a few questions from colleagues who were working late as to why he was back to work a day early and powered up his computer.

Edward Brand had taken the bait. He had instructed Brent Hawkins to check out the CIA connection. Kelly knew this because he had placed a tracer in the file that would ping anyone who entered. The only hit on the file had come from the San Francisco office of the FBI. As of eleven o'clock tonight, that file would cease to exist. Its usefulness was at an end, and he intended to erase it from the computer's hard drive. The less evidence they left for Brand and Hawkins, the better. In fact, even the slightest shard was too much. Brand was no fool, and he would be looking for who had ripped him off. Kelly was sure he had covered his tracks.

That left the human element. Ricardo and Adolfo needed to convince Brand that they held the key to a great treasure. They needed to get Brand to instigate the wire transfer for five hundred thousand dollars. Then they needed to get the hell out of there. Because once Brand knew he had been scammed, there would be the devil to pay.

Taylor was directly in harm's way. She would be at Monte Alban, scrambling along a dangerous mountainside, trying to evade the guards as they came running to see the cause and the extent of the fire. Her timing had to be perfect. Adolfo would have seconds, not minutes, to link up with her and for them to get back to the vehicle he brought to the meeting. Then they had to get off the mountain and back to Oaxaca City. From there it was overland by secondary highways to Minatitlan, on Bahía de Campeche. If all went well, Ricardo would travel back to Oaxaca City with Brand and Carlos, then steal away in the middle of the night. He would also head for the Caribbean coast. Nothing to do with Mexico City. Once Brand knew he had been taken, he would be watching. If Taylor were right, what they were doing would almost demolish him financially, but he may still have some resources to come after them. That's why Brand could never know who was behind the con. Ricardo and Adolfo were the front men. They would have to meld back into Mexican society and keep a low profile because Brand would be targeting them. Things would be very different if Brand managed to tie Taylor and him into this.

Very different. Probably fatal. They could never hide from him.

Kelly took a deep breath and stared at his computer. It was all there, waiting. The program that would track the call from the satellite phone, then capture the millions of bytes of digital information between the man at Monte Alban and his banker. The program that would initiate a second transfer. The program to decode the data in case it was encrypted.

In theory, everything was perfect.

A fully loaded Browning pistol sat on the bed. A second clip, complete with bullets, lay beside it. Across the expansive hotel room, Carlos Valendez was sitting by the window oiling a Smith & Wesson 1911. A classical guitar CD played on the stereo. The music was barely audible to Edward Brand, on the balcony overlooking the gardens. The quiet of the late afternoon was exactly what he wanted. Time to sit and reflect.

He closed his eyes, the waning sun still warm on his skin. He had just checked his watch and knew it was six-thirty. Five and a half hours until the meeting at Monte Alban. There were certain aspects of this deal he liked, certain ones that he didn't. Ricardo's story was believable—stuff like this did happen. There was an abundance of undiscovered treasure out there, the actual amount unknown simply because it had yet to be found. Everything and everyone had checked out just fine. Brian Palmer, the murdered CIA agent, was real. He had filed a report indicating the treasure at Monte Alban not only existed, but it was substantial. Worth well into the millions. That was one of the deciding factors that had convinced him to get involved.

The second was Manuel Sanchez. Brent Hawkins had

called an hour ago with the news. Manuel Sanchez was the Director of Antiquities, stationed in Mexico City. He was out of the office on holidays. By all appearances, Brand had stumbled onto a goldmine. That was what worried him. He didn't like packages that fell in his lap. All neatly tied up, no loose ends. It reminded him of what he did for a living. When things looked too good to be true . . .

Brand hoisted himself out of his chair and wandered back into the cool of the air-conditioned room. A fan beat out a slow tempo, and the music was slightly louder inside. He walked over to the bed and stared down at the gun and the extra bullets. Would he need them tonight? He had no idea. Would he use them if he had to? Absolutely.

Ricardo Allende had better be exactly who he said he was. Manuel Sanchez had better produce once the artifacts were out of the tomb and safely stashed. He had already rented a panel van and would pick it up the next day around noon. Then, tomorrow night he would return to the site and plunder the cave. He didn't like waiting an additional twenty-four hours, but there was nothing he could do. This was Sanchez's show, and it moved at the speed he wanted. Ricardo was simply the messenger boy.

Brand reached down and picked up the gun. The metal was cool in his palm. Cool and reassuring. He wondered if anyone would die tonight.

CHAPTER SIXTY

Taylor left the hotel at ten o'clock. She drove a Suzuki 4x4 she had rented earlier in the day during her only outing from the constricting stone room. The ride was bumpy, the suspension in the five-year-old vehicle completely shot. The streets of Oaxaca City were lively, many locals just finishing their evening meal and sitting on plastic chairs in front of their small adobe and brick houses. The smell of fried beef and onions was heavy in the still night air.

Once out of the city and on the road to Monte Alban, the traffic was light. The drive took her less than fifteen minutes, then another ten to find a suitable place to conceal the Suzuki. She tucked it in an overgrown pull-off, about four hundred yards from the top of the road. From there, she hiked along the side of the road until she could see the tops of the north palaces. The museum and parking lot were directly ahead—and the guards. She veered off the path to her right and followed the edge of the plateau until she reached a point opposite the museum. The light from the half moon silhouetted the guard house against the sky as she crept along the far west side of the ruins. The guards' outlines were visible through the windows. If she could see them, they could see her. Taylor cut off the edge of the plateau onto the rocky mountainside, trying to stay out of their line of vision.

From here on, it was dangerous. The rocks were uneven and often loose, the cliff beneath them steep and unforgiving. One wrong foothold and she was dead. The moonlight, which had moments before acted against her, was now on her side. She could see where she was stepping, and as long as she concentrated on her footing and didn't hurry, she was safe. About halfway along the six hundred-yard plateau she checked her watch. Five minutes after eleven. She should be okay for time.

Twenty minutes later, she was almost at the south end of the ruins. She started to break twigs off the dead and dried shrubs that had sprung up between the cracks in the rocks. By the time she had reached the far south end, she had a good armful of wood for the fire. She piled it on the edge of the plateau, to the east of the south platform so the location was visible to the guard shack. Then she checked her supply of matches, turned on her walkie-talkie and sat on a rock.

Half an hour and it would happen. So close now.

Adolfo drove the Jeep to a place close to the top of the road, turned it around so it was facing downhill, then parked. He didn't worry about concealing the vehicle as Taylor had; Brand would expect him to drive. He walked up the incline to a position about fifty yards from the parking lot and sat on the side of the road. He pulled the walkie-talkie from his suit pocket and turned the dial to the on position, then adjusted the squelch. He swore softly in Spanish. The button that needed to be depressed in order to talk didn't have a switch on it to hold it down. He had not brought any tape with him to keep it in the talk position. Taylor was on the other side of the ruins, expecting him to leave the line open so she could hear what was happening. How was he going to do that? He couldn't keep his hand in his pocket with his thumb on the button. What to do?

A small bush, mostly dried twigs with an occasional sign of green, was growing beside the rock. He snapped off one of the dead branches and then broke off the very end so he had a tiny piece of wood in between his fingers. He depressed the talk button and gingerly slipped the twig in the narrow gap between the housing and the button. When he released the pressure with his finger, the button stayed down. Taylor could now hear everything. He glanced at his watch, the hands readily visible in the moonlight. Eleven-fifty-three.

He didn't have long to wait. Another set of headlights pulled up close to where he had parked, then went dark. A moment later, he saw three figures walking up the side of the road. Ricardo was in the middle, flanked by Carlos Valendez and Edward Brand. He took a deep breath and said a quick prayer to the Almighty. This was it. Time for the performance of his life.

There was the sound of gravel crunching under the men's feet, but other than that the night was entirely silent. It was eerie. When they were ten feet away, Edward Brand gave a nod.

"Good evening, Senor Sanchez," he said. "Is everything okay?"

"Everything is fine."

"Then let's have a look at what you've found."

Sanchez shook his head. "We wait for the guards to leave. I have something planned."

Brand's face changed slightly—took on an ominous look. "What have you—planned?" he asked.

"I'm not sure in English of the word. A fire. To take the guards away."

"A distraction?" Brand asked.

"Yes, that is it." He glanced at his watch. "Any minute now."

Almost on cue, exactly at twelve o'clock, there was activity in the guard shack. The two men began talking excitedly and pointing. A few seconds later, they left the shack, heading south at a good pace.

"Now we go," Adolfo said.

The four men moved quickly, Ricardo leading the way. They skirted the parking lot and museum, then dropped over the edge of the plateau onto the thin path leading to the cave. Single file, and moving now with more caution, they snaked their way along the worn rocks to where the boulder they had embedded in the cliff side hid the entrance. Ricardo carried a crowbar and used it to lever out the smaller rock. He set the stone aside, against the cliff and away from the edge.

"Don't knock it over the edge. We need it to reseal the cave," Ricardo said.

He crawled through the tight opening and turned on his flashlight. Behind him came Adolfo, then Carlos. Then they got lucky. Edward Brand's shoulders were too wide to fit through. No one had thought of Brand's size—whether he would fit through the small aperture. It had always been assumed that both Brand and Carlos would be in the room looking at the treasure.

"For Christ's sake," Brand said, extricating himself from the hole. "Carlos. Come here."

The Mexican stuck his head through the hole. "What?"

"I can't fit through. I need you to check things out. Don't fuck this up. I'm relying on you."

"It's okay. I'll make sure everything's okay."

"You do that."

Carlos slipped back into the cave. "Where's the treasure?" he asked.

Ricardo pointed to the back of the cave. "This way." He walked carefully on the slippery rocks to the alcove at the back of the cave. Water dripped from the ceiling and made plopping noises as the drops landed in small pools. They reached the opening to the smaller room and Ricardo shone his light on the contents. The gold reflected the light and scattered the beam throughout the alcove, showing the rest of the artifacts they had carefully placed on top of each other, then covered with the tarp. Carlos stretched his arm out and grabbed the top piece.

"Don't move them," Ricardo said. "They could spill all over, and the guards might hear."

Carlos ran his hand over the smooth surface and pulled on the tarp. It dropped away a touch, revealing more golden objects beneath. He touched each of them, feeling the unmistakable coolness of the precious metal. He wet his lips and grabbed the edge of the tarp, ready to yank it back.

"That's it," Ricardo said, clamping his hand on the man's arm and pulling it back. "We're out of time. We have to go."

"I can't tell how many pieces there are," Carlos said.

"Hundreds," Adolfo said. "Many, many pieces."

"But not now. Tomorrow," Ricardo said. "Now we leave before the guards return."

They piled out of the cave and Ricardo busied himself with replacing the stone. Brand looked at Carlos and shrugged. "Well?" he asked.

"There is definitely treasure. A large mound of what appears to be gold. But I don't know how many pieces there are. It's in a small room in the back of the cave—difficult to tell."

Brand turned to Adolfo. "How many pieces?" he asked.

"At least one hundred and twenty, perhaps as many as one hundred and fifty," he replied.

"The back portion of the cave is very restrictive," Ricardo said. We've been in a few times now and have yet to get to the bottom of the stack. I think that Senor Sanchez is correct. One hundred to one fifty."

"You will catalogue them?" Brand asked.

"That is included in the price," Adolfo said.

Brand was quiet. Handing over a half million dollars without seeing the merchandise was risky, but then again, it was only a half million. The upside to the deal was potentially huge. He had little to no time to make up his mind.

"All right," he said. "Let's do it."

Ricardo pulled out the satellite phone and handed it to Brand. With the phone was a slip of paper with a transit number and an account number. Adolfo's secret account. Brand took the phone and the paper, moved a few feet away and dialed a number. He spoke into the receiver for a minute, then returned to the group.

"The money has been transferred," he said.

Adolfo took the phone and placed a call to the bank where they had set up the account to receive the half million dollars. He entered his code on the keypad and pushed one for account balances. The money was there. He smiled and killed the satellite link.

"All is good," he said.

They retreated along the narrow path to the far north end of the excavation. The guard shack was still empty, but there was no sign of flames at the south end of the plateau. The fire was out, and the guards would be back soon. Brand dropped behind the other three men and aimed his flashlight at the north palaces. He flicked it once. No one noticed. He fell in behind them, and they continued down the road at a brisk pace. They were eighty yards from the northernmost tip of the parking lot and just out of sight of the guard house when another figure appeared from the direction of the north palaces. In the moonlight it was obvious the man was a *gringo*, his blond hair swaying as he moved at a fast pace toward them. At fifty yards, the man's facial features were discernable.

Walking toward them was Alan Bestwick.

CHAPTER SIXTY-ONE

Kelly Kramer picked up the link from the phone to the satellite the moment the connection was made. He locked his computer on it and listened. One voice was Edward Brand, the other a man with a pleasant tone and a lilting accent. The two men talked briefly, enough time for Brand to tell him the transfer was legitimate. Then the banker switched over to the automated system, and Brand began entering numbers on the keypad.

Kelly knew he was in trouble by the fifth number. As the numbers Brand entered on the phone came up on his screen, the software immediately tracked the transit code. By the fourth digit, the number of banks with that transit code, worldwide, had slipped to ten. As the fifth digit was entered, the screen went blank. The bank he was dealing with had encryption software that time-delayed the numbers Brand was entering by one millisecond and scrambled them at the source. The only way to get the real numbers was to find the right decoding algorithm. And fast. He had a window of maybe one minute before the automatic transfer system would shut down and any additional transfers would require another call to the banker.

Kelly initiated the decryption software and hit Enter. The supercomputers at the National Security Agency rank among the fastest in the world, at over five trillion computations every second. With it being after one o'clock on the East Coast, there were very few users and the systems were running fast. It took eighteen seconds to find the right algorithm and apply it. A series of numbers, five with a gap followed by sixteen more, a hyphen, then another twelve, scrolled across the screen. The transit code, the account number and the numeric password. Kelly hit the print button and jotted them down on a piece of paper. He had lost data before and that wasn't going to happen tonight.

He switched from decryption to identification. The response time was almost zero. The account was in a bank in the Seychelles. The Greater Seychelles Financial Institution. He keyed in a request for an account balance. When the number hit the screen he sat back in his chair and sucked in a deep breath. The funds were registered as American dollars. The amount was staggering.

Two hundred and sixty-four million dollars.

He leaned forward, keying furiously. Seconds now and the window would close. Then the user requesting the withdrawal would have to speak with someone at the bank. He initiated an electronic withdrawal form and typed in the necessary account information. It asked for his password, and he entered the twelve-digit code. The cursor jumped down to the line asking what amount to withdraw. With shaking hands he entered two hundred and sixty-three million dollars. He hit Enter.

Nothing happened for about two seconds, and then a prompt came on the screen. *Destination.* Kelly could hardly breathe as he typed in the numbers to start an electronic transfer that would send the money bouncing off eight satellites and in and out of thirty banks in as many countries. Every time it hit a destination, that bank's security software would throw up a firewall for anyone trying to trace it. Moving the money through the satellites disguised where it was going. The satellites were just about untraceable.

He touched the enter key and stopped breathing.

Seconds passed. The machine beeped. The money had been transferred. He let out a whoop and killed the programs. Then he opened a direct link to Taylor's account in the Bahamas—the ultimate resting place for the funds. The balance read twenty-three thousand dollars. He stared at the screen. What the hell was going on? Where was the money? He keyed in a request for recent transactions. There were two. A deposit of two hundred and sixty-three million dollars, then a debit for exactly the same amount. Both transactions were within the last two minutes.

"Christ Almighty," he yelled at the screen. "No, no, no."

Edward Brand must have had some sort of program in place to immediately retrace the steps and redeposit the money unless the transaction were verified. Kelly grabbed his head in his hands for a second, then moved back two screens and tried to reactivate the initial transfer out of Brand's account. A note popped up on the screen that any debits would have to be cleared through the bank by calling a banking representative.

"Oh, my God," he said, leaning back in the chair. "Oh, guys, I am so sorry."

The only explanation was that the money was back in Brand's account. They had failed. And right now, thousands of miles to the south, a deadly game was being played out on the top of a rugged Mexican mountain.

CHAPTER SIXTY-TWO

"What the hell are *you* doing here?" Alan Bestwick asked as he approached the group. His gaze was firmly fixed on Ricardo Allende.

Brand glanced between the two men. "You know him?" he asked Alan.

"From Mexico City. He drove me around one night. Remember?" Alan asked Ricardo, now only inches separating the two.

The pistol appeared in Brand's hand, and he flipped off the safety with the fluid motion that only comes when the user knows the weapon well. Carlos backed off, the Smith & Wesson out of his waistband, and covered the group from a few yards away.

"What's going on, Ricardo? You and your little friend here trying to pull a scam of some sort?" Brand asked quietly.

"I met this guy one night. So what?" Ricardo said, faking bravado. Tough to do with a pistol aimed at his chest. "I drove him about the city. I haven't seen him since."

"You trying to say this is a coincidence?" Brand said. "I don't think so."

Silence engulfed the group. Brand backed off a few feet and watched both Alan and Ricardo. A slight breeze stirred the air and rustled the leaves on the few scraggly plants bordering the road. The moonlight played off the men's faces, casting shadows on their eye sockets and masking the fear and the hate. Edward Brand didn't need to see Ricardo's eyes to know. Ricardo was in on the scam. He and Adolfo had five hundred thousand dollars of his money. Brand toyed with the idea of killing Ricardo on the spot, but the shots would only attract the guards. He made a motion toward the road leading away from the ruins.

"Move," he said. "Down the road."

"This isn't right," Ricardo said.

"You've got that right, you fucking moron," Brand spat. When he spoke it was with emphasis on every word. "Get moving or I'll kill you. Both of you." He waved the gun at Adolfo.

As they started to move, a shout cut through the night air. The language was Spanish and even without Spanish as a native tongue, it was clear who it was and what they wanted. The guards had returned and were standing on the rocks yelling at them to stop. Carlos spun and yelled back, trying to encourage them to get back to work and leave well enough alone. The two uniformed men started down the hill, their guns still holstered.

"Oh, for God's sake. Is everything going to fuck up tonight?" Brand yelled, spinning about and leveling the gun at the guards. He pulled the trigger, and five shots barked out. Two hit their target, and one of the guards grabbed at his stomach and fell, rolling down the hill, bouncing off the rocks. The second guard pulled his gun and returned fire, then dove behind the nearest rock. The bullets churned up the dirt at their feet, and one caught Carlos in the calf. He took two steps and crashed to the ground, writhing in pain. Ricardo pounced on him and grabbed his right arm, trying to wrestle the gun from his grip. Brand turned and leveled the gun at Ricardo's head.

"You fucker," he said. "Try to rip me off, will you?" He pulled the trigger.

Ricardo had grown up street smart and street wise. One thing he knew was when someone was pointing a gun at you, get something or someone between you and the gun. Fast. He wrenched on Carlos's left arm, taking the man by surprise as he was protecting the gun in his right hand. Carlos rolled from the force, right into the path of the bullet. It ripped through his right shoulder, the trajectory and power of the pistol driving the bullet through his lung before lodging in his chest cavity. He shuddered from the impact and blood poured from his gaping mouth. Brand tried to find a target but Ricardo had pulled Carlos on top of him, giving the man nothing to shoot at.

Adolfo was running down the road, and Brand swung about and fired two quick shots after him. Adolfo stumbled and fell, clutching his side. Brand turned back to the scene just a few yards from his feet. Three shots, fired in rapid succession, whizzed by, just missing Brand. He ducked and dove for the edge of the road, training his gun on the approaching guard. Two shots smacked into the rocks close to the guard, who dropped to the ground, his gun in front of him. He fired another two shots before the hammer clicked on an empty chamber, one of the bullets ricocheting off the rock Brand was hiding behind and showering him with razor-sharp shards of stone. He grimaced in pain.

That wasn't the worst damage from the last two shots. Alan Bestwick, running to the same side of the road as Brand, had taken one bullet in the neck. He was sprawled on the dusty road, clutching at the wound. Blood spurted out, leaving strange mottled patterns on the dirt. His hands slowly stopped grabbing at his neck, and his body went stiff.

Edward Brand leapt up from behind the rock and ran toward where the guard was hunkered down behind a large boulder reloading his gun. He had just finished re-loading when Brand rounded the edge of the rock, and pumped three bullets into his chest. The impact knocked the guard over the rock, and he hit two more on the down slope before falling in a crumpled heap. Brand shot him once more in the head as he walked past.

"Asshole," he said, looking down the road for Adolfo and Ricardo. He saw them, about two hundred yards along. Ricardo had his arm around the older man's torso and was helping him. They were almost at the Jeep, parked facing down the road. Brand started to run, a fast jog at first, then an all-out sprint as he realized they were at the vehicle. When he was about sixty yards away, the lights came on and the Jeep lurched onto the road. He stopped and took careful aim, firing twice before the magazine was empty. He flipped it out and jammed in the replacement. He raised the gun and then slowly low-ered it. The Jeep had rounded a corner.

Brand turned and surveyed the carnage. Alan and Carlos were both dead. He had lost a half million dollars. The bastards who had scammed him had gotten away. He stood on the road, the pistol by his side, the half moon reflecting a strangely luminescent light on the scene. It seemed almost surreal. He sat on a rock, his mind alive with the irony.

So many times he had taken people's money. Some of those times it had turned ugly. People had died trying to protect what they owned. Until tonight it had always been them, never him. He didn't like being on this end of things. He sat in the silence for a few minutes, then re-trieved the car keys from Carlos's pocket and returned to the car. He had to get out of Oaxaca before the Mexican police discovered the two dead guards. They wouldn't give two shits about Alan or Carlos, but the guards would have them searching every house and stable in-side a hundred miles.

CHAPTER SIXTY-THREE

Everything had gone so wrong.

Kelly Kramer sat in his living room, soft piano playing on his stereo, the Boettger acoustics perfect as always. The mug of tea was warm on his hands. He stared at the time. Ten-fourteen in the morning. Nine days since the snafu at Monte Alban. Nine days of wondering how the wheels had come off so badly.

Ricardo had phoned him once, to give him a cell phone number where he could be contacted. That was his only link to the events of that dark night. It had come three days after the slaughter atop the mountain—the call originating in Villahermosa, an oil-producing city set in the swamps and banana groves of southern Mexico. He and Adolfo were on the run, laying low. They spent one night in Minatitlan, but the city was too small. Eventually word would get around that two men had shown up early on the morning of January 3, one with a bullet wound. That would be an invitation for Edward Brand to come sniffing about.

Kelly sipped his tea. Ricardo had taken a couple of minutes to fill him in on what had happened. He and

Adolfo sold Brand on the treasure and Brand made the call. Then, when they were getting ready to leave, Alan Bestwick showed up. That's when everything went from good to horrible. He described the gunplay—Alan and Carlos both killed on the dusty road, the guards' bodies splayed on the rocks, dead from bullets fired from Brand's gun. Then their run for freedom. The two bullets crashing through the rear of the Jeep and smashing the windshield only inches from his head. The terrifying drive down the road and the difficulty in finding a doctor to treat Adolfo's wound.

"What about Taylor?" Kelly had asked.

Ricardo didn't know. Taylor lit the fire exactly on cue at midnight. From that point on there was no indication she was anywhere on the mountain. Which was Kelly's fear. Taylor had slipped while navigating her way along the treacherous west side of Monte Alban. One misplaced footstep in the jumble of rocks, and she would have fallen to her death. And the mountainside was so rugged that it could be months or years before a local, scavenging for firewood, would find her body. By then she would be just a skeleton, the bones bleached white by the tropical sun.

The last thing Ricardo had asked was about the money. "Did you get it?" he had asked, his voice eager.

Kelly explained the transfer back of the money. That, to the best of his knowledge, Edward Brand had managed to reroute the funds back to his account. There was nothing to split. It was too dangerous to touch the five hundred thousand dollars. It had been sent directly to an account in the Caribbean, and Brand's bank would be able to trace that in ten minutes. Brand would be watching. Any attempt to get money from that account would only result in Edward Brand at your doorstep in record time.

Ricardo had repeated his cell number in case something changed, then hung up. Kelly had gone back to work at the National Security Agency. It was business as usual. No one had noticed the quick blip of computer time he had borrowed to track the money. No one was the wiser. Nothing had really changed, except for the five people who had lost their lives. He felt some remorse at the thought of two Mexican police officers being gunned down while simply doing their jobs. He felt nothing but loathing for Carlos and Alan. Every time he thought of Taylor, trying so desperately to get back to the north end of the ruins, falling to her death on the sharp rocks, he felt a wave of sadness and despair.

He finished his tea and took the empty cup to the kitchen, rinsed it out and dried it. He had worked late the night before, and no one expected him in before noon. He switched the stereo over to his favorite FM station and caught the weather forecast. Seven degrees and snowing. He shrugged into his coat, slipped on his boots and opened the front door. A blast of cold air hit him, stinging his lungs as he breathed. The tip of an envelope stuck out of his mailbox, and he opened the flap and dug out the mail. He went to throw it on the stairs, then stopped. One piece caught his attention. He closed the door, the wind and snow trapped outside.

Kelly set a handful of mail on the stairs and held the one of interest in his hand. His name was handwritten in scrawling text and the postmark was from Vienna, Austria. He knew the handwriting—he had seen it many times while at G-cubed. There was no return address. He took off his boots and coat and returned to the living room where the light from the front window was strong. He sat on the sofa and fingered the envelope for a minute before opening it. He suspected he knew who had sent it.

Please God, let it be her.

He ripped open the end of the envelope and pulled the single sheet of paper from inside. With trembling hands he unfolded it. There was very little printing on the page, but what was there was of incredible value.

> *Kelly,*
>
> *Sometimes life can be a little twisted. Things not always what they seem. Kind of like those street performers who put a peanut under one of three shells, then mix them up and have you guess which one is hiding the peanut. They always make one move you don't see. That's why you can never guess which shell it's under. Maybe that's why they call a con like this a shell game. Hope you understand.*
>
> *There are three account numbers on this page. The one marked 10M is yours. 5M is for Ricardo. 500K is for Adolfo.*
>
> *A good rate of pay for a night's work.*
>
> *Sorry about the transfer out. Should have warned you I'd be doing that.*
>
> *Thanks for all your help.*
>
> *Taylor*

Kelly held the single sheet of paper in his hand, a slow grin creeping over his face. Taylor had set up Edward Brand. It was not at all the way it appeared. Brand had never held the aces in his hand. Taylor had perpetuated one of the largest frauds he had seen, and he had been witness to some pretty brazen schemes. And she had done it with total anonymity. To this day, Brand didn't know she was the one who stole his money. How could he? She had left no clues.

Taylor was alive. And she had the money. Two hundred and sixty-three million dollars. And ten million dollars was sitting in an offshore account—with his name on it. Five million for Ricardo. A half million for Adolfo.

Taylor had done it. Taken a con man for everything he was worth. And survived.

He walked to the kitchen, found the scrap of paper and reached for the phone. He dialed a long-distance number. When the voice answered, he said, "Ricardo, it's Kelly. I've got some good news for you."

CHAPTER SIXTY-FOUR

The Caribbean sun was wonderfully strong. She glanced down at her arm and poked it with her index finger. A tinge of white showed, like a dot on a piece of colored paper. Time to get out of the sun. But finally, for the first time in her life, she was tanning. Red hair was nice, but the pasty white skin that went with it was a pain in the ass in a tropical climate. Taylor retreated to the giant palapa next to the pool and poured a glass of lemonade. She sat in one of the wicker chairs and stared out over the teal waters of the Caribbean.

What a ride. The last three and a half years had been everything she expected. And more. With the exception of Alan's death, she couldn't have scripted a better ending. No, there was nothing else she would change. And that was saying something, considering the whole thing had started so innocently so long ago. She let her mind drift back.

Alan Bestwick had tried to pick her up in a bar while she was having drinks with a few of her staff after work one night, but she had shut him down on the spot. A week later he reappeared in a more appropriate setting—

one of her favorite restaurants. He stopped by the table, talked for a while, then left. With her phone number. He had called—and they started dating. And that led to them getting married. All pretty simple, but for one thing.

Taylor had known from minute one what Alan Bestwick was doing. She checked his name in the Alumni records at Stanford—his Master's degree in Electrical Engineering was a fake. Then she paid a local private investigator to dig up the facts on exactly who Alan Bestwick really was. And what she had found was more than a little interesting. Alan Bestwick's real name was Francois Vallencoure, an American with strong ties to France. And he was joined at the hip with a man named Robert Zindler—a very successful con man who went by numerous aliases. In this case, with the NewPro scam, he had chosen Edward Brand.

Taylor knew from the start what they were after. Her money. And from that moment on, she was a lioness on the hunt. She called in a favor and had G-cubed grossly overvalued. Its actual dollar value on the market was less than six million. But Alan and Brand would never have bitten if that were all she was worth. So she played the game, knowing all the while that her turn would come.

Kelly Kramer was her ace in the hole. When she interviewed him, his résumé was convincing, almost too perfect. She contacted his previous employer and received a glowing reference. The little things were setting off warning lights, and she looked deeper. She had a private investigator check the company on his résumé, and after considerable digging about, he discovered it was a front for the American government. A department of the country's security forces designed to give references to previous employees of the CIA and NSA. She knew she had an in to one of the agencies. She didn't care which. She hired Kelly on the spot.

From that moment on, it had been her game, not theirs.

She let Edward Brand and Alan guide her through the various stages of the con, from the antique dealer in Mexico City to Alan's apparent death on the cliff near Cabo San Lucas. She traveled to Paris, knowing his strong ties to the French capital. The trip was necessary, otherwise how could she have convinced Kelly that she knew Alan was alive? From that point on, Kelly and his co-workers at NSA were very accommodating.

Most importantly, she had always stayed in character. She convinced herself that she had been taken, that her life was in ruins. She became the woman everyone thought she should be—the widow, the victim. She vilified herself—actually stretched the game to the point where she believed her own falsehoods. She walked a dangerous line between reality and the fiction she was creating. That believability was the key. Brand, Alan and Hawkins all saw her as the grieving widow who had lost her money and her husband. They never suspected. Not even once. In retrospect, her performance was nothing short of brilliant.

Cashing the million-dollar insurance check was the most difficult thing for her. It was fraud, and she knew it. But not to cash it was folly. By that time, Kelly had uncovered Brent Hawkins, and he would be watching. So the money went in her account.

Then, in mid-December, when the right amount of time had slipped by, she suggested to Kelly that they go after Alan and Brand. Beat them at their own game. When Kelly agreed, she knew she had the resources of NSA at her command. The rest had simply been a series of logical steps to the inevitable conclusion. Get Edward Brand on top of that mountain, on a satellite phone, and have Kelly intercept the call. She knew that all the information Kelly needed to empty Brand's accounts would be transmitted digitally during the call. It was up to Kelly from that point on. He had to produce. And he did.

The two hundred and sixty-three million dollars had

gone directly into the account she set up right after discovering what Alan and Brand were up to. But that account was simply a front. It was coded to immediately forward any deposits to another Caribbean account, through a complicated and untraceable series of satellite transactions.

Taylor finished her lemonade and set the glass on the counter. It had been a long, tough grind. Living with Alan as his wife had been incredibly difficult. She knew now that it was because she lived the lie, that she had been successful in becoming the woman Brand and Alan expected her to be. She felt an overpowering sense of guilt over Alan's death. It was something she lived with every day—the one thing she truly regretted. She justified it by telling herself that he never loved her—that he had just used her to get what he wanted. It felt strange to finally admit to herself that she had done the exact same thing. They had both known the risks going in.

Risk. It was the key word to the one clue she had given Alan. She vividly remembered her exact words when sitting in their living room with Sam Morel, the DA and the two FBI agents. *When I see something I consider to be risky, I check it out. If it falls within my boundaries of acceptable risk, I go for it.* I, not we. She had given all of them the opportunity to catch on. Not one of them had noticed. Not the slightest blip on the radar.

What had transpired atop Monte Alban was not what she had wanted or planned. If Alan had stayed out of the picture, things would have ended that night with a respectful parting of the ways, and Brand wouldn't have known he'd been scammed until the next day. Too late to find Adolfo or Ricardo. And no mention of her and Kelly. Despite the heat, she shuddered when she thought back to Alan arriving at the ruins. Adolfo's walkie-talkie was still open, and she had followed the entire conversation as she made her way back along the west side of the mountain. When Alan arrived and recognized Ricardo, she thought her cover was blown. But Alan said that Ricardo had driven *him* around Mexico City, not *him and Taylor*. She had dodged a very real bullet. If Brand ever tied Ricardo back to her, he'd be searching. And he'd eventually find her. When Alan died on the mountain, that connection back to her had died as well.

She had stolen two hundred and sixty-three million dollars from a thief. Then she paid back the buyer of G-cubed the seven-point-five million-dollars they had overvalued the company, plus a two million-dollar bonus. She deposited fifteen and a half million dollars into three accounts to cover her debts to Kelly and Ricardo and Adolfo. The final ends were tied up; the deal was done. Now she could live her life as she pleased.

One of her live-in staff approached the palapa, a cordless phone in her hand. "It is a call for you," she said. "He asked for Taylor."

She smiled. He'd found her. She knew he would. She took the phone and punched the talk button. "Hello, Kelly."

"Hello, Taylor. How are things?"

"Very well. And with you?"

"Couldn't be better."

"So you found me," she said, a tinge of feigned surprise in her voice. It was solely for Kelly's benefit. He had probably worked very hard to locate her.

"It wasn't easy. Took a couple of months. With the resources of the NSA behind me. I see you put your life in San Francisco on hold. New name, new life. I guess that's the way it has to be. If Edward Brand ever caught on to your little shell game, he wouldn't be happy."

"My shell game. I think it's a good description, Kelly. Sums things up nicely." She took a couple of deep breaths of the fresh sea air. "What are you up to these days?"

"Well, I'm recently retired from my job with the government. Don't need the money anymore. I seem to have more time on my hands than I know what to do with. It's a problem."

She laughed. "Do you want to visit?"

He didn't answer for a few seconds. A light breeze blew in from the sheltered cove. Finally, he said, "I'd like that, Taylor. I'd like that very much."

She smiled, but simply said, "Do you know where I am?"

"Yes."

"Then I'll see you in a day or two?"

"Give me a week."

"A week, then. Bye."

"Bye."

Taylor pushed the talk button and set the phone on the table. Three and a half years ago she had seen an opportunity. She had gone for it, and she had won. And to the victor came the spoils. She glanced about the beachfront house, a marvel of white stucco and glass touching onto the soft sand that ran down to the warm waters of the Caribbean. A Lamborghini and a Porsche sat in the driveway. Amazing what cash could buy.

And the money in the bank. More money than she would ever need. She could donate to charities, travel, try her hand at writing a novel—whatever she wanted.

Ahh, the spoils were nice. Very nice indeed.

ACCIDENTS WAITING TO HAPPEN
SIMON WOOD

Josh Michaels is worth more dead than alive. He just doesn't know it yet. When an SUV forces his car off the road and into the river, it could be an accident. But when Josh looks up at the road, expecting to see the SUV's driver rushing to help him, all he sees is the driver watching him calmly...then giving him a "thumbs-down" sign. That is the first of many attempts on Josh's life, all of them designed to look like accidents, and all of them very nearly fatal. With his time—and maybe his luck—running out and no one willing to believe him, Josh had better figure out who wants him dead and why...before it's too late.

SMOKE

LISA MISCIONE

A late-night visit from an NYPD detective rarely brings good news. But true-crime writer Lydia Strong is especially surprised to hear that one of her former writing students has been missing for more than two weeks. Before she disappeared, Lily had tried to get in touch with Lydia, seeking her help. Could it have something to do with the death of Lily's brother, the one Lily refused to accept as a suicide? If she wants to find the truth, Lydia will have to follow the trail Lily left behind, a trail that—like Lily herself—seems to disappear like smoke.

SHAME

ALAN RUSSELL

Gray Parker's execution is front-page news and his case inspires a bestselling book. Everyone wants to hear about the man who strangled all those women. Everyone except his young son. As soon as he is old enough, Caleb starts a new life and denies any connection to his infamous father.

But now new bodies have started to turn up, marked just as his father's victims, and all the evidence points to Caleb. His only ally is the sole survivor of one of Parker's attacks, the woman who turned his crimes into a bestseller. Together, these two must desperately try to prove Caleb's innocence—before the law or the killer catches them.